TASTE THE
GUNPOWDER.

SWALLOW THE
BLOOD.

FEEL THE HEAT.

OUT OF CONTROL

HOT, TRASHY, MAN-ON-MAN EROTICA

OUT OF CONTROL

HOT, TRASHY, MAN-ON-MAN EROTICA

EDITED BY
GREG WHARTON

suspect thoughts press
www.suspectthoughtspress.com

Cover photography and design by Shane Luitjens/Torquere Creative
Book design by Greg Wharton/Suspect Thoughts Press

First Edition: November 2005
10 9 8 7 6 5 4 3 2 1

Library of Congress Cataloging-in-Publication Data

Out of control : hot, trashy, man-on-man erotica / edited by Greg Wharton.
    p. cm.
 ISBN-13: 978-0-9763411-3-0 (pbk.)
 ISBN-10: 0-9763411-3-1 (pbk.)
 1. Gay men--Fiction. 2. Erotic stories, American. I. Wharton, Greg, 1962-

PS648.H57O98 2005
813'.01083538088642--dc22

                                                        2005027364

Suspect Thoughts Press
2215-R Market Street, #544
San Francisco, CA 94114-1612
www.suspectthoughtspress.com

Suspect Thoughts Press is a terrible infant hell-bent to burn the envelope by publishing dangerous books by contemporary authors and poets exploring provocative social, political, queer, spiritual, and sexual themes.

PUBLICATION CREDITS

Grateful acknowledgment is made to the following publications in which these stories originally appeared:

"Shiftless Mind Matter" by Rusty Canela first appeared in *suspect thoughts: a journal of subversive writing* (www.suspectthoughts.com), Greg Wharton, ed. (Issue 5, 2001).

"Blue Boy" by M. Christian first appeared in *Embraces: Dark Erotica*, Paula Guran, ed. (Venus or Vixen Press, 2000) and *Dirty Words* (Alyson Books, 2001).

"Ten Apologies" by Wayne Courtois first appeared in *suspect thoughts: a journal of subversive writing* (www.suspectthoughts.com), Greg Wharton, ed. (Issues 4-6, 2001-2002).

"Toad" by Ian Philips first appeared in *Velvet Mafia* (www.velvetmafia.com), Sean Meriwether, ed. (Issue 13, 2004).

"Hurts Like Hell" by Mel Smith first appeared in *suspect thoughts: a journal of subversive writing* (www.suspectthoughts.com), Greg Wharton, ed. (Issue 8, 2003) and *Nasty* (Alyson Books, 2005).

"A time comes when silence is betrayal."
—Martin Luther King, Jr.

"Annoy them...survive."
—Lark Lands, PhD

CONTENTS

BLOOD, TATTOOS, LEATHER JACKETS, AND FAST CARS: A SHORT INTRODUCTION

Out of Control: Hot, Trashy, Man-on-Man Erotica is about love gone wrong: love with the wrong man at the wrong time and the wrong place that takes you places you never dreamed you'd go, not even in your hottest, wrongest wet dream.

All you wanted was a drink, some conversation, and a little attention, perhaps the warmth of another body pressed to yours. Preferably a sane one. But the weight of his hand on your cock silenced the alarm buzzing loudly in your brain. Perhaps you dismissed the fact he had a gun. Or maybe you knew the car was stolen, but he was so handsome. You wanted him more than you have ever wanted anyone, or anything, before. And you couldn't pass up the chance to have him, no matter what it took, where it took you, or what the consequences might be.

Out of Control: Hot, Trashy, Man-on-Man Erotica is that heavy hand, that loaded gun, that long ride over the edge of a cliff. It features over-the-top tales of the wild evening that turned into several wild days, the date that turned psychosexual, the perfect lover that turned obsessive, crazed, and vengeful. It's about road trips full of fast cars and bumpy rides, and lots of beautiful, man-on-man, out-of-control, hard-core sex. The stories in this anthology are wild, original, imaginative, crazy, sexy, graphic, kinky, and surprising—the stuff of some sweet dreams and also a few nightmares. Will they be your nightmare, sweet dream, or wet dream? That depends on you.

Here are some of the characters: single men, married men, and sweaty men; straight boys, nelly boys, and smelly boys; brothers, fathers, cousins, leather daddies, clown daddies, and dead daddies; psychopaths, sadists, masochists, and sluts; sex junkies, sex workers, butch queens, and drag queens; terrorists, bank robbers, coaches, ghosts, and toads; runaways, hillbillies, and hoboes.

Sexy or scary? Both!

Here's a short list of the props: fists, guns, razor blades, and bombs; nipple rings, safety pins, dildos, feathers, ropes, and handcuffs; pot, speed, Vicks VapoRub, and raspberry moonshine; pancakes, cum, Moon Pies, and green chile burritos; blood, tattoos, leather jackets, pool tables, and fast cars.

Taste the gunpowder. Swallow the blood. Feel the heat. Let go. Give in. Enjoy the ride.

Yours in danger,
Greg Wharton

JOKER'S CANYON
THOMAS S. ROCHE

It was a .38 Smith & Wesson; it said so right on the barrel. Bright, like quicksilver, like shining molten metal, its constantly shifting patterns of light and liquid.

"Where the fuck did you get it?" I asked Ray, eyeing it with the fright that came not from the gun but from the hand wrapped around it. "Is it loaded?"

"Mike, Mike, Mike, you stupid fuck. There's nothing more useless than a loaded gun," said Ray, pointing it at me. I could see into the cylinders and it looked fucking loaded to me, and I put out my hand and pushed the gun away.

"Don't fuckin' point it," I said. "Where did you get it?"

"My dad keeps it hidden under the floorboards in the den," he said. "He won't miss it. I've got six extra rounds of ammo. Let's go shooting."

"We'll get in trouble," I told him. "Your dad will fuckin' kill you."

"No, he won't," sneered Ray. "He doesn't even know it's gone. Come on, let's go out to Joker's Canyon and shoot some squirrels or something."

"What did squirrels ever do to you, motherfucker?" I asked him.

"Not a goddamn thing," said Ray, sticking the gun in his belt. "So let's go kill them."

He pulled out his tight white T-shirt and smoothed the hem over the butt of the gun, not doing a very good job of hiding it.

I was the one with the car, an ancient Dodge a cousin on my mother's side had sold me for $100. I took the keys out of my pocket and fondled them, looking at Ray nervously and still kind of hoping he would change his mind. "Isn't it illegal to shoot guns without, like, a license?"

"Stop being such a pussy," said Ray, and snatched the keys from my hand. He headed for the door and down the stairs. I followed him, rolling my eyes.

When he got to the car he fired the car keys back at me. I missed the catch and had to scramble to pick them up from the long grass of the front lawn. Ray got into the passenger's seat and took the gun out of his belt, laying it in his lap.

"Nobody better try to fuckin' carjack us on the way," he growled. "They'll be fuckin' sorry."

"Grow up," I said. "Stop playing *Dirty Harry*."

He picked up the gun out of his lap and pointed it at me as I got in the driver's seat. "Feel lucky, punk? Do ya?"

MAN-ON-MAN EROTICA

"Cut it out!"

"Thirty-eight Smith & Wesson. Most powerful handgun made."

"No, it's not," I said, starting the car.

"Close enough," he said, peering down the barrel. "Blow your head clean off. 'Course, a pussy head like yours..."

"Shut the fuck up," I told him, and slammed the car in reverse, hoping the gun would go off and blow his dick clean off.

"Fuckin' man with a gun can have anything he wants," cooed Ray crazily, giggling.

I reached out and turned on the radio, just to shut him up. The tape deck had broken months ago, and with the antenna broken the only radio station I could get was this crap-ass country station that played twangy bullshit whines by bummed-out truckers who needed a fucking blow job so bad they sounded like they were going to blow their brains out.

We drove up the state road to Joker's Canyon, Ray pointing the gun out the window and making "pow" sounds. I felt my stomach churning, half-convinced he was going to start shooting from the window. I prayed we didn't run across a state trooper, but we made it to the canyon without incident, unless you count Ray pointing the gun at my head and growling "Feel lucky, punk?" as an incident.

I drove the car up the dirt road and parked at the edge of the canyon.

"Hey, you know the faggots come here?" asked Ray.

"No shit," I said. Faggots had been coming here, or so the legend went, for as long as I could remember, and so had we. We'd still never seen any.

Ray got out of the car, stood there at the edge of the canyon, and held out the gun.

"Feel lucky, punk?" he said, and squeezed off a round into the canyon.

The noise blasted my eardrums, and I rubbed my ringing ears as I followed after him. "Fuck," I said.

"I left it loud," growled Ray. "Scare any pain-in-the-ass innocent bystanders."

"Stop quoting fuckin' gangster movies," I said. "Let me shoot it."

"Fat chance, faggot," said Ray, and pointed the gun at a tree ten feet away. When the bullet hit, fragments of wood went blasting everywhere and rained down around us, dusting the summer air.

"It's, uh, powerful," I said stupidly, and Ray looked at me like I was the dumbest fuck on earth. He pointed the gun at me and made a "pow" noise.

"Stop fuckin' doing that," I shouted. "The fuckin' thing is going to go off."

"No judge would convict me," said Ray, and whipped around, shooting another round into the canyon.

"Don't waste them," I said. "You said you only have six more bullets."

Ray squeezed off three rounds in rapid succession, blowing holes in trees all around us. There were no squirrels in sight.

"You're wasting them," I said.

Ray tipped the cylinder out and dumped spent rounds into his hand. "Feel them," he said. "They're hot." He threw them at me and I caught one of them. It was kind of warm.

"Let me shoot it," I said, holding out my hand, more because I wanted to take the gun out of crazy-ass Ray's hands than because I genuinely wanted to shoot the fucking thing. Ray fished in his pocket for bullets and I heard them jingling with his change. He found them one at a time and loaded the gun methodically, looking around for his next target.

"Please?" I asked him.

He ignored me. "What should I shoot next?"

"Let me shoot it," I pleaded.

He clicked the cylinder closed and fondled the gun, peering at it. "What do you think it's like, faggots coming here? They suck each other's dicks and shit?"

"I don't know," I said nervously. "Who gives a fuck?"

Ray swung the gun up at me and giggled.

"You tell me," he said. "Come on, you said you didn't think it was gross. You said you'd done it and it was no big deal."

"Fuck you!" I spat. "I never said that!"

"Bullshit," he said, his face twisted with a smile. "You offered to do it. That one time we were drunk at Jenny Michelson's house."

My face went red and I felt dizzy. "I was joking," I said.

Ray giggled. He pointed the gun at me and said, "You were drunk. Come on. Find out what it's like to suck a real dick."

"You were drunk, too!" I said. "You even..."

He pulled back the hammer. "I even what?"

"Nothing," I said.

Ray smiled, that freaky crazy smile I never could resist. "Come on," he said, his voice gone from gunpowder to chocolate.

My balls clenched up and my heart pounded.

I could feel my cock getting hard.

"You won't tell anyone?"

"Why would I tell anyone?" he said. "That you sucked my dick with a gun to your head."

"Don't point it at me," I said.

"Oh, I'll point it at you," he said, giving me a perfect view of the big black eye of the barrel. "If you don't suck my dick."

I opened my mouth to say something, changed my mind. My cock was so hard it hurt, pointed the wrong direction in my tight cutoff jeans and aching under the thick material. I felt hot all over, and it wasn't the summer sun. Ray reached for his fly and unzipped it, reached in, and took out his dick. It was already hard—fully hard. Ray never wore any underwear.

He held out his dick, using the same hand he was holding the gun in. His fingers curved around the shaft of his cock and let the gun hang half-dangling, his thumb hooked in the trigger guard. I could see his dickhead glistening.

"All right," I said. "Just don't tell anyone."

"Come on," he said, gesturing at his dick with the revolver. "On your knees."

I went over and knelt down, taking his dick in my hand and tentatively licking the shaft.

I felt the weight of the gun against my head. "Come on, faggot," said Ray. "I know you know how to do it better than that. Cocksucker like you?"

I took his dick in my mouth and my own cock surged in response. I swallowed half of him and started sucking, my tongue working in circles around the head. I was so fucking hard, terrified that he would notice. I was wearing this old pair of cutoffs I'd made last summer. The fabric was so tight against my cock that when I rocked forward on my knees, I could feel my dickhead grinding against the fabric. I was so hard I could have come if I'd just barely spanked it. I sucked Ray's cock deeper and even pushed it into my throat a little bit.

"Yeah," he said, the gun hanging loose at his side, his hips rotating under me, forcing his cock deeper into my throat. "Fuckin' deep-throat it. Just like the bitches in the pornos. Take it all down your throat."

I choked on it, but didn't stop. He pushed deeper until it was filling my throat, and then he started to kind of fuck my face. I glanced over at the gun to make sure he wasn't pointing it, because he was all moaning and loud and shit, like he was about to come. I rocked back and forth and worked my hips, and I tried hard not to let Ray know I was about to do it. I came so fucking hard with his cock in my throat, soaking the front of my shorts in a single hot flood of pleasure. When Ray shot in my mouth I swallowed it all, my eyes watering from the rough fucking he'd given my throat.

I looked up at Ray; his dick spent, his whole body was hanging kind of slack, his eyes glazed. He looked a little scared.

I let his cock slide out of my mouth; I sniffled, licked my lips, wiped my chin. I looked up to him expecting him to put the gun to my head, smack me, call me a faggot. I could feel the wet stain of cum soaking my shorts.

"I'm fuckin' bored with this," he said. "Let's go see if we can score some beer."

"You've still got six bullets," I said.

"Fuck it," he said, tossing the gun through the window onto the seat so he could zip up his pants. "I want some fuckin' beer."

I got into the driver's seat and started the car, backing out slowly and then doing a Y down to the state road. Ray just sat there staring out the window.

"Hey," I said. "I won't tell anyone."

He seized the gun and pointed it at me. "You better not tell anyone!" he said.

"I won't! I won't!"

Ray went limp again, staring at his pants, the gun hanging loose in his lap with his hand on the trigger.

"Good," he said softly.

"I *won't*," I said, and when he didn't say anything I just shut up and thought about his cock. See, I hadn't just *said* I would suck his dick at Jenny Michelson's house. I'd sucked it all right, and he'd sucked mine, three fucking times and twice with my fingers up his fucking ass lubed with Jenny Michelson's mom's KY Jelly. I thought about it whenever I jerked off. Ray was the one who brought it up, all the fucking time, telling me I'd said I'd suck his dick and that meant I was a fag.

I always played along, pretended that was all I'd done—said it. "I was drunk," I told him. "I was kidding. I'd never suck dick," even though I fucking prayed for it every night, stroked my cock remembering Ray down my throat, my fingers up his ass. I could still fucking smell him on them, sometimes.

I looked at the gun, still smoking a little, glistening silver in the sun in Ray's lap. His hand twitched on the trigger.

I said gently, "Why don't you give me the gun, Ray."

He looked up at me, his eyes all red and weird-looking.

He lifted the gun and held it out to me. I took it from him and let the hammer down delicately, then stuck the gun under my seat, steering with my knees down the state road.

"Gotta get that back to my dad," he said.

"I'll take care of it," I told him.

He looked up at me, blank and vacant.

"Thanks, Mike," he said weakly. "You take care of everything."

"Yeah," I said, looking away and watching the road. "Yeah. Sure. Whatever."

I turned on the radio, but all we could get was that shitty country station. I turned it as loud as it would go anyway and hummed along.

DRUNK, STUPID BLOND
SIMON SHEPPARD

He was a stocky little blond. Just your type. Handsome, looking like tough trash. A stocky little drunk blond with a ponytail. He came up to you in the back of the bar, back where guys were feeling each other up, where furtive blow jobs were accomplished in dark corners. Obviously way fucking out of it—the way he was jumpily sweating was probably from speed as well as booze—he came up to you, wrapped his arms around you like you were his daddy. Fuck, you were old enough to *be* his daddy, almost. He was short, maybe only five-two or five-three. You held him as he laid his head against your chest. You sniffed his unbathed maleness and sized up his body through his shirt. A tough, meaty slab.

You ran your hands down over his torso, down to his crotch. His long, curved cock was soft. You knew it would most likely stay that way: crystal-dick. Still, you could feel the bulge of the prominent cockhead through the grimy denim. His hands, for their part, wandered aimlessly over your body, looking maybe for a grip. You knew if you kissed him you'd regret it, so instead you ran your hands up under his shirt. Almost hairless. Prominent nipples. He really was fucking short, hardly tall enough to lick your armpit without standing on his toes. And drunk. He was drunk and probably stoned. His hands finally reached your dick. Started kneading it through your jeans as he mumbled something incoherent. He unbuttoned your fly and fished out your hard-on. That's when you grabbed his fucking white-trash ponytail and pulled. Pulled pretty hard. He swayed a bit, but then, he'd been swaying anyway. The little blond slab dropped to his knees, "dropped" being the operative word. For just a little while, while he was being cuddly and needy, you'd begun to feel the glimmering beginnings of some kind of protective affection. But now, as his handsome, tough face enveloped your dick, you felt pretty much absolutely nothing. He gave lousy head anyway, all teeth and gagging. The crush of people around the two of you became too much. Like flies to carrion, the smell of sex had attracted the crowds. One guy reached for where your dick met the blond's mouth. You pushed his paw away, hoping his sulkiness wouldn't turn belligerent. The situation was saved by the bartender's shout of "Last call!"

You cleared a space with your elbows, then pulled the piece of boy to its feet. A trickle of drool, unfocused eyes, but otherwise fairly passable. It licked its lips, mouth almost too wide, nearly pretty as a girl's. You dragged the drunk blond through the thinning crowd, out through heavy black curtains to the chilly street, and found out that he—conveniently—lived within walking distance. He slurred his words. He wobbled on his feet. When he walked, he wove. Still and all, he didn't live too far away. And unbelievably, all-too-believably, your dick remained hard all the way there. En route, you saw a couple of crackheads sharing a pipe. Nice neighborhood. The fucked-up boy lived at a cheap residential hotel. You were disobeying the no-visitors-after-10-p.m. rule, but the pimply kid at the desk didn't seem to give a shit. He went back to his stupid Game Boy before you'd even gotten to the elevator.

On the way up, you noticed he had tattoos on each of the fingers of his left hand: I, H, 8, U. It made you want to slug him, right there between the third and fourth floors.

It was a room with no bathroom, a stained sink on the wall. Cheap pictures taped above the crappy dresser. Brad Pitt. Some Herb Ritts model. A watery painting of Jesus exposing His sacred heart.

Blond boy was turning all affectionate again, grabbing at you, purring. Well, kind of purring. Gurgling. You looked into his handsome face, tugged at his ponytail, forced him to his knees. You both took your dicks out, him pulling away at his long, limp piece of uncut meat, which you could in fact smell from above. You shoved your hard, kind-of-interested dick into his mouth. You already knew he gave lousy head. You didn't care. His tongue started in on your cock. You had to pee, you'd had to pee since before you left the bar, so you started pissing down his throat. His body sort of stiffened. There might have been a look of surprise in his blank blue eyes. But he gulped down your piss, and you gave him more, draining yourself into his throat as he struggled to keep up, to gulp it all down without gagging. The piss coming out of your hard cock felt good, like one long continuous cumshot. Then he was gagging for real, pushing you away, struggling to his feet, reaching the sink just in time to lose it all down the drain. Watching him puke out what he hadn't wanted in the first place, you began to feel what might have passed for sentiment. Then he was done, leaning over the sink with his pants around his ankles. He wasn't wearing underwear. He washed out the sink, rinsed his mouth, turned back to you, and smiled. Your dick gave a jump. He shuffled back over to you, looked up, and his smile turned fuzzy. There was still barf on his breath. You shoved his stupid body across the room. He landed face down on the unmade bed. His ass was chunky, hairless, and pale.

You lubed a couple of fingers with your spit and eased them up his hole. He was loose and willing. And—surprise—it felt clean in there. You got a third finger in him before he started to resist. So you slid in your pinky, too, and rooted around inside him, inside his stupid, meaty blond butt. He moaned for a while, then became so still you were afraid he'd passed out. But when your other hand pulled his head up by the ponytail, his eyes and mouth were both wide open. You pulled your fingers out of his warm guts and shoved them into his mouth. He sucked greedily. You shoved farther, feeling the back of his throat. He gagged again. You let him off the bed, back to the sink. Dry heaves. While he was standing there trying to puke, you unrolled one of those black rubbers over your dick. He was still leaning against the sink when you entered him, sliding your hard prick into his pussy. Fucking that tough little piece of ass. When you looked up, there was Jesus on the wall.

You put your hands around his throat and squeezed as you pumped your shiny black hard-on into his hungry white ass. For a few seconds, he was rasping for air, till you relented. You fucked him for what—ten, fifteen minutes? Till your legs began to tremble from the strain. The smell of used asshole was in your nostrils, pretty pungent. Still fucking away, you reached around and punched him in the gut, not all that hard. He let go of the sink, reached his arms back, and tried to hold you tight. He looked back over his shoulder and opened his mouth for a kiss. Enough of that. You pulled out, whirled him around so he was facing you. His dick was hard at last. For a second you jacked at it, the silkiness of his long foreskin as it slid over his cockhead. Then you reached down between his thick thighs and grabbed his nuts, wrapping your hand around the base of his loose sac. Even standing up, he only came up to your shoulder. But a rough pull at his balls and he dropped to his knees, down to the dirty, uncarpeted floor.

You pulled at that stupid, trashy ponytail again till his head was thrown back, his lips open. You slid in your dick, the rubber glistening with his pungent assjuices. He sucked at it, sucked it clean. When you pulled out of his mouth, he thanked you. You kicked his nuts with your right boot. It wasn't the sort of thing you usually did, not really. But you did it. You did it. He winced, smiled, wrapped his arms around your legs, rubbing his dumb, gorgeous face against your jeans. You kicked again. A third time. That must have, you figured, hurt. He was still holding on, purring, gurgling, whatever.

He was gazing up at you like a lost little boy. Some other time, you might have gotten sentimental, like some asshole looking at a puppy in a cute TV commercial. As things stood, you didn't give a shit. You weren't a monster, not really. But you slapped his face, slapped it hard. And then you hit the other cheek: White-trash Jesus on the wall would have been proud. The boy's pale little face was turning bright pink. His eyes, already kind of blank, were getting blanker. Trying for a snarl, you told him to open his fucking mouth again, and when he did you shoved your cock back in. Ordinarily you didn't fuck face with a rubber on, but you'd gotten clap from some guy's throat a couple of months ago, and you weren't going to go through *that* again. Fuck, just being in that lousy hotel room made you itch like you had scabies.

You were relieved to notice his teeth weren't scraping your dick any more. The rubber helped, probably. Or maybe his mouth had just gone slacker; he was, in fact, starting to drool again. You leaned over to grab his hair. Your other hand resumed slapping his unfortunately handsome face, kind of softly, then harder. You started having thoughts, fantasies of punching his face, maybe busting his cheekbone, breaking his nose so it wasn't so pretty any more. Blood would run out of his nostrils onto your cock, and he'd lap it up. If you were a smoker, you could burn him with a cigarette. Fantasies like that, things you wouldn't really do, at least not probably. You weren't a fucking monster.

The blond piece of meat sensed something was up. He backed off your dick and looked up at you, lost, drool running down his fucking chin. You hoped to hell he wouldn't say something about love. Then you *would* have to bust his nose. For real.

You thought about fucking him again, maybe slapping his ass while you did, but it was getting late. Enough. You pulled the rubber off your dick. With one knee, you shoved at him till he let go. You pressed your boot against his chest. He leaned back on his haunches, lost his balance, sprawled on the floor. He slurred something. You thought you misheard. But then, you didn't really care about what he had to say, one way or the other.

It was easy enough to jack yourself off, to shoot on him, to cover his blank, unattainable, cheap-whore face with your hot cum. It ran down his cheeks. He stuck his tongue out and hunted for spunk. You gave his once-again-limp dick one more medium-hard kick. For good measure. For auld lang syne. For the hell of it. Because you could. And get away with it.

It was getting late. You tucked your meat back inside your pants, turned and found the door, stained hotel rules thumbtacked to the splintery wood. As you were walking out, you thought you heard him say "thank you" again. What an asshole. You didn't look back.

HOLE
MOSES D'HARA

Unlike women, generally speaking, when a man disappears—it's because he's decided to. Even the shadow has a shadow. And everyone lives with the saboteur.

"Go for it. You fucking deserve it. Besides, you're doing it."

Sometimes I disappear.

Permission granted.

The pendulum swings out of sync for some small reason. Some seemingly insignificant event that begins the odd turn. The spin. The spiral inward. Gaining momentum—and suddenly I'm gone.

The buildings that were new when I first got to L.A. are being torn down now. No great loss. I stopped at a red light on Rossmore and Melrose and swallowed a handful of mushrooms—'cause I was almost there, and I prefer my hallucinogens be organic, whenever possible. Then I washed 'em down with a big gulp of chai iced tea spiked with an airplane bottle of vodka. My stomach wrenched. Living on protein bars and breath mints to lean down for the hunt. I watched my stomach contorting under my T-shirt until the light turned green.

Flex is your average run-of-the-mill Los Angeles bathhouse. Nothing special. It's clean—pretty much. And it's got a pool. Basically it's a cement box of mirrors surrounded by a quarter acre of hurricane fencing, jammed in perilously close to an anonymous off-ramp of the Hollywood Freeway. Very romantic. I turned up the radio and turned off the headlights. Blood. Sugar. Sex. Magic. And I couldn't believe I actually snagged a parking space. My stomach growled.

Exactly.

You gotta get a membership and check your ID at the door. An oddly appropriate metaphor. There are no bags allowed. Some guys get a room, but I've never been one of those. Standard issue—white cotton towel and a key. Hang a coupla lefts. And you're in. The locker room floor is red linoleum. It's very pleasing, and the guy getting dressed next to me was a complete thug. So I was happy as shit. Watching those big hairy balls swaying back and forth between his legs when he bent over—and that's when the first wave hit.

My heart began to race, my dick swelled (although I don't think that had anything to do with the mushrooms), colors started to intensify. Intensely. And I couldn't wait to get out of my fucking clothes. I shoved down my jeans and struggled to get 'em off but for some reason it wasn't working. I sat back down on the bench and smiled. Shoulda taken my shoes off.

It takes a certain lack of judgment to show up at a bathhouse. Exactly what I was looking for. A loss of judgment. No judgments—and a shower, 'cause there were two guys fucking in the one across from the steam room and actually what I really needed to do was take a piss. A shower just seemed like the most convenient outlet. Yet somehow I wound up outside the gym.

Mirrors; blindingly, excruciatingly bright lights; and a guy in Jockey shorts. All by himself. Lifting weights. It was a whole other world in there. I mean inside him—you could tell. Caught in his own reflection, soaked in sweat, and there was just something about the way he carried himself or handled himself or handled the fucking weights— I don't know what the fuck it was exactly, but my dick definitely responded. It swung out in front of me. And there's something about a half-hard dick that always seems to get a guy's attention. I watched his eyes trace up my abdomen and over my chest. We looked at each other—cool, copacetic. We were both on the same page.

He ditched the barbell and let his hand drop to the bulge in his underpants, then he hooked his thumb over the top of 'em and pulled down until his pubic hair was pushing out over the waistband—and then he smiled. 'Cause he liked being in the spotlight. I started massaging my dick.

Pale skin and you could see every muscle in his body. Not that he was your typical bodybuilder type. He wasn't. But man—he was fucking ripped. His hand settled on the big mound of schlong forcing its way out of his briefs. Those fucking briefs. He yanked 'em down under his balls and I swear there musta been birds singing 'cause I sure did wanna fuck him. I braced myself against the doorway for some serious stroke action.

And that's when I noticed him. The other him. Another him at the far end of the hall. In a shaft of flickering blue light. Watching me— watch him. And playing with himself. He dropped his towel. Anime guy. Strobing silhouette—shaved body with a shock of jet black hair jutting straight out of his head at an eighty-degree angle, superhero arms, and a glow-in-the-dark wristwatch. Wow. It disappeared into a blur as he jerked himself off. At one point actually seeming to erase himself. And I could respect that. I turned back to Gymbo—still pumping. But somehow, it just didn't seem the same. I'd glimpsed the future—and it was *hentai*. Besides, like I said, what I *really* needed to do was take a piss. So I shoved off into the darkness.

Dark wood, closed doors, and more mirrors. Barely lit. I like being anonymous. People are much more honest when they're anonymous. Just ask anyone who's ever taken a survey. And the truth. I mean what's ultimately intimately inside someone is just about always a fucking trip.

I love getting inside someone. And then fucking them. It interests me. A flush. The promise of immediate gratification—and just the sort of positive sign I'd been hoping for. I spotted the men's room.

I never get sick of seeing stiff dick. Ever. It's amazing. I used to think maybe there was something wrong with me. Briefly. Then I wised up. I pissed my heart out. I'm an animal. And a god—I love my fucking life. Thank you. I also tend to like ugly guys and rough trade.

No Anime. Damn. Musta jerked himself into oblivion. I looked to the space that was formerly him. *Illo tempore*. Outside time. No clocks. No windows. Purposefully disorienting—not that I needed any help in that particular direction. Seems I turned a corner. Full-on body rush. Doors open—open doors. Like vacancy signs. Color. Guys hanging out in rooms like girls in the windows in Amsterdam. *Fetish de Straat*. Foot traffic. The crawl. And the best thing about living in L.A.—total ethnic diversity. The whole fucking world at your fingertips. Literally. Wanna fuck an Israeli? How 'bout an Ethiopian? Ever blow an Arab? I have.
They're usually not cut.
And body types. I mean, c'mon. I like to fuck men. Even when I was a kid I liked to fuck men.
Don't obsess.
It's always the weird thing that makes you cool.
I felt fucking awesome.
Guys milling around. I slowed down my breathing. The reformatory dorm at porn camp. It was the first thing that came to mind—musta been the carpeting. I noticed a feather and bent down to pick it up. And that's when he fell on me.
Dropped outta the fucking sky.
...or maybe he tripped over me. Either way—I ended up under him. Icarus. Just to wreck my fucking time.
"It was HIS fault!" and he points to an open door that immediately slams shut. So he picks up his shoe and hurls it at the door. "BASTARD!"
Then he bursts out crying. "Now I have a rug burn."
And I'm like barely conscious.
"Don't cry." It was as much out of disgust as sympathy, and he was wearing eye makeup. Mascara or eyeliner or something—whichever one runs. Ninety-five pounds soaking wet. Which he was. And you'd swear he was melting. I swear. Trust me. I have no reason to lie.
He looked over at me. "Just 'cause I wouldn't lick his ass."
It was a moment.
He sniffled. "You're bleeding."
Which somewhat explained the ringing in my ears. "Oh." It was

worse when I touched it.

"Oh no!" He grabbed his throat in a panic. "I think I swallowed my gum." And his eyes started to well up again. "Oh. Never mind. There it is." He pulled it off my towel and stuck it back in his mouth.

"Get offa me." And I meant it.

"I beg your pardon?"

"Get the fuck off of me."

And that scared him. Something in my voice. It made him nervous. And not the kind of nervous I like to make people.

"Look, kid. Relax. Really. It was my fault. You couldn't see me." Guess that's the thing about disappearing.

He studied me for a second. "You know, I think you're awfully handsome."

"I'm old enough to be your father." Then it dawned on me. That was probably actually true. I saw his dick jump. Oh, fuck. Here we go.

So I handed him his key—and his other shoe. "Maybe you better sit this one out."

"You'd." He smiled. "You'd better sit this one out." And he smiled again.

Punk. I coulda punched him.

Enter the obligatory unattractive best friend.

"So *there* you are." Delivered in classic "unattractive best friend" fashion.

"I think your ride's here."

He kissed me on the lips.

"Bye." And he looked back over his shoulder.

Where was I? Oh, yeah. Archetypes. I love the way men think. It's in big block letters—with pictures. And none of the words are very long. As if to illustrate my point, *El Diablo*. Mohawk and a goatee. Skate goth tattoo *"Papi"* across his whole fucking stomach and I'm rock hard instantly. *La Loteria*.

We wrapped our hands around each other's puds right off the bat. I fucking love making out with a guy. More than anything. He bit down on my bottom lip. I mean, fucking forget it. I love men.

Of course, you probably picked up on that.

I shoulda fucking killed him when I had the chance.

I'm covered with scars from my misadventures. I took a left and then a right and then passed through some kind of no-man's land. It appeared. The pool at Flex is surprisingly secluded considering there are thousands of cars whizzing by at ninety miles an hour. I think you'd like it. I saw a shooting star—and then another.

I've always been the luckiest guy I know, and I don't know why. I lie and I cheat—and I just don't get it. I did a half-gainer into the deep end and slammed my hand against the bottom. Maybe God just feels bad 'cause I'm so incredibly fucked up.

Tropical plants, floodlights, and some unlikely dude getting his ass plowed on a white plastic chaise—my eyes stung. Too much chlorine. And then there was them.

"Hey, man. Feel like fucking my boyfriend?"

Couples—go figure.

"No, I don't wanna fuck your boyfriend." I grinned. "But I'll fuck you."

He wasn't expecting it. "Or I could fuck him—while he sucks on your dick." It was like negotiating a deal with Michael Eisner. "Okay." Obviously, either way it was the boyfriend who was gonna get fucked.

Every porn movie has a hole. The receptacle. Some guy whose sole function is to take it. Take it up the ass—take it in the mouth. Take it wherever. To just plain take it. Of course, so do most relationships.

Me and the underdog. He had a mouth that came on tight as a pussy with a mind all its own, and all the time I'm watching him get fully penetrated by this...brute. And I'm telling ya, it was almost enough to make me come. Almost. I pet his face, which only got his ass slapped. Boys. No wonder people don't know what the fuck to make of us. So I ran my fingers through his hair, and then I grabbed him by the head and forced my dick into his throat. Me and Brutus. Two tin cans and a piece of string.

I think the average guy falls in love with just about whatever he's looking at when he comes. At least momentarily. I fucking *love you*—and then it passes.

Not that that makes it any less real. I could see it in his eyes. I fucking love you. And he came all over his boyfriend's back. Welcome to my world. Thing is, bizarre as it seems, just for that moment—I think I probably loved him too.

Not that I was gonna come over it or anything.

Splash. Slam. Back in the swim. Another experience experienced. Waist deep in the water, I heard the telltale clickity-clack of his Dr. Scholl's and suddenly the air was thick with the unmistakable scent of Youth Dew.

"I see you've met the neighbors."

"Icarus." I turned around.

"Icarus...I like that—sounds exotic." He pondered it. "And that way I wouldn't need a last name."

"Last name'd wreck it."

"Absolutely." He tried it on for size. "Icarus. Thank you."

"Don't mention it."

"I just got myself a Pepsi-Cola. Would you like a sip?"

"No. Thank you." Shooting star. And who the hell says Pepsi-Cola?

"Vicodin?"

"Sure, what the hell."

He sat down on the edge of the pool and dangled his legs in the water, took the leather cigarette case that hung from a long cord around his neck, and emptied it onto the cement. Tic-Tacs, some pills, a small mirror, eyeliner. Three cigarettes.

"No lighter?"

"I prefer to let the gentleman light my cigarette."

Then he giggled. "I can see your willie." And that cracked me up. It truly did.

Utterly ridiculous, outrageous, absurd, and totally unabashed—you couldn't get him to shut up if you tried. He had an opinion on everything. And the gossip.

"Jamie Lee Curtis was born hermaphrodite."

"Where the fuck did you hear something like that?"

"I know people—and you have a potty mouth. Smart people don't swear."

Starlight. Star bright. Nine-hundredth fucking shooting star I've seen tonight. I wish I may. I wish I might. Send me a black guy with a big fucking dick.

Amen.

Deep inhale.

"Yo. Bobo! Toss me your lighter." He was smoking a joint under a coupla garage-sale palms, and we'd already made some serious eye contact.

One-handed catch—always the crowd pleaser.

"Why, thank you." Chipped blue nail polish. He picked up one of his cigarettes and smiled.

His *ears*. They were fully torn. Both of 'em. Healed—but even so. Somebody—or something, actually ripped the fucking earrings out of his ears.

"You can fuck me if you want." Totally out of left field. All cavalier and full of abandon. He was right. The word had a lot more impact if you didn't use it all the time.

"Icarus. What is your *deal*?"

He shrugged. "What's yours?"

Good question.

"So *there* you are." The return of LaRue.

You could see Icky's face drop. "We're having pizza delivered."

"*Here*?"

He nodded.

"Well, then. I guess you'd better go eat your pizza." I boosted myself up on the edge of the pool and kissed him on the cheek.

MAN-ON-MAN EROTICA

I actually kissed him on the fucking cheek.

Sap. I oughtta have my frigging head examined. Maybe next time I could just ask him to the prom.

"See ya, Icky."

I don't know what the fuck I was looking for. I really don't. I mean, besides Bobo—strictly to return his lighter. You understand. But anyway, I'm walking down this path—and all of the sudden I'm in the Poconos. Hot tub honeymoon. Big orange moon. Strings of colored Christmas lights and all the water glittered bright turquoise. Ah...peaking. There was a big gust of wind and the air turned purple with jacaranda blossoms.

Fucking magical.

No wonder I take drugs.

I've always had a soft spot for hairy guys in boxer shorts. Call me sentimental, but there's just something about armpits and big muscular asses that makes me wanna jerk off. And I can never remember a time that that wasn't the case. I used to look forward to going to the Y with my Dad, like—all week long. Just for another shot at it. Or of it. Naked hairy men, including him. Who'da thunk?

"Hey."—Bobo.

"How's it going?"

And that's pretty much all it took. The proverbial match made in heaven. X and Viagra—and we were all over each other. Dick hanging outta his fly—he got the blow job of a lifetime. Full-body blow job. Shorts around his ankles—pubic hair all thick with cum. The guys in the hot tub musta loved it. But I shouldn't have smoked that second joint with him. I really shouldn't've—never mind the poppers. Wretched excess. It's always been my downfall. One of 'em anyway. "Too much cookie dough" syndrome. I came plummeting back to earth. Honeymoon over.

I wiped my mouth on the back of my hand and headed inside.

Trying to take a shortcut. That's what screwed up the Donner party. I had no fucking idea where I was. Peaks and valleys. A tangle of rooms off an endless winding corridor. Banks of video monitors and an orgy room—which seemed a little redundant. I looked in the mirror. Nope—still there. But, oh my God, my fucking eyes were bloodred. With huge black pupils. It's easy to get lost in the dark.

Late night and the walking wounded, survivors of some terrible crash. I got groped by some guy in a wig and baseball cap. The proverbial toad—complete with genital warts. Hallucinogens and warts. Bad combo.

Permission revoked.

And now all I wanted to do was take a shower.

Lukewarm hot water. A three-quarter wall of ice-cold tile facing an open hall, two half-ass nozzles, and absolutely no soap. Starving and I still had a raging hard-on. I looked down at it. Go away. I woulda fucking stabbed someone for a dry towel. And that's just about the time I realized he switched keys.

Icarus.

Oh. You'd better fucking run.

Knock knock. It's your life passing before your eyes.

He opened the door with all the nonchalance of a bad actress. "Well, hello." I swear all he was missing was a negligee.

"Gimme my key."

"Oh—do I have your key?"

"The innocent." I brushed by him. "Yeah, me too." And stopped dead in my tracks.

The place was more decked out than my first apartment. A scarf over the lamp, quilt on the bed—flowers. There was a transistor radio playing "Magic Carpet Ride." All he needed was a hot plate and some lace curtains. But there was an electric candle and some kinda shrine to Buddha. I turned to him.

"I'm in my Buddhist phase—freedom from desire and all that."

"Yeah, well. Just don't mistake repression for freedom. Doesn't work—leads to acting out...take my word for it."

I tried to take it all in. "How did you get in here with all this stuff?"

"I told you. I know people."

A stack of fresh warm towels.

"Well—at least stay for a piece of pizza."

Cold pizza. Yes. "Okay."

At least he had all his bases covered. I'll have to give him that.

Sitting on the bed watching porn and talking with a mouth fulla pizza—and I can't tell you how wrong it felt when he grabbed me. Hand all slicked up with lube and I honestly didn't see it coming. I really didn't. So, I mean, how stupid am I? Icarus. Oh, fuck. The explosion. Which doesn't even begin to do it justice. Jizz dripping off his eyelashes—and I'm like...speechless. Not a good scene.

"I gotta go."

Then I thought about it for a second, turned around, took his face in my hands—and kissed him, in a way...I've kissed very few other people in my life.

"Listen to me. I'm gonna see you on the other side of the game. And I'm expecting something of you. Get your ass outta here. This is no place to set up camp. It's slumming. Don't get stuck. Don't get defined. Don't let this place define you—not that it doesn't have its charms. But you're better than that. You're a survivor."

He smiled at me. "Know what? I don't even know your name."

"Moses." And suddenly I got a flash. "Icarus & Moses" inside a heart — tattooed on his scrawny white ass.

I smiled back at him.

And we left it at that.

Sunrise.

A chain-link fence and you only had to wonder what the fucking neighbors thought. And who they were. And who we were. Us. And who that was.

And them.

I got back in the car. Thank God for Visine. 'Cause you know — sometimes I disappear.

IDENTITIES
CARY MICHAEL BASS

At 7:30 a.m. on Tuesday morning, Jeffries Parsons left home in Coral Springs in his 2056 Osprey and entered the Chiles Bulletway to glide two hundred miles to his office in Orlando. He always left home early because the Bulletway was rarely crowded until past eight, and at this hour he could usually expect to be at his desk by eight thirty, if he didn't stop along the way.

As the Osprey sped along, he pulled down the driver's mirror and sprayed his teeth with bromide, careful to cover the insides and the gaps between the teeth. After he finished, he kept the mirror and assessed his looks. His fortieth birthday was rapidly approaching, but he was still as handsome today as he had been ten years ago. Unlike his dad, who'd already been shaving his head at thirty to compensate for early hair loss, Jeffries still maintained a full covering of his own original blond locks. He wore his hair in the more conservative '50s fashion, parted down the middle and just long enough to cover the upper rounds of his smallish ears. In back it was cut high and tight, like that of most of his contemporaries. He kept his boyish face clean-shaven except for the sideburns he maintained to give him a bit of respectability, preventing him from appearing too immature.

Jeffries pulled the mirror back into place, and looked at the gold wedding band on his left hand. What was love ten years ago seemed to be nothing more than comfort now. He and Alex hadn't been intimate in more weeks than he cared to count, and now they barely spoke at home. It only made sense that Jeffries should seek out extramarital sex every once in a while.

Jeffries pushed the "*" and "3" keys simultaneously on the screenpad in his console. In seconds, a mechanical voice surrounded his vehicle.

"You have reached the..."

His fingers cut the voice off, selecting "1" and "4."

"Rosanne," a voice soon identified herself.

"It's me."

"Jeff, what's up?"

"There's an accident on the on-ramp here in Coral Springs, I'll be a bit late this morning."

"It's okay, boss...I'll clear things here for you. Be careful." Rosanne's voice was non-presumptuous, but Jeffries could tell that she knew he was lying.

"See you later," he responded with detachment, then hit the

DISCONNECT button.

Okeechobee had been a farm town, stuck in the twentieth century until the Bulletway came through, but within weeks after the hyposonic expressway's opening, it experienced a boom, becoming a haven for the high-speed traveler. The Simulcurion Adult Gay Emporium was located about three blocks off the Bulletway, an easy on-and-off for Jeffries. He pulled into the parking garage, a thick, concrete edifice that was designed to prevent external global positioning sensors from discerning vehicular location.

The easy and anonymous sex available at the Emporium was a compulsion for Jeffries. Trying to stop from acting on it was an effort in futility, and Jeffries now just accepted the fact that he simply needed to go with it.

The tinted glass door slid open as he glanced at the retinal scanner, and a computerized voice welcomed him, by name, back to the Emporium. Jeffries passed through the DHD title section without looking at either the attendant or any of the holovid customers, toward a dimly lit passageway beneath a neon sign reading Shower Rooms. Once he made his way through the steamy entry, red arrows lit up the walls, directing him to booth 27, which would be prepped with a freshly laundered towel and tiny bar of deodorant soap. It was all just cover— the Emporium was a legitimate sex club and only pretended it was something else to appease small-town sensibilities.

On his way to his booth, Jeffries passed several men in various degrees of nudity, none that especially titillated him. He was looking for a quick fix, however, some release from the stress of too much work and not enough love, and most of the men would suffice for his needs. Then, as he opened the door to his cell, Jeffries shared a brief but intense stare with a wiry man in his early to mid-twenties. The man was not close enough for Jeffries to get a reading on his attractiveness. He smiled crookedly, offering Jeffries a telltale glow of magnesi-capped teeth, popular among Punk-aa-Funk band members and the welfare class. Jeffries nodded his head and closed the door to undress, laughing at the circumstances.

When Jeffries finally reopened the door, the same man was standing right outside, a devilish smile on his face.

"What's up?" the young man said.

Jeffries responded dumbly, "What do you think?"

The man nudged Jeffries back into the tiny cell and said, "I'd sure like to find out."

Jeffries smiled. The man's forwardness was turning him on. "I think I could get into you."

The wiry man dropped his towel, revealing a nice piece of meat, then turned around and replied, "I was hoping you'd say that."

His ass was nice and small, perfectly proportioned for the man's size. Jeffries dropped his towel, spit on his hand, and rubbed the saliva around the head of his cock. As the boy watched him, his butthole expanded and contracted in anticipation, inviting Jeffries inside of him. Jeffries did not hesitate to lick his finger again and push it inside of the wiry man. He seemed to already be lubricated. Jeffries bent him over the bed, pushed the head of his cock into the eager asshole, and began fucking him slowly.

"Oh, man, I like it big like that. Split me open!" the man moaned.

Jeffries could tell by the ease with which he took him, that the boy was used to a fat cock. Jeffries was so tired of all those so-called size queens who made for him every time they saw him only to complain furiously when he finally got into them. It felt good to give it to someone who knew how to handle what he had to give.

It only took fifteen minutes for Jeffries to spill his load inside the young man, and then they were off to the showers.

"My name's Nico," the young man offered.

"Good to meet you. I'm Rob," Jeffries lied without hesitation.

"Listen, I live close by, you have some more time?"

Jeffries was tempted by Nico's allure, but he had responsibilities elsewhere. "I have a busy day ahead—I've got to get going."

"Let's be fair now," he said. "You've already gotten off. I deserve a chance too...why don't you come on over?" The sparkle in Nico's eyes was hard to resist.

Opportunities like this didn't come along every day and Jeffries knew he could arrive another half hour later at work. "You said you live close by. Can we walk it?"

"Sure. If that's what you want to do."

Jeffries eyed the young man up and down. His smooth, olive-skinned body was worth a little more consideration. He briefly considered calling back to the office, but he didn't want Nico to see the kind of car he drove and besides, Rosanne would already have some idea what he was up to and would cover for him.

Along the way, the kid asked if Jeffries was healthy, something Jeffries found odd after he had already taken his load. Nico went on to ask if Jeffries ever had any seizures or brain trauma, making it seem as if it were normal conversation among tricks. Jeffries laughed and responded that, no, he was in perfect health.

Nico's apartment was indeed close, an efficiency in an old motel called the River Inn. The room appeared to have the original motel room contents, with very few actual personal items about. Jeffries doubted that the browning nineteenth-century prints of Parisian Expositions adorning the walls belonged to Nico, considering them more likely some twentieth-century idea of ambiance for weary travelers. It didn't look much like a home.

Nico went straight to the room's kitchenette. "Could I get you something to drink, Rob?"

Jeffries wanted to get right down to business, and was already unbuttoning his shirt. "No, that's okay, I don't want to trouble you."

"C'mon, Rob, I've got some ice-cold soda in here. You drink soda, don't you? Let's talk for a few minutes? What's the rush?"

Had the man not heard him earlier? "I've got a pretty busy day, man. I do have a job."

Nico walked out of the kitchenette with two glasses of cola in his hand. "I just need to unwind a bit." He handed one to Jeffries, who sat on the edge of the bed.

Jeffries took a sip. It tasted stale and a little bitter. "You seem pretty relaxed to me," Jeffries said to him rather than offend the young man's hospitality. He took another sip.

"Yeah, well, you know," Nico said, "I really don't do this sort of thing that often."

That surprised Jeffries because the boy's motives were clear. "Well, you seem to be a real pro." He took another swallow of the drink and leaned over to kiss Nico. The young man took the kiss with what seemed to be some apprehension. Jeffries sat up, surprised. "You were certainly different at the Emporium."

Nico simply shrugged. "Just give me a few minutes."

Jeffries suddenly realized his head was swimming. "What did you give me? I don't use drugs." He stood up and threw the glass at Nico.

The kid began to sputter. "Give you drugs? What are you talking about?" Nico's eyes and behavior betrayed the deception, but there was nothing Jeffries could do about it. Whatever Nico had slipped into his soda was working quickly. Jeffries felt his legs give out, and then blacked out.

Jeffries awoke with no sense of time and a feeling like his head was in a vice. Groggily he opened his eyes and realized he was on the same floor, in the same position he had fallen. Nico was staring at him anxiously.

"Claude?" the concerned boy said. "Claude?"

Jeffries could not move his limbs. What had this kid done to him? He had heard of the legend about people being drugged and their organs harvested, but he was not in a bathtub of ice, and Nico was still here. There was, however, something pressing against Jeffries temples.

"Can you speak, Claude?"

"What did you do?" Jeffries managed to mumble. He managed to move his arm. The drug Nico had given him was beginning to wear off.

"I brought you back, Claude." Nico's eyes were teary. "The Hyptoral should wear off shortly. Try to move."

The kid was nuts! Jeffries thought the best thing he could do was play along. With what little strength he had, Jeffries managed to put his hands to his head and felt metal and wires attached.

"Don't touch that, Claude, here, I'll take care of it," Nico said, reaching over. "How do you feel?" There was some relief of the pressure against Jeffries' temples.

"Like I've been drugged," he replied. "What happened?"

"There was an accident. I don't know what went wrong. But... you're back now. Here with me." Nico was holding the object that he had removed from Jeffries' head. It looked like a homemade combination of a beauty-salon dryer and short-wave radio, a dome of metal covered thickly with wires.

"What is that?"

"A low-frequency neural recorder. It's a black-market device. I saved enough to buy it, from the Serbians. I know how you feel about them, but they got it for me to collect your thoughts and memories and implant them in this fellow. You're in a coma."

Jeffries was horrified. He'd read about neural recorders in *Popular Science*. They were used to collect information from people who'd been in accidents and to help quadriplegics communicate. He couldn't fathom that they could be used to rewrite another person's memory. He felt violated, and anger strengthened his limbs. He stood up and yanked the recorder from Nico's hands, throwing it with all his might against the wall, shattering the glass from one of the prints.

"Well, I'm not this Claude you want me to be! Who the fuck do you think you are? What kind of person kidnaps and drugs someone to replace him with someone else? Well, whatever you did, didn't work."

Nico's face had blanched from the moment Jeffries stood up, and he was now backing away from him.

Jeffries continued. "How stupid are you? I should beat you senseless right now!" He pushed the kid against the bed and ran from the apartment. All he wanted to do was escape from the efficiency as quickly as possible.

His anger was turning to confusion, and he again felt the effects of the drug and staggered away from the motel, down the road, back to the Emporium and his car, looking back every few seconds to see if Nico had followed him. He dialed his office and left a message for Rosanne that he was too sick now to come in and would be returning home. His work didn't seem all that important today.

Jeffries was grateful to be alive, and took deep breaths of relief on his trip back down the Bulletway to Coral Springs. He was still disturbed by being violated so horribly and hateful thoughts of retribution continued to linger.

His spouse, Alex, was surprised when he returned home, and questioned him. His only answer to the inquiries was that he had seen a terrible accident and been so sickened by it he could not go into work. He went into his bedroom and closed the door, brooding for much of the morning, ignoring Alex's expressions of concern at the door.

By noon he had lost the feelings of victimization and no longer felt guilty about the indiscretion. In order to maintain peace in his relationship, he emerged from the room and joined his perplexed spouse for a healthy lunch. Although Alex seemed apprehensive at first at Jeffries' sudden change of heart, he readily cooperated. While Jeffries did not let on that anything extraordinary had happened, he felt oddly invigorated by the morning's experience. He felt somehow changed by the event, as if inhibitions had fallen away from him. He saw his spouse with fresh, new eyes. As they finished lunch, Jeffries arose and took Alex's arm. Alex opened his eyes wide in surprise when he realized what Jeffries' intended.

Although Jeffries was familiar with every aspect of Alex's body, each touch felt novel. Perhaps it had been too long since they had been intimate. Jeffries fucked Alex furiously, during the afternoon, coming inside of him once...twice...copulating in unusual positions and bizarre joins until he came once more and the couple collapsed into an exhausted heap.

As he lay looking into the blue eyes of his spouse, Jeffries thoughts turned to Nico. Alex was here smiling at him, but vivid fantasies of Nico were invading Jeffries' conscience. Fucking Nico on Fort Walton Beach, taking Nico's cock into his mouth in the woods south of Daytona, Nico sucking him off while they were driving a car down a dark road through the Everglades. Jeffries realized when he imagined he and Nico in bed with an unnatural clarity that his fantasies were, in fact, memories that he should not possess.

Whatever had occurred that morning with Nico, the purpose of the horrible device had not, in fact, failed, only been delayed! The novelty that Jeffries was feeling with Alex was not a product of going too long without sex with his partner. It was the result of Claude's complete lack of familiarity for Alex.

Memories were flowing into Jeffries' head of another man's life. He began to see visions of Claude's debauchery and Claude's crimes. Instances of performing robbery and rape, violent acts against other men, ingestion of massive quantities of narcotics—these recollections overwhelmed Jeffries and he stood up, pushed Alex away, and returned to his bedroom, closing the door behind him.

Jeffries looked in his mirror at the man standing naked before him.

The blond hair, blue eyes, reasonably well-kept shape, hairy chest did indeed belong to Jeffries Parsons. But it was no longer who he was: Claude Chevre.

Claude could feel Jeffries' identity buried deep inside of him, but the man's personality was so revolted it had withdrawn. Claude could not remember much of who Jeffries was. The only memories belonging to the man whose body Claude now possessed began with his awakening in Nico's apartment.

What had become of Claude? Nico said there was an accident—but Claude could not remember anything about it.

Claude had a memory of Nico and him in Atlanta, in March of 2057. He knew that it was past September now. Had he only lost six months, or was it even the same year?

Claude looked down in the mirror at the size of Jeffries' cock. Nico had certainly been careful in his selection of bodies for this bizarre transformation.

The sensation of occupation was too strange for Claude—he had to find Nico and figure out how and why the boy had done it. Had Nico become so lonely and desperate that he would do anything, no matter how callous, to bring Claude back to him? He opened up Jeffries' closet door and was disappointed by the man's overly conservative taste in clothing. Leaving the room, Claude nearly ran into Alex, who'd been standing there.

"I can't wear any of this shit. You're about the same size. What have you got that's not so stuffy?"

"What's wrong, Jeffries—why are you talking that way?"

"I'm not feeling myself right now," Claude quipped. "Give me something of yours."

"Stop acting that way! Why are you doing this?"

"Never mind, I'll find it myself." Claude ran into Alex's room, and rifled through his belongings, finding an adequate-looking chemise and loose-fitting slacks. Ignoring Alex, he ran out to the Osprey, the younger man right behind him.

"What the hell happened today?" Alex grabbed his spouse's shoulder.

Claude shrugged the smaller man off. "I'm a new man," he responded as he put his palm on the Osprey's door.

The door unlatched and Claude hopped into the driver's seat. He looked around the cab of the vehicle and quickly realized he did not know how to operate the vehicle. The one time he could remember driving it was away from Okeechobee, when Jeffries had been completely preoccupied.

He yelled at the man outside. "Do you know how to move this?"

Alex hesitated before he cried back, "You never let me drive! How would I know?"

"You want to drive it?" Claude shifted over to the passenger seat. "Get in!"

Alex appeared indecisive, as if he would be damned by the admission of knowledge.

"I want you to drive right now, Honey." Claude smiled as he bluffed Jeffries' response. "Come on, you've seen me do it a hundred times."

Alex looked apprehensive, but slowly got in and sat down next to Claude. Then Alex looked at his spouse, his mouth agape with consternation.

Alex pushed two buttons on the console that were camouflaged as stylistic indentations. The Osprey purred to life. Claude smiled at Alex. "I knew you knew how to do this."

"So where do you want me to drive it?"

"It should be in the travel log for my previous destination."

Alex's eyes furrowed in incomprehension. "But you said you were going to work when you..."

"Go ahead, baby. You'll see I've been a very, very bad boy."

Alex was silent and teary-eyed as the Osprey glided down the Bulletway to Okeechobee. Claude did not know the first thing to say to comfort Jeffries' spouse, although he had dealt with lies and betrayal on a much larger scale. He doubted Jeffries' escapades could be more than insignificant in comparison.

Alex broke the silence as they arrived at the Emporium. "I don't even know why I'm going along with you on this. What's going on, why won't you tell me?"

"I don't want to go here," Claude responded unsympathetically. "Keep going down the road just a bit more. See the motel up the street?"

Following Claude's instruction, Alex repeated, "What's this all about? I demand that you explain it to me."

Arriving at the River Inn, Claude said, "Let me out here. Go home and do what you have to do. I can't stand your whining anymore."

Alex stared at him for a second, then huffed and drove off.

Claude made his way to Nico's room. The door was unlocked, but Nico was nowhere to be found. The evidence of the morning's disaster was also missing, the pieces of the device and the broken glass, but Nico's personal belongings still remained.

Claude rifled through a stack of paper on the floor beside the bed, hoping for some evidence as to Nico's whereabouts or even the solution to his own mystery. An unpaid invoice caught his eye—sent not to Nico but the "Guardian of Claude Chevre." The sender...a nursing home located nearby.

Claude opened the door to the hospital room where his body lay resting. Nico was there, spread over his stomach.

"So you want to tell me what happened?"

Nico looked up. "Rob?"

"His name's not really Rob, you know."

"Claude? Is it really you?"

"Claude's memories, Claude's feelings, Claude's personality. Yes, I've got all of that. But am I Claude?" He pointed at the body lying on the bed. "No, that's Claude. You've made a terrible mistake." He walked to the body, looking at the face. The eyes were open, staring out into space. They were his — Claude's eyes.

"Of course you're Claude...I can see it in your eyes." Nico stood up smiling, and threw his arms around him.

He held Nico tightly. The young man felt comfortable. Claude wanted so much to make him happy, to let things be the way they were at that moment. But none of it was right. He pushed the young man off of him.

"How did I get...how did Claude get like this? I can't yet remember..."

Nico said, "We were ready to leave. Going to get away from everything here — go to Europe."

Finally, the memory that was on the edge of Claude's conscience completed itself. Claude continued for Nico, "Everything was planned, wasn't it? We had made all the arrangements." The younger man nodded his head. Claude turned away from him, toward his body. "But we weren't completely safe, were we?" He looked at Nico again — the young man was averting his eyes. "There was that government agent. I never had the pleasure of meeting him. You stopped him yourself...all by yourself. So we could leave the country." Claude raised his voice. "You killed him, Nico. You killed him and got rid of his body!"

Nico looked at Claude again, his eyes wide open. "I had to do it for us, Claude. So we could be together."

Nico had been such an innocent when Claude met and fell in love with the sixteen-year-old. What had that love done to the young man? Claude had taken the child and corrupted him into a killer. "Did you think you were doing what I would do? I have never taken a life! That was murder! It is wrong...and what you have done to Jeffries is wrong now!" It was all Claude's fault. *He* made Nico. He pulled a pillow from the bed and pushed it on top of the face — *his* face — before him.

"Claude, what are you doing?" Nico tried to yank his arms away, but he was no match for Claude's determination — and Jeffries' strength.

"I'm finishing what I started — I left you, drove off a bridge because

I could not live with what I...Claude had made of you. You were trying to be like Claude—but Claude was never able to do those things. The murder you performed—it *revolted* Claude!" The body beneath the pillow—the real Claude—remained motionless.

Nico gave up his struggle and crossed his own arms. "It does not matter. You are still Claude."

The body shuddered, and then went limp and an alarm went off in the room. "You fool! Claude is dead! I am not, nor will I ever be he!"

"But I know you love me!" Nico cried in anguish.

He threw the pillow to the floor and looked at the young man. Did he love him? What existed of Claude's personality now saw the man that Nico had become. And Jeffries? What Nico did to Jeffries was worse than rape. "Love you? I don't even know who you are! I loathe you!"

The door to the room slid open, and an automated attendant passed to determine the cause of the alarm. Within minutes, a living nurse would be present and then explanations would be beyond him.

"Claude, please! Tell me you love me!" Nico's eyes were filling up with tears.

The older man knew who he was. No matter the memories he possessed, the personality that seemed to exist, for a time, the underlying individual was still Jeffries Parsons. "My name isn't Claude. Claude is gone. Goodbye." Jeffries Parsons passed through the opening without looking back. He heard Nico sobbing behind him as the door slid closed, but he continued walking until he was out of the nursing home, and well down the street. Claude's personality was fading fast. The guilt of what he had done to Nico and the resulting evils Nico was able to perform, were too much. It had made him entirely unwilling to exist as Claude, and Jeffries was able to finally reassert his domination.

Then tears started rolling down Jeffries' face. He didn't know what felt worse, Claude's corruption of Nico or his own abandonment of his marriage, but at that moment, Jeffries felt like he deserved to die.

The memories, however, remained intact, and contrary to his actions, Jeffries did indeed feel some residual compassion for Nico. But he was not in love with Nico—that belonged to someone else.

Jeffries didn't know if he could ever fix it.

Jeffries hadn't realized that Alex had pulled alongside him until he suddenly spied the Osprey's skids next to his own legs.

"Are you done, then?" Alex yelled out through the opened window with a sarcastic tone.

Jeffries couldn't look up and face Alex. He remained still.

"Well, I'm not going to leave you up here. Besides, this is your glider."

Jeffries opened the door and sat in the passenger seat, next to his spouse—the one man he truly loved.

"Are you going to tell me what happened?"

"You wouldn't believe it," Jeffries responded.

Alex fumed in silence as they pulled away from the curb. Then, "Well, I've already made an appointment with an attorney."

"I understand." Jeffries stared ahead of the Osprey as they entered the on-ramp to the Bulletway. "Alex..."

His spouse turned and looked at him through squinted eyes. "What?"

"I love you."

Alex's mouth was pursed—he looked like he was about to explode. After a long moment, he responded, "It's not going to be that easy."

"I know," Jeffries answered.

SHIFTLESS MIND MATTER
RUSTY CANELA

I was melting into the sofa. I'd smoked so much dope I could feel the hairs on my hairless face tingling before they were born. I could feel each drop of urine drop into my bladder. I could feel my asshole pucker up wanting dick. *Fuck*, I thought, *it's late*. It must've been one or so. I was going to get the munchies. The store a few blocks away was going to close and I was going to go to sleep hungry from both ends of my body.

Precious luscious seconds slipped by and seemed like an eternity. I should've done some cocaine or some acid. Hell, it was Friday night, time to be out on the town partying with my friends. Friends I kept my most guarded secret from. I was a nerd with dirty underwear. God I hadn't changed them in weeks. They had urine stains and little brown streaks where the underwear would go between my cheeks and rub my asshole. I wasn't stupid enough to take them off and get them washed. What, and air out my laundry? Hey, I was stupid, but not an idiot.

I thought of a big, fat, long dick, and my straight friends. *Bitch*, they called me now and then, not knowing that I really was. The sky looked green through the sheet rock ceiling. I couldn't remember when I had started seeing through it. I looked down and saw the tile on the floor peeling as if it had a life of its own. I looked at the walls of my ten-by-ten hole.

There was a cockroach eating out of a plate and another one dancing to the *Steve Miller Band's Greatest Hits*. He'd folded his leg to the rhythm and turned around and around then stood up, skipped around the plate, made a fist, and yelled, "Yeah!"

I got up from my creaky bed with the sagging springs and the swaying mattress. I held onto the wall and wondered how long it would take me to get to the store and back. Thirty minutes? I walked to the rest room and took a piss, letting out all the little drops of urine that had accumulated in my bladder since last I'd pissed. I could hear the roar of a train, but there were no trains in the vicinity. I couldn't remember how close the closest set of tracks was. I could feel the walls bend as I walked by them to walk out of the house.

Diamonds were scattered across the black sky. The streetlamps were bright. I was blinded by the passing cars. *Munchies, munchies!* my stomach screamed. I had to have another fix. My heart was throbbing and my stomach was empty. My hair was a mess and I knew it. I thought of what my mouth wanted to eat. Mouths are funny when you're stoned. They want to eat delicious food: soda pops, Twinkies, chocolate Moon Pies and saucy cherry pies, burritos, tuna-fish-salad sandwiches. I wondered how much money I had in my pocket. Would it be enough to buy half the store and eat it in the parking lot?

I got to the store and purchased a green chili burrito, chips, a chocolate Moon Pie, some sodas, an orange juice, and some jellybeans. I walked back with my treasures thinking the only thing I wish I could've purchased was a big long extra-saucy dick for desert, or was it dessert? I thought long and hard, and my mouth watered. I could imagine this cute young guy attached to this wonderfully big dick. He'd be tall, muscular, with big arms and thighs, a huge chest and a six-pack on his stomach. I'd drink the six-pack, then I'd suck his dick, bend over for him, and give him the ride of his life.

That's how I would do it if I had one.

I walked to the post office and realized while I was walking by it that it wasn't on my way home, and I wondered what had brought me to that place. You know the one with all the letters going everywhere. I thought a minute, looked right and then left, and wondered if my hole had fallen out of my pocket, and I worried where I was going to sleep if I didn't find the bed with the creaky springs and the swaying mattress. I headed right and decided that the streetlamps didn't look right. Something about the light didn't seem right. They had a yellow haze and the ones near my house were white and bright. I looked left and didn't see any familiar landmarks and thought I should go back where I came from, but I couldn't remember that either, so I sat on the curb, popped open a soda, and ate a Moon Pie, only it wasn't chocolate like the one I had bought; this one was not very cool; it was yellow and tasted like bananas. I ate the damn thing anyway.

I couldn't remember when I had started having delusions. I must've been very young, like a year or two before, but I couldn't remember before that.

I sat and listened to my thoughts of the people that lived in my head. Yeah, there were people living there. All kinds of people. My favorite was this cute guy with the big long dick.

I walked straight, straight into hell, that's what I did. I just kept walking. And when I came to the park I realized I was only a block from my house, but there were these three guys there drinking beer and I felt like screaming, *Hey motherfuckers, who the hell wants to get their dick sucked or fuck me!* But I didn't. I kept walking, pretending that I wasn't hungry at all for those great-looking guys. I couldn't really see them in the dark, but I knew they were great-looking.

As I walked I felt as if they were looking my way. I turned quickly to look at them. One of them looked over and motioned *what was up.* I shook my head and kept walking. I walked a few blocks when I realized I was being followed and this one guy says to the other, "Lookit, I thank ees quiyor?"

The other guy says, "Yeah, lookit how he moves his little butt."

"Reckon we oughtter get us a little?" the first one says.

"I reckon so," the other says.

I started walking faster, only I didn't know why. I wanted dick. They followed at a faster pace and suddenly I realized they were catching up with me.

I walked faster and faster and finally reached my house, which was a few paces away. It was dark, and I fumbled with my keys. One guy reached for the doorknob and I caught his wrist. The other grabbed me from around my neck and pushed me forward. I couldn't remember why I was looking for my keys when I hadn't even locked the damn door.

The guy who had me by my neck shoved me onto the creaky bed with the swaying mattress. The other guy pulled on my belt and figured I didn't have one because he couldn't find it, so he said, "Stupid punk."

He undid my pants and pulled them down with my stinky underwear with the yellow urine stains and the streaks of brown where they had crept up my ass and rubbed my hole.

No, stop! I yelled in my mind. *I'll let you, I'll let you, just let me loose.* But they didn't let me loose. I remember seeing the chickens in the yard earlier. They looked so beautiful. And just then this guy sticks his big, thick dick in my mouth and I could hardly breathe, so I began breathing through my nose, and I didn't have to throw up. The guy in my rear stuck his dick up my ass and it burned, and I wondered if he had used Vaseline or Vicks. It felt like the day I had eaten too many jalapeño peppers but instead of going out it was coming in, and at that very moment I wondered if I had eaten my green chili burrito or if I still had it in the bag that I had dropped when the guy had caught me by the neck on the way in. The guy in the front fucked my mouth and the guy in the rear fucked my ass, and I wondered where the hell the third guy was going to put his dick.

The guy that fucked my mouth came. His cum was delicious; it tasted like the white cream inside the donuts from the donut shop up the street, the one with the yellow lights that said Open 24 Hours, and god, thinking of that donut made me hungry, and I wondered if I would have some hot chocolate to go with it or if I would drink it with my orange juice.

Well, the next guy who entered my mouth did not taste at all like orange juice; it was more like a wienie from Der Wienerskitsall or whatever you want to call it. The guy in the rear was moving around like he was on a pogo stick, and I said, *Shit, can't you fuck like a man,* in my mind because my mouth was being occupied by this dick that tasted like a wienie and with all that flavor I wish he'd put mustard on it to make it taste even better. I was thinking all along about what had happened to my green chili burrito. If any of these guys ate it, I'll kill the mother-fuckers. I'm a black belt in Karate.

You fuck me good or I'll beat the shit out of you motherfuckers, I thought.

The guy in the rear finally came and he sat down and had a beer. I cussed him out because he hadn't offered me one before fucking me. *Who do you think I am? Your dada? Piece of shit son-of-a-bitch*, I thought. *You leave me some beer.* Then the guy in the front comes and he holds me tightly by my hair and shoves his dick to the back of my throat. Son-of-a-bitch didn't even let me taste the motherfucking cum, and here I am fantasizing about all the cream inside a donut and the motherfucker doesn't even let me taste it.

When he finished, he shoved my head sideways. I hit my head on the bed and conked out.

I woke up naked with the sun in my face. My head was pounding, and I saw the green chili burrito wrapper on the floor and I thought, *God damn it, they ate my burrito. They could've at least left me that.* I got up and when I turned around to look for my stinky underwear, the one with the yellow stains and the streaks of brown, there was this big good-looking naked body on my bed.

How could I have slept next to that gorgeous thing and not have known it?

"Hey," I said, "time to go home, the ride's over, motherfucker."

He turned toward me, and it was one of my best friends, Jas.

"Fuck, how'd you get in here?" I asked.

"The door was open," he said smiling.

"God, I smoked too much last night and I had this horrible dream," I said looking away and feeling that it hadn't been a dream because I felt like I had Vicks up my butt.

"Isn't Vicks cool?" he asked.

"Fuck, that was you, you stinking son-of-a-bitch," I said angrily.

"Humped you good, didn't I?" he said.

"You ever try that again and I'll kill you, you queer son-of-a-bitch," I said wishing he'd do it again.

"Bend over, you queer," he said laughing.

"Get out!" I yelled.

My other friend, Mark, comes in and asks what the problem is.

Jas is getting up and putting on his clothes.

"Thinks I fucked him with Vicks or something," Jas says.

"There he goes imagining all this queerness again," Mark said laughing.

"Hey, guy," Jas said leaving a dollar on the bed, "I ate your green chili burrito, get another one, and quit smoking so much dope, man."

UNSAFE SEX
STEVEN SCHWARTZ

I didn't realize how much I'd changed. After all, I was still the same man who'd come into the Ram plenty of times before. I'd buy a pack of condoms and give the man behind the counter ten dollars more than they cost, to get into the back room. I was just another man getting a quick suck-and-fuck before going back to his nice apartment.

This time, I just took out a ten-dollar bill, and the attendant barely looked away from the Bulls game to grab it and nod toward the turnstile.

I'm not a nice guy, tonight. He didn't see sweater and slacks, or a fashionable T-shirt. I left those at home. Instead, I was wearing a leather motorcycle jacket, aviator sunglasses, tight blue jeans, and a shirt advertising a local leather bar. The cap and gloves topped it off; I hoped that all the clerk would register was "leatherman." I was a different man than the last time I'd come here: I'd washed out the hair dye; there was gray at my temples now, not much, but some. I'd let my beard grow. It's damn hard to wait, to let it get from scratchy nuisance to actual disguise. I'd had customers come in and ask why I was growing it out. "It goes along with the rest of the outfit" was my usual response, and they'd laugh. At the metal shop, I wear a plaid flannel shirt and jeans, so that people feel like they're dealing with a real craftsman. It's amazing how much people judge by clothes. I'd be the same person at work in a pink polo shirt and white slacks, but I'd get requests to rearrange furniture, rather than build it. Jack, my ex-lover, did that kind of thing. Not me.

As I walked past the wall of toys and magazines toward the turnstile, I lingered a moment to stare. I should have come here sooner, I thought, as I looked at the dildos in their glass case, and I could feel my ass tighten and relax, like it was trying to pull some lover's cock farther up inside me. I wanted one of those dildos. One that doesn't have a curve, though, one nice and straight and long that'd fill me up, fill up the empty places inside me. No curves. Jack had a curved cock; great for making my prostate happy, but the rest of what came with it I could do without, right now. And my prostate doesn't overrule my brain very often. What color would I want? Not DOA Caucasian, for heaven's sake. Jack might be DOA soon enough, and I didn't need any reminders. But all the black ones looked like someone just dipped those same dead white guys' dicks in India ink. Wonderful.

Tonight, though, I don't need a dildo. I was the top, and I had something that'd be perfect for what I wanted to do. I reached under the bulky leather of the jacket to make sure it was still there.

The turnstile had a new slew of safe sex warning stickers on it, matching the posters all over the walls just on the other side. I'd always hated that turnstile; it was narrow enough that unless you watched your weight, and kept your hips slender, you'd feel awkward as hell getting through. Jack, of course, had never had a problem. I shuffled my way through it, thanking God that my old jeans weren't as stiff as my new jacket, as I felt the cool metal of one of the turnstile arms press against my thigh. Inside, it's darker, so I stuffed my sunglasses in my pocket. I found a corner by the entrance, quickly, and slipped my hand inside my jacket. When I'd had the harness made, I'd had this in mind, so it wasn't that difficult; my fingers brushed T-shirt, then leather, then steel. I touched my dildo, my fill-him-up and get-me-off dildo one more time, checked that the safety was still on, that the magazine was snugly seated. It was ritual more than any kind of precaution, like straightening your tie one last time before a job interview. My dildo and I had an appointment.

More than anything else, it was leaving the chain off the door that made me want to kill him. We had a goddamned open relationship; we'd even both gone to the Ram together more than a few times. He went more than I did, sure, but people are different. And we'd made a deal; always leave the chain on when you bring someone home. That way, at least you'd be sure not to bring some surprise houseguest home to find your partner and his trick already fucking on the couch.

We had some other rules too; safe sex rules, mostly: no penetration without a condom, no rimming without a barrier, no letting them leave marks on you. The sort of things that a responsible couple sat down and talked about seriously some early weekend afternoon, felt better about, and then went and had a romantic dinner and cooed at each other about how close they were and how good they were.

And so we trusted each other. Which was why, when I opened the door easily, as if it were just any day, I figured Jack would be ready to sit on the couch, listen to a few of the CDs I'd picked up on my way back from the workshop. I'd left work early; a shipment of metal was late, and there's no point sitting around with nothing to do. So I thought I'd come home and surprise him.

Even when I heard the man who wasn't Jack moaning, I trusted him. We had our collection of pornography, after all, and I hadn't told Jack I'd be coming home. If he was getting himself off, I wouldn't object.

"Oh, yeah, I'm gonna come..." So one of the actors was about to come. Good. Jack liked cumshots. Maybe I'd get to see Jack come, get to look down the length of the sofa to see him splayed out, stroking himself.

I turned the corner from the entrance hall and looked into the living room, seeing Jack, indeed, sitting on the edge of the couch, his pants open, pumping his cock with his left hand. His right hand, though, was wrapped around the base of this blond gymboy's cock, the ring made of his first finger and thumb meeting the ring of his lips each time his head bobbed forward. I stood there, stunned, while the other man stood there, hips straining forward toward my lover's face, and announced his impending orgasm to the world.

"Jack?" The name was a question, since I couldn't entirely believe what I was seeing; I didn't want to believe it, and I was sure there simply had to be a perfectly reasonable explanation for why I was seeing my lover sucking this man off in the middle of our living room.

His first response was muffled by his trick's cock, but he managed to pull his head back far enough to say, "I didn't know you were coming home..."

My answer caught in my throat as, with one last loud "Yes," the other man started to come, the white strands splattering onto Jack's cheek, into his hair, some into his open mouth.

The goldfish imitation that damned gymboy did, when he realized that he'd just been dropped right into the middle of a screaming argument, stays with me. He couldn't have looked more surprised if Jack had tried to bite it off. What the hell was I supposed to do about him? I wanted to hate him, make him into some temptress, wanted to think he'd dragged my lover up here, but that was just ridiculous. He was cute, more so to Jack than me, but not so cute he could waggle his ass in someone's face and get whatever he wanted. I let him leave, with his cock still outlined against his shorts; he hadn't waited around long enough to put his underwear back on.

Jack was babbling some kind of explanation, facts and figures about what was and wasn't safe, about how he wouldn't have swallowed anyway, that this was an aberration, that this would never happen again, had never happened before, etc. I wasn't interested.

"Damn it, Jack, we had an arrangement!" After about the third or fourth time I said that, he finally began to understand.

He sighed, and all the apology leached out of his voice, replaced by scorn. "Oh, Michael, I can't believe you're so petty."

Again I was struck speechless for a moment. "Petty?" was all I was able to croak out.

"Yes, petty. You don't even care about some matter of life or death, just about some silly little arrangement. I mean, it sounds like you wouldn't care if I sucked off Death Himself, so long as I used a condom and put the damn chain on the door, but some nice farmboy, never had his dick in anything more menacing than his hand, well heaven help me if I decide that if I don't swallow, it's all right, and forget to put the chain on." Jack was playing it for all it was worth; he knew he was right and was going to rub my nose in it before we were done.

That was the last straw. I was over by the fireplace, and had the poker in my hand before I fully realized what I was doing. Jack does interior decorating, and lets other people move the furniture; I weld and work with large iron sheets. I didn't need the poker to be threatening, not at all. I saw Jack start to flinch, but didn't care. "First, you fucking idiot, you don't know where he's been sticking it. Second, that wasn't any goddamn farmboy. Third, if that's trivial to you, then get the hell out of here. You could have gotten yourself killed doing that!" I emphasized each point with a dramatic twitch of the poker, like some demented university professor.

He stuck up his nose, trying to wrap himself in bravura. "And I suppose I'm not going to get killed with you waving a poker about like some Neanderthal? Fuck you, Michael. That wasn't Death Himself I sucked off; I trust the boy."

It took most of my strength not to take a swing at him with the poker. Instead, I just pointed with it at the door. "You may trust him, but I don't. And I'm damned sure I don't trust you any more. Get out."

He did. And that was it for us. Oh, he came back to get his things, to work out details, but that was it for us.

There's a taste I get in my mouth—I've been told it's adrenaline—when I know I'm doing something I shouldn't. I could taste it as I surveyed the dark room. It seemed stupid at first; after all, it's not like I haven't been here more times than I can count. But this time, it was different.

When you're looking for someone in a back room, all the old habits go by the wayside. I had gotten so used to not looking at people's faces, or, if I did, for only that moment of eye contact that says "Yeah, sure, I'd like to suck your dick" that it was hard to let my eyes linger. So many people don't want to see faces. Many's the time I've thought back here that if they could get away with it, if the laws didn't come oh-so-close already to shutting them down, they should just put in a single long wall with holes, so that if you wanted to get sucked, you'd step up to one and stick your cock through the hole to the side where all the hungry people waited. It'd be simpler.

This time, though, I was looking for someone, not something. A specific person, not a specific body part, though some of the body parts I saw certainly were tempting. Even if things went perfectly, even if I did do it and got away, I could never come back here again, so why not enjoy it one last time? My cock certainly thought so, and it clearly wished I'd worn the old, ratty pair of jeans I sometimes did when I was feeling like a slut, with the hole torn in the crotch. So, to calm my nerves, keep my cover, and see what was up, I started walking around.

First I scoped out the glory holes; that's where I was going to catch him, later. They look like someone had taken a row of men's room toilets, divided by wooden boards, and put video screens in them instead of the plumbing. And they all had holes in those dividers, perfect height to stick your dick through. They seemed only somewhat busy tonight, only a few adjacent doors closed, which was just what I wanted. An even better chance I could get to Jack.

On one side was the maze: the same wooden closets, except with no glory holes, no video screens except above, where the people waiting in the aisles, cruising, could watch. Jack wouldn't be here — I was fairly sure of it — but I did the turn through anyway, trying not to notice other people's expressions. I didn't want them to lust after me, didn't want their eyes burning holes in the front of my pants.

The last area to check out was the rooms: benches, locking doors, same flimsy wood construction as everywhere else. People could hear you while you moaned, and the video screens just had images, no sound to go along with them. These had always been my favorites; I liked to see the person I was with, liked to get to know them to the extent, at least, of a few words of conversation, a few sentences that weren't just, "Oh, yeah, do that more," or "Fuck me."

As I walked down the aisle, I saw some rooms with their doors closed, and paused to listen, trying to hear Jack's voice. I didn't hear him anywhere, but heard enough to make sure my cock stayed hard. Other rooms had open doors; men were sitting in them, waiting to see if anyone paused outside the door, with the excuse of watching the same video screen. They'd look at each other; one would gesture, or smile, and they'd either close the door behind them, or one would wander on. None of the men sitting there was Jack; he wasn't there yet, it seemed.

I felt like such a top; I didn't just have one dick, I had two, and the one that everyone could see was hard as a rock. But I had to save my dicks for someone else. One guy, just my type too, kept scoping my ass as I passed the room he sat in, looking at me rather than watching the video screen. It was hard to resist; he had a long face, and long fingers, and a long body, and I wanted him to fuck me, but I couldn't let him. I wasn't even going to think what would happen if I let him take my jacket off, revealing the rig underneath. And he didn't look, in his button-down shirt and slacks, like the sort of person who'd want a quickie.

Then again, up until tonight, I never thought I was the sort of person who'd want that kind of sex. I'd changed in a lot of ways.

Knowing shops that do custom work helped a great deal. Male Hide Leathers was more than willing to make the straps and harness I wanted, no questions asked, from the drawing I'd sketched out. Well, no questions save, "Do you want that in latigo or patent," and "Do you want studs on that?" Latigo, no studs, and they might have been able to deduce what it was for, but it would have taken some guesswork on their part.

There were a lot of people around Chicago and the suburbs now who might have been able to guess what I was up to, if they'd tried. One was the gentleman I bought the pistol from, a Colt .45 automatic that had been modified to within an inch of its life, a marksman's pistol. The issue of discovery, after I killed Jack, was one I couldn't avoid; I'd done my best, and bought a second barrel, swapping it in before I left the house. It was a faint hope, but better than nothing. If I had time to get home, I could change the barrels back, and all the police would find would be a match pistol, with its custom barrel, and the barrel that shot Jack would be in some dumpster. I wasn't interested in a tragic opera finale; if I shot Jack, I was not going to look dramatic and wait for the police to arrive.

I was surprised, though, that the salesman was not more suspicious; after all, I wasn't a member of any of the initial-laden shooting organizations he named. So why the hell was I spending thirty-five hundred dollars on such a custom job?

Because Jack didn't deserve less. To give the son of a bitch credit, he'd made me happy for a long time. We'd gone to shows together, to the opera, whispered to each other about our sleazy exploits late at night, cooked, cried, everything. He deserved the best, and a little more besides. I couldn't feel halfway about Jack. I'd loved him, and now I hated him with a hatred fit for a Wagnerian hero. Everything had just come crashing down the night of the argument, as his clay feet had proven to go all the way up to his eyebrows, or so it seemed. At least, that was how I'd felt at the time; and I couldn't be neutral about him. Whether it was the Linn-Sondek turntable I'd bought him to listen to his old 45-rpm opera recordings, or a custom Colt .45, Jack would get the best.

The hardest part was assembling the pieces for the silencer. That took time and persistence. There are mail-order places that will sell you a fully assembled, phony silencer, designed to make you look tough, or "supply all your film and stage needs," as one said. From a place in the south suburbs I bought the filter material, and I had more than enough scrap metal in my workshop to finish the job. It was a long afternoon's labor, but I had one; a nice seven inches of polished steel silencer, going on the end of the already big and heavy pistol. There was no way I could carry this thing under my arm or at my side. The only thing I could possibly do was carry it on my back.

While I was waiting for the parts of the silencer, though, I hadn't been wasting my time. I knew where Jack lived, since I was still forwarding mail to him. And so I'd watched him. Watched and seen his habits, when he left the house, where he went. I saw him bringing in the new furniture, new decorations; everything new, everything fit to appear in a glossy home-design centerfold. I saw him bringing in new tricks, most of them in awe of his car, his cash; Jack had always had a thing for white trash, outdoorsy types, and boys fresh off the farm. I'd kidded him that the only reason he stayed with me was the flannel shirts. After we broke up, I'd worn them half as often.

Even with his tricks, it was only a matter of a few days before he went back to the Ram. After that, he did it again and again, almost like clockwork.

One night, he did catch me, as I followed him toward his weekly glory-hole fix. He was walking near a tapas place we'd eaten at together countless times. I was crossing the street, trying to keep up with him, when he noticed me. He smiled, and waved, flashing far more teeth than he needed to. It wasn't a pleasant smile or a pretty wave. It was a wave goodbye. To avoid watching him anymore, I'd walked quickly into the restaurant, and tried to bury my anger in good food and Sangre de Toro wine.

That was what first led me to Male Hide Leathers, though; I didn't want to get caught like that again. I went in determined to look like someone else; and after the jacket, the boots, the cap, and the gloves, I felt like I should pose for leather beefcake shots or the Colt Men calendar. I was quite sure, however, that I wouldn't be caught again.

I could tell that I was losing it: losing my nerve. My cock whispered to me from my pants, "Look, you're excited, you're ready. Damn, man, I've never been this ready before; why are you saving me for that son of a bitch? There's plenty around here you'd like, I know you've seen it, so why don't you just get off and get out of here? You've got to start living a normal life, man, so why don't we just start now?"

I headed for the bathroom; the only place in here I could be alone and not cruised, not surrounded by men wanting sex, having sex, either live or on video. Otherwise, to pull myself together, I'd have to leave, and I certainly wasn't going to do that; I'd never have the courage to come back.

I had to wait a few minutes for whoever was in there to finish. When they came out, it was with the same furtiveness, the same speed that you saw people leave the standup booths. It meant "Me? No, I was never here, no one saw me leave." I went into the bathroom, closed and locked the door, and tried to get a grip on myself.

The only light was a single bare lightbulb; it was a dingy enough room that when I'd come here in the past, I'd avoided it, crossing my legs until I got home if I had to. Tonight, though, it felt right, a small, grungy space where nothing was clean, nothing was any good at all, from the toilet seat with the broken hinge to the mirror hanging cockeyed. If I'd sunk to this, why was I going on? That's what my cock wanted to know, what the part of me said that wanted to shrug it off, try and forgive the bastard. You've wasted thousands of dollars, hours and hours, and ended up in a stinking bathroom with a case of the shakes. This can't be worth it, can it?

I reached into my inside jacket pocket and pulled out my wallet. The condoms came with it, falling on the floor, and I left them there. I didn't need condoms for what I was doing, I thought, and felt my cock twitch. Instead, I focused on getting my wallet open, right-side up.

It opened on a picture of the two of us on the day we'd moved in together, trying to look proud and relaxed, like we were on some kind of vacation, while all around us there were boxes. We'd had our friends' help to move in, but this was after they'd left, the timer on the camera clicking the shutter. Later, that night, we'd done it in the living room, since the bedroom didn't have overhead lighting and was a maze of boxes. That first time when we'd locked the door, put on the chain to make sure neither the landlord nor the friend with the emergency key came in to surprise us, was a wonderful time. It meant that we had somewhere private, somewhere we didn't have to worry about other people walking in on us, or knocking petulantly on the door wondering how much longer we were planning on taking. And we'd used a condom that night. We'd been tempted not to—oh, hell, we had been—but there was always something to make us pause, whether it was my banging my head against the corner of a book box, or the wind outside rattling a branch against the window. And so we stopped, and he put it on, and then we went back to what we were doing. After that condom was on, though, I knew I'd hit my head a few times, and the wind didn't stop blowing through the trees. We just stopped noticing.

And later, on a sunny day, with all the time in the world, that smiling bastard standing next to me in the picture hadn't bothered to stop to put a condom on.

I took the photograph out of its plastic sleeve, laid it on the sink. I was tempted then to pull out the gun, blast a hole in the picture, right through that smiling face, but that might get me caught, and I didn't want to get caught, oh no. I had an appointment with Jack, and no matter how long I needed to wait, now, I'd keep it. Just looking at that smiling face, remembering those lips around that blond trick's cock, the cum dripping down his cheek, the white drops on his tongue; that was enough. That was more than enough.

I tossed the picture in the wastebasket, on top of all the condom wrappers, cigarette packs, and tissues. Taking one last look in the mirror to steel myself, I rubbed my hand along my cock, and felt it twitch again.

With that, I felt ready, and I left.

It wasn't more than a few minutes later that I spotted him, coming through the turnstile looking fresh and hungry, and an hour and a half late. He started to saunter down the line of glory holes, and I followed, slowly, trying to look side-to-side just as he did, not cruising him, just following him.

I had to admit he'd taken good care of himself; he still looked good enough to eat, with his ass tucked up tight in those jeans, his tan clear over his T-shirt. Unless he'd gotten another that same color, that was his "Cheap and Easy" shirt. How like him. I could taste the same rush in my mouth as when I'd first walked in here, could feel my cock throb. "Soon," I whispered to myself, at first not sure I'd done it. When I realized I had, rather than speaking in my mind, I looked around, hoping no one had heard. If they had, they looked away now, not interested in me.

I just hoped Jack was in a hungry mood. Sometimes he'd come here and pick through them all like an overzealous rabbi, trying to find something *treyf* in everyone he ran across, until he'd leave, and go home and masturbate, thinking about what might have been, if only Mr. Right had been there.

Today, though, I was in luck. Without looking at anyone, he ducked into one of the glory-hole booths, with empties on either side. I picked up my pace, striding across the gap between us so fast my boots clacked on the concrete floor. He'd be inside there, kneeling, and unzipping his pants so he could beat off while he sucked. He'd have one hand at each of the holes, fingers through, signaling that he wanted cock. When he got it, he'd just keep his mouth on that hole until the other man came. From all the nights we'd teased each other in bed with the fun we'd had here, I knew what he'd be doing, his whole routine. He'd gloried in telling me, and I'd gotten off, thinking about it. But that was when I trusted him.

Now we met here, and I stepped into the booth next to his, seeing the fingers there. I closed the door behind me, remembering at the last minute not to slam it, and unzipped my pants. Now I was scared; he'd had my cock in his mouth hundreds of times; if he recognized it, everything would be over. It was hard and ready, though, and so I teased his fingers with it a bit first, until I heard him whisper,

"Come on, man, let me have it..."

And I felt his tongue licking at me through the hole. So I let him have it, leaning up against the wall of the booth, feeling his tongue run all over my cock. I thought I could hear him moan with satisfaction, though that might have been me. It wasn't as if he'd never sucked me without a condom before, but this was different. This time it didn't feel like the little tease at the beginning, the appetizer, before we made the preparations for dinner. I knew that was what it really was, and that I had the main course all planned, but he didn't, and that made all the difference. I could feel his hunger, his tongue not afraid to touch me anywhere. I'd always been a bit nervous when he seemed close to coming, my mouth on his cock, a little afraid of the precum. Jack wasn't, and he certainly wasn't now. I could feel it oozing from me, feel him lick it up thirstily, his hand massaging what he couldn't fit in his mouth.

I had to shake myself, to try and come back to earth. I wasn't just here to shoot a load in my ex-lover's mouth. That wasn't the plan. I pressed my fingers hard against the wood, feeling the harsh grain of it, to bring myself back down to earth. Then I let my hands drop to my sides, my hips still pressed hard against the barrier. It was time to shrug off the jacket, moaning at the same time, to make Jack think my movement was a reaction to what he was doing, and reach back, lifting the gun from the holster's embrace, grip already warm from the heat of my body.

I checked, brushing the silencer against the slim strip of exposed flesh where my pants had slid down. It was warm, from my body and the leather jacket, but cool enough; cooler than my cock—and harder.

"Man, let me put a condom on..." I whispered, trying to make my voice sound different, lower, rougher.

I felt his head withdraw. "You don't need to do that..."

I know I don't. A condom wouldn't make a bit of difference; less than a millimeter of latex won't stop a .45 bullet. But I need to do it this way, Jack. I need you waiting for me with an open mouth. "Damn, it's all this safe-sex shit. Need it to relax."

I heard him chuckle. "All right. I'll stay right here. Just slide it right back in."

I drew my cock back, and I could see his teeth and tongue through the hole, so close he must be waiting, pushed up against it. His tongue flickered out for a moment, as if he wanted to lick the taste of me from the wood.

I knelt, quickly, and slid the silencer through the hole, as far as I could get it gently. He started to rear back, but I spoke, my own mouth practically touching the gun, with my voice just loud enough to be recognizable:

"There, Jack; there's death. You'd said that it wasn't like you'd sucked off Death Himself, wasn't that the phrase? Well, this is close enough. Death's got a gun for a cock, Jack. Suck it, Jack. Love it. Can you taste the steel, Jack? How does it feel, Jack, sucking off Death? How does it feel, metal against your teeth? You know what this is, Jack? You'd appreciate it; you always did like high class with a touch of trash. This is a Colt competition gun, Jack. I could have shot you from two blocks away and you'd never have known, shot you from the alleyway behind your new apartment. Taste it, Jack." I couldn't see Jack's face, just a bit of his lips, the hairs of his mustache around the silencer. He'd pursed his lips around the silencer, and they moved. I could feel the tug of his tongue as it did as I told him. "And the silencer? It's homemade, Jack, just a bit of homemade junk; but it makes the whole damn thing longer, now, longer for you, Jack. It's your damn nine inches. I know you've got your hands in your pants, Jack. You always said you did. So do it, Jack. Pull out your cock and start stroking." He did, I could hear it, a slapping noise. "How does it feel now, Jack? Grab a hold of your cock, get a good feel, because it might just be your last. Keep on sucking, Jack. You know, I've heard people can catch bullets in their teeth. But not their throats. Suck it, Jack. Suck it good; love it. You know, suck Death off well enough and maybe, just maybe, he'll like it so much he won't come yet; he'll wait, and let you go on sucking live cocks, cocks that aren't hard and cold as bone in the grave; and then he'll be back, and someday... someday..."

I felt a tightening in my balls, and a twitch as I started to shoot, my cum staining the walls underneath the video screen, one more set of white streaks on the dark wood. I heard him moan as well, and the noise of his beating off stopped. I could still hear his breathing as I pulled the gun back through the hole, the silencer warmed by the heat of his mouth. "See you around," I said, and stood up, zipping up my pants. I draped the jacket over my hand, over the gun, and strode out, not looking back, not looking at any of the other men. I'd walked out of the Ram like that many times before, and anyone looking at me would have thought the same thing: that I'd done what I'd come for, and now wanted to put it behind me.

I went through the turnstile like greased lightning, past the garishly lit dildo rack, and out into the night, turning north to walk home. My boots clacked against the concrete, in half-time to my still racing heartbeat. It wasn't until I'd rounded the corner, and was no longer in sight of the Ram, that I could stop walking. I leaned against a post, breathing slowly, trying to calm down. For several minutes I stayed there, feeling the wind against my skin, the sweat evaporating from my arms, my forehead, making me feel cool and clean. Then, as I started to walk back home, I said a silent prayer. I prayed that Jack didn't suck Death off again for a long, long time.

MY HERO: A WILD BOY'S TALE
TRISTRAM BURDEN

This boy has time. Got an old god behind him; a throwback, primordial beast of the deepest waters, the furthest reaches of space. Came to him in a dream one day and said: "Boy? Boy? You gotta ride. You gotta fly." Whispered all heavy, middle-of-sleep sweat hanging off the balls, hard-on all juicy-tipped from the emanations of this creature. This Titan.

"You gotta ride. You gotta fly." On the road, thinking that old priest ain't nothing on a god, and if I gotta fuck something, I'd rather it were he. Fuck Mary. Fuck the Holy Ghost. Jesus is all right, all that blood and all nice and slippy, got the lube all fixed up there. Just rear into that holy mound of thin, sinuous tortured muscle. Cock hard as nails, that fucker gotta love being crucified, face so peaceful'n'all, like he just came a big, wet, slippery one and laid down to rest. Hell, I'd fuck the wound in his wrist.

"Now just push forward and swallow." Wasn't the meanest sumbitch in town, I'd taken worse. All grunting with his fist. He coulda just asked me, and I'd a been ready for the taking, but this fucker di'n't have nobody's permission. No style or grace. Something had to give, and it weren't gonna be my asshole.

"Boy, you gotta reputation round these parts for bein' an ass-kissing, devil-worshipping, glue-sniffing pretty boy with a cherry on top and there ain't nobody in this town whose gonna give a fuck about what I'm about to do to you, so settle down and pucker up, fuckhead, cos I got a long way to go." Couldn't figure then whether it were that sumbitch or my god talking, cos the voice made allota sense, like some oracle from the deepest reaches of me.

When I talk to my cock he got things to say that nobody should know, but I gotta get him all hard first, make him spurt and glisten, then his mouth moves, gurgling silver jelly down over my purple dome, talking in riddles. Dunno why I got hard when the sumbitch was pumping into me, but I looked down an' there it was smiling up at me, all dreamy and blind. "Come on, kill him, Hero, he's asking for it, and while you're here, don't let that fucker touch me, or I swear I'll do it myself..." And I always does what it tells me, cos it always makes good sense to.

So I ride. I don't belong in this shit-hole town, anyway. And if I stay, I die.

Joshua would hear a thousand voices in as many different tongues, over the days the nights, invading his young mind. A dry heat hung everywhere, scorching even the mouth, dust settling into the eyes, as he made his journey beyond home into a wasted planet. Joshua's parents never told him much of what had happened, just that the white light had killed the sky.

In the vast encampments and the rundown cities that Joshua passed through, pockmarked throughout the desert, he remained in the company of beggars and thieves. He traveled bare-chested, red-and-blue-checked shirt tied around his waist, jeans and loose, beaten trainers on his feet, blistered now from walking this distance. His hairless skin wrapped itself tighter and tighter over his bones as the days passed. Walking, hitching, stowing away. He felt hands and eyes all over him, suspicious of this creature, of his absence of disease.

Everywhere he traveled he looked for signs, cash for hard graft. When he asked a toothless woman, walking on her elbows and knees, in some tent town gathered around gray, still water, she gurgled at him, "Place you wanna go is Morntlik. Plen'y a steel thar." He'd work at almost anything, so that was where he headed: running on beastly atavisms, bearing the red-rimmed, wild eyes and harrowed face of a runaway. Head down, he kept his dry throat from suffering by keeping conversation to a minimum. One thing he could always guarantee was company, enquiries. But never of the sort he wanted.

Now that I tear myself away from death, I draw nearer to whatever life has to offer me. He read about positive affirmations from a bookstall he found in one of the encampments; he stole the book and devoured it in an hour, then gave it to a drunk who lay beside him.

When he reached Morntlik, he found the quietest place he could, part of a small tunnel overlooking an empty riverbed. Night cloaked the sky, and he'd have to wait until morning to find work. He began his nightly ritual, and under the half-moonlight, he reached into his battered satchel to pull out the yellowed, dog-eared, coverless and crumpled book he'd once found in the trailer park when he was twelve. He'd never shown it to his parents, always remembering the first time he wanted them to read him something...

"MA! PA! What does this mean?"

"I dunno son, looks like devil talk to me. MARLEEN!!! This here boy's got his hands on some proper satan-speak! It's burnin' time!!!"

So Joe lit the fire in the barrel, showing his son just what to do in these cases. Every time Marleen and Joe Hero burned a book they got excited, twitching, knowing they were secure in doing the Lord's work.

"You see this, Joshua? This is the only way you'll ever get to heaven. You don' wanna be botherin' with readin'. Readin's shit! There ain't nothing but the devil's word when it's writ on a page!"

"But what about the Bible, Pa? That's words, ain't it?"

"You back talkin', you li'l sumbitch? L'il sumbitch's backtalkin', Marleen!"

"Oh, now, Joshua, you know better than to back talk your father."

"Jus' you come here, boy!!!"

And Joe wrapped a fat oily hand around his young boy's neck, and pushed him toward the barrel.

"FEEL THAT HEAT, SON? THAT'S THE HEAT OF HELL AND THERE AIN'T NO SON OF MINE WHO'S GOIN' NEAR THERE! ONLY WRIT WORD'S ALL RIGHT IS THE ONE'S THAT TELL YA WHAT KINDA BEANS YER BUYIN'!!!"

Joshua's ear singed against the hot metal; whining a five-year-old whine, he tried to control his anger and fear.

"Okay, Pa...I won't read nuthin', I promise..."

He broke his promise as soon as he'd found someone to teach him.

Joshua crunched open the book, and spoke the words in his mind:

Nineteen. Throw away holiness and wisdom, and people will be a hundred times happier. Throw away morality and justice, and people will do the right thing. Throw away industry and profit, and there won't be any thieves. If these three aren't enough, just stay at the center of the circle and let all things take their course.

Wish the old man were here; he'd have something to tell me. Not like my daddy. Wish he'd never found out about us.

"You been fruitin' around with that priest again, boy?"

Every time he said that, I shoulda said: "Yes, Daddy, I have. He's got a whole lot more to offer me 'an you, you fucked-up, cocksuckin' redneck—how'd I ever come outta your balls?"

Tha's one thing a never did understand. But I couldn't talk to him or mamma 'bout that. They woulda killed me for sure.

"That's a smart mouth. Learn to keep it shut. Won't cause you nothin' but trouble round these parts."

Old man was always right. 'Cept about killing. Never did kill no one before, but it don't feel so bad. I feel kinda like a god. All them rules, Sunday school's for shit. Only good things the preacher taught me weren't out the book. He had something else going on. He always taught different when he were alone wi' me. Never taught me how to kill a man, though, and look at me now. Fuck all them rules, them commandments. Never did nobody no good; they ain't natural. Gotta kill sometimes to survive; gotta stay alive. That's all I got.

Joshua felt his exhausted mind and body beg for release, then sleep. Sure there was no one close, he slipped his hand into his jeans, gently rubbing the head of his cock, until it was rock-hard and pushing uncomfortably against the tightness of denim. As he unzipped and let his hard cock spring out into his palm, he heard a voice behind him and jumped, belly twisting with shame.

"You know, some people say the male body uses almost half its energy producing sperm. As wasted and tired as your body looks, I dunno if that's a price you wanna pay 'til you get some food inside you."

The tunnel was pitch-black, but Joshua, sensitive as he was, could sense no danger; he heard and felt the body rustle closer to him. Relaxed. *He's got a nice voice. He don' seem diseased like the others. I'll play 'im.*

"How long you been watching me?"

"Since I saw your face scope out this place. Geez he's bony, I thought, when was the last time he had something to eat?"

"Why'd you wait till now to talk, then?"

"Well, I wasn't really expecting you to get off in front of me. That only happens in dreams don't it? Good ones, of course."

Joshua could feel breath against his hair now. His hardness hadn't gone away. It pulsed thicker; he could feel it beg for release in his palm, solar plexus tingling, heart beating faster. Instinctively, he thought that this man was looking for an excuse to beat him. But he could sense in the air that catching Joshua about to wank had turned this person on. He went with his gut.

"Can I see you?" He gasped as he said it, trying to hold the moment off for as long as possible.

"No."

He felt the body move closer, and heard a zip come undone, fumbling with pants. As hungry as Joshua was, he thought about his situation, and backed away. "If I can't see you, you gotta pay. You said I needed something to eat."

Joshua could feel the tension subside for a moment, felt his partner close off. Then: "That's not what I had in mind, but if I have to pay to fuck you, that's okay with me. You'll go down on me, right?"

Joshua didn't have to answer, eager for the feel of thick hard meat in his mouth. His partner had already worked himself up, and inhaled hard as Joshua worked his tongue over stiffness, precum sliding onto his tongue. He wrapped his hand around the cock and worked the skin back and forth.

"You ain't had any of this for a while have you?"

Joshua heard a guttural inhalation, and then felt a jet of cum spray over him; he put his lips over the gushing head and felt his mouth fill with salty ejaculate. He licked his lips and swallowed every drop, feeling it tingle on his tongue, like butterflies all the way down into the belly.

"No. I haven't. I woulda lasted longer, usually..."

Joshua kissed the cock. "It's your money. Don't worry 'bout it."

But Joshua couldn't help feeling disappointed. The cock slipped out of his hand, and in its place he felt a wad of money pushed into it, warm hand clamped around his. "Well earned. You do his often?"

"Never for money."

"Maybe you'd better get used to it. Unless you have something else to offer the world. "

As sudden as the body and voice had entered it departed. He was alone again, feeling hollow, cheated. But less panicked now that he could afford breakfast. He eased his own cock back into his jeans, but felt it stiffen with attention. On his knees he quickly worked it up again, felt it convulse against the sweaty flesh of his palm, and moaned, coming all over the wad of notes, before he collapsed into dreamless sleep, panting and lonely.

Waking in garbage, he felt the cool damp of a small tunnel, and then he remembered where he had drifted off. Sun twinkled off gray-green slime that clung to the walls of his bedchamber. He rubbed his eyes and put his shirt on, then slung his satchel over his body, making sure the money he'd made was tucked into it tight. He hadn't counted it. He'd wait.

It was a pink morning; the gray clouds bore the tincture and spilled it over the riverbed, which had become littered with activity. Knotted strands of people weaved all over, shifting around market stalls, skyline thick with heads and shoulders. As Joshua stepped out of the tunnel, the smell of so many people in one place made him gag; he gasped for breath and pushed his way into the crowd, clocking distant shop windows when they parted enough for him to see. He still needed work. He wasn't going to suck cock for dollar until he knew he had no choice. When he got to the edge of what he saw now was a town square, he looked in shop windows—NO HOMELESS—OVER 21 ONLY—NO CRIPPLES. These words accompanied most offers. The other jobs, Joshua didn't even know what they were. He knew he'd have to start lying sometime. He scuffled and pushed, looking for somewhere he could buy some good food. Feeling hot sweaty bodies push against his own, tired and weak now, barely able to stand, he decided to pick up the job search later.

The crowd cleared slightly, and Joshua's body was free to feel the sun's heat, piercing and clinging to the dust that mingled with his sweat. He saw some tables and walked toward them, empty but for two women who ran their eyes over him in disgust. *Gawd, women never used to look at me like that back home...I must need a shower something bad.* The café beyond them looked more inviting than anything he'd seen for the week he'd traveled. Mirrors lined the walls and four tables were crammed together. At the bar a man swirled a gray-brown drink around a muggy glass. He was dressed all in off-white with a panama pulled low and a walking stick hanging next to him off the bar. He was the only customer in there. Joshua walked in, took out a note, and got the atten-

62

tion of the barman, who slipped in and out of focus.

"Can I get some breakfast?" Joshua's voice was cracked, and he felt his stomach lurch but he kept his back straight, and struggled against the urge to pass out.

The barman didn't answer immediately, seemed to be polishing something, out of sight. Joshua guessed it was a glass but it was passed to the company and discreetly pocketed. "What kinda breakfast?"

Joshua was about to speak when the other man spoke for him, without looking up from his drink. "For god's sake man, can't you see the boy is ravaged?"

The man had a strange accent, spoke well.

"Eggs and bread it is then..."

The man spoke again. "And room and board perhaps. A shower?"

The man turned now, lazy and calm, one hand in his pocket fingering something.

Joshua spoke with an aching mouth. "A shower's something I need all right, but I can't afford a room. At least I don't think I can."

He still hadn't counted the money.

"Don't worry about that. They know me here, I'll see that you get what you need."

Joshua felt himself weaken, and tears of relief welled up behind his aching face. Before everything he could see turned white, he saw the man jump off his stool and hold out his arms.

When Joshua came round, he could smell the eggs in the room, and before he had opened his eyes fully was upon them, ignoring the knife and fork that lay wrapped in napkin. Instead he covered his filthy hands in runny yellow, which he sucked off with eyes wide and feral. The plate was empty in under a minute. Joshua belched, almost vomiting, but he held it down and sat with his back flat against the wall, legs spread out breathing relentlessly deep, still chewing, mouth flinching against flavor. He rolled his head in ecstasy against the wall, and looked about the room. He remembered the look he got off those women.

Well, I ain't gonna find work if I look that disgusting.

The soap burned his sun-smouldered skin, but the towels were soft, and he began wondering, for the first time, how far he'd made it from home. Perhaps the man will know. If he hadn't left. He'd ask the barman when he got downstairs.

He gathered up his clothes from where he'd dropped them, but noticed a new pair of jeans and a light blue shirt, neatly folded with a note on top, next to where he'd lain. Joshua read the note aloud to himself:

You talk in your sleep. If you want to find work, you'll need

OUT OF CONTROL

these, and I suggest you go to the steel works. They'll take anyone. Just lie about your age.
Regards,
B.C.

Don't feel right trusting just anyone...but this man...he may have saved my life. I hate that blue though. Reminds me of babies.

He looked at himself in the mirror, deciding he didn't look that bad at all. He found his satchel hanging on the door, and looked in it, counting the money. Twenty dollars all together. He packed up his old clothes into it and made his way out the door.

The barman was reluctant to tell Joshua anything about his benefactor, who Joshua couldn't see anywhere. All the barman had time for was to give directions, the café was filling with people. Joshua guessed it must be midday. He noted the name of the café and moved off, following the barman's directions to the steelworks.

Sweating from the heat, cold hard grind of steel behind him, sparks rained in a hot shower. Joshua was referred to a rotund, bald, and snarling man, Bullner.

Bullner Vulgar Vulgar Bullner. Fat, ugly fuck. How can I work for him? Joshua felt bad the moment he thought it.

"So, how old are you son?"

"Twenty-one."

"Twenty-one? Bullsheeeet. You ain' even got hair on your chest, boy."

"All right so I ain't. But I can work real hard; just show me what to do, I'll bet I can do it. If I don't, I don't get paid, sounds fair to me."

"Sounds fair to you? And who the fuck do you think you are?

Joshua stuck his chest out. "My name's Joshua My-Hero."

Bullner laughed, spraying spittle over Joshua's face. "What kinda fucked name is that, boy?"

He put his eyes to the loose dirt. "I dunno. It's what my ma and pa called me." Joshua felt the man soften to him.

"Well, we do need another man. But you're on trial. If you fuck up, boy, I'll tear your ass in three."

Touch my ass an' I'll kill ya, fat ugly fuck.

"Done."

So he shows me what to do. Pull the lever, drill the hole. Easy enough. Fat grimy fuck's outta sight now, left me with these bastards. All in a row. Pull the lever, drill the hole.

I know these sneers. Cockeyed sumbitches not a brain between 'em, staring at me. Can feel their hate and anger but I gotta work, I gotta do something, or I'll jus' die. Pull the lever, drill the hole. Pull the lever, drill the hole. A fucking robot I ain't. Pull the lever, drill the hole. A fucking robot I am. Thinking about muscle now. Wonder what these boys are packing, whether they like a tight young bit like me. Could make more money being drilled than drilling this fucking hole in steel.

Pull the lever, drill the hole. A room of flesh and sweating muscle, organisms the likes of which this Earth may never have seen. Civilizations rise and fall, brains work on insolvable mathematical problems, and AI grows in the shadows. Sweat and toil. And Joshua began dreaming.

Cock's singing a tune now. Growing and growing, trousers busting, my cock just growing, so big now it's pushing over the machine, twisting steel to snap, iron to burst, these fuckers have stopped working now, and having a good look at what's growing toward them, pushing them over now, just growing and growing, me at the end, struggling to stand, to take the weight of my growth. They're shouting now, "That ain't natural; run, boys, run!" and my cock grows over them all, so heavy, thick veins like water pipes pumping blood so hard these fuckers are getting squashed, machinery pushed out to make room for this growth, suffocating these sons of bitches, growing and growing now, and the walls cave in and the roof comes off and dust flies an' my cock grows and grows as the red sunlight spills into the room through the breaking plaster and fucked machinery, swelling gargantuan hard-on growing and growing toward the sun, out into the sky, growing and growing, ripping up tree trunks an' causing tidal waves as it thrusts into the ocean an' over the edge of the world, growing and growing so huge now I can feel the chill of space on my purple head, an' I fuck the cosmos, spunking wet comets that cripple planets with the force of their exit, destroying worlds, fucking up the earth's orbit an' sending it flying into that red-yellow fireball so we's all on fire now, all screaming and yelling for whatever god to have mercy on us, and we all die, apocalypse now by my raging hard-on.

Trance broken by screeching and grinding, steel on steel, the foreman shouting: "Watcha doin', fuckbag?!"

Joshua's drill had somehow jammed, twisted up, and buckled. Joshua could sense everybody's eyes on his skin.

"What d'ya call this? This ain't work, you jus' gone fucked the drill up, boy, an' nobody could do that even if they tried! You ain' been doing this ten minutes an' you already screwed it up! You're gon' havta pay for this, boy! Get the fuck over here an' you other boys get back to work."

And they pulled levers, and they drilled holes.

Back in his office, he sat down and pulled out wads of paper. "Dunno what I'm gonna do with you, boy, but those drills don't come easy. It's gonna cost a fortune to work that bill off, let me tell you. I'll find you something you can put your back into, you'll pay it off boy let me tell you—"

The reply was quick, inspired. "I can suck your cock."

"WHAAAT!!!" Bullner looked up from his paperwork, fat red angry face, disbelief all over it.

Joshua cowered, but repeated. "I can suck your cock; I've had lots of practice." Then Joshua heard it, the lips didn't move but a voice from somewhere:

Pretty little mouth. But no one must know.

Bullner looked at Joshua's lips.

I heard him think. An' it looks like he's agreeing. Hope this fat ugly fuck washes sometimes. Christ, I pity his wife with that shrunken piece of shit. Okay, here we go. On my knees now. Here's to the future.

"Hunngghhhh..."

Jets of cum hit Joshua's throat. He grimaced against the force of it; tasted bitter, diseased. A primal fuzz hung thick in the air. Before Joshua could get off his knees, Bullner threw his fist into Joshua's young face.

"Tell no one, little shit."

He put himself away, pulled up his trousers, looking down at Joshua as he wiped blood from his mouth, blood specks on the face. After the fear, Joshua felt a rush of anger within him, and spat silver rain on Bullner's straight beige trousers.

"NO! Little shit!!"

Bullner grabbed Joshua's ear, before he got time to run, and pulled him into the dust outside. "The Englishman'll know what to do with you..."

THE BINDS THAT TIE US
SEAN MERIWETHER

No matter how long each session lasts—sometimes hours of questions that bleed into one sound, one voice—they always return to the one they need answered. *Where is he now?* The battalion of men in ill-fitting suits use different tactics to elicit a response, from wheedling to manhandling, but I remain mute, as stubborn as you.

The heavy-set cops circle the table, their enraged voices insisting that I know all, tell all, tell them everything to save myself and stop you for completing your mission. I shout at them to *shut the fuck up*—but only inside, where my unspoken words mirror their frustration. I stare down at the scarred metal table and spit out my empty curses with each breath, hating the men but understanding their impatience—it's only a few hours to your self-imposed deadline.

I watch a curl of smoke escape the overflowing ashtray, the cheap plastic bowl crowded with a dozen cops' leavings. One cigarette butt rises above the others in the heap, a defiant figure standing apart, daring to be plucked out and destroyed. The yellow filter darkens and smolders, spinning a coarse ribbon of acrid smoke. The cops take no notice, but barrage me with a litany of new questions. I close my eyes and invoke your memory.

If I'd known it would lead here, abandoned and jailed for a crime you've yet to commit, would I have approached you in that pisshole of a bar? My eyes were instantly drawn to your rough-hewn profile. The riot of red hair that burned across your skull should have been a warning instead of a beacon, but I was intoxicated by my own youth and beauty and knew you were mine for the taking. You weren't an attractive man, Nash,—your war-scarred face was lined and pitted with life—but you wore the guise of outlaw as easily as the oily denims you lived in, and you radiated a dangerous knowledge I wanted to steal from you; I was an ambitious Prometheus.

My head rocked with cocky fantasies as I approached. I anticipated overwhelming you with the offer of my body, of you, impatient and surly, taking me at the bar with no preliminaries. I pictured the two of us, limbs entwined as you pushed home, eliciting jealous catcalls from the men you'd spurned with your smoky frown. I could already feel you in me, that fiery cock making my ass twitch and burn. I stood at the bar and waited for you to notice me. Impatient with an eclipsing desire, I demanded your attention by taking hold of your arm. You acknowledged me with a warning exhalation, daring me to bother you again.

I sputtered, my confidence challenged, but demanded you look at me. You grabbed my shirt and yanked me to you, your swarthy face one sweaty inch from mine, and snorted over me like a bull. You burrowed into me with your eyes, those violent brown cinders flashing past my ego and plunging deeper than any man had ever fucked me. I stared back with the same scrutiny that you invaded me with, but found a solid wall of resistance. You dropped me, unworthy of further attention, and I slipped to your feet. You towered over me, a rumbling volcano, and I knelt, bringing my head level with your threadbare crotch, hoping to appease you with the application of tongue and mouth.

There was a challenge in your glare that made my mouth water for your cock, which was straining the worn fabric of your jeans; but you held me in check with those eyes and I froze. The bar went silent as we faced off; the other men faded into the walls as you flared above. One blinding moment and I would be yours. I tilted my head back to receive you, but you were already gone, leaving only the raunchy smell of you to fill my lungs. I stumbled to my feet and trailed you out of the bar, running to keep up as you strode into the squalid industrial neighborhood beneath the highway. You disappeared into a monstrous garage, but I waited outside, certain you would open the heavy door and admit me into your lair. I watched your shadow move through the darkness within, saw blurred moments of flesh as you stripped down by the window, but then you evaporated from the dirty glass as if you'd never been there.

My visions of you faded with the coming dawn, and I wandered home, reeking of sweat and failure. Uncomfortably safe in my own apartment, I could only think of you, those scorching brown eyes assaulting me. My cock was on fire, but I couldn't relieve myself, needing to save it for our future moment together.

It was not the second night, or the third, or the tenth that you took me into that garage, a cathedral of abandoned metal and tires. I spent more than five weeks building your trust in my need for you before you allowed me into your sanctuary. You didn't speak a word—that was your way—but ordered me with your body and those searing eyes that glinted with all you could bestow upon me. You grabbed my insignificant waist in your thick hands and stripped away my jeans and shorts. You pulled me to you, thrusting a solid finger deep into my ass until you alone possessed me. *This is how it is*, you said with your breath, *this is what you are to me.*

I gritted my teeth and accepted your contract.

The policemen with their pasty faces and potbellies hanging over their belts know that you fucked me. They have evidence—hundreds of pictures of you. You'd been under surveillance for months, they assure me. These wife-fucking cops spread out a portfolio of images: you bending me over, your face twisted like an animal, mine in passionate pain; me at your cock, a blur between your furry legs; you with other men, each one so different from me, but all taken in our garage. A jealousy wells up in me as they show me photo after photo of you fucking teenage boys and construction workers—a brief history of your sexual conquests laid out in black and white—but I know they are using any means necessary to turn me against you and reveal your target.

They try to destroy your power with facts and dates and your real name. Not Nash, a cop sneers, but Walter Van Dorn, Jr., the unruly son of an overbearing judge who may have beaten and molested you. Your mother, Bridgette Kelly, gave you the stocky build and flaming hair but never any refuge from your father's violent temper. Then a litany of offenses: petty larceny, grand theft auto, arson. The juvenile detention center. A decade in prison. The state nuthouse. They use your history to build a case against you, show me that you were always a liar and a thief, make me understand that I had no hope of laying claim to you. But what of that now? What does it matter who you once were when you meant more to me, offering freedom from my own past?

I break my silence to defend your honor. I tell the men about the smell of you, a wild odor of sweat and semen, of fetid earth and grease and the dangerous bite of something more, something explosive and angry—the men cough and turn away. When I speak of the taste of your cock, its copper tinged by the forbidden flavor of my own asshole—they back away from the table. When I reveal the way you filled me, your heat bursting into me like a judgment from god, leaving me wounded and raw—they are finally muted. Even in your absence you have the power to intimidate.

All those months I waited on you, wandering the Minotaur's maze of rooms above the garage, an endless warren of abandoned tools and car parts, paperwork and forgotten things—like me. You worked nonstop for hours, the scrape and screech of disfigured metal echoing through the deserted building. At night you'd call me down into your world. You'd be dirty and stained, reeking of some volatile charge that you had absorbed and needed to release. I'd strip myself bare beneath the swinging chains dangling from the dark; the reek of gas and explosives rich in my nose, overpowering the smell of you until you became those vapors. I breathed you in, my head reeling, as you took me against the side of the van that housed your work, pressing my sweat-stroked body into the cool metal.

You spoke only then, once your cock was buried inside of me. Your manifesto began with the coming civil war; the forgotten masses who'd been beaten down by wealthy fucks and would rise up to take the reins of the world, showing their oppressors no mercy. Chaos, you prophesied, your hips bucking against mine, ruled the universe and would reclaim the earth. All it needed was a catalyst, a spark, the first volley of fire. All it needed was you.

Your pace quickened, the slap of flesh against flesh, as you described the bomb, an elaborate structure woven into the van beneath my pummeled body. The unnecessary engine parts removed, the passenger and rear seats razed to make more room for your creation. You panted against my ear, singing of the biblical fire you would rain down upon the lawmakers and politicians, freeing us from their tyranny. Biting my ear, drawing blood, my legs shaking as you thrust into me, you called upon a future that we could own, a landscape of smoke and fire and retribution. As you pumped into orgasm, driving deep inside of me until my ass burned like the fire you heralded, you exalted the bomb, a steady prayer that ended with a shudder as you flooded me. You'd stagger away, quieted, leaving me sore and stained with your sweat, my blood, our cum — the landscape of your foretelling.

Did I ask why? Why start a war to save the masses when you lived outside the boundaries of society? Your only connection to humanity was me, and the men before me, naïve players who wanted to experience the dark world you offered like a ripe fruit. Who were you intending to save with your creation?

The cops gladly explain your motivations, paraphrasing doctors' reports and newspapers to fill in the gaps. They describe your patterns as if to write a self-concluding end to your story, of events that turned you against the world. Your abusive father, judge and jury, your distant mother. The fire that swept through the house, killing them both, and you only thirteen. The rapes in the juvenile detention center, the boys you beat up, landing you in jail where worse rapes occurred. The forced commitment to the psych-ward where they kept you so drugged up and restrained that you lived in your own piss and shit for days at a time. Pictures of you, your nose and eyes twisted and purple, your younger face mauled, but those flaming eyes staring out at me, holding me in place. *This is the face of a madman*, they tell me, but all I see is you.

A commotion in the hallway as the clock ticks down to your golden hour, 3 p.m. You are somewhere out in the world, Nash, in that van, once white, but painted black by your own hand. Have you arrived at your final destination, waiting to begin the next chapter of society? A knock at the door, hurried whispers, the cops leave the room together, looking back at me as if I were responsible for the interruption. With them gone, the room is too quiet, only the whir of the camera behind the mirror, taping every second of my time here. The door to the investigation room is ajar, and I consider standing up, walking out...but to where? There's no home to go to from here.

Our last night together, I knew it was the end. You'd perfected the device and were ready to set us free, spark the revolution. You were different that night, quiet while you fucked me, slow where you were normally fast, grunted out my name which you'd never used before. I knew you were pulling away, sensing it through the placement of your callused hands on my waist, on my back, touching my cock for the first time. You jerked me off while you worked into me, pulling cum from me that you had never spilled in our time together. In that moment, I thought you were doing it for me, to free me from the life I'd chosen in you.

Perhaps it was feminine of me to believe I could save you, that I could reach out across the chasm you'd placed between us and save you from the brink of self-destruction, but it was only a dream, one that evaporated the moment you pulled out. I watched as you wiped your dick on a stained rag and tossed it carelessly to the floor. It landed in a pool of iridescent oil and began to darken, and in it I saw my new future, one without you in it. I demanded that you stop and stay with me, the only time I'd ever asked for anything. You didn't even pause, but circled behind the van and closed the back doors to your creation. I begged you to let me come with you, be with you in your last moments, as you launched yourself into the driver's seat. You stared down at me, just like the first night, those intense brown eyes drilling through to my soul, searching for an answer. Then you turned away and started the engine, activating the bomb. The garage door opened with a squealing thunder; the wall rose up into the void. You pulled away, never looking back, only forward. My last memory of you: the blazing red taillights as you turned onto the street and drove away.

It was there that the police found me hours later, standing at the threshold of your future. They filed into our sanctuary like a band of greedy ants, taking me into custody and demanding I tell them where you'd gone. They ransacked the garage, the Minotaur's maze above, tagging and bagging all our meager belongings, finding the hand-written proclamation declaring the beginning of the war, listing the date and time of the first strike, but not the location.

I've been here since, in this small interrogation room, the walls so white and flat that it hurts to look at them. I'm the key to you, Nash, the last one who saw you, the scapegoat should you succeed. They won't want a corpse to blame, Nash, but a living human being they can splay open like a biology frog, a spectacle for public consumption. *Was that the role you assigned me, Nash?*

The cops return all at once, dragging me to my feet and ushering me out into the corridor. They escort me down numbingly bland hallways, the florescent lights blanching their flushed faces. They have new demands for me, not questions, but instructions, as they haul me out the front door onto the stairs outside. The overtly bright day burns away my vision, and I find myself surprised to see the sun, as if it had not existed before this moment. The cops are holding me, shoving a bullhorn in front of my face, yelling at me to talk to him, to you.

My vision fades up, and I see you behind the wheel of your van, parked diagonally in front of the building. I wonder how you got there, past the security gate, into the parking lot, to this position. There are dozens of armed men surrounding you, dressed in police blue and army green, poised like plastic figures a child would own. Someone is telling me to talk you out of it, to get you to step out of the van, but words would only ruin the moment.

At first you don't seem to recognize me, and I'm almost glad you don't, but then that brown-eyed glare penetrates the windshield and dissolves the distance between us. I stare intently at you, driving past your defenses into the meat of you. I see the beatings and the torture, I hear the voices of the dead berating you, the eternal ache of needs unfulfilled. I see the sex, an arena of cocks and asses that you have possessed, that have possessed you, granting momentary reprieve. Beneath this is the knowledge that this lone act will come to nothing, spark no revolution, no uprising, but only set you free.

I close my eyes and break the connection between us, like a rope snapping its tether. I sense you alone out there in the parking lot, your hand on the ignition key. I reopen my eyes and see you for the first time, the blank stare of a doll. You are looking past me to the building, to your target and all that it represents. The silence of the afternoon is punctured by a single shot, knocking you forward into the windshield of the van. Your hand slips, the harsh jingle of keys, and the cops nervously congratulate each other for saving the day.

They seem to forget about me as they swarm the van, dragging your body out into the parking lot, spilling your blood onto the warm asphalt. I stumble down the stairs, my feet deadly weights impeding my progress. I approach the passenger door as a body of blue and green rushes to the driver's side. I open the door and see your blood on the steering wheel, puddled on the dashboard. The smell of you is ripe inside, your sweat and the explosives all around. I crawl over the boxes that replaced the passenger seat, and sit in the driver's seat, still warm from your presence. The keys dangle from the ignition enticingly, catching the late afternoon sun with a blinding glimmer. The bomb is already armed, though they won't know that until I kill the engine. I hold my breath and count down from ten, doing this for us, for me. You're already gone but I can catch up to you. My hand shakes as I grip the key, twisting it down, staring up at the building you wanted to eradicate. I ignore the shouts and warnings of the men around me as the key slips into the final notch, my eyes open, staring you dead in the face. *I'm coming, Nash.*

AT GUNPOINT
DEBRA HYDE

I'm an old man now but in all my years I ain't never understood why Case hopped the train with us that day, ages ago. He should've done what any self-respecting, gun-toting bank robber did back then—he should've stolen a car. But instead, he hops our car, yelling and waving a gat around. Christ, a gat. None of us carried a firearm back then. It just wasn't done among us gentlemen hoboes. But there Case was, threatening to shoot us if we came after his loot.

The surprise was on him though because instead of finding a destitute and defeated bunch fresh out of Hooverville, he gets me and Redder going at it, my head bobbing in the old man's lap. I guess cocksucking was the last thing Case expected to find 'cause he just stood there slack-jawed, gun suddenly hanging loose in his hand. Whole thing just about done shut him up. Redder looked his way just enough to say, "Take that corner over there. Heeber Joe won't be here for a couple days yet."

Redder. Some say he was riding the western rails from the get-go. Maybe that was true, but all I knew was whenever I hopped the "anything goes" car out of Seattle, there he was. Just the sight of him was enough to make me eager for his dick.

Even with Case there, I kept sucking Redder's cock. It was the least I could do, what with my belly full of his food. But honestly, I would've done it anyway. Redder always came hard and loud and had the sweetest tasting spunk you ever had the pleasure of swallowing. 'Course Case almost blew his top when Redder jammed his dick deep into my throat and yelled, "Fuck, yeah. Take it, Bo! "

Case just about climbed out of his skin over me fellatin' Redder. I remember laughing at him as I asked, "What, you ain't never seen this before?"

All he could do was stammer, "You gaycats?"

Redder snorted. "We're not thieves."

But I knew what Case meant. He wasn't using gaycats the old way like Redder was. He was using jailhouse terms. And, yeah, to his way of thinking, we were gaycats. We were homos and I told him as much, despite Redder's elbow telling me to shut up.

"Shit," was all he could think to say.

Far as we were concerned, Redder and me thought his kind was the worst: the criminal type who tramped only to avoid the law. His type was worse than the filching yeggs who sought out unsuspecting pockets. His was one step meaner than a pete man with his hands in an open safe.

Like I said before, he should've stolen a car. He wasn't meant to be among our kind.

Redder, though, he knew his way around Case's type. As the sunlight faded and the shadows grew deep in the boxcar, Redder just said, "Put that damn gat away, fellow. We're not going to risk a bullet for what you're hauling."

It never failed to amaze me, but Redder always spoke close to proper English, even in the face of what these days you'd call a hardened criminal.

Case, though, he was suspicious. "How do I know you ain't gonna boost me?"

Redder stiffened at the implication but rather than explain it out, he just observed, "I doubt us 'unfortunates' could sneak pass a big man like you. Especially when he's holding a loaded pistol."

Unfortunates. Back then, that's how people viewed us. Born with a man's body and a woman's instincts, a scurvy trick of fate if ever there was one. At least Redder and I had it easier than most; we had each other, even though it took me three years riding the rails before I realized he actually wanted cock. Mind you, it wasn't easy to find another homo among hoboes back then. Few of us were itinerants. And it was hard to know the sincere cocksucker from the thieving prushuns all around us. Them petty punks did cock only because their jockers had taught them it was expected.

Case didn't know all that, though. In fact, it was painfully obvious that he didn't know much of anything. All he had on his person was his clothes, his gat, and his bag of loot. Christ, he didn't so much as carry a canteen. So when Redder portrayed us as a couple of unfortunates, what he didn't tell Case was that soon enough, Case would need us. He'd need us homos for food and drink at the very least. Redder's advice to Case was simple: "Do yourself a favor while you're on the lam. Don't refuse anything that's offered to you, hear?"

Me, I wasn't so sure. I'd heard about these burgling types—heard that they flew off the handle at the least provocation. And although I'd seen a lot among tramps and hoboes in my few short years on the rail, I hadn't seen a loaded gun before, and I wasn't warm to the fact that one was on board with us now. It spooked me, that gat did, and the more I thought about, the more I wanted to be rid of it.

Looking back now, it was a fool's errand, I suppose. But at the time, I thought I was protecting me and Redder. I thought I knew best.

It didn't take much to push Case toward dependence. Just the full bladder and empty stomach he woke up with the next morning. Of course, he woke skittish and set to clutching his loot in one arm while patting his coat for his gat. I was pissing away my morning wood into a big ol' coffee can. Wasn't 'til I heard Redder scoff, "We aren't interested in your wealth," that I checked Case out and saw him all jumpy.

"You need this?" I asked him, raising the can. "It ain't full yet."

Case looked from me to Redder and back again with squinty squirrel eyes. Man, but he didn't trust. "No?" I asked. Case didn't move so I shrugged my shoulders and made my way across the boxcar and tilted the can to the wind. As the piss streamed away, its pungent smell reached me, a smell I love so much that it still reminds me of the road whenever I'm lucky enough to happen upon it today.

Smells of the road—they were strong, all of them, and I loved them. Especially the delicious stench of a bo's ripe package when he ain't had a decent bath in weeks, after he's been sweating on the rails in the summer heat of a boxcar. Redder smelled of decades of travels, and I swear but my dick got hard if I so much as caught a whiff of him. God, but that was the best of it.

Anyway, Redder was rummaging through his pack, looking for breakfast fixings. I stashed the can back in the corner and went to my own pack. "I got bread," I volunteered. "And dried fatback."

"You did well," Redder said.

"Well, you were right. Ol' Mrs. Hannity was good as your word."

"You dishwash for her?"

"Nah. She already had someone, but when I told her you sent me, she wrote me up a good word and sent me to a warehouse. Packed crates for a week."

"Lucky," Redder observed. "Plum job."

"Yeah, I owe you."

Before Redder could downplay his good reputation, I tossed an orange his way. "Earned me a few prizes," I told him. "Hey, Case." I tossed an apple his way. It was an obvious slight—his apple to our oranges—but I wasn't about to welcome a guy with a gat just yet.

Redder divided the food among us. As elder bo, it was his right to decide the portions, but I always liked his spooning out best. With Redder, the food always seemed better—the fruit tasted sweeter, the bread more filling, and the meat salted just right. I suppose I loved him as much with my stomach as I did with my cock.

The train stopped in a gray and muddy little city, one just big enough to warrant a rail yard. When Redder and I climbed out, Case hung back, but we looked over our shoulders and suggested he'd best follow if he didn't want to get chased off. Or discovered.

"Bet the radio's told everyone about a bank robber from up north," I surmised.

That got Case moving.

Redder had us head for the river where an "anything goes" hobo camp stood ready. Anything goes? For us, it meant we didn't have to worry about being faggots. For Case, even though he didn't know it, it meant no questions asked. You knew anything goes by its hobo marks, two slanted slashes. Which appeared on the stone bridge overpass a hundred yards or so before the camp.

We found Heeber Joe there, and a bad cough had gotten hold of him, a real bad cough. Another bo's brandy had kept the worse of it out of his lungs, and he had a dry spot in California Slew's lean-to, but we knew it didn't look good. He needed medicine—real medicine, not them concoctions we hoboes pretended would keep the croup away.

Redder and Heeber went back a long ways together, and seeing Redder distressed, I gave him all my money. It didn't matter that my pockets were empty again. Better to do well by him and his. Besides, Redder had the respect of all the bo-friendly folk in every town up and down the Pacific Coast. He'd know which doctor to go to for Heeber, and he'd tell that doc that an able body back at camp had forked over all his cash for a sick man's medicine. I'd be filling my pockets again in no time with good words like that.

Redder glanced over to Case, concerned.

"Don't worry," I volunteered. "I'll keep him busy and thinking about other things."

After Redder left for town, I fetched up a fishing pole and said if someone was willing to gut some pan fish for dinner, I was willing to spend the afternoon fishing for them. And I took Case with me, away from camp.

We settled along the riverbank far enough downstream to be well away from camp. I took a bit of bread from my coat pocket, dampened it, rolled it into a ball, and put it on the hook. "Lazy man's worm," I told Case as I cast the line. I knew the fish wouldn't bite fast and furious. It was cloudy and damp and fish always seem to lose their appetites on gray days. So I settled in next to Case and started explaining a few things to him.

"Look, I know you're just hiding," I told him, "and I ain't got a problem with that. But some of the boes will and you got to understand this: We help each other. We share our food and when one of us is down, we care for him."

Case didn't say anything. He just kept one hand on his loot. I got up and collected fallen leaves, talking as I worked.

"It ain't gonna take long for the others to figure you out. They'll size you up and they'll know something's in that bag."

"I ain't sharing my money," Case said flatly.

I walked away from the bank and stooped to make a small bed of the leaves.

"Look, nobody's gonna be angling for a share. We don't care about that. We only care about our own. Let's say we run out of coffee, or a gang of punks beats on one of us in town. That's when you fork over a little of what you got. Just to help out. It's what we do. And you remember what Redder said last night?"

Case nodded. "Don't refuse anything offered."

"Yeah. Exactly."

I sat down next to him and, seeing a tug at my line, picked up the pole and gave it a quick jerk. A sunfish started fighting me right away. Damn, I love them. They ain't stupid, laying flaccid on your line the way young trout do—they fight you real good. When I got the fish off the line, I tossed it over to the bed of leaves and left it there to flop around. I baited up and threw the line back out.

"Look," I continued. "You should've figured out by now we don't ask questions, and we leave well enough alone. But you gotta know, even hoboes have their ways and if you're too selfish to help a fellow bo, some will turn you in right quick, just to get you out of our camp. So do yourself a favor. Show some respect."

Case grunted some kind of agreement, and I set to watching the river go by. I had other things to offer Case, but the time hadn't ripened just yet.

Three fish later, I asked ventured, "You been in the pen?"

Case startled. "How'd you know?" His eyes squirreled up again.

"Oh, hell, Case. Don't go looking all suspicious on me. You talk jailhouse. 'Gaycats.' Dead giveaway, the way you used it."

Before he could argue with me about it, I added, "Been out long?"

"Just long enough to see how broke and miserable this country is."

"Yeah," I agreed. "Lots of folks living poor and tragic. Hell, I'm glad I'm a hobo. I've been poor so long that I already know how to be happy about it."

My pockets might've been cash poor, but they still held the fixing for a cigarette so I rolled us some smokes. Handing a cigarette to Case, I lit us up and together we enjoyed the draw of tobacco into our lungs. Fleetingly, I wondered if Heeber would get well enough to ever enjoy another smoke, but I didn't stick with that thought for long. Something else was on my mind.

"Good, ain't it?" I needed to move my plan along and sharing a smoke was letting me get my nerve up. One last drag and I screwed my courage up. "You had any cunt since you got out?"

Case didn't answer at first. I guess he knew where this was going.

"No. Been too poor."

"Yeah. Pussy ain't cheap, 'cording to camp talk." I shrugged. "But I ain't one for women..."

Case didn't say anything, but it wasn't spoke about back then anyway. Mum was the word, and if you were a cocksucker, you waited until dark and when camp settled down to sleep, you simply went to whomever you wanted and undid their pants. If they didn't resist, you sucked. If they did, you knocked off. Men being what they need, I wasn't made to knock off very often, but still, you never, ever spoke of it.

But I had to. It was part of my plan.

"...you saw what I like."

"Yeah, I saw."

"You get any of that in the pen?"

"Sometimes."

Case lay back on the riverbank and stretched out with his hands behind his head. Which told me that he'd gotten it often enough to know how to signal for it—and that he'd accept some right there and then.

I hurried to get into his pants, not out of eagerness, but to get him into my mouth before he changed his mind. I mean, I just didn't know if he really meant it, what with it being broad daytime and all—and us boes have been beaten and bloodied over less. Case let out a groan when he felt my lips close around him, and I knew I had him when I took all of him into my mouth and sucked. I knew we were a go when I tongued that sweet spot of his stubby, thick dick and he went rock hard over it. He welcomed it and, soon enough, his cock swelled even more against the roof of my mouth. Case groaned, then let loose. His jism was thick and plentiful, and I couldn't help wondering as he filled my mouth how longed it'd been for him.

I knew not to linger over him. You could linger over someone like Redder—you could keep your head in his lap, admire his withering cock, and let him stroke your hair if it was just the two of you around— but a straight guy's cock you put away as quickly as possible. No loitering.

Returning to my fishing pole, I told Case, "You can have that any time you want."

I figured that the more cocksucking I provided Case with, the less trigger-happy he'd be and the safer my fellow boes would be. Redder decided to see Heeber Joe through his sickness and he moved into the lean-to, to care for him. I didn't mind because I had a job to do too, but when I told Redder as much, he narrowed his eyes and warned me to be careful. "Guys like him will turn," he said. "Jail does that to them."

Wished I'd known then what he meant.

But until I learned, I let Case take good advantage of me. I sucked him whenever we went fishing or snaring—and, man, camp had a lot of fish and rabbit for eats. I even came to like the man, sort of, but only after I got to where I liked sex with him. Sure, sometimes he'd just lay out and wait for it, but just as often he'd put me on my knees, grab the back of my head, and piston my mouth with his cock. That he bullied me with insults as he fucked my mouth only made it wilder. He even badgered me into showing him my cock, had me jerk to stories he told about fucking and sucking in jail. I never before met a guy brazen enough to show any interest in my dick or who liked watching me come, but man, if I didn't shoot hard and strong when he told me his smutty stories. Man, he could be a thrill.

For a time, my plan worked. I kept Case, his gat, and his suspicious nature away from camp. I protected my own. But one day, he wandered off, only to return empty-handed. He had stashed his goods.

After that, Case grew restless. He got tired of our ways, of our scrounging to live with less than his bag full of money could buy, so it wasn't any surprise when the sex stopped working for him. It wasn't a surprise when he told me to show him into town.

Mostly that meant showing him the way to the nearest saloon. I left him there with its girls, figuring he was going to get some that night. I assumed the time had come to part ways. I assumed we'd put Case behind us without incident.

We hadn't. Two days later, Case tore into camp, mean with drink and shouting for me.

"You snake. You left me there, knowing I couldn't get back."

I was handing Redder some broth for Heeber and I barely got out of the lean-to before Case rushed me and started throwing punches and yelling about me stealing his money. For a time, I ducked him just fine but I took that wrong step and fell flat on my face. Case was on me then, all fists and accusations. He pummeled me about the ears, bashed my nose into the ground, and when I tried to fight back, he pinned me down.

"You fucking shit," he cursed. "I'll show you to skip out on me."

He cuffed me hard enough to see stars. The pain was suffocating—made it hard to see or breathe. But I wasn't completely oblivious. I could feel Case pull my pants down. I could feel him tug at his own. He cursed and called me a nancy.

He shoved his dick up my ass. Brutally. The way he forced me open felt like I was tearing in two. I never felt anything like it and started crying like a baby. I sobbed as he fucked me raw and rough as he spat vicious insults and threw punches at my head just to see me blubber as he used me.

"You fucking shit."

That's when I heard it—the gat, at my ear, cocked for action. Thrilled, scared, I didn't know whether to piss myself or come.

"I'll kill you."

The words froze my blood. I couldn't breathe.

Another time and another place, and, hell, I probably would've welcomed him to rough me up and sodomize me. I would've shot my wad to hear a fucking gat at my head. But it was different back then. Danger and sin were real. This was real. And I was going to die with his dick in my ass.

Suddenly, Redder's there, yelling and pulling Case off of me. I remember it, clear as day: Case tears out of me, ripping and hurting like a son of a bitch. Case curses at Redder. I panic — Redder ain't seen the gat and he don't know it's cocked. Instantly, I stop crying. I forget my pain. I try to scramble to my feet, but my pants keep me down. I feel something leak from me — blood — but I have to get to Case. I lurch after him, hitching up my pants as best I can.

I grab Case and tackle him. I bring him down but the gun goes off. It's so loud, it's deafening. I wrestle him for it and win, but only because Case suddenly decides he needs to get his dick back in his pants. But I had the gun now. I had it.

That's when I see Redder — laying on his side, clutching his arm, wounded. Holding my half-hitched pants to my waist in one hand, the gat in the other, I fumble to his side on my knees.

"Redder..."

His face was scrunched up in pain. Blood seeped from the wound, up through the fingers he gripped himself with.

"Redder..."

He pulled himself into a half-seated position, breathing heavily. I could tell by the way his arm swung limp, bone had shattered.

"Redder..."

"Shut up, kid." He gritted fury through his teeth and I knew that, if not for the pain, he would've spat at me.

I did the only thing I could — I told Case to take a hike. "Get out of here, you sick bastard," I said, aiming the gun at him. "Your loot's wherever you left it. Get it and get lost." I knew it wasn't enough to regain Redder's good graces, but as I stood up, staring down the point of the gun at Case, I vowed to myself that I'd care for Redder from that day forward. I'd never let another bad thing happen to him.

I held my aim as Case circled around us, ready to shoot if I had to, but it wasn't necessary. Case hightailed it out of camp, finally putting whatever common sense he had to good use.

For months afterwards, I paid for my shortsightedness, but I kept my vow. I spent every waking moment paying off my sin — I got Redder a good doctor, took a job, and got us rooms at a flophouse until he mended. And I paid for my sins at night in the form of vivid, gruesome, and hateful nightmares. It wasn't easy, being unforgiven.

It took time, but Redder eventually did forgive me. It happened when we saw Case again — on page one, all shot up from a botched heist. I felt pretty queer that day, seeing the picture of a corpse, obliterated by gunfire, knowing that I'd sucked its cock. But Redder downright celebrated, seeing Case dead as a doornail. He passed a whiskey bottle around camp that night, full of a drunk's glee and cheering that the man finally got his due.

That night, in the dark, Redder came to me and forgave me. It was the only time he ever sucked my cock.

We saw better times after that. Redder and I wandered up and down the Pacific Coast and even saw ourselves cross-country a couple of times. When the war came, we settled down. I got myself a job with the city and Redder sat home to watch the fog roll in off the bay. It was a good life. Maybe not as free as the road was, but it was pleasing enough and I got to care for Redder and see to his comfort and security.

I suppose I was always paying off that debt from a mishap with Case. I always felt some measure of guilt about what had happened, and no matter how often I saw happiness in Redder's eyes, I never forgot the pain and anger on his face that day. I never forgot his suffering.

Yeah, I spent all of Redder's remaining years paying off that debt to some degree, but so what? I had been one pull of a trigger away from death and somehow I'd gotten a second chance. With Redder. I took it.

And you know what? That, I don't feel one bit guilty about. No, sir, not one bit.

BLACKOUT LEATHER JACKET
MATT STEDMANN

The next thing I knew I was flat on my back in the middle of the street. Angelique was kneeling on my chest, her tall pink wig swaying back and forth as she yelled to someone above my head, "Get it off him! Get it off him!" There was a tugging on my arms and then something came free, causing my shoulders to rise up and then fall again, my head thudding against the pavement.

"Ow!" I yelled. Angelique leaned down and peered into my face, her long, glitter-encrusted eyelashes fluttering. "Abe! Abe, can you hear me?" She snapped her inch-long candy-apple red fingernails in front of my eyes.

"Of course I can hear you, you ditzy queen, get off of me!" I said. Several hands took hold of me and hauled me to my feet, where I lost my balance and stumbled forward.

As I fell I was caught by a pair of hands on my arms, and found myself face-to-face with a pair of astonishing blue eyes. I was pushed back onto my feet and my view zoomed outward, until I could see all of the face of the man holding me. He was young, maybe late twenties, with dirty-blond hair and a neatly trimmed goatee. But his eyes, cobalt blue and intense in the afternoon sunlight, were what held me enthralled.

"Hi!" he said brightly, flashing me a dazzling smile. His smile quickly turned to a frown of disappointment at the incomprehension on my face. "You don't remember me, do you?" His frown deepened.

"Uh..." I looked around for help. Then I shook myself, and looked again as I finally took in my surroundings. Blue-Eyes and I stood facing each other, as Angelique stood nearby with her hands on her hips. She was backed by her three drag-queen cronies, the Andro Sisters: Eva, Deva, and Feva. The Sisters wore their trademark matching sequined jackets and miniskirts in turquoise, lime green, and flame red. We were all standing smack in the middle of Fifth Avenue.

I looked down. All I was wearing was a pair of tight black jeans, torn and scuffed at the knees, a studded leather belt, and a pair of black army boots. There was a black leather jacket lying in a heap near my feet that Angelique had apparently torn off me when she and her crew had tackled me.

Lost, I looked up again. Way up. Behind us was a huge float, covered with rainbow tissue paper and a five-foot-high banner that read: Straight but Not Narrow: Daughters and Nieces of Clean and Sober Lesbians of Color of the Bronx, Brooklyn, and Staten Island. Bands played, confetti flew, and excited crowds lined the sidewalk.

Oh, fuck. I had somehow stumbled—literally—right into the middle of the New York City Pride Parade.

Quite a few people in the crowd had noticed our little tableau. Some of them were pointing at us, and a number of them were applauding, apparently thinking that we were engaged in some sort of impromptu queer street-art performance. Just down the block, two cops began striding toward us.

As I stood gaping around me in shock, Angelique spoke up. "Abe, honey, let's get you out of the street and try to get this all straightened out. Come on," she said, turning and starting to lead the Andro Sisters toward the sidewalk.

"Uh, sure..." I looked around, hugging myself self-consciously. I didn't have a shirt on, and I wasn't used to showing off my chest in public like some guys are.

Blue-Eyes saw my discomfort and bent down to pick up the jacket, which was still lying in the street. "Here," he said, handing it to me.

"Thanks." I smiled sheepishly at him and began to put it on.

Angelique half-turned and saw what I was doing. As I shrugged the jacket onto my shoulders, time seemed to slow and stretch as she threw out one hand toward me shouting, "Abe...no...wait...don't..."

Blackout.

"...down here NOW!" Angelique was shouting. This time, I came up out of it with my body moving, and another body pressed close against mine, slick with sweat and heat.

There was another pair of eyes staring me in the face, jet black this time, and as I jerked my head backwards in surprise I realized that I recognized the young man I was apparently dancing with.

I'd never seen him in broad daylight, only in the half-lit dimness of bars where I'd seen him dance atop bartops and pedestals. He had a broad Asian face, smooth and unlined, and warm brown skin. I'd spent one hot summer evening a few weeks after Ramon left me, just watching him from the semidarkness, nervously folding and refolding a dollar bill, but never finding enough courage to approach him.

Now he was shirtless, his body shining with scattered glitter in the warm sunlight. He smelled of cocoa butter and fresh male sweat. I looked down to where our hips were locked together, gyrating to the throbbing sounds of techno that surrounded us. He wore only a pair of silver Lycra Speedos which clung to him as we dry-humped each other. I still wore the black jeans, but my belt was now missing, and the top button was open, a few tufts of my pubic hair poking out. My arms were pinned behind me as he held me by the wrists, the leather jacket pushed down around them.

As I slowly came to my senses I stepped back from him and looked around, stunned. I was standing high atop a float with the name of one of the city's many boy bars—Inferno!—emblazoned on it in blinking letters. Around us, muscle boys similarly attired in glitter and Speedos were clapping to the beat, egging the two of us on. Below us, the crowd was in a frenzy, men and women alike waving up at us and enthusiastically shouting, "Go, go, go!"

The only person who apparently hadn't been enjoying whatever show we'd been putting on was Angelique. "Abraham Martin Jefferson Davis DuPree," she screeched up at me from the street, "get your ass down here this second!"

Uh-oh. When Angelique starts using my full name, that's when I know I'm in real trouble with her.

I smiled apologetically and a little uneasily at Asian Guy as I continued to back away. "Uh, gotta go," I mumbled, and began to shrug the jacket back up onto my shoulders.

"No!" Angelique yelled, freezing me mid-motion.

"What?" I yelled down to her.

She was waving her arms. "Drop it!"

"Drop what?"

"The jacket!" she shouted. "Drop! It! Now!"

I allowed the jacket to fall the rest of the way off my arms, looking at it quizzically, then tossed it down to her.

She caught it clumsily in one hand. "Now get your ass down here and stop making a spectacle of yourself!"

I peered cautiously over the side of the float, then turned around, grabbed the edge, and began to climb down.

"Hey, wait a minute!" A pair of boots came clomping over to me, and then Asian Guy squatted down in front of me, his knees level with my ears and his crotch staring me in the face. I stared entranced at the outline of his obvious hard-on through the clinging silver briefs, watching as it actually pulsed a few times, brazenly straining against the fabric.

I looked up toward his face to see him grinning mischievously at me, and then he bent down, grabbed me by the back of the neck, and kissed me.

Time stopped again, but, mercifully, this time I didn't black out. He kissed me as if he was fucking me, lips locked tight against mine. His tongue probed my mouth, first teasingly and then with a growing insistence. It slid into me like hot silk, alive and pulsing. His tongue wrapped around mine, squeezing and then pulling it deep inside his own mouth. I hadn't known that you could even do that with your tongue. When he let go of my head again my ears were ringing. Over the ringing I could hear a fresh round of raucous cheering from the crowd.

He leaned in so that his lips brushed my ear. "Come see me sometime," he whispered. Then he pulled back, winked at me, and gyrated his way off to the other side of the float.

Still dazed, I watched his Lycra-clad ass bounce away from me, then shook myself and scaled my way down the side of the float. As I jumped the last few feet to the ground the crowd broke into a final round of wild applause.

Whereupon Angelique grabbed my arm and yanked me out of the street and onto the crowded sidewalk. As she pushed her way through the crowd with me in tow, quite a few men smiled and winked at me, and at least one older woman who I think was somebody's mother.

"Wait a minute!" I called after Angelique as she pulled me along. "Where are we going?" I could see the Andro Sisters and Blue-Eyes waiting for us a little way ahead.

"Brunch, honey. Brunch. Everything makes more sense over brunch. And you," she said, turning and fixing me with an evil eye, "have got some serious explaining to do."

The bored waitress didn't even bat an eye as the six of us crammed ourselves around a corner table. We were only three blocks off the parade route, but here it seemed like an ordinary Sunday in New York, with no hint of the wild bacchanalia going on only a few streets away.

Since we couldn't get a table while I was shirtless, Eva had lent me her turquoise sequined jacket. It barely closed over my chest, and left me feeling utterly ridiculous, especially under the steady gaze of Blue-Eyes. He had finally been introduced to me as "Chad" and he never took his eyes off me for a second. I wanted my leather jacket back—Angelique's jacket, actually—but she was clutching it as if she were afraid to let me near it.

No one said much of anything until we had all placed our orders and sat with steaming cups of coffee before us. "Much better," said Angelique, finally breaking the awkward silence as she sipped her coffee with extra sugar and cream. "It's been a long night, no thanks to you. Now," she fixed me with a glare, "what's the last thing you remember?"

The rest of the table turned to me with a breathless anticipation that made me nervous. "You mean besides you sitting on me in the middle of the street?" I asked.

"Yes, dear," she said patiently. "Before that."

"Well," I said, "before that I was...I was..." Chad was watching me even more intently than before. "Uh–oh. I don't really know...well, the last thing I remember we were in your room..."

"I don't know," I said, turning this way and that before the full-length mirror in Angelique's room. "I feel kind of silly."

"Trust me honey, you look hot," said Angelique. She was reclining on her narrow bed, her face already made up to perfection, wearing a silk dressing gown. Beside her on the bed she had carefully laid out her outfit for the evening, a green dress slit halfway up the leg. Most people don't understand how I can put up with having a drag queen for a roommate, with all the attendant drama that it inevitably entails. The truth is that I like all the excitement; it feels like it livens up my own rather drab life. In fact, I like Angelique better as herself than when she's being plain old Andrew, though of course I'd never tell her that.

"You really think so?" I was wearing black jeans, black boots, a studded black belt, and a new black T-shirt about a size too small for me. I cringed. "Christ, this shirt is so tight you can see my nipples."

"That's the idea. What did you do all that working out for, anyway? I thought it was to be able to show off what you've got for some new man." That was true; when Ramon had left I'd drowned my sorrows at the gym, reasoning that I'd have at least something to show for all those months of heartache.

"And besides," she added, "it's Pride weekend, it's time to let loose and show it off a little."

I turned back to the mirror, resisting the old urge to suck in my gut. I didn't have a gut anymore, but it sometimes still felt like I did. Right. Show it off a little. I gave myself a little shake and tried to look at my body objectively. No hint of my old belly showed; it had been replaced by a new washboard flatness. The black fabric of the T-shirt stretched over a chest that now looked powerful and massive. I flexed my arms, watching my biceps and triceps pulse, my forearms corded with new muscle. I smoothed the legs of my jeans, watching how they clung to my quads and gave me a nice bulge at the crotch.

I had worked hard to build the kind of body that would project raw power and sexuality, and as I posed in front of the mirror in my new clothes, I tried to look the part. Reckless. Mysterious. Dangerous.

I sighed. It wasn't working. I still felt silly.

Angelique was watching me, considering. "Hmm. I think it needs just one more thing," she said. She rummaged around in her closet until she came up with a black leather jacket, encrusted with chains and slightly weathered.

I raised an eyebrow at it. "You have a leather jacket?"

"Well, it's from my younger days," she said, patting it fondly. "Let's face it, leather's just another kind of drag anyway. My, I certainly had some wild times in this thing." She was lost in thought for a moment, then shook herself. "Here," she pushed it toward me, "try it on."

I recoiled as if she were brandishing a snake in my face. "Oh, no.

Uh, thanks, but I couldn't."

"Abe?" Angelique said, puzzled. "What's wrong? It's just a jacket."

"Well..." I stammered. "I know. And it looks great, it really does." The jacket hung in Angelique's hands, limp yet also somehow powerful. I could smell it from here, the unmistakable scent of leather that, for me, always carried the suggestion of something darker. Strangers half-glimpsed in dark alleyways, and imagined nights of animal abandon, and back rooms where I'd always been afraid to go.

"I've always wanted one, but...well, this sounds really foolish, but I've always been afraid that I couldn't handle it, you know? It's like it's *too* sexy for me, like I wouldn't know what to do with that much power. Like if I put one on I'd just go wild, end up turning tricks or working a phone-sex hotline or...or something," I finished lamely.

Angelique was waiting for me to stop talking with a little half smile on her face, and I winced inwardly, cursing myself for my stupid outburst and bracing for an example of her famous cutting wit. But instead she only smiled a little sadly and said, "Abe, honey. Let your best friend the drag queen tell you a little secret. You can pump all the iron you want, and you can buy all the tight jeans you want, but the only thing that's going to help you project a new image is up here." She tapped one temple. "You have to *own* it, honey. If you've got that, then anything you wear can be drag. I think that if wearing this jacket can help you feel that way, then you should try it.

"And really, honey, I hardly think that if you put on a leather jacket for one evening that you're going to go off on some kind of monstrous sexual rampage. And, Abe?" she said, suddenly completely serious, "I think maybe if you loosened up just a little bit and allowed a tiny bit of wildness into your life, it might really be a good thing."

I bristled. "Just because I'm an accountant...," I began.

She cut me off. "It's not that, honey. But you remember what Ramon said when he left you..."

Ouch. I looked away, back to the mirror. Ramon had dumped me because he said I was too boring, too controlled. Actually, "like a mayonnaise sandwich on Wonder Bread" had been his exact words.

Well, look at me now. I had a hot new body, and some hot new clothes. Maybe it was time I had a new attitude, too.

"Fine." I turned back to Angelique. "I'll try it."

"That's the spirit!" she said. "Here," she held out the arms out for me, "let's slip this onto you and take a look."

I put my arms into the jacket and Angelique pushed it up onto my shoulders where it settled firmly, heavy and faintly warm. As the jacket enfolded me, I smelled the mingled scents of it, of whiskey and cigar smoke and old sweat. I turned back to the mirror, and...

"... and that's all I remember," I finished.

"That's all?" Chad asked. He was looking at me with real disappointment. "Nothing else?"

"Well, nothing else until you lot jumped me in the middle of the Pride parade."

Chad bit his lower lip and Angelique reached over to pat his hand. "There, there," she said. "I think this is all becoming a little clearer. Why don't you tell Abe here how you happened to meet him last night?"

Chad blushed. He looked nervously at the Andro Sisters, who were breathlessly following the conversation, then over to me before dropping his eyes again. "Come on, dear," Angelique coached.

Chad nervously cleared his throat. "Well," he began, "it's Pride weekend after all. So it's time to cut loose and have a little fun, right? It's not like I went out looking for trouble. Well, not exactly..."

I didn't know Jamal and Eric well or anything, but I thought when they invited me to their party it would be the chance to meet someone different, you know? Someone interesting. Or at least interesting enough for Pride weekend.

Anyway, when I got there the guys all looked pretty much like us, but they were more different than I expected. They all had *money*. I mean, I make a good living, but these guys all had vacation homes, fancy cars, the works. One guy actually asked me who my "personal banker" was. I laughed and told him it was the ATM machine down on the corner. He thought that was really funny, until he realized that I wasn't joking. Then I realized that he wasn't joking either. Then he excused himself for a drink and never really came back. I saw him talking to some people, and after that no one paid any attention to me. It was like I didn't exist.

Well, when I couldn't take being invisible anymore I left—I think Jamal and Eric were actually relieved to see me go. I went home, threw on some shorts and a tank top, and went back out again to see what I could salvage from the night. The problem was, it was so late that now all the good places had huge lines. I ended up at some sleaze bar down in the Village; I figured with the city overflowing with guys from out of town I could at least meet someone no matter where I went.

But there was still a huge line. It actually wrapped around the side of the building into an alleyway. Well, after an hour of waiting, I was bored and ready to give up. Everybody behind me had already bailed, leaving me the last in line. At this rate, I figured I wouldn't be getting in until the Parade started Sunday morning. Then I heard a commotion around the back of the building. I looked at the guys ahead of me in line. None of them were paying attention to me anyway, so I figured, "What the hell?" I slowly stepped back from them, deeper into the shadows of the alley.

I slid through the shadows to the back of the alley, where a rickety wooden fence screened it from the backyard of the bar. My heart was thumping in my chest. It's not like I was exactly doing anything wrong. Well, maybe I was, but it was just dangerous enough to be exciting. As I crept closer I could see that the slats of the fence were loose, so I put one eye up to the gap.

I blinked in the sudden glare of a bare lightbulb that hung above the bar's back door. The area behind the bar was unfinished, just some gravel, weeds, and two rusty dumpsters. Pinned in the glare of the single bulb was a man in a black leather jacket.

All he wore was the jacket, a pair of black jeans, and black boots. His jeans were open at the crotch, where his cock stood up, straight and stiff. Another man knelt before him in the gravel, red hair bobbing as he slowly licked the underside of the man's cock. A third man's head was busy beneath the open edges of the jacket. Brown hair shot through with gray, his head moved back and forth, lapping at the chest of the man in the jacket.

Just a few other men stood in the backyard, watching, their forms hidden in the shadows. From time to time the back door of the bar swung open and then shut again with a bang. My own cock had gone achingly stiff, and I reached up inside the leg of my shorts to finger it. I looked behind me toward the mouth of the alley. There was still no one watching me. So I unzipped my shorts and pulled out my cock and began to pump my fist up and down the length of it.

The man in the jacket suddenly thrust one knee forward, shoving it into the chest of the redheaded man blowing him, who sprawled backward onto the ground. In a flash, the other man who had been licking his chest was on his knees before him, drawing the cock deep into his throat. Beneath the edges of the leather jacket, a tightly muscled chest glistened with sweat and spit, until another man quickly stepped forth from the darkness, lapping hungrily at it.

The man in the leather jacket wasn't large or imposing. He was well-muscled, but not massive or tall. His face was backlit by the bare lightbulb, hidden in shadow.

Yet a clear aura of power radiated from him, one of both mastery and intense sexual hunger. He was utterly in control, taking his pleasure in each of the men in front of him. And they all seemed to sense it; you could see it in their eagerness to serve him.

It was so hot. I was gasping now, pushing myself forward, humping into my fist as I pressed my chest against the fence. I'd never watched anyone have sex before, except in a porn film, and never anything like this. I risked a glance behind me again; still nothing. I put my face back to the hole. I wanted to be back there, with him, yet at the same time the thought that no one knew I was watching felt incredibly dangerous and exciting. God, I was going to come.

There was a sharp crack, and the fence gave way in front of me, spilling me onto the ground. Everyone froze, looking at me curled on the dirt with my hand wrapped around my cock. It was painfully obvious what I had been up to.

I looked up in time to see the man in the jacket free himself from the men who surrounded him and come striding toward me. With one powerful hand he dragged me to my feet. There was a frozen moment as he studied my face and I finally saw his clearly, black brows, black eyes that burned with a maniacal fire. Then he grabbed my tank top, stripping it roughly over my head, and turned me around, shoving me up against one of the dumpsters.

One of his arms came around my neck, pinning me, and my nose filled with the scent of leather. The other hand shoved my shorts down around my feet, trapping me, and I felt his cock press against my naked ass. There was a rustling and a fumbling behind me, then I heard the distinctive crinkling sound of a condom being opened. The pressure on my ass loosened for a moment, and then it was back, the hard rod of his cock poking insistently between my cheeks.

He wasn't gentle. Time stretched as he first slid into me, and then he began to pound into me with long, lazy strokes. He moved slowly, taking his pleasure in me, but he was relentless, withdrawing and then plunging himself deep into me over and over like a machine. My face was pressed harder against the rough metal of the dumpster each time he pushed into me, and soon I felt myself pushing my ass back with each thrust, anticipating it, welcoming it.

Then I felt myself lifted away from the dumpster and turned, the sudden coolness of the night air against my naked skin. My head hung down over the arm at my neck, but then a hand came up and grabbed me by the hair, pulling my head up and forcing me to see.

We were surrounded by men. Their faces hid in shadow by the light behind them, they stood quietly in a semicircle around us, the edges of the crowd lost in the darkness. All of them were watching me. My body gleamed with sweat in the pool of light, shaking with each thrust as they watched me get fucked by the demon behind me.

Slowly, almost reverently, the silent crowd of men inched closer. I could feel the pressure of their attention like a physical thing. One reached out and touched my chest, the mere pressure of his hand causing me to moan and then the hands were everywhere. Stroking my chest, pulling on my nipples, stroking my cock. First one man knelt before me and I felt the warm wetness of his mouth envelop my cock. Then another knelt beside him, and the two of them trapped my cock between them. Their lips played up and down the shaft, alternately sucking on the head of my cock and passing it back and forth between their mouths.

Other men came forward, and then there were hands on me everywhere and then tongues, licking my legs, my chest, probing my armpits. Shuddering, I gave myself over to them, allowing my head to fall back against the man behind me, feeling the leather slick with sweat between us, feeling the zipper of the jacket press hard against my back. With each thrust of him into me, my own cock moved deeper into the mouths of the men kneeling before me. Each time he shoved into me, my own body bowed outward, pushing itself into the hands and mouths of the men who surrounded me.

I vanished into it, feeling the man in the leather jacket pushing insistently into me from behind, feeling the men before me hungrily pulling me into them until at last a river of fire pulsed upward, out of me, spraying from between my legs and onto the men before me.

I stared at Chad as he finished his story. He was flushing bright red, but he still held my eyes. My cock was throbbing so hard it was painful. I was ready to come in my own pants. Was that me — really me — that he was talking about?

"Anyway," he continued, still not looking away. "It took me a while to come back to my senses after that. When I did, I started looking around for you, but you were already gone.

"Apparently, I ran into you when you were just getting started for the night. I missed the show a few minutes later on the pool table."

The pool table? I winced, but managed to keep my eyes locked with his.

He saw it, and grinned a little. "Yeah, the pool table. Then you left and went looking for another bar. Once I started asking around, trying to follow you, I heard quite a few stories. That's how I ran into your friend here; she was out looking for you too."

I turned to look at Angelique. "Oh, no," I said. "Don't tell me the drag queens know about this." Even in a city the size of New York, tell one drag queen something and you might as well publish it in the daily paper.

"Well, honey," she said, "how else was I going to find you? I got worried after you just up and strode out of the apartment as soon as you got this thing on." She shook the jacket. "Besides," she continued, "it's not just the queens who know about it. Apparently you were quite the busy boy. Honey, *everybody* knows about last night."

"Although I don't believe that story about the triplets," Eva supplied.

"Oh, I do," Neva said, grinning wickedly at me, "You can't make up stuff like that."

"And I know at least four people who saw what happened with those two Teamsters down by the piers," Feva put in.

I looked back at Chad while Angelique and her friends nattered on around us, recounting my apparent adventures of last night. He was still looking levelly at me, his blue eyes shining. He'd followed me all over the city last night because I had become something for him, something I'd only dreamed of being. I looked at the jacket, still in Angelique's hands, and knew what I wanted to do.

Before she could react, I leaned over and plucked the jacket out of Angelique's grasp. While she gaped at me, I took off Eva's sequined number and handed it back to her, finally uncaring of the fact that I now stood there shirtless or that everyone could see the obvious boner in my jeans. While the Andro Sisters tittered, I leaned down to look into Chad's eyes. "You're with me," I said. I yanked hard on the back of his chair and he scrambled to his feet.

Angelique was, for once, speechless as I pulled Chad out of the restaurant and onto the street. I looked at the jacket, turning it around and around in the sunlight. It was just a black jacket, just leather and cloth. Yet somehow it had allowed me to go to a place I had never dared to go before. Maybe this time I could go there without forgetting, without trying to deny who I could be.

I looked at Chad and smiled. It was a wild and reckless smile. Mysterious. Dangerous.

"Come here," I said to him, pulling him close as I began to shrug the jacket on.

After all, it was still Pride weekend.

TOAD
IAN PHILIPS

Toad's wig was askew. A retreating wave of blonde leaving hairless sweating skin in its wake. The stoat fucking Toad's slimier ass didn't seem to notice or care.

Toad's wide face—wide with horror, wide from tadpole-tail–like twists in his genetic code—banged against the baize of the pool table. A wet green *O* was slowly filling in each time his slobbery open mouth kissed it.

"Do—you—know—whom—you're—fucking!" he managed to shriek during an especially vicious series of thrusts.

"Yeah, some green-skinned bitch who can't sing," grunted another stoat who stood on the other end of the pool table frantically jacking his prick, as slick and as red as a clown's patent leather shoe.

"High—Olive!" shouted Toad in reply.

"Hi, Olive, yourself, cunt," the stoat said as he shot at Toad's face.

"My—eye—my—eye—not—green—olive—my—eye—my—eye—it—burns!"

Sccchhhreeechbangbambambambambambambambamsplash.

Toad was going a hundred kph down the wrong side of the road—*Damn Yanks, have to do everything their own way and that's why I love them!*—toward the glint of fallen gold steaming from the asphalt in the hot, slanted light of the midafternoon sun. The faster he sped, the farther it retreated. Till it leapt in dazzling flashes from rearview mirror to rearview mirror on the row of bikes parked in front of the bar known and feared far and wide as The Wild Wood. Toad squinted, blinded by the fierce light, raised his hands to his eyes, and slammed into the first bike. As they toppled like a set of $10,000-a-pop dominoes, Toad hurtled, limbs flailing like an epileptic starfish, over the twisted steel and rubber, bleeding gas, into a gravel-rimmed containment pond.

Toad kicked and flapped off his leathers before they dragged him into murky depths forever. Naked, he floated to the surface. He rolled over and spat water and gulped air and choked on both. Even without opening his eyes, he could see the white hot sun. And then a large shadow passed across the lids of his eyes. It circled back.

"Bird of prey! Bird of prey," Toad screamed and splashed out of the water and ran for the cool dark of the treeline. He punched at branches of trees and tore at green choking leaves of that plant with the name of some African animal he'd shot on safari once—*Kudu? Kudzu?*—as he rushed toward something that looked like shelter. It was a circle of campers, huddled close together. *What do they call them here? A park of trailers?* Before he could answer, a voice croaked from behind a screen door, "Ruby? Ruby, is that you?"

A face that resembled a painter's palette, thick with freshly squeezed oils, and surrounded with metallic red curls peered through the mesh before it was swung out from behind the door. The face shielded its eyes from the sun and looked hard at Toad. It leaned forward and the rest of its body followed until the unnaturally ripe breasts nearly rolled up and over the tube of pink cotton keeping them and a little bit of the torso covered.

"Shit, girl. Deek's gonna gut you if he sees you looking like that. What'd I tell you about going out of the trailer without your face. Hell, girl. You all right? You're soaked. And buck naked as the day your mama spat you out! I don't even wanna know how. Just git in here. Deek's been asking where you got to. Soon as he hears you're back, it's payday. And you're gonna have to be on your back all day if you don't want him beating you all night. Well, don't just stand there, staring all bug-eyed at me. Git in here and let Krystal clean you up. C'mon, girl! I got a john in half an hour and I ain't gonna make him wait just cuz you've been out joyriding."

The painted face, the red curls, the round breasts, the pink cotton, bounced up to Toad. Long nails pinched his skin as the hand they grew from pulled him inside the trailer.

"I'll be back with your smokes, Shugah," Toad drawled, stretching each vowel into a slow-motion aria. He pushed against the door, and the wall of heat that greeted him with a gut punch secured the leopard-print sundress to his skin with a thin paste of sweat. He staggered under the weight of the hour-from-setting sun. He teetered from atop the heights of his heels. He took each lower step as gingerly as if he were dipping his entire foot to test the temperature of his evening bathwater.

"Take your time, Ruby," Krystal hollered after the door banged shut. "And don't come a-knockin' if you see the trailer a-rockin'." She cackled and the trailer sounded like a coop of demon chickens.

"Girl, you know I will," Toad warbled back in his sweetest sing-song voice. He was delighted that he'd made it to the bottom of the steps, soaking from every pore, but alive.

Toad tried to walk a foot on the loose gravel in his heels. Each step twisted his ankles. Pebbles crammed their way into the opening of the shoes and under his toes. He bent to unfasten them and the ends of his blonde hair stuck themselves to the fresh coat of lipstick.

He spat and wiped the hair from his mouth with one hand as he took off his shoes with the other. With a hop, he left the heels behind him, sunk in gravel. He headed back to the treeline and toward the open road.

He sniffed his way to the parking lot of the bar. His bike and all the other mangled metal skeletons had been dragged away the steps of The Wild Wood and toward the highway. They'd been heaped together in a bonfire that said "Fuck you!" to the pissant sparks that were campfires and belched story-high flames when another gas tank exploded.

This almost drowned out the *pap-a-pap-pap* of gunfire and Toad's hysterical weeping. The mascara mixed with Toad's tears and sweat began to bead up like toxic dew. As he wiped the sludge from his eyes, and into his eyes, Toad hopped and reeled toward a new row of bikes and up the steps and into The Wild Wood.

He nearly fell backwards as his skin slapped up against a wall of cold as diabolically unnatural as the heat outside.

"Help me—help me—it burns—please, somebody help me—it burns!" Toad hiccupped through sobs.

"Ruby, is that you?" a stoat in a leather vest said before he fired a shot into a moaning heap of weasel.

"Hey, Ruby! Who fucked you up, girl?! I'll kill him!"

Toad aimed his wet, stinging eyes toward the voice. It was a high-pitched squeal that silenced everything in the bar but the CD-jukebox. *At last, someone in charge*, Toad thought. He would recognize Toad as a fellow pillar of the community. He would help him get home.

He shivered and stepped his way over the broken bottles and glasses and fallen barstools and cracked pool cues to get closer to the voice shrieking, "Ruby, Ruby, what the fuck happened, baby?!" Toad failed to notice the bloody weasel carcasses slumped in booths or draped like furry bunting from the bar until his foot flopped into a pool of dark thick water. It came from the freshly made weasel stole the voice, a grizzled stoat, was shouldering with difficulty.

"Damn, woman. You look worse than Big Daddy Zel," he said patting his wrap. Toad wiped the sludge from his eyes. Just enough to see without squinting. He dimly realized what that was, where he was, what must have happened here. "Oh," he sobbed. "Woe," he bawled. "Oh, woe is me!"

"Did Ol' Zel fuck you over, girl, did he?"

All Toad could do was blubber and mutter either "Oh" or "Woe."

"Well, he sure as shit ain't never gonna touch you now. Come here and let Stoat Force One make it all better." The stoat raised his arms to embrace Toad and the skin and fur of Ol' Zel began to slip-slide away.

Ka-thud.

The pelt landed in its own congealing pool of blood. What was still viscous splattered across Toad.

"Doooooomed!" Toad screamed and screamed and screamed until

Stoat Force One slapped him silent.

"Baby, getta grip." He pulled Toad into his arms. "Get Ruby something to drink. Something strong. And none of that weasel piss beer." His gang snickered and looked behind the bar for an unbroken bottle. At last, they found a large label-less mason jar. They scratched and bit at each other as they tried to unscrew it. Snout after snout sniffed it, dipped into it after it was open.

"Everclear, Mr. President," said the one not shoving his tongue deep in the jar.

"So get Ruby a fuckin' drink, already!"

The stoats scrambled again and came up with a "Gulp 'n' Blow" supersized plastic vat. They poured almost half the jar into it. And two of strongest stoats struggled to carry it toward the trembling Toad.

"Drink up, Ruby," Stoat Force One said. Toad noticed the shoulders of his leather jacket were dull and cracked with dried blood. The fur around his neck tangled and black and wet. "This'll wash all your pain away."

"My eye! My ass! It burns! O Woe! Woe! Woe!" Toad caterwauled against the stiff, indifferent belly of the pool table, his face held down as Stoat Force One came closer and closer to landing.

"Shut the fuck up, bitch!" he shouted back, his hand gripping and yanking on the back of Toad's dress like reins. "Nobody gives a fuck what you feel. Trying to sneak in here disguised as Ruby and kill us all." The rapid thudding of his hairy balls against Toad's slick backside punctuated nearly every syllable. "Trying to kill us with that goddamned harpy singing of yours!"

The leader of the stoat gang had been right. The Everclear did take all Toad's pain—even the hibernation-inducing chill of the cold dry air!—away. Not since Toad had pulled out of the dealers to test drive the Harley-Davidson Low Rider, not since the second before he was blinded and crashed it, had Toad felt like his old self. Fortuitously, he thought, the CD-jukebox began to play "Freebird," and so Toad began to sing. He was alive, and once he liberated one of the wicked stoats' bikes, he would be as free as a bird on the open road.

Somewhere in the refrain, those still alive in The Wild Wood turned on Toad. Turned Toad over and onto the floor with a few slaps and punches and kicks. Heaved up and turned Toad over the edge of the pool table and fucked him. One stoat after the other. Stoat Force One was the last. As soon as he came, he planned to slit this spy-bitch's throat and find the real Ruby.

"You're never gonna walk straight again, bitch. You'll be bowlegged till the day you die," he panted, the pitch of his voice growing even higher as his balls came to a boil.

Ka-bam! Ka-bam! Ka-bam!

"What the fuck?!" the stoat yelled as he frantically spurted into Toad. He could barely hear himself yipping over the exploding bar windows, the blaring music, the screaming not-Ruby beneath him.

Pap-a-pap-pap!

Rat, Mole, and Badger entered the bar firing.

"Am I dreaming? Do my stinging, weeping eyes betray me? Is that you, Badger? Mole? Dearest Rat?" Toad croaked. His words were too loud and bumped against the now-silenced jukebox, against the steaming bullet holes in every stoat but one, against the cold caked blood on Ol' Zel's fur. In the distance, he heard the whir of the straining air conditioner and the roar of the flames from the still-burning bikes.

"Had your fun, Stoat?" Badger asked. "You have three seconds to pull out of my friend before I pull the trigger. One, two..."

"Three! Three! Three, three, three," wailed Toad. "Pull the blasted trigger."

"You're welcome, old man," said Badger as he waved Stoat toward him with his Glock 9mm.

"Oh, Badger. It really is you. You've come to take me home."

"All in good time," Badger said calmly as he motioned Stoat to kneel before him. "Mole, Rat, do help our long-lost friend off the billiards table and out of that frightful wig."

"Yes, Ratty. Please help me. My back is broken I think."

"More like his asshole," Mole tittered into Rat's nodding ear.

"You there," Badger growled at the stoat, "suck on this while I think of what to do with you. Even though I can't imagine you going to the authorities, dead rodents tell no tales."

Stoat Force One, aware that he was just that, a force of one, reached to unfasten Badger's belt.

"Oh, how predictable. Do you really think I need a weapon to get blown? No, the gun."

Stoat trembled, his large black eyes watered, and he pressed the thin pink strip of hairless skin around the mouth of the Glock.

"How very prim. Now suck."

And suck the nearly convulsing stoat did.

"So, Toad, what to do with you?"

"Me?" Toad snorted. He waved away Mole and the handkerchief he'd been dabbing at various reddish streaks that may have been blood, may have been makeup. "I've been raped god knows how many times, and you want to chide me like some tardy schoolboy?!"

"There, there, Toad," Rat said as he lifted Toad's arm across his shoulder. "We've come across the great pond to find you. We were so worried," he added as he helped Toad hobble from the pool table toward Badger.

"I know, I know," Toad said as he stopped to lower his head and let it bob on his chest. "I know. Oh how I know. Woe, woe, woe...," he sobbed.

"There, there," Rat whispered as he reached for the handkerchief Mole had nearly tucked away in his breast pocket.

Toad snatched it up and wiped and blew.

"Thank you." He handed the damp rag back to Rat who daintily pinched the end of it between his right claws and passed it on to Mole who sighed before bending to lay it over the open eyes of a very dead weasel. "Thank you, one and all. Once again, I've been an ass and paid for it. And once again, you've saved me from my ways. I'm so terribly sorry. I'll never get near anything powered by an engine again."

"Toad, old fellow," Badger laughed, "there's plenty of time for apologies later. When we get back to Toad Hall."

"How is my ancestral home?" Toad asked, recovering his spirits at the very mention of his riverbank mansion.

"In frightfully better shape than this bar," piped in Mole.

"Oh, Mole, you are priceless," said Badger.

"Bar?" Toad asked. He remembered where he was. "Oh, my. Guns, blood, wreckage? Yes, of course, bar. I'm in America. How ever did you find me here?"

"Water Rat," said Mole.

"Beg pardon," replied Toad.

"My friend the Water Rat," said Rat.

Toad only smiled, his eyes as empty of reflection as the windows of The Wild Wood.

"We asked the Water Rat the name of the worst bar he'd come across in his travels in the U.S."

"We knew," added Badger, "you'd grow tired of the rides at Disney World—none would be wild enough for you, eh?—and thus stray. But really now, to stray several states away." Badger harrumphed, thrusting the gun deep into Stoat's mouth till he choked.

Toad pursed his lips into an obscene pout.

Badger busied himself fucking the stoat, trying as best he could to ignore Toad's growing glumness. But Badger knew a quiet Toad was a dangerous Toad. Who knew what even more toad-brained schemes he could be plotting. At last, Badger broke: "What is it, Old Man?"

"I want to choke the stoat," he said. "After all, I was the one he fucked." He sighed and let his eyes and chin drop in one well-rehearsed, well-used move.

"Oh, blast it all, Toad. Here." And with that, Badger grabbed Toad's hand and placed it around the warm heavy handle left behind by his own retreating palm and claws. "Now do be careful. The safety's off.

And I haven't decided whether to kill the wee wannabe weasel yet."

The stoat squealed. From fear or outrage? No one but the stoat cared enough to ask. And his squealing didn't last for long because Toad had begun to ram the muzzle as far into his mouth as it would go.

"That's right, boy. Lube up Ol' Toadie's gun. Get it slick, boy. Gotta keep it cool. Because it's overheating. Like me. I'm mean and high olive and ready to blow." Toad howled with laughter as he pumped the gun faster.

"Toad. Toad! Is that really necessary?" cautioned Badger, who was also nodding away the worrisome looks that Rat and Mole were shooting him.

"Yes, it is necessary," Toad countered, never slowing his arm. "I'm the one he and his gang fucked. Me. Toad of Toad Hall. You have no idea what it was like, Badger. The abuse! The indignity! All those little dicks in me. Barely opening my asshole. Barely tickling my prostate. And each one lasting but seconds! The only blows to matter coming from their little fists and feet. And one shot in my eye. My eye. My eye that has taken in all the wonders and horrors of this wide world and never once blinked. Oh, my noble eye. It still burns, Badger! Burns like the white-hot hole at end of this big thick gun when I fire it..."

K-plap!

"Bloody hell," exclaimed Badger, retrieving his own handkerchief to wipe the bits of brain and bone from his whiskered face.

"My eyes! My eyes!!" keened Toad as he dropped the gun onto the headless corpse and wiped the blood and gore from his face.

"Rat, old fellow, do help Mole there. He seems to be doubled-over and retching. And once you've helped him clean himself up, find some water and towels to wipe up this mess." At "mess," he pointed to Toad, who was nearly slapping his face as he wiped it hand-over-hand, managing only to smear the ooze more evenly across his skin.

"There, there, Toad," Rat cooed as he dried Toad's still-twitching face.

"There, there indeed, Rat," harrumphed Badger as he pocketed the flask he'd just shared between himself and Mole. "Don't mother him so. He's not Otter's little boy."

"Whatever Toad's faults, he's in shock, Badger," said Rat.

"As well he should be. Shocked at what he's done."

"You planned to kill the stoat too."

"Perhaps. We'll never know now, will we?"

"Oh, really now. I'm as angry as you to be thousands of miles from our river and rescuing Toad from this slaughter house—"

"Rescuing?" Toad moaned. "I saved you all from this foul beast. He could have overpowered Badger and then raped and killed each of us."

"How?" snickered Mole. "By swallowing the gun and belching out bullets?"

"How dare you!" roared Toad.

"How dare *he*?!" Badger shouted. "Oh, that is quite enough, Toad. Quite enough indeed. I'm going to leave you with such a bitter taste in your mouth that you will never dare insult your rescuers—yes! rescuers!!—and friends again!"

"Who are you, Badger, my father?!"

"If you're father were alive, and not felled anew by the spectacle of you as you appear this very moment, he would tan your hide to a most hideous shade of *green!*"

"Gr...gr...*green!!!*" Toad wailed, pressing his hands to his ears and waving his head from side to side.

"Yes, green, you ill-mannered amphibian!"

"Why...I...why...my...oh...Fuck you, Badger!"

Rat and Mole gasped. Badger snarled and then broke into deep and menacing laughter.

"Strip him," Badger said.

"What!" shrieked Toad, swelling at the threatened indignity. But Rat and Mole seized his arms and with their free hands tore away what remained of his dress, a patchwork of dried blood and cum and fabric.

"On your knees, boy," Badger hissed.

"What! No! You wouldn't dare."

"If you wish to ever leave these ruins and return home, you'll kneel this instant and give me the best fucking blow job you've ever given in your long wasted life."

"Why...I...never..."

"Then you'll need to learn quick. It's the only apology from you I'll accept."

"Ap...ap...ap...apol..."

And as Toad stuttered, Badger unzipped his tweeds and thrust his dick hard and fast into Toad's mouth as it tried to spit out "ogy."

"Rat," Badger grunted, "do be a friend, and push the back of his head to remind him of how a blow job should go. And Mole, would you be a good fellow and root about my ass with that snout of yours?"

"Certainly," Rat said as he gave Toad's head a shove, then gripped the sides of it and began to push it back and forth.

"My pleasure," said Mole as he sniffed and licked and squeezed his snout deep into Badger's crack.

"Oh, Rat! Oh, Mole! Never have I had such dear friends."

Rat shoved, Mole dug, Toad sucked, and Badger grunted and moaned. This continued for quite some time till Badger realized that he was not the only one who'd been slighted by Toad.

"Rat, Mole, can you ever forgive me?" he exclaimed, startling the three other living souls around him. "In my anger, I thought only of my slighted and sullied manhood. Yet Toad has slighted all our manhoods and thus should unsully each one of them. At once."

"At once?" asked Rat.

"Aphmunce?" mumbled Mole.

"At once. Indeed. At-one-and-the-same-time at once! It's the only way to put Toad's big mouth to good use."

Rat let go of Toad's head, and Mole kissed Badger's warm hole goodbye, and both soon stood on either side of Badger with their pants and undergarments around their feet.

Badger flicked a finger sharply against the top of Toad's head. He opened his mouth as wide as he could to shout his protest. "Now," commanded Badger and in went the dicks of Mole and Rat.

"Now suck, Toad, if you ever wish us to forgive you. Use that cunning tongue of yours if you ever want us to take you home. Not since public school have you sucked so many dicks in one sitting—and this time all at once. Think of how you can work this into another of one of your poem songs. What do you call them? Raps?"

"Yes, raps," huffed Rat as Badger stroked his tail.

"Oh, yes, rap me, Toad," wheezed Mole as Badger twisted his nipple.

"Oh, good and merciful Pan, I can hear it now. Suckle, suckle little Toad," rumbled Badger, his voice somewhere between a groan and a sob.

"Suckle," said a fevered Rat as he fingered Badger's hole.

"Suckle," said a dizzied Mole before he bit Badger's tit.

"Suckle...suckle...suckle," chanted Badger until he and Rat and Mole all came fiercely and together, one howling and two squealing, "Toad!"

And Toad flopped about on the floor as he swallowed the wide mouthful and shot himself. For the memories of public school and his acclaim as a singing slam poet—for he felt he sang too much and too beautifully to be a rapper—had made his dick stiff and his hand eager to jerk it off.

"That'll do, Toad. That'll do." Badger patted Toad on the head to calm his flopping. He then zipped up his tweeds.

"Time to go home?" Toad asked shyly, rubbing what little was left of his lipstick and cum from the edges of his mouth.

"Indeed," Badger said as he smiled at Toad as he slowly rolled from off his knees and onto his ass. "And once home," he whispered to Rat and Mole as they dressed, "I'll call the doctor and have him cut off those runaway legs of Toad's for once and for all. Then we can put that new French chef of his to good use and feast on our good fortune that at last our dear Toad will stay put."

Badger guffawed, Mole tittered, Toad, ever-in-the-dark but hating to be left out of any bit of good cheer, burst out with deep, gut-jiggling ribbits, kicking the floor with his feet. Only Rat smiled politely, already imagining his remaining twilight years hobbling after old Toad, rumbling down the country road in his motorized wheelchair. "Oh, Toad," Rat sighed as he watched him vanish over the cresting macadam.

"To my liberators!" Toad boomed in the here and now as he leapt to his feet.

"Here, here!" the trio of heroes cheered.

"To the brave hostage who killed the worst of them!" Toad crowed before taking a bow.

"Here, here!" the trio cheered a little less enthusiastically.

"Let us drink to their good fortune!"

"Here, here!" the trio shouted, their good spirits revived by the thought of even better spirits.

And all rummaged through the ruins of the bar and drank until the rising of the new moon, a sliver in the night sky as thin and curved and luminous as a nail clipping askew on the star-flecked bathroom floor of God Himself.

ANDREW'S SHIRT
REUBEN LANE

I pick the phone up. He says: "Baby, are you passive? Are you feminine? Would you dress up for me? Do you think you could pull it off?"

The fevers of three o'clock in the morning sweating the ceiling of my bedroom. Stalactites of the mind dripping into my hair, cold and clammy.

I watch the different options for suicide, surfing the TV channels. A crocus blooms in stop-start freeze frame. Then fades, wilts; corpses. Waiting for the man from the night before who met me on the corner outside the Great Eastern Hotel — in a black suit and black T-shirt. Took me through the lobby, up in the lift, along the silent carpeted corridors to his room. Apologized for the smoke; opened the minibar fridge and asked me if I'd like a drink. "What are *you* having?" then "Let's have a beer." He reached for two bottles of Beck's.

Three years ago Daffyd was a foreman working on the refurbishment of this hotel — he'd come back in the evenings, complaining about the hostility between the Kosovan and Russian builders on his team.

We sat on either side of a round shiny black table. He said he was organizing a press conference for his company.

"Do you have a partner?" he asked.

"Not at the moment. Do you?"

"Yes," he smiled. "We've been together for ten years now."

"Wow," I said.

"I—I mean we, neither of us, wanted a monogamous relationship when we started out. I think it's not very realistic. Just..."

"As long as you don't rub each other's noses in it."

"Exactly."

"Do you mind if I take off my shoes?"

"Of course — you need to ask?"

He undressed me and carried me over to the bed where I sucked on his cock for a bit before he fucked me. Long, black eyelashes and big, dark, brown eyes. He stopped when there were flecks of blood appearing on the bed linen. Then he asked me about the scar on the back of my neck.

Stars in glycerin falling from the shop assistant's eyes. A calculator and a felt tip pen in his shirt pocket. Haunts me with a look that will be a question once I've turned my back and am stepping through the glass door out onto the chewing-gum-splattered pavement.

"No strings."

Yesterday afternoon the *Evening Standard* boards wired up that the company he works for "DIPS £194M INTO THE RED."

Last night, on leaving my flat, I caught eyes with an incredible-looking man — walking in the rain in a white vest and combat camouflage trousers. I cut back around the corner and our paths crossed again on Goulston Street. He waited, looking back from under the glass atrium of the shop that sells smiley-face T-shirts. I stood in the gloom of the tunnel under the flats. Then he came back, doubtful as to my worth, into the shadows, scouting out a doorway in which he'd open his fly to have his cock sucked. But then — a wrinkle of contempt across his lips — he passes back muttering and goes out into the rain the way he came. And I go through the white fluorescent strip-lit expanse of the car park and wait for the number 40 bus at the Aldgate garage, get off at East Street market, and walk down East Street, which feels dangerous even though it's only ten thirty.

I find the block of council flats the man told me about. I ring him. He comes down to let me in. He's watching a documentary on TV. He pours himself a glass of red wine into a tumbler that's already seen the rest of the bottle pass its way; slices of lemon edged with the tannins.

He says, "Yes, I'm an alcoholic. It gets to this time of the night and I'm thinking I've either got to go the office to get myself something else — or then after eleven, I'll have to go to a bar in town. Only in this country, mind. You don't have that problem in Italy. There you can go out any hour of the night and buy yourself some wine."

He doesn't stop talking. It's a tiny room — the bed in an alcove, washing drying on a wooden clotheshorse. Drawings on the wall.

"Did you do those?" I ask.

"No. Though that one's *of* me. I've been a model in art schools the last four years. Before that I was a chef. Then I had a breakdown. Now it's the holidays. I'm thinking of going to live in Turin. I'd rent the place. I've had enough of it round here. There's more and more — what do you call them? — Nigerians — moving in."

When the documentary is finished he says, "So, are we doing anything then?"

"No — I don't think so." I laugh.

"Well I'm sorry about that — and you coming all the way over here."

"No, it's fine."

Outside the block of flats there's a young black woman screaming at a white woman standing in the doorway of her flat in her dressing gown. The white woman slams her door. The black woman goes up to the door, flings open the metal grille and begins yelling at the door. An old weary Jamaican man's voice comes from above and slowly calls, "Lorraine, Lorraine, come on inside."

And I walk back. It's barely scratching midnight but there's hardly anyone around. A man sleeps bundled up at an angle of forty-five degrees against the inside of London Bridge. At least I talked to someone.

At ten past three I ring the man who says he's going to cycle over from the Elephant. He whispers: "Baby, it's like the dress is in this room—and there's someone standing outside it. Would you wear lipstick for me?"

I ask him if he's bi.

And he says "Baby—basically I'm straight."

"What's your name, boy?"

I stared over his balding head at the blackboard.

"*You.*" He glared.

"Me?" I raised my eyebrows.

"Yes—you. Stand up."

I got up. "Rooley, Sir."

"What were you talking about?"

"Nothing, Sir."

"That's an impossibility, isn't it? What did you say your name was?"

"Rooley."

"Aren't you interested in geography, Rooley?"

"Yes, Sir."

"Then why do you choose to talk in my lessons when I'm trying to explain the extraordinary phenomenon of ley lines to you?"

"I don't know, Sir."

"You don't know?"

"No, Sir."

"Well if you don't know, I don't know who is going to know. A hundred lines. To be delivered to me in the staff room by the end of break. Write this down, Rooley: 'I must not put my head in the lion's mouth.' You may resume your seat now."

At the start of break, Steve Manhood, Paul Reeves, and Mansur Patel crowded around my desk. I started writing out my lines on a sheet of ruled A4.

Paul Reeves seized my pen.

"You better hurry, poofter boy."

I stayed still watching my purple Platignum pen in Paul Reeves' fist as he towered over me.

"You're in trouble now." Mansur Patel bent down to whisper in my ear.

Natasha King and Julia Markham shouted out, "Leave him alone" and "Give him back his pen" as they hurried off for a cigarette in the girls' toilet.

"All right then." Paul Reeves lowered his hand toward me, but then threw it across to Steve Manhood.

"Catch."

"Whoops." Steve Manhood missed, and the pen went clattering across the wood floor. He went to pick it up. "Oh dear," he said, "looks like the nib's got bent."

"Not the only bent thing around here." Mansur Patel whispered an inch away from my ear. The other two laughed.

"Here," Steve Manhood held the pen two feet above my head. I looked up. Then he pulled the fill-up lever and a huge drop of blue Quink fell on my forehead.

"What's going on in here?" A boy from the second year stood at the door of the classroom. "You lot shouldn't be in here. Give him back his pen and fuck off out."

His name was Dawkins, and his dad had a car repair workshop in Crystal Palace. I knew—we all knew—the only reason that he had intervened wasn't that he disliked bullies but that he had it in for Mansur Patel.

I rushed down my hundred lines in the fifteen minutes left of breaktime. I ran to the staff room, knocked on the door. Mr. Hawley, the geography teacher, appeared.

"Can I help you?" he asked.

"I've brought you my lines. I held out the two pages of "I must not put my head in the lion's mouth."

"Who asked for these?"

"You did, Sir."

He looked at the papers quizzically and then handed them back.

"Very good, very good," he said. "Are you in one of my classes?"

"Yes, Sir. 1S Geography."

"Have I told you about the time I met Paganini's ghost?"

"No, Sir."

The bell rang for the end of break. Two years later, on the day of Mr. Hawley's retirement, four senior boys grabbed him, ran with him down to the swimming pool, and threw him in. He almost drowned.

After break was French.

Mr. Nott had big poppy eyes.

"Who haven't we heard from recently? Ah yes—Mr. Rooley hiding away at the back there."

I was dying for a piss because I hadn't had time to go during break.

"Yes, Sir?"

"What is 'some milk'?"

"Du lait."

"What?" he barked.

"Du lait."

"Rooley, I want you to stand up on top of your desk."

There was a rustle of laughter around the class.

"Sir?"

"Go on. Stand on your desk."

I did as I was told.

"Now," said Mr. Nott sitting on the front of his desk, "I want you to shout at me so I can hear you."

The whole class was staring up at me.

"I want you to shout at me..." Mr. Nott scratched his head, "I want you to shout, 'You Great Big Fat Green Wally,' all right?"

The whole of 1S was waiting. This was much better than French.

"Come on, Rooley."

I clenched my bladder. "You great big fat green wally," I said.

"WHAT?" Mr. Nott boomed, "I didn't hear you."

"You great big fat green wally." I said louder—all the time feeling the hot urine burning inside me.

"You MUST be able to do better than that." Mr. Nott's face was going puce. Everyone was laughing. "Come on Rooley—SHOUT!"

"You GREAT BIG FAT GREEN WALLY!" I screamed.

"That's it." Mr. Nott danced about. "Again—again—do it again."

"You GREAT BIG FAT GREEN WALLY," I yelled. The class laughed and laughed.

The face of Mr. Collins, the lower school headmaster, appeared at the porthole window in the classroom door. He frowned. Mr. Nott said, "You can get down now, Rooley."

I stepped off the desk.

"Homework." Mr. Nott announced leafing through the textbook. The whole class groaned.

As soon as the bell rang and Mr. Nott had left, I ran as fast as I could down the corridor, down the stairs to the boys' toilets in the playground. The piss came out for a whole minute: fierce, acid yellow, and steaming.

"What are you into? How far do you want to go?" the man who never gave me his name asks on the phone. Sunday morning.

"I don't know. I'm up for anything." Then I remember, "So long as it's safe. Anything that's safe. Where do you live?"

"Bethnal Green. Along the Roman Road. You can catch the number 8 bus."

"I'll walk," I say. "I'll just have a shower, get dressed, and be on my way."

"You can shower here. Save yourself time."

"I'll be there—no later than an hour—twelve thirty."

"You better not be. I'm bored."

Why do they always say they're bored—as if it's meant to turn you on?

Put on a pair of clean underpants. I walk. Baking hot in my street. An elderly West Indian woman talking to a younger man.

He asks, "So, what are you doing here?"

She says, "I've just been to church, and I'd thought I'd come and have a look at the market."

He says, "I haven't been down here for years."

Up Brick Lane—a cappuccino from the Portuguese man with his coffee cart—along the Bethnal Green Road. A memory of walking along here one winter day ten years ago with Ethan who wanted to find a barber for a number-two crop.

Up the Roman Road past the Buddhist Center and the Globe Town estate—hanging baskets with unwatered and now-dead dwarf conifers and heathers. I get to the turning he told me—and call from the phone box. He directs me to his block. It's a new block. I press the buzzer on the ground-floor entrance, aware that I'm being judged and evaluated: the picture on the wrapper, through the eye of a CCTV camera.

"Top floor," his voice clicks over the intercom.

Up three flights and out along a balcony.

He appears at a door.

There is a blackness smudging beneath the skin under his eyes. No preliminaries. No "Hello, how are you doing?" No names. Just: "Did you have a shower?"

I tell him, "No. I came straight here."

He stares into me, standing three inches away. "So, do you want to stay?"

I nod.

He starts kissing me. His breath smells like boiled cabbage with a last-minute addition of mint toothpaste. I bet he cleaned his teeth after I rang him from the phone box. I hope he has healthy gums.

"Come on then." He leads me next door into his bedroom. It's a tip—worse than my own—with a week's trousers and shirts piled, dragged off, and thrown on the floor; printed out emails and magazines along the skirting board.

He pulls me onto the bed. He's got tin-gray, inquisitive eyes, a small mouth. He undresses me. Flicks my bollocks, smacks my ass. I wait—I show it in my eyes—the way my mouth is parted ready for him to kiss me. He hovers over me, then hawks up a throatful of flob that he spits into my mouth.

"So, what do you do?" he asks without much interest.

"I'm a writer."

"Do you make money from it?" They always want to know that.

"No—not really. It will do." I promise his eyes, "Not lots, but enough. And you?"

"I work for the BBC. I'm a talent manager."

He shoves his nose under my arms; first one side, then the other, whilst pulling on his cock. "You've got horny pits." Climbing on top of me he asks, "Are you close to coming?"

I nod and ask him, "So, were you out partying last night?"

He says, "Why? Do I look as bad as that?"

He has a picture of a young man and woman sitting with Richard Maddeley and Judy Finnigan on a shelf. The young man appears in another photo behind. Ex-boyfriend or sometime-boyfriend — now does too much coke; bored with his job; has lots of sex.

He comes.

"I thought you were going to come." He's pissed off.

He watches: lying back as I wank myself and then climb onto him. I make a milk lake in the hollow where his ribcage ends and his stomach starts.

Immediately he reaches out for a towel — always a bad sign when they want to get mopped up straight away. I go for a wash in the bathroom. It could do with some serious Jif and Vim. And by the time I'm dressed, he's in the living room turning the pages of *News of the World*.

"Right then," he says — as in — *Right, off you go.* A dry chaste peck on the lips.

"Right then," — as in — *That's all you're ever going to find out about me.* Rewind.

On the way back I swerve off to do my shopping in the Sainsburys. An Indian man tells me, "There's one of those for 99 pence on the other side," pointing at the boxed carrot cake I'm staring at, my head a million miles away.

"Thanks," I say, smiling back at him, laughing to find myself back in the aisle of the supermarket.

My sister had a boyfriend from the church youth group. His name was Andrew. He was beautiful. He used to come around to our house a lot after school. We'd all have toast and Rice Krispies together. Andrew liked to talk.

For Valentine's Day he bought my sister a scarlet shirt with popper buttons down the front and pale blue piping along the shoulders and arms.

He told us, "I went into the shop, and there were these two girls in there, who I could tell were eyeing me up. So I went over to the woman at the counter and I said in a loud voice: 'I'm looking for something nice to buy for my *girlfriend* for Valentine's Day.'"

We went and sat on the bench in the garden even though it was cold and getting dark. My sister went up to her bedroom. We could hear her Bananarama and Duran Duran records playing. She'd left her new shirt behind, still in its tissue wrapping.

"You try it on." Andrew said. "It'll fit you."

I took off my gray school cardigan, undid my inky tie and slipped the T-shirt over my head.

It felt nice on.

"You look good in it," Andrew laughed, "Those colors really suit you."

A week or so later I asked my sister why Andrew hadn't been over since.

"We had a row. I dumped him. He talks too much."

"Oh," I said.

"Yeah—oh." My sister vanished up to her room and then reappeared holding the shirt he'd given her. "Here," she said, flinging it on the table, "you can have it if you like. It's a boy's shirt anyway. The stupid twat."

Yesterday evening, and all week I'd been planning to go the White Swan in Limehouse with Eli. But then when I rang Eli yesterday morning he said he'd forgotten and he'd got a date with a man off the Internet. So I thought—I'll go on my own. I had a travelcard.

I was expecting it to be the disco night, but when I walked in, the black-painted room was almost empty. I got myself to the bar and turned to see what was happening. It was ballroom dancing, with couples waltzing around the room in a circle. I got my pint of Stella and found a dark corner from where to watch.

About halfway through the pint I shed my disappointment that the place wasn't heaving with East End lads dancing to Beyonce and Justin Timberlake. I followed the steps of four feet gracefully drawing order across the air. A man came over and sat next to me, said his name was Jackson, and asked me if I danced. I said, "Yes—but not to this kind of thing."

Jackson said, "It's easy; there are eight basic steps and all the rest is just decoration."

Everyone was friendly in there; they all knew each other. It was like a club from the 1950s. Jane, a tranny sitting across the table, got talking to me. She pointed to an elderly woman in a shimmering green blouse dancing: "That's me mum," she said, "She's eighty, mind. She's a few sheets short, if you get my drift. I bring her along here. Ever since me dad died a coupla years back. He used to tell her she was no good at dancing—*he* was the dancer. But truth is he was a nasty piece of work: a bigot; chased any woman in a skirt; a toerag; used to knock *her* around. The last few years when he was stuck in bed I used to go round the house dressed up like this—rub it in—there was nothing he could do.

I bought Jane a Newcastle Brown and cadged a roll-up off of her.

She was the best bit of my evening. The reason I tell myself to wait and see what's going to come to me.

Jackson, the graceful dancer, sat in close and we started flirting and pawing each other. I said, "You can have a cup of tea back at mine," and said goodbye to Jane.

She said, "Come again."

Jackson and I caught the Docklands Railway. We seemed to be getting along fine. But then inside my flat—in my bedroom—he became quiet. We undressed and he laughed at my purple underpants: "Where *did* you get them? They're not exactly your standard gay white Calvin Kleins are they?" And it was as if the sight of my underpants was a signal to him to leave.

I asked him if he felt okay. He grunted. I sucked his cock—and quickly, without warning, he shot into my mouth. All he wanted to know was what track on my compilation CD had been playing when he'd come.

I handed him the cover whilst I went to spit his spunk out in the bathroom. Then he left hurriedly; all friendliness, flirtation, kindness drained away. And I felt I hadn't had a good evening after all.

I phoned the chatline and wanked off with a Dutchman who was fantasizing about being gang-fucked; and a guy in Wimbledon who makes up stories about teenage boys he lures to his from internet chat rooms. It's late and I'm tired and smaller than I used to be—and I know it would be possible in this state of mind to walk to the edge of the world and step off it.

My sister changed schools at thirteen. She went to the girls' school at Tulse Hill. Mum and Dad, who were both now in their fifties, couldn't cope with her. As soon as she was home from school she was off and out with the wild boys in the street, like Dean and Charlie who'd both been expelled from their schools. Dad tried to stop her seeing them. When Dean rang the doorbell, Dad would bellow at my sister, "Stay in your room" and then he'd march to the door, open it, and tell Dean "She can't come out tonight. She's got her homework to do."

My sister would be in her bedroom screaming at Mum and Dad: "You can't STOP me seeing my friends." Mum going: "You want to bet on that?" The screaming got louder; then the sound of a hand slapping her face. It was like the three of them had no way out—trapped in my sister's bedroom with her posters of Simon LeBon and Kajagoogoo on the walls.

I listened guiltily at my bedroom door—part of me wanting my sister to get hit and another part terrified at the realization that Mum and Dad could so quickly lose control. My sister's screaming got momentarily louder as her bedroom door opened to let Mum out. I listened as she went down to the bathroom on the landing, filled a bucket at the bath tap with icy cold water, carried it back up to my sister's room, was let back in—the continuous screaming rising a pitch and then shuddering into a horrid silence as the bucket was emptied over my sister's head.

I will never forget that sudden silence, followed by wimpering and sobbing. I ventured out onto the landing. "I HATE you," my sister said, her voice shivering, "You're not even my REAL mum and dad."

I then scurried back into my room. The door of my sister's bedroom opening, my mum and dad—breathing heavily—shifting down the staircase. I felt guilty; guilty that I'd listened and heard it all and not done anything to help my sister; but much more guilty that I'd actually felt pleased. Because I was jealous of my sister; of her wildness, her willfulness, the way she fought back—while I felt myself to be too much of a coward, too shy, picked on, unable to run with the after-school boys, to come home—loudly boasting of french-kissing them.

A white-sheeted tent over the body of a man in a field in Oxfordshire. Claimed by the government to be the leak in the Ministry of Defence; he set out for a walk and doesn't return.

In Tokyo, a reporter calls out at the morning press conference with the Japanese and British Prime Ministers—a question to Tony Blair: "Prime Minister, have you got blood on your hands?" Tony Blair stares straight ahead, his lips sealed—as a Japanese official steps up to the microphone to call an early close to the press conference.

Stumbled into a wood two miles from his home, feeds himself a packet of painkillers, and then rips open his left wrist with a sharp blade.

In Brockwell Park, an overweight fifteen-year-old boy and a thirteen-year-old girl pick on their eleven-year-old brother—pinning him to the ground and kicking the shit out of him. The boy with a strawberry blond crewcut struggles and kicks back. He grabs the girl's jeaned leg as he crawls on the grass, makes to bite it, and with his other hand grabs and squeezes her crotch. The girl screams. The older boy yanks at the small boy's shoulder. One of the girl's three friends comes over and starts kicking the boy: "Let go of her." He releases his grip. The big boy picks up his little brother and shakes him until his gray tracksuit trousers fall down his skinny legs.

Setting up the fun fair—lorries and vans—gray tarpaulins over the cars of the Twister. The yellow-and-red-striped canopy over the bumper cars faded with a dozen summers. Blue and white marquees. An open-back truck drives by my tree trunk, on the back a young man with bottle-blond shaggy hair, squatting as he holds on. The Waltzer; the

Rocket Ride; the House of Fear.

Candy floss; toffee apples; hot dogs. Simply the Best Tasties. Supreme Fast Foods.

The two brothers come and sit on the trunk just along from me. The fat boy orders the little boy: "Alan, see if you can jump from one trunk to the next"; "Alan, see if you can dive over it head first" — like the boy's his slave, or stupid. He says, getting out his mobile: "You know that girl I was seeing — I'm going to give her a ring." He wanders out from under the branches of the beech tree — holding the Nokia to his head: "Are you still going out with me?" Pause. "I was just wondrin' cos I ain't seen you for a coupla days."

I want to shout at the fat bully: "Don't you ever touch that boy again."

Walking here from Trafalgar Square — through Parliament Square past the heroic man who's been camped out with his banners for two years now, pricking the consciences of the warmongering MPs across the road. Kennington, Brixton. Growing up in South London.

And now here I am trying to salvage some confidence. Stop me from becoming bitter and curmudgeonly. Not scared by the hooded black teenage men-boys who brush my sleeve as they cycle past me on the pavement.

This wish to vanish; click my fingers and be gone.

THE PANCAKE CIRCUS
TREBOR HEALEY

Clown Daddy bussed dishes at the Pancake Circus, a popular, tacky breakfast joint on Broadway in Sacramento. I only went there when I was depressed and, in my half-baked noncommittal self-destruction, craving food that would kill me if I ingested enough of it. I wanted a steamy stack of buttermilk pancakes with that weird whipped butter they use that melts slowly and thoroughly, sort of like my psyche does when it's heading south. (It does not have the same effect on your arteries however, which slowly harden like dogshit in the sun.) And I wanted that diabetes-inducing syrup of course. Two or three shots of it—lethal as sourmash—surreptitious, sticky, and sweet as it vanishes into the spongy cake, absorbed like a criminal into the social fabric.

Clown Daddy began as a tattoo of a tiger jumping through a ring of fire—a tiger with a pacifier in his mouth. A tiger caged in a mess of plump blue veins—veins like the roots that buckle sidewalks. Straining as they held the pot poised over my cup; straining like my throat suddenly was; like my cock caged in my drawers.

"Coffee?" It was Josh Hartnett's sultry bass voice.

In an effort to compose myself, I drew in a breath and followed those veins up that forearm, down through the dimple of its elbow and up across the creamy white bicep, firm and round as a young athlete's buttcheek, before the blood-swollen tubes vanished into his white polyester shirt, reappearing at the neck and passing the Adam's apple, which was nothing less than a mushroom head pushing boy-boisterous out of his neck skin like a go-go dancer in Tommies. *God have mercy*, my soul muttered, as my eyes, having lost his veins somewhere under his chin (and damn, what a beautiful charcoal-shadowed chin), slowly crept up his clean-shaven cheek, savoring the pheromonal (and I mean *moan*-al) beauty of him, deadest for his eyes like a junkie tightening the belt. And bingo, like apples and oranges lining up in a slot—oh my God, I won!

I'm a homo and you know where I'd look for the coins. I felt my sphincter dilate and my buttcheeks, for all intents and purposes, were suddenly like open-cupped palms, holding themselves out to him.

I came in my pants. And then, a bit unnerved to say the least, cleared my throat. I'm not sure I would have even been able to answer him if I hadn't relieved the pressure somewhere. Fortunately, God had mercy after all.

I whimpered, "Yes, please." I couldn't even look at him, so I watched the cup as he filled it to the top and then some. It crested the brim and ran down onto the saucer—and then I watched the pot move away, off to the next table.

Jesus H. Go-Go Dancing Christ. My drawers were soaked and cooling. I felt like a kid who'd wet his pants. This had happened to me only once before, in junior high, when Greg Vandersee had stretched, lifting up his arms and revealing a divine cunt of underarm hair that made me lurch forward as my cock emptied its copious boy-fresh fluids into my little BVDs.

Fortunately, Clown Daddy was a busboy and not my waiter. I could handle *yes* and *no*, but *the buttermilk stack, with sausage and one egg over-easy* wouldn't have been pretty—or perhaps even possible.

"Hi, I'm Edna. What'll you have?" She smiled.

A bed, some lube, and an hour with your busboy would have been the honest answer. Or a fresh pair of undergarments. But this wasn't about honesty, this was about self-destruction. Wasn't it? I ordered the low-cholesterol Eggbeaters in a vegetable omelet with whole wheat toast. Say what you will—lust leads to healthy choices. Doesn't it?

What I hadn't realized as I sat back gloating, my penis clammy in my damp, semen-soaked briefs, was that when I'd looked in Clown Daddy's eyes my days as a law-abiding citizen had abruptly ended. Choices? Choices had nothing to do with it.

But ignorance is bliss. While it lasts. And while it lasted, my head wobbled like one of those big-headed spring-loaded dolls that look just like Nancy Reagan, swinging this way and that, watching for him, rolling up and down and around like an amusement park ride, taking in the Pancake Circus as I did so, its paint-by-number clowns adorning the walls, its circus-tent decor, its uncanny ambience of a sick crime waiting to happen.

I watched him move about while my fly tightened like a glove over a fist. A wet fist, sticky and greedy for more of whatever messed its drawers. My mind played the sideshow song as I imagined Clown Daddy behind the curtain, Edna up front barking for him, "Step right up, see the man who makes you come in your drawers!"

I gulped the coffee down, which drew him back to my table like a shark to wet, red, bleeding bait.

He didn't look at me until I thanked him, and then it was just a shy, straightboy grin. God, but his features were sharp, angled, and clean. His dark, deep-set eyes, the long lashes, the wide mouth with its full lips, the arresting pale blue-white of his skin and the night-black hair— that goddamn shadowed chin. And his eyes: dark as crude oil, raw out of the ground. He was undeniably, painfully handsome. Prozac-handsome because he cheered me up. Wellbutrin-handsome because one saw one's sadness disappear like a wisp of smoke—and those pesky sexual side effects? Gone. Every woman in the place blushed when he cleared their plates. I probably wasn't the only one stuck to the vinyl seat in my booth. Thank God my cock has no voice, or it would have been barking like a dog.

But I felt the letdown all the same. He's probably straight. Though he ignored the blushing dames. He seemed even a little annoyed by the attention. But we knew who each other were, the girls and I. I eyed them, and they, me. Did I look as greedy as them? Like there was one Cabbage Patch Kid left, and they'd kill to wrest it from whatever fellow shopper had his or her eye on it? Fact was, we all had holes we wanted his cock in. Simple as that.

I gulped my food like a scat queen falling off the wagon. Delirious, my diaper soiled, I paid my check and left, one gaze over the shoulder to see him bend to pick up a fallen fork. Damn, Clown Daddy had a butt like a stallion. My dog leapt, knocking over the milk dish again. Jesus H. Cock-Hungry Christ. I lurched out the door as my piss-slit opened like a flume on a dam.

Clown Daddy sent me home in a frenzy, is what he did.

I rushed home, needing to get naked. Onto my back on my bed, my legs kicking like an upended insect as I pulled like a madman, again and again, on my slot handle, hitting jackpot after jackpot until my bed was plain lousy with change.

From then on, he filled my nights and days like a cup, brimming over.

He had no name in the beginning, of course. He was just the dude at the Circus. I went for more pancakes two days later, but he wasn't there. On the third day, he was, with a beautiful zit on his cheek. Clown Daddy looked right through me when he recognized me, and then he pulled himself back out.

I lurched. Shit—I came again.

"Coffee?"

"Uh, yeah," I half-coughed.

"Cream?"

I nodded. The greed. My shorts were already full of it.

"Sugar?" He's talkative today.

I regained my composure. "No sugar—sugar's for kids," I answered flirtatiously. I don't know why I said it. I had to say something. I wanted to talk to him, relate to him, hold him there, even if for only a few seconds.

He smiled the brightest smile, and walked away.

My head swiveled. What was that? Had he flirted back?

I sat there at the table, waiting for my waitress, reading the ads urethaned into the tabletop: ads for vacuum repair, van conversions, credit counseling, body shops, auto detailing, furniture, appliances, and bail bonds. The clues were everywhere. It occurred to me then that he was the only white busboy in the place. The rest were illegal Latin guys who didn't have a choice. What would a citizen take a job like this for? Maybe he was Romanian or something. But he had no accent. What could he be making?—four, five bucks an hour? Hell, his looks alone could get him ten doing nothing for the right boss. He could hustle at two hundred an hour, do porn for a few thousand a feature; he could wait tables and fuck up and they'd still forgive him because the doyennes of Sacramento would return for the way he made them feel against their seat cushions. *What* was he doing here?

Love is blind, fools rush in, whatever. So I misread him. Just let me fuck him. Shoot first, ask questions later.

He was as aloof as ever when he came back with the coffee. Three cups later, I asked for sugar. He smiled again. "Sugar's for kids. You like kids?"

"Sure, kids are all right."

He nodded in the affirmative, and raised his brows with just a hint of a grin as he said sort of stoned-like, "Kids are all right." And he walked away.

Go figure. I scribbled my phone number on the coffee coaster, with a little cartoon kid, waving.

And he called. But he never left his name.

"This is the guy who likes kids, down at the Circus. I can't leave a number, but meet me at the Circus at three on Wednesday."

This was Sunday, so I had to navigate three days of my imagination on overload: Clown Daddy's tiger jumping back and forth through my ring of fire; Clown Daddy's sidewalk-buckling vein roots making a mess of my street; Clown Daddy's chin knocking on doors; His voice arresting me amid flashing lights; His brows like awnings in the rain; Clown Daddy's lashes in all the falling leaves; Clown Daddy profoundly fucking me with the wisdom of the ages. I went through four bottles of lube.

I jacked off at two thirty Wednesday, not wanting to repeat my little Pancake Circus habitual jackpot when I sidled up to shake his hand. My knees might buckle, and then what? Would I hold onto his hand and pull him down with me? Would I beg him to clean up my shorts with his tongue? Would he do it? Anything is possible—I've learned that much in thirty years.

I needed to get hold of myself. I turned the key in the deadbolt as I left the house. I pushed the key in hard, my mouth agape. In and out went the key. I reached for the knob. Good God, I've lost it.

I saw him from two blocks away. He sat on the low wall of the planter that had endured, neglected and falling to pieces with its ratty bushes and weeds, between the sidewalk and the parking lot.

He wore black boots, Levi's, and a camouflage winter coat. Not a promising fashion statement for what I had in mind.

He nodded when he saw me coming, but ignored my hand when I put it out to shake. He just said, "What's up?" And then, without waiting for an answer, added, "There's a playground about five blocks from here."

"What?"

"Come on, I'll show you."

I feigned having a clue, but I really didn't until it occurred to me he might be suggesting a place to have sex—some doorway maybe, or a clump of trees out of view that schoolyards were notorious for. But it was 3:00 p.m., school would still be in session. I'd done schoolyards, but always after five.

I could see the schoolyard fence from a couple blocks away as we approached. Stepping off a curb, he abruptly grabbed my arm by the bicep, and my cock leapt like a Jack Russell terrier.

"Stop here," he stated flatly.

I looked at him inquisitively, at a loss. He dropped his gaze and I followed it as, with his left hand firmly in his pocket, he lifted his pant leg slowly to reveal a plastic contraption surrounding his ankle. A small green light pulsed intermittently. He studied it, then backing up three feet, got it to stop pulsing and simply glow a constant green.

"This is as far as I can go," he stated matter-of-factly.

It took me a minute to realize he was under house arrest. Then there was the crowd of thoughts, like people at an airport, ornery about a cancelled flight and vying for the next option: What does it mean? I didn't know anything about law enforcement. Drunk driving? It must be some kind of probation.

He's probably a rapist or a killer, a thief or a drug dealer. Nah, too cute to rape. But if he's fucked up enough, what would that matter? Too smart to kill. Thieves are a dime a dozen, and I'm only carrying twenty bucks. Drug-dealing? Humbug. So what. But none of these possibilities were in any way convincing. He was just too sexy to fit any criminal stereotype which shows you what a dumbfuck I was. For my part, I didn't really care. I could only wonder if he were queer. He ignored the blushing dames at the Circus. He looked almost tired by the attention. Of course, he'd sneered at me too.

I may have misread him, but I wasn't completely foolish. Not completely. I knew he was a criminal, so I figured I'd need to find out about the ankle bracelet before taking him home. Just in case he was going to murder me or steal my stereo. The logic of queers. On top of all that, I assumed he'd tell me the truth, which was preposterous—except that he did. More or less.

Ignorance is not only bliss, it's a bit disorienting too.

He retired to a sloping lawn in front of the house on this particular corner, offering, "This will be fine." I was getting more and more confused. Sex right here?

Within minutes, we heard them: the cacophony of tykes, who were now streaming down the street in little gaggles. They reached the far corner, stopped, looked both ways, and then proceeded across. Group after group of them: little Koreans and Viets with rolling book bags; Mexican kids burdened by overstuffed backpacks; white kids on skateboards; little black kids strutting.

"Aren't they beautiful?" He said out of nowhere.

"Sure they are," I concurred, "kids are like flowers."

"Flowers?" He looked at me like I was stupid.

"You know, those colorful things? New life? All that?" He wasn't buying my poetry.

"I mean beautiful like meat," and he ran his tongue lasciviously across his full upper lip as it occurred to me, amidst my throbbing erection, that he was a pedophile. My cock was like a poised spear now, but not because of what he'd just confessed about his sexual orientation—it was his tongue and what it had just performed. Take me, you beast. I must confess, moral repugnance was not the first thought that entered my mind, nor the second. The tongue being the first, what followed was my sudden disappointment that not only was I possibly the wrong gender, but I was most definitely not the right age. I hadn't a chance. My cock still reached for him, fighting against the binding of my jeans—not to mention the limits of his orientation—like a child having a tantrum, refusing to let go of a cherished teddy bear. But I felt the sweat on my asshole cool.

He lay back, a sprig of grass in his teeth, smiling at the kids—a pedophile cad. They smiled back. Jesus Wayne Gacy, we were cruising!

I tried to get a foothold. "Uh, would you like to go grab a coffee?"

"Nah, I'm happy right here."

I said nothing more, paralyzed with ineptitude. We sat there for just fifteen minutes, until the herd had passed. "Damn, I gotta jack off. Come on."

Speaking of come-ons—was this one? I'm not sure I was interested anymore, but of course my cock still was, throbbing like a felon in chains. I followed.

Back to Broadway and to an ugly stucco motel-looking apartment building streaked with rusty drain runoff, its windows curtained and unwelcoming. Clown Daddy said nothing. He simply keyed the lock, and I followed him into one of the saddest apartments I'd ever seen. A mattress lay in the middle of the living room, with a single twisted blanket lying across it. There was an alarm clock on the floor, and in the kitchen, fast-food trash in the sink.

OUT OF CONTROL

The toilet was foul and ringed with dark grime. There were no pictures, no kitchen utensils, plates or cups, no toaster, no coffeemaker, no books, no phone. Other than the bed and the roof and plumbing, there was but one thing that made the place habitable at all: a TV with a VCR.

He pulled a video cassette out of the back lining of his camouflage hunting jacket and placed it in the VCR. He sat down on the bed, suddenly eager and animated. "I just got this from a dude I met. It better be good; it cost me thirty bucks." There were no credits, no title, not even sound. There were a lot of kids though, doing things that got people put away.

"I think I better go," I muttered, when all at once, with his elbows now supporting him on the bed, he leaned back and yanked his jeans down, revealing an enormous marbled manhood which slapped back across his taut belly like a call to prayer. His eyes fixed on the TV, never even acknowledging his handsome cock as he grabbed it full-fisted. "Jesus God," I muttered to myself, staring at one of the most stunning penises I'd ever seen: nine inches, wired like the backside of a computer with mouth-watering veinage, and nested in the blackest of hair, which right now was casting deep forested shadows as it worked its way under his well-stocked jumbo-sized scrotum. I never had a choice. It was in my mouth before I made any decisions or even considered whether he wanted it there. He didn't protest, bucking his hips and driving into my whimpering mouth as he glared at the TV set. I shot in my pants without so much as touching myself, just moments before my throat filled like a cream pastry, hot gobs of his God-juice leaking from the crust.

I tongued it clean before he quickly grabbed it like a hammer, or anything else I could have been borrowing, to put it away. He didn't even look at me as he hopped up to his feet, yanking up his jeans in one fluid motion. It wasn't fear of intimacy like I'd seen with other guys. He was simply done, and more or less emotionless — in his own world. God knows what he'd been thinking as he bucked his manly juices into my craving body, which for him had become just one big hole to propel his antisocial lusts into. I can't call it my mouth; it was just what was available. I'd have torn my skin back like curtains if it were possible and let him drill through whatever part of me got him off. I had to restrain myself from crying I was so devastated by his beauty.

"That tape sucked," he casually related. I was still sitting on the bed, stunned, not knowing what to do, licking the remnants of his now cooling semen off my chapped lips. "I gotta get to work," he informed me, pulling the video cassette out and handing it to me, without making eye contact.

"Uh, I don't want this," I said as my hand opened to accept it.

"No? Don't you like kids?"

"Uh, I think you know what I like."

He said nothing. Then: "Keep it for me till next time." And he grinned.

"Next time?" I was in a daze, but hope springs eternal all the same.

"Yeah, next time I see you." I lit up even though I was nearly consumed with dread from what, other than the amazing cock action, was a profoundly depressing social interaction.

"I'll just leave it here," I said, balking.

"No can do, guy. I'm on probation. Can't have that here. Keep it for me."

"Uh, yeah, sure, till next time."

I didn't think myself an accomplice as I walked home. What did I know about such legal machinations? I only knew I was no longer depressed and had just had one of life's peak experiences. Had his cock literally trounced thousands of years of science that had eventually developed selective serotonin reuptake inhibitors? Imagine the clinical trials. I'd seen a lot of cocks, a lot of naked men, like any fag. But Jesus H. Priapus Satyriasis, I had never seen such a beautiful manifestation of the male organ anywhere—in print, on film, in my bed, even in my fantasy life, which was no slacker when it came to cock. I imagined what it must have been like for explorers coming upon Yosemite, Victoria Falls, the Grand Canyon. Unimaginable and sublime beauty. I leaned against a wall at one point on the walk home, needing to catch my breath, my cock once again tenting my jeans. The fact of the matter was: I was strung out on his cock. And I didn't even have a phone number.

No matter, he called, thank God. It was either that, or I was in for a lot of pancakes.

"I got some more tapes. Wanna come over and check them out?"

I didn't hear any of it but the *come over* part. "When?"

"Now."

"I'm on my way."

The door was cracked when I arrived. When I opened it to step in, I lost my breath. Splayed across the bed was Clown Daddy, his substantial manhood like the clock tower at some university—everything converged toward it.

"Oh, baby," was all I could think to say, which was oddly appropriate considering what was happening on the VCR where his gaze was fixed. My brows furrowed. Good God, they can't be more than three.

"Come to poppa," he said with a fatherly grin.

I was like a panting puppy with the promise of a walk. He held the leash. Or the staff as the case may be. I was sucking on his teat like a hungry lamb before you could say *baahhh*. My mouth had never produced so much saliva. It knew as well as I did: for this I came. I had never wanted anything like I wanted his cock, lapping up and down the hard shaft, savoring the throbbing gristle of his veins, weeping at the sweet softness of the massive velvety helmet. I was aware of what felt like a tear rolling down my inner thigh. My asshole was sweating like a day laborer who was in danger of not making the rent: more baskets, more peaches.

I knew I needed to strip but balked at taking a time-out for fear he'd lose interest or lose control. I hopped up and stripped quickly. He didn't even notice, his eyes locked on the romper-room shenanigans stage-left like a baby enthralled with a mobile.

I knew all I had to do was get into position, and in no time was on my knees, facing the TV, blocking Clown Daddy's view. He didn't miss a beat as he hopped up on his knees and grabbed my waist, ready to plunge.

"Lube, Clown Daddy, lube." That was the first time I'd called him that. He wouldn't tell me his name, and nicknames are born of such ignorance. So be it.

Of course he didn't answer my plea, though I heard him spit. I opened like sunrise, pulled him into me more than he plunged. I heard him as he vanished into my sleeve, which I offered as if to warm his very soul: "Uuuuuuuuuuuuuuuhhh." And I matched him like a chorus: "Aaaaaaaaaaaaahhhhhh." I dropped my face into the mattress as he pounded me, knowing I'd be unable to maintain any balance with my arms, which were not only shaking with excitement, but were seriously challenged considering the slams he was delivering—and the fact that my body's focus was pretty much solely directed at the contractions of my rectum as it greedily grabbed at what can only be described as the bread of life. A baguette of it no less.

He sent me onto the floor by thrust ten or so and then he emitted an enormous Josh Hartnett, "FUUUUck," as my asshole filled with his ambrosia.

He pulled out with a pop and wiped off his cock with the blanket and fell backward onto his back. "That's a great age," he wistfully concluded, staring at the ceiling.

I felt a momentary sinking feeling as I looked at the video monitor, realizing all at once the makeover I would need to employ if I was to hold onto Clown Daddy past the duration of his probation.

"I gotta go to work," he quipped. I nodded; I knew the protocol. He popped out the tape and handed it to me. I staggered down the walkway of that shitty apartment building past dried out cactuses in pots and a pair of roller skates—good God, did his or her parents know who was living next door? What about Megan's Law? I was lost in a strange milieu of overarching lust, revulsion, horror, responsibility, and that unique postfuck feeling of *that was great; everything's gonna be just fine*. But I wasn't stupid. I'd just had unsafe sex with a child molester on probation next door to an apartment where a child lived.

I walked home bowlegged, my asshole seriously misshapen and in need of rehab. While my mind meandered through this new strange and dangerous frontier I'd happened upon, I fumbled through my bathroom drawers for the Flobee and set to work shaving my body clean of hair. I didn't miss a beat. While my mind remained a stew of anxiety, and I winced at the razor nicks I was inflicting on my balls, I reveled in how I was going to finally incite his lust as he had mine.

Next, I got out my sewing machine and set to work on a new wardrobe: a sailor suit, a Boy Scout uniform, a large diaper, Teletubbies briefs.

I put on the briefs and sailor suit, looked at myself in the mirror. Ridiculous. *Don't be so negative*, I self-talked back. I did a striptease, attempting to be convincing. I worked on my little boy shy look. But when I finally dropped my trousers and gazed at my hairless cock, I was sorely dismayed. I have a big cock, huge really, and the shaving had only made it look bigger. How am I gonna convince Clown Daddy I'm a child with this thing? How many grade-schoolers are packing eight inches? Then there was my chest and arms. I worked out, for God's sake; I was a mess of secondary sex characteristics. I needed to gain fifty pounds, maybe take some hormones. *One step at a time*, I calmed myself.

I'd done what I could, and I wanted to see him, to show him how I'd be whatever he wanted me to be. I don't think at that time I was considering saving him and reforming him. I just wanted to please him, make of myself a gift. Woo him.

Chocolate. I bought a box of Le Petit Écoliers and went for pancakes. He smiled big when he saw me. The hostess looked askance. The crowd wondered. It occurred to me I was exposing him. I blushed red as a swollen cockhead. I left as quickly as I'd come, racing back up the street. Whatever happened, I didn't want to hurt Clown Daddy. Goodness no, I was interested in his pleasure.

There was a message on the machine when I got home: "Nice suit, hee, hee. 8:00 p.m. Wear it." Click.

The shirt never came off as Clown Daddy's maleness hovered over me and he ominously climbed up on top of me, his lead pipe of a cock bobbing like a tank gun, my legs held behind my ears like the spring-loaded pogo stick I would soon be playing the part of as he bounced me off the mattress. I was a toy to be played with until it broke.

"You look fucking great," he smiled, and he kissed me this time, full, his tongue like a tapeworm, bent on my intestines, determined to reach all the way down to where his cock was reaching from the other end to meet it in a hot sticky mess of saliva and semen.

"Daddy, daddy, daddy," I yelped. We growled, we lost ourselves, and rode our dicks like runaway horses. His final thrusts were so divine, my hands digging into his firm white buttcheeks like talons holding their kill. He split me like a piece of wood and my cum hit his chest so hard it bounced and splattered like blood would if the ax of his cock had buried itself in my forehead.

I'd brought the diaper in my backpack.

"Daddy...please...diaper me."

He guffawed, and then with an eagerness I'd never seen, yelped, "Yeeeeaaah!"

He diapered me. Patted my ass. Told me to pack up and get out.

My God, I'd done it. I'd seduced Clown Daddy.

He didn't kiss me goodbye, of course, nor invite me to brunch. But I walked away without a videocassette this time. Progress.

I guess that's when it occurred to me I could save him. And maybe not just him. Maybe I'd just found the treatment for pedophilia. God knows, no one seemed to give a damn about these people. The last sexual minority. I could rehabilitate them all. My shaved asshole, a rehab center. What would we call it? A Thousand Clowns Rehab Center? More like a million.

What was I saying? It wasn't rehab at all, what I was doing. It was just a way of accommodating his pedophilia. And how better? We all had to accommodate our sexuality. Why couldn't they be treated the same? Maybe hormones and plastic surgery were a better idea. I felt like the guy who'd invented acid, a whole new world of enlightenment was opening up before mankind and I was poised at the apex of human evolution.

That's when I saw the squad car. Parked in front of my house. Next to the undercover white Crown Royale. Three men in dark suits. It was *The Matrix* and I was Neo, standing on a street corner in a sailor suit, my hips bulging from the diaper that swaddled my manhood.

I knew what they'd found. I knew my chances. I ran. It wasn't much of a chase. At least it would make them look bad. I know cops do important work, but I hate them and consider it my job to embarrass and sabotage their work.

I had nowhere to go, had no chance of escape. All I had was a shot at making it back to Broadway where the great voting public could witness four cops tackling a child — a rather large child to be sure — in a sailor suit.

I felt the tug as one of them got hold of the back of my shirt just as I reached the intersection of 23rd and Broadway. I screamed as high-piercing a preadolescent scream as I could manage.

I was interrogated at length. I assumed they had Clown Daddy somewhere. How else would they have nabbed me? I drank coffee, got knocked around, but through it all I endured by dreaming of meeting Clown Daddy — when I was finally convicted — in some filthy prison cell where we could pursue our love affair in peace — me trading cigarettes and gum for razors to keep my cock and balls soft as a baby's behind for my Clown Daddy and his meat-eucharist, truly a transubstantiation of all the misery around us into an Elysian field of bliss.

"Where did you get the tapes?"

I refused to tell. "I found them."

"Where?"

I had to place them as far away from Clown Daddy as possible. "In a trashcan in Vacaville."

"What were you doing going through trash in Vacaville?"

"Someone on the Internet told me he'd put them there." It sounds strange I know; I was indicting myself. I thought I was saving Clown Daddy. If I had to lie, even to the point of destroying my own future, I'd do it for Clown Daddy — blinded by love, or myopia for his cock. Same difference. And to think, I didn't even know the details of his crime. We'd never discussed it. I didn't want to know. He wasn't telling besides.

I'd asked him once, after he diapered me. "Can we talk, Clown Daddy?"

He'd smiled and said, "I don't talk."

"Who?" The cop was demanding, but in a boring, annoying, non-sexual way. Why couldn't Clown Daddy be my interrogator?

"He didn't have a name. It was one of those throwaway names."

"What was it?"

"Bob."

"Goddamn it! Bob who?"

"Bob1 at aol.com." (I hoped to God there was no such person as Bob1.)

Whack! And he backhanded me across the face.

They threatened me with a stiff sentence if I didn't give them something. I only considered that their sentence could never be as stiff as Clown Daddy's meaty member, so I was unimpressed with their threats.

They gave me five years.

Clown Daddy did not appear in my cellblock, though I looked and waited and pined. It had been explained in my trial that the videos found in my home had been coded with a tracking device which had led the authorities to my house. Not unlike an ankle bracelet such as Clown Daddy wore. It had even been suggested that Clown Daddy was a narc, or had used me as a patsy. The judge put a stop to those conjectures, admonishing the defense: "Whoever gave him the pornography is not on trial today. Another day. Right now, we're trying this man." And he pointed at me like Clown Daddy's member used to do; like Uncle Sam on those old war posters. How I wanted to beg of him: *Have you got my Clown Daddy somewhere in a dungeon too?*

But Clown Daddy never appeared. I met other people in the big house in his stead. Vernon, for instance. He was my cellmate, and he informed me, as a skinny white fag, I'd be wise to do his bidding. I've done it, though he lacks both Clown Daddy's girth and length, not to mention all the other characteristics that gods wield over man.

Ah, but the gods are kind, for they have blessed us with imagination. And so when Vernon slicks his member with Crisco I steal from the commissary and mercilessly impales me, I close my eyes and see a circus tent populated by clowns, and the circus music begins, and all the clowns drop their baggy pants and out pops Clown Daddy's blessed cock! Then the tigers and lions turn, lifting their tails, and the dwarves and ape-men offer up their tight behinds, hands firmly gripped to their ankles—all of them anxious and elated to do the bidding of the clowns. And the crowd cheers, and then goes *AAAHHH* when Clown Daddy himself in all his naked, huge-dicked, grinning, Josh Hartnett–throated glory comes swinging through on the trapeze spraying his jism all over the clowns and animals and the whole damn crowd, who bathe in it like the blessed waters of Lourdes.

And Vernon is proud. He thinks he's made that mess all over my chest and belly. Let him think it. The truth is hardly important at this point. I'm an innocent man doing time for kiddie porn; the police are fools; Vernon's a chump, and he's still committing crimes. And my asshole's just a 7-Eleven that he holds up every Saturday night. As for the cash, I hand it right over. In fact, I leave the register open. No way to run a business. But I, unlike Vernon, am not proud. For I have seen God.

I spend all my time with him. Vernon that is, not God. We even eat pancakes together. I stuff my face. I'm fattening up for Clown Daddy, while Vernon goes on and on with his theories.

"The earth is a plate," he tells me. "Mankind sat down and is eating. When he's through, it'll be over."

"Where are we now?" I ask, bored.

"Somewhere deep in the mash potatoes; maybe halfway through."

"Are you gay, Vernon?" I like to get a rise out of him.

"Not at all," he explains. He tells me men are pigs, and this is why you can't call him a faggot. Vernon says if it were legal, most men he knew (and he knew a certain kind, though he always meant every man) would fuck everything in sight, and what's more, they'd never let their sex partners survive to betray them (as they always will by his reckoning—something to remember when I get out of here). Therefore, he's of the opinion that men "would drill holes in their sex partner's skulls if they could, and fuck their brains out. They'd drill holes in backs and arms, thighs, through the bottom of feet, right through the front of 'em, core the motherfuckers like apples," he says drolly, "leave them like the dough after all the cookies have been cut out of it. But the screaming would be annoying, so you'd do the brain first."

"Do you like the circus, Vernon?"

He shrugs his shoulders. "I don't like those clowns. Creepy."

"I knew a clown once."

"Shut up and eat."

I pour more syrup on my pancakes and watch it vanish, falling into my endless reverie: Where's Clown Daddy? Is he still free, wowing the clientele at Pancake Circus? Did I save him? Rehab him? Is he placing ads now in gay weeklies for shaved, pudgy boys who look like children? Is he waiting for me? Or is he passing off coded porn to some other sucker with a willing hole? Is he doing it to save his own beautiful blue-white skin—or is he doing it for the Feds?

What do I know of the ways of the world? I played the slots and won. And who can say whether I'm a lucky man or no? There are those who might say: be careful what you wish for. I say: get it while it's hot, and if the opportunity comes along, run away and join the circus.

BLUE BOY
M. CHRISTIAN

"Sure you won't?" Mr. Oleander asked, fondling the fine, supple neck of a sweet young thing. As a boss, Oleander was a lethargic mountain—slow but unstoppable in his decisions. Luckily for the firm of Oleander, Destar, and West—designers of fine imitation antiques—his mountain was formed by tried and true decisions. Luckily for Prosper, Oleander considered gestures just that—and not a personal affront if refused.

So Prosper could, and did, shake his head: a slow tired movement of boredom.

Oleander continued to trace the contours of the young girl's lovely neck and shoulders. Even Prosper, who had seen his share of lovely necks and who rarely would have looked this one's way, had to watch—hypnotized by the subtle geometries of her throat and beginning slope of chest.

The girl was in a perfect lithograph dress. She was an ideal Alice, a snapshot Dorothy, or an identical Wendy. She was crinoline, lace, and tiny cream-colored shoes. Her dress was a slightly bluer blue than her skin. Her sunset glowing hair was highlighted by a pink silk bow.

"I know she's not exactly your type—but you positive?" Oleander asked again. The girl was balanced perfectly on his fat knee. Together, the girl and Oleander were another picture—he a rolling surge of dark, strong meat, pressed into a fine Osaka suit. The picture wouldn't have been pretty, if the girl hadn't been—

—such a lovely shade of blue.

Prosper had enjoyed his share in his quite young life. Maybe not Dorothies, Wendies, or Alices but many Hucks, Rudolphs, Troys, and Rocks. A great many. A great many—far above the national average. Still, this one, this one girl, was such a lovely shade. Despite the lack of interest in her sex, Prosper still had to watch her if just for her magnificent shade: early dawn, shallow ocean, a lovely bird's wing.

Lovely, lovely blue.

With refinement and dexterity, as if cautious not to disturb the girl, Oleander reached out a fat, walnut-colored hand. Prosper knew from twenty years of Hucks and Rocks and the rest that she wouldn't bat an eyebrow. Letting a lemonade and peppermint smile play around her porcelain features, she absently kicked her little legs—balancing on his massive knee—as Oleander moved. She didn't hesitate, or even pause, as Oleander picked up the finely crafted wooden box from his desk.

Simple in its beauty. Teak. Oleander skillfully opened it with one hand, a gesture rehearsed by endless repetition. In another age, it would have been lighting a cigarette, producing identification, or checking a pocket watch.

Oleander took the young girl's head and tilted it back. Animated with a girl-like glow, she complied. Then he kissed her fine throat, just a grazing of his thick lips along the cerulean column of her neck.

"Don't know what you're missing."

Again, Prosper shook his head. He knew exactly what he was missing. Exactly; he knew what had been in the box and what was now in his boss' hand, knew the antique straight-razor's weight, its contours, and even its oily smell—if not precisely, then its very close kin. Prosper knew the way it fell into the skin, the way the steaming blood poured out and onto the hand. He knew the feel of rope, the greasy mass of a pistol, the heft of a candlestick, and much, much more.

He knew the smell, after: copper and salt. Knew it all very well. Twenty years well.

Mr. Oleander slit the girl's fine blue throat. The razor slid back into her skin, two inches at least. A very fine knife. A good razor. The kind of quality that one would correctly assume for the leading partner of Oleander, Destar, and West. For a beat of his heart, Prosper was caught by the act of Oleander slitting the girl's throat—but it was a catch of reminiscence rather than attraction.

Seen one, seen a thousand.

The girl's blood poured out of her, running down the razor and over Oleander's hand. The leading partner had an expert's, a connoisseur's, touch—as the blood ran, he tipped his razor just-so and pale blue blood, even paler blue than the girl's skin, flowed and splattered onto the same-colored carpeting.

A gourmet's touch: none of the new sky, robin's egg, blood fell on his lovely suit. Instead, it soaked her dress, all but making it vanish with the flow—fainter blue against fainter blue.

As the girl died, Oleander put his lips to her cheek, kissing her softly as she drained of fluid, potential, future, and resale value.

Oleander tipped the dead girl from his lap with a practiced movement: gripping her neck from behind and pushing her slight body away from him—till she dangled like a cold puppet at the end of his huge arm. Being careful to avoid the quickly evaporating pool of azure blood at his feet, Oleander took the small corpse to a carefully unfurnished corner of his vast office and dropped her with a tumble of flaccid limbs.

Dabbing at his immaculate hands with a lovely lace handkerchief, Oleander sat down again and smiled, a contented play of dazzling eyes and widely grinning lips: "Much better—does wonders for the blood pressure, you know. Doctor's orders."

Prosper nodded, smiling back but feeling nothing. Nothing at all.

"Now—" Oleander said, knitting his large fingers together over his belly and fixing Prosper with calm eyes " — about the redesign of those Jivaro skinning knives..."

Somewhere, he was unsure of where, exactly — some program or other (television background), paper article (lying around the office), or just common knowledge ("You know...") — Prosper had heard that certain occupations were manufactured en masse. Street cleaners, simple clerks, clowns, prostitutes, ticket collectors, repair people, etc., stream out of one of the huge upstate factories.

The newspaper vendor in the lobby was different from when he entered that morning. He remembered his slightly lopsided head, his slight facial twitch. Abnormalities both subtle and gross were a common design theme: what better to exorcise the hate and fear of the unusual than on disposable, and easily replaceable, Blues?

For some reason he remembered his irritating (another commonality) voice and his scowling eyes. Someone must have blown out his brains, stabbed him, slit his throat, crushed his skull, or any one of a thousand other outlets early in the day: his stall was clean, immaculate — without even the telltale of another Blue mopping up his cerulean blood.

Prosper bought his evening paper without even a thought for the old proprietor — after all, he'd only been there since last night. Someone had stuck a sawed-off shotgun into the belly of his predecessor the afternoon before. Prosper remembered it clearly, mainly because he'd had to walk through a pool of his quickly evaporating blood to buy a nicotine stick.

Outside, Prosper let the city wash over him: the usual sights and sounds of his way home blurring into a endlessly repeating kaleidoscope of storefronts, smiling commuters, flickering advertisements ("20% Discount on All Custom Blues!" "Blue Quick Learn — Don't Waste Valuable Training Time!"), and diligently working street cleaners, simple clerks, clowns, prostitutes, ticket collectors, repair people, ...etc., who were replaced as soon as someone killed them — from that huge manufacturing pool.

The frustration was a wire in Prosper. As he usually did, had done, for almost three months now, he thought about killing. He thought about it as he entered the subway, looking at the pleasant-faced girl in the ticket-booth, at her sparkling smile and firework eyes. He thought about taking her head in his hands and banging it, again and again, against the pink-tiled wall of the subway platform. He knew exactly how it would feel: the echoing vibration of each *smack!* of her against the wall. The way her head would shake in his hands, how the feel of it, the solidity of it, would change as her skull cracked, changed shape with each fevered impact. He knew exactly how the sound would change as the back of her head flattened then seeped blood—blue, quick-evaporating blood.

He knew, after a point, as he slammed her harder and harder against the tiles, that her blood would seep and then splatter. He knew that there was that special, magical moment when her skull would just simply collapse from his passionate, diligent pounding and in one instant he'd go from holding an intact head in his hands to holding a globe of broken plates, mushy tissue, brains, and seeping, squirting blood.

Done one, done a thousand. Prosper passed her his ticket, and she let him onto the platform.

He knew he should still be thinking about work, mulling over the nuances of Mr. Oleander's timbre and choice of words—but all he could seem to summon up was a overwhelming sadness and a deep, all-but-hidden whipcord of painful frustration.

Again, he debated killing. There were several Blues on the platform: an old-looking couple scowling at all the young and energetic, an arrogant buck in a leather jacket, a tiny boy in a (naturally) blue sailor suit who cried hysterically and annoyingly, a very pleasant-looking young man in an white shirt and tight jeans.

Looking at the latter, he ran a quick fantasy though his mind—with the perfect detail that came from many, many (too many) real experiences. The platform wasn't all that crowded, more than enough room for a quick one. The details rolled through his mind in perfect clarity (Done one...): walk up to his perfect, bountiful Blue form; a quick slap to knock him off balance; a tear at his shirt to view the perfect geometry of his chest; a shove to bring him to his knees; jam his too-hard cock in his mouth; feel him swallow and gulp it down through his artificial moans and complaints (yet with that spice of "he really wants it"); maybe he'd fuck him, turn him 'round, yank down those jeans, and home his cock in his warm and also expertly designed asshole, or maybe he'd just crush his throat around his cock as he sucked at him till he was gripping his own pulsing cock in a steaming bath of blue blood (...done a thousand).

Done a thousand, why do one more?

The train pulled into the station, sliding in with no noise save for the screams and wet sounds of the little boy's body. Prosper blinked, joining the queue to enter, suddenly realizing he had missed whoever had tossed him onto the tracks. Distracted...

On the train, he took his usual seat. Across from him, a pair of Blue workmen in stained and dirty coveralls were bagging the corpse of a old lady and cleaning the wall and seat where she had been sitting. The map of the brilliantly colored routes was all but obscured by her rapidly vanishing blood. With the absentness of trying to remember the next line of a popular song, or what he'd had for breakfast the day before, Prosper tried to figure out the murder weapon. He had all but decided on a *katana*, because of the very clean way her head had been separated from her body, the way her blood (vanishing quickly into the subway car's rarefied air) had fanned onto the route map, but then noticed the tall, thin black man sitting two seats back—and the Maori ceremonial knife in his lap (still a faint blue). One of their own products. A very successful line.

Again, Prosper remembered his therapist. He'd selected Gordon more or less on a whim, after visiting three or four of his profession. Gordon had an easy voice, a sleepy style that went completely against the hysteria that Prosper seemed to feel day after day. It made it easier to talk to the man, to have a still pool to drop his sharp, rattling angers and frustrations into for an hour.

"Set a goal, Josh. Make it simple. No big plans, no immediate reward. The strangle-job is a good one, but you still think about it too much. Just do it. Set yourself a time limit—say tomorrow at lunch or the first thing in the morning. Carry a knife if it'll make you feel better. Be spontaneous rather than plotting. When you feel like it, then just do it. You take the subway, right? Just push one onto the tracks. The more you wait, the more frustrated you'll be. You'll be surprised at how much better you'll feel—"

The others hadn't worked out, and Prosper wasn't sure if it was because their analyses were too accurate, disturbing ("I want to prescribe you something...", "...I think you should consider more extensive therapy..."), or simply because he didn't find them at all attractive.

But Gordon he did. He liked, more than anything, to just stare into the man's pool eyes and think about kissing his cheeks and stroking what must be his finely shaped chest and back. He never really thought much about his suggestions, if at all—just his eyes, and how he might move and smile stripped of his professional demeanor, as well as his usual cotton drawstrings and leather sandals.

Westerberg. The neighborhood smelled of dusk, the slow-moving Mongusti river, and bad Chinese food. Once again, walking home, Prosper thought about killing. Even though the Gung Ho had been closed since someone had machine-gunned down the Blue staff one night and the owner hadn't gotten around to replacing them or reopening the place, the neighborhood, by law, had its proportion. A boy in plus-fours and suspenders bounced a ball on one corner; a panhandler (all drug palsy, missing teeth, and aggressive palms) moved through the commuting crowd; a Playmate of the Moment lounged against one of the Gung Ho's boarded-up windows, Spandex skirt hiked high to show off a lack of panties as she scowled her disdain at them all.

The only one who caught Prosper's direct attention was a cop icon, who watched them leave the station with mirrored-sunglasses and an abusive "Fucking homo queer" to Prosper.

He thought about killing him: automatic and fully detailed. The cop would be slow, since he was an icon: easy to push him over his bike, simple to fumble his revolver out of his holster (against his surprisingly feeble protests), click the hammer back, and fire three or four rounds into his helmeted head. He guessed that he would scream and plead as he clicked the hammer back. He supposed that the cop would soil his immaculate uniform with blue piss as he cried like a tortured baby. He knew, fucking knew, that his head would explode with the first round, his face blooming forward against the shock wave of the bullet passing through his head, confined by the helmet.

Prosper shook his head sadly and entered his building. He was surprised, pleasantly, to find that the lobby and elevator were free of the evidence of murder. It lifted his spirits somewhat to have a clean slate for once — a unique situation — and he felt his muscles relax against their gripping tightness of frustration. *Yeah, maybe*, he thought. *Maybe tonight. A fresh start — something unique.* He started to think about his kitchen, his sample case of half a dozen finely crafted weapons. Hadn't done a circular saw in a while, hadn't done a spear since two years ago (at the Mass Murder Street Fair); shotguns were fun and he had the one, unused, that his father had given him for his birthday two years ago.

But it vanished, evaporating as everything seemed to do, in just a few moments as he put his key in his door and went in.

"The first developments in Blue technology..." went the announcer from his blaring television "...was, of course, in the fields of nanomolecular engineering, leading to the first prototype fetus in 2015..."

The channel flipped as he hung his coat. "Cerulean Industries today announced a new line of Blues dedicated to less-represented ethnic types. As part of the Stereotype series, Cerulean plans a modification of the current Gook, Kike, and Nig—" The announcer was, as always, new: Prosper caught sight of her as he walked in, noting the standard Saccharin smile and glittering eyes. He doubted, again, if he'd turn in to watch the audience poll of how to kill her at the end of the broadcast.

"Oh," said Troy from the couch, taking his eyes off the flickering set for just a moment to nail Prosper with arrogant boredom, "you're home." The television flipped, again and again, till it finally settled on a flashy commercial for a new line of Sex/Death Blues called *Come Hither*. Strobed with whites and royals, the commercials painted Troy's normally dark blue skin almost purple.

Prosper went into the kitchen and poured himself two fingers of scotch, kicking back the flames and closing his eyes. From the living room, Troy said, "So, shithead, are you gonna kill me tonight or what?"

Prosper smiled till his cheeks hurt and knocked back another drink.

"So how was work, dear?"

The liquor burned, a flaming trail from the back of his throat to the unknown depths of his stomach. The sensation felt good—feeling anything felt good.

Prosper shrugged, breathing heavy over the sink. He didn't see, didn't care, if Troy saw the gesture.

"Had a very exciting day, myself. Saw a *Life Without Hope* I hadn't seen before."

"Happy for you," Prosper said, panting into the sink, fighting the liquor that was struggling back up. Troy had been an indulgence. Oleander, Destar, and West paid well enough that he could easily afford someone every few days or so. He'd had Troy for three months. An eternity for a Blue.

"Almost enough to get out of fucking bed for."

His breath was acid; breathing burned his sinuses. The pain was real and sharp. He panted till the room started to tilt—enjoying the sensation. Troy had originally been part of something—elaborate. But the way things had been recently, it had never materialized. Troy became almost like furniture. Almost—but not as comfortable.

"You would have loved it. Tristan—you know, the illegitimate son of Vera-De and Despar Cosmo, heir to the Cosmo fortune—has this problem. A kind of intimate, manly problem. And he was having all these kinds of troubles keeping people from finding out. That is till this one person, and, you know, I can't recall completely if he was Blue or not, just happened to speak to just the wrong person." Troy *tisk-tisked*, still staring, fixated, on the flickering screen. "Poor Tristan—"

The knife's handle was cold, and that surprised Prosper. Maybe it had been from keeping it in the dark kitchen drawer or maybe it was just that his blood was so hot, hammering with heat.

He took it out of the drawer (cool, cool in his hand) and walked the four steps from his kitchen to the living room. Troy started to turn his head, as if on finely machined bearings. A movement beyond anyone save his make and model. Pulse jumping his vision, Prosper still managed to ponder, as he walked and raised the knife, that he didn't really understand their mechanics, the details of them. You didn't need to know exactly how a bus worked to ride on one, or how a screen worked to watch it—or even turn it off.

Tension thrummed in his arm as Prosper stabbed down. The leather of the couch drank the blade till it hit something more solid that its stuffing. The impact jerked up his arm, echoing the real pain of the scotch.

Troy looked at the vibrating knife then turned back to the screen. A sound, something like a sarcastic sigh but without enough real care to voice it, slipped from his azure lips.

Prosper swung hard, slamming his knotted fist into the side of Troy's head. The sound of thick eggshells cracking was sharp, a voltage spark in the room. Troy's whole body jerked to one side with the blow, and a deep-toned groan grumbled from his chest.

In one practiced move, Prosper had the knife again, and had one strong hand knotted in Troy's silk shirt. Hauling the Blue up, he expertly flipped the knife around and brought it with a blurring fury to his throat.

Troy breathed deep and slow, eyes straining up toward Prosper. Prosper looked down at the tip of Troy's nose, just visible beyond his perfect hair.

Prosper's cock was stone, iron. He ground his pelvis against the thick resistance of the back of the couch, relishing in the feeling, the humming frustration coming from the Blue.

After time had passed, glacial and tense, Troy pushed forward, sliding his neck along the knife blade. Prosper saw him move, felt the knife glide across his alluring neck and smelled Troy's blood mixing with the stale room air. Salt and copper adding to dust and stale sunlight.

Prosper pulled back on the knife, moving it away from Troy's straining neck.

When he had gone so far that his muscles were straining in his right arm, and Troy was leaning so far forward that his forehead was beyond his knees, Prosper crumpled his fingers into a shaking fist and slammed it into the back of Troy's head, at the same time snaking the knife out of the way as he fell.

"Motherfucker," panted Troy from the narrow valley between the screen and the couch, panting and rubbing the side of his head. Even from where he stood, Prosper could see that his neck was softly bleeding.

Leaving him there, Prosper went back to the kitchen and put the knife away. Troy wouldn't touch it. Blues couldn't. The thought of killing Troy churned Prosper's stomach, knotting his guts with frustrated boredom. Troy would just have to wait. Living to die, Troy was aching to. Killing him might be deadly dull, but keeping him breathing was, at least, not.

Crossing the living room with heavy steps, Prosper claimed his coat and opened the door. "If you kill anyone else I don't want to fucking hear about it," Troy said, glaring up at him with brilliant blue eyes.

Without looking back, Prosper stepped outside and slammed the door behind him.

Dust danced, revealed by dying sunlight. The stairwell was old and echoing, carrying a heavy drumbeat tune from the machines in the basement. It was a place that Prosper liked to go. He kept it on reserve against the heavy boredom—intentionally going there only when things got Very Bad. He'd been there maybe five times since his...problem first started. He wondered, feeling the depression and anger rise in his chest like warm lead, how many times he'd visit it again. Hundreds? Thousands? And isn't one trip pretty much like them all?

Labor was cheap, since life was. A dirty and all-but-abandoned stairwell was rare, a priceless gift. Hanging on the cool metal of the railing, Prosper kicked at some of the crumbling stonework that had fallen on the landing from high above. One. Two. Three. The impact bounced up to him, a wet and harsh sound. With it, he caught a vision of thin, standing water over tile; of rust inching up the banister; mildew like slow, red ripples crawling up the walls.

Go out, he told himself. Just do it. Go out. Walk someplace, anyplace. Get a gun and do it. Don't worry about freshness, uniqueness—just break out of it. You know that's that way, you can feel it.

Anything. Remember that young one two years ago, the one outside the museum, how you slid the knife in under his ribs and watched his pale blood trickle out? Got soaked all the way through, holding him in your lap and letting his blood leak. Remember how you held him, and rocked him as he bled early morning sky onto the sidewalk?

Or that one you surprised last fall. Remember him? Bodybuilder icon, all full of himself and his royal muscles. God, what a monster—all bluff and steam. Remember how you dragged him out of that bar, smashed him to the street with a barstool then stood there, on his head, as he screamed and tried to reach up and knock you off? Remember your little improv dance number, till his skull gave up and you fell through a spongy turquoise brain, landing with a jar on the cement. Laugh riot, that one—

Remember the boy? Looking maybe, just barely, eighteen? Such a delightful present to yourself. A special treat, a glorious gift. He lasted all night. You were so skillful with the scalpel, the cuts. From sex to sapphire blood, from the wetness of his mouth, his ass, to the wetness of his wounds, his holes. He was so good, remember, that you just snapped his neck with the dawn—applause for a night in purest heaven?

How many glorious others, Prosper? One? Two? Three?

The splash broke him from his self-examination. Looking up from his internal gaze, Prosper's knees prickled from crouching too long at the railing. The sound bounced around him, finally landing on his ears and then his thoughts. Standing against the pins and needles, he looked down the stairs.

"Hello." Black leather pants, a thin coating over a finely honed body. White T-shirt over a perfect ribbed chest—nipples showing through as he moved. Streaks of blond eyebrows drawing perfect attention to pale blue eyes. A finely shaped face, a pleasant fall between full and thin. Good bones. Lips like a perfect stroke of a brush. They looked like they might taste, and feel, like silk.

"Fine night for it," he said, smiling at Prosper, bathing him in light, despite the fading sun.

"For what?" Prosper managed to get out, still trying to climb back into the real world from his thoughts and his ennui.

"Navel-gazing," he said, smiling a flash of white teeth.

"'Fraid I've been doing way too much of that, of late. Hard to climb back out sometimes."

"Problem?"

"Nothing that won't get better, I guess."

He was standing close. Prosper could feel the burning between them. His eyes hummed from going from his delicious shape to his ideal face. Blue eyes. Nice teeth. Tight body.

"If there's anything I can do—" He went to the railing and stared out at nothing—maybe hypnotized by the dust dancing in the fading sunlight. Maybe just standing there, waiting for Prosper.

Even though it wasn't exactly his style, Prosper ran a finger up his spine, tracing the bumps of his bones with a gentle touch. He made a soft sound and smiled back at Prosper, grinning lights.

Prosper stepped up and in, bathing his chilled, nervous self in his warmth. His cock was metal—iron or steel—and ached with a good kind of muscle ache. It felt good.

He brought his hands around his chest, feeling his tits—flat and hard—with his palms, the tips of his fingers. Prosper hadn't felt anything like him for...he hadn't felt anything like him. Ever. He was dazzling, alive and sparkling. Prosper found it hard to look at any one single thing about him—his blond hair, the lovely slope of the back of his neck. He kissed the back of his neck, feeling his nipples with his gently stroking fingers as his own grazed his strong, tight back.

He moaned, high and sweet, pushing back against his straining cock.

Hands falling to his waist, he pulled his T-shirt out of the tight pants. Giving permission, he lifted his hands above his head. The shirt came off.

Turning 'round, he smiled. Chest, firm and cool. He had a silken belly, a gentle patch that played so well with the strength of his muscles: something gentle mixed with the strength.

Prosper kissed him, feeling a faint lingering of wine, a memory of...garlic?...from dinner. Their tongues touched and danced, a ballet of warm and wet, firm and course. Prosper felt them burn, ignite.

Distantly, he knew he was rubbing his cock through his pants, knew he was tugging at his own waistband, pulling down Prosper's zipper.

The stairwell was cool, touching cold, but his cock was still hot as his hands explored him. Like a fever, Prosper felt his desire blast through him. He started working at his own pants. "Take 'em off," he managed to say between their kisses.

He helped, doing magic with his own zipper and buttons. They were tight, so he backed up against the railing for leverage before managing to work them down over his strong hips, corded thighs.

Kissing him again, as penetrating as a fuck, as aggressive, he turned and bent over the railing.

He was like an oven inside. A wet, tight, oven. Prosper fucked him, feeling almost afraid that the heat of his asshole was going to burn his cock, was going to light him like a fuse and blow him away.

So good, Prosper managed to think; so hot, so new.

Then he let go, his orgasm mixing with a high point in his own moans and near-screams. Relief and the little death surged through Prosper as he managed (barely) to step back and shove his still-hard cock into his pants.

So hot, so hot—he thought. So nice and refreshing. Only one thing to make it better—perfect...

Quick and hard, he knocked him off-balance by kicking the back of his knee. Dropping hard, hand skipping across the rusted metal railing, he collapsed. Feet perfectly aligned with his head, Prosper then kicked in his face. The impact was hard and meaty, traveling up Prosper's leg like electrical current—straight to his cock and his smile (both very hard).

The man moaned and whimpered, clutching his mouth. He looked up at Prosper with shocked and scared blue eyes.

Prosper kicked him again, aiming for his jaw. He connected again, and the stairwell echoed with the wet gong of skull bones on the railing.

Kneeling down, Prosper took his wheezing, gasping face in his hands. "So new," he said, as he slammed him back, again and again, against the metal. It became a fevered blur, a motion like walking, like pedaling a bicycle (you, after all, never forget how)—impact after impact, gong of metal after gong. One flowing perfectly, hotly, into another. One. Two. Three. Four. On and on. It was like a kind of tempo, a background rhythm.

Then there wasn't enough of his head to pound. Prosper was kneeling in a slowly growing pool, holding thick fragments of bone and sticky blood.

"Very nice," he said, in an absent kind of voice, standing up.

Brushing his hands on his pants, he was startled by how sticky they were. Looking down, he saw the mess his pants had become.

The roar came up from his gut, his stomach, his balls. It tore through his lungs and up his throat. It escaped as nausea, and he felt the liquor boiling up.

Then the impact. From behind. A flash of an azure hand and he fell, down to his knees, onto the sticky floor, the red blood.

Red.

Pain woke him. Pain and the strangeness behind his eyes. He remembered being given something, and having something taken.

What was gone wasn't obvious, glaring, but he felt it. It was like something had been moved beyond his reach, pushed back so he could see it—maybe even understand it, distantly—but couldn't do it. That part of him was gone. The humming frustration, the ability, was gone—exorcised from him. He couldn't, ever, kill—or even fight back.

Something given: he brushed a brilliant blue hand across his brilliant blue brow, feeling the sweat the hot sun brought to his forehead.

Looking down and up the alley he saw people moving to and fro at either end. Some looked his way but most didn't even notice him. It was early, most were too busy going and coming to walk down, to indulge in anything Blue—in killing him.

Slowly, dancing back into the shadows, Prosper thought: *unique.* Smiling: yes, *unique—*

RASPBERRY MOONSHINE
JEFF MANN

I liked to look at the blood.
That blood was part of my love.
—C.P. Cavafy, "The Bandaged Shoulder"

"Sorry, this is my seat," I say politely.

A poofy-haired Jennifer, my buddies would call her. She's about to sit down when I tap her on the shoulder.

She stares at me. "Whatever!" she mutters, rolling her eyes and moving on down the aisle. The smell of her perfume lingers, so strong I can taste it on my tongue. Sickeningly sweet. I'd much prefer smelling James' pits after a hard afternoon of putting up hay.

There's a reason I really, really want to sit here: I can study James better. It's one row over and a few seats behind the spot where he customarily sits. Since his focus is always on the teacher, he's never caught me harvesting him with my eyes. From this angle, I can see his bearded face in profile, admire the thickness of his arms, and today I even get a peek of his underwear because he's wearing a tight gray T-shirt that rides up when he bends forward to pull a book from his backpack. I glimpse, above the belt of his jeans, the white fabric of his briefs, and, maddeningly, a tiny strip of his lower back. Just the right place to drip a little buckwheat honey, slowly lick it off, my tongue working through that dark sweetness down to the taste of skin beneath.

Fat chance. I don't know how to get closer to him. We haven't even spoken. Only reason I know his name's James is that's what he answers to when the professor calls the roll. Despite the big curves of his arms and chest—he's kind enough to wear clothes that show all that off—I never see him in the campus gym. I only see him here, in Introduction to Appalachian Studies. It's only the third week of class—early September—but being in the same room with James for seven fifty-minute class sessions has been enough to convince me that I'd give up my fucking soul to have him naked in my bed, my mouth and hands all over him.

I think he's in this class for the same reason I am: because Appalachian Studies is a topic we can relate to. He looks local, somehow, and the few times he's spoken in class, he sounds local too. Hell, for all I know, maybe we grew up in adjoining counties. Might be that we have a lot in common, though I'm guessing he isn't gay—the cosmos isn't kind enough to allow that. Hell, I'd settle for being beer-buddies. Anything to spend time with him. Maybe if I got him drunk enough, he'd even let me suck his dick.

James is scribbling on a piece of notebook paper now, and from here it looks like a list. Then I remember that today's the day the professor has asked us to hand in a list of topics we'd prefer to do our oral reports on. "Choose five topics from this master list," he'd directed, "then tell me if you'd like to be partnered with a classmate with similar interests."

If only, I think, pulling out my list with "Appalachian Ghost Stories" at the top. Similar interests? Like getting really drunk with a guy, then tying him to a chair, and sucking on his tits till he screams? Not on the master list of topics? Just my luck.

But even my sad luck can change. James finishes scribbling, stretches his arms — the T-shirt sleeves pull back, revealing biceps bulges so large I'm reminded of the curve and slope of a mountain above my granddaddy's farm — and then, since the professor hasn't arrived yet, he strolls out of the room, probably for a cool sip from the nearest water fountain.

That's when it occurs to me. We're fatalists, we mountain folk, but I want to give fate a nudge, so I stand and stretch too, show off what muscles I have to no one in particular — I'm pretty well-built, though not half as buff as James — then head toward the door, as if after a drink of water too. As if water could quench this thirst.

That's when I peer over at the paper on his desk and make a mental note of his list of topics. The word at the top of the list is "Moonshine," followed by "Harlan County Mine Wars," "*The Dollmaker*," and "Bluegrass Music."

Passing James in the hall, I meet his eyes and nod. He nods back, solemn, unsmiling. By the time I've had my drink of water, the professor has walked in, unpacked his briefcase, and asked for our topic lists. I have just enough time to rip out another sheet of paper and write down the topics James chose.

A week later. There's some confusion, and, for me, bitter suspense. At first it's announced that James will be partnered with Britney, who turns out to be the perfumed, big-haired harlot who tried to take The Viewing Seat from me. I figured that being partnered with James in any way, shape, or form would be beyond the realm of happenstance. Goddammit. He looks so hot today, with black hair curling over the collar of his beige T-shirt, like a pine forest impinging on a pasture. I can even see the points of his nipples against his shirt, which only convinces me that I'd take any risk to get them between my teeth.

But then Britney squeals, in high dudgeon — I haven't heard a sound that unnerving since my uncle castrated a calf — and explains that she wants to be partnered with Jenn and forgot to put that information down. So the professor fumbles with some papers, then says, "Okay, so it's Britney and Jennifer on Quilting. James on Moonshine. James, did you want a partner?" The professor starts shuffling again, then looks up at James over his eyeglasses.

James shrugs. God, I wish my shoulders were that broad. "Sure. That'd be fine."

I nudged Fate. Now it nudges me back. I rub my beard, prop one hiking boot on one knee, slide down in my chair a little bit, and open my mouth. I'm amazed. Not only because the voice comes from me, but because it sounds not shaky but strong.

"I'd just as soon do Moonshine, Dr. Kinder," I say casually. "Sounds like more fun than the topic I have."

"Hmmm, okay. James and Greg. Moonshine," mumbles the teacher, making a note: our names, no doubt, bunched up together, with a tight circle around them. Like barbed wire wrapped around a fencepost. Like those heart-bound names that lucky lovers cut together in smooth, gray trunks of beech bark.

"Well, there's the easy way. Real safe. Then there's the fun way. Kinda risky."

James is sucking on a cigarette and mapping out our options. There are scrawled legal-pad notes on the table and a couple volumes from the campus library, including *The Foxfire Book*, that compendium of Appalachian folklore. We're sitting in Champs, a sports bar, and drinking some draft Guinness he bought. When he licks beer-foam from his moustache, I want to grab my crotch beneath the table.

This urge is only encouraged by the stained wifebeater he's wearing. Chest hair tufts over the top of the ribbed white cloth and smoulders out the sides, around the swell of his pecs, like black smoke rolling off a wood fire. There's a scorpion inked into the skin of his inner right forearm. Thick gold hoops glimmer in each of his earlobes, and, from what I can see through the cigarette haze and the dim gray light typical of bars, there's a very small nipple ring in his left tit.

That's the last detail I need. I fucking love pierced tits. This partnership was a mistake. I want him so bad I'm sick with it. Yet I've made my bed. I've got to sit here and make conversation and talk about copper stills and worms and sour mash and other moonshine-making jargon.

He's saying something about risk. Okay, Greg, concentrate.

"Now, we already got enough here for a good report," James drawls, an accent so much like mine. Grayson County? Dickenson? Tazewell? He's got to hail from somewhere close. "But I gotta get a real fine grade in this class to pull my GPA up, and I'm thinking that ole Dr. Kinder would be real impressed by personal testimony, instead of just book or online research, and since we got a good month to work on this..."

He's leading up to something, all right. I take a swig of stout. He crushes out the butt of his cigarette and lights another. I study his face in the brief flare of the lighter. Thick black eyebrows meeting over his nose. Long, ridiculously long, eyelashes. Close-trimmed beard, a lot like mine.

We look a little alike, it suddenly occurs to me: same thick dark hair, same height, same basic build. What am I, a narcissist? Looking for a twin brother to fuck?

James lets out a sigh of smoke and closes his eyes. Then he sits up suddenly and rummages through his backpack.

It looks like pewter, with Celtic swirls across the front of it. James hands the flask to me and slowly I make out the design: two bearded warriors holding between them a flaming cup.

"Give it a try," says James, and pushes an empty water glass in my direction.

Ain't much he could offer I'd turn down. Hell, I'd drink his blood, if that was the only option. For just a second, I see myself on my knees gulping down his cum. I want my black beard streaked with it: mistletoe berries, spruce boughs rimed with new snow.

I tip the flask and something red runs out into the glass.

"That there's raspberry moonshine," James says softly.

I look up at him, unsure. Every country boy knows bad moonshine can kill you. Some cheap bootleggers run it through old car radiators or dilute it with formaldehyde. You've got to know it came from a reliable source before you drink it.

"Go on, Greg. Take a taste. It's safe. I'll show ya." James pours a little out onto the table and pulls a matchbook from his backpack.

I know what he's going to do. Just about everyone who grows up in the mountains knows how to test moonshine. You light it. If it burns yellow, it's full of impurities. If it burns blue, it's safe.

The match catches, and then the tiny puddle on the tabletop. We bend over it and watch the transparent blue flame waver between us. "See?" whispers James. I look up at him. His face is only inches from mine. His eyes in this light are a glistening black, like that volcanic glass I saw in geology lab last week. He reaches across the table and gently shoves my shoulder. "Trust me, buddy. I ain't gonna give you any bad booze."

I nod and drop my eyes back to the dying flame, unable to hold his gaze any longer. My mouth's suddenly dry, so I grab that convenient glass of moonshine and take a good swig. It's surprisingly smooth and not too sweet, sort of like Bacardi rum. "Pretty fine," I mumble.

"Take it all," says James, and I do.

"Good boy," he laughs. "Most folks choke up a little."

"Naw," I say. "Not me. This is easy stuff. Not like the rusty-razor popskull I've had before. Besides, I was born to swallow flame." Something about the sight of this big scruffy guy makes me want to break some rules, take some chances, run a little wild.

James laughs again, nudges my knee with his beneath the table, and then bends forward. "C'mere," he mutters.

Again our faces are only inches apart—I can smell the tobacco on his lips—and for a crazy split second I think we've suddenly slipped into a parallel universe and he's going to kiss me, but instead he says, "Here's the thing. I know exactly where this moonshine was made."

Essential Steve Earle. Perfect CD tunes for two hillbilly boys four-wheeling up and down the mountains of McCormick County.

The road's muddy and narrow, and leaves from the surrounding woodland slap the side of the truck. James is driving fast, cursing every time he hits a pothole. It's a beat-up Toyota pickup he bought off his daddy, and I'm envious. Four-wheel drive and extended cab. "This bitch can get us anywhere," he shouts over the music, taking a curve so fast my stomach staggers.

Earle's singing, "You never come back from Copperhead Road," which makes me a little nervous, since he's talking about revenuers who spied on a moonshine still once too often, and spying on a still is just what we're about to do. On the other hand, James has assured me that the still's run by a good buddy of James' distant cousin Steve, so even if we're caught, we'll make it back to campus alive. Besides, to get my courage up and to tolerate being in such close quarters with a man I want so goddamn much, I've been borrowing sips from James' flask for the last hour. The moonshine goes down easier and easier, and it's hard to be afraid when you're this buzzed.

"He's pretty good-lookin', isn't he?"

I look up, off guard. James has caught me admiring photos of Steve Earle on the CD's liner notes. Good-looking? With that beard and those full lips and that long black hippie-hair falling down over his eyes? Hell yes, he's good-looking. But that's not the kind of thing a straight guy would admit to noticing.

The bagpipe note that ends "Copperhead Road" puts a little shiver up my spine, despite September humidity. "Uh, yeah," I reply. "He's handsome." I hesitate, then say, "Could I have a draw off your cigarette?"

"Sure," says James. "Didn't know you smoked."

"Uh, sometimes," I lie. I've never tasted tobacco in my life, except for one peach-flavored mouthful of chaw my cousin shared with me last year.

"You want your own? I got a few nice hand-rolled ones here."

"Naw, just a few puffs off yours." James hands me the cigarette, and I put it between my lips, feeling his mouth's moisture on the paper. Jesus, I want to kiss him. Instead, I tentatively suck in a little smoke. Don't want to take too much, then go off on a coughing jag and look like a pussy.

"Very fine," I say, then hand it back. His mouth would taste like tobacco, booze, and raspberries.

"Shit, it's hot," I say, and pull off my T-shirt. We're both wearing boots and jeans, ready for the spy-hike to come, and James is wearing the same damn wifebeater he's worn the last couple times we've met— I can tell because there's an oil stain I've noticed before just under his left pec. James doesn't change clothes very often, it seems. He doesn't use deodorant much either. I can smell him from here, even with the windows rolled down and late-summer air pouring through the truck cab. I want to push my face in his pits, give him a good long tongue-bath.

"You look like him, y'know," I mumble. I scratch the sweaty hair matting my belly and take another sip of 'shine from James' Celtic flask.

"Huh? Who?"

"Steve Earle."

"Oh. Yeah?" James swerves to avoid a mudhole, hands me back the cigarette.

Then he looks at me. "You know, you do, too."

Our eyes hold for about three seconds, then he clears his throat and turns up the music. Earle's singing, "I Ain't Ever Satisfied."

The truck's parked off the road, a good ways down the mountain, half-hidden by rhododendron thickets. James and I have been trudging up the hill for a good half hour, through stands of white pine and tulip tree, where no one's likely to spot us.

The trees end with the hilltop, and now we're looking over a sloping pasture. The sun's low in the sky, tangerine-colored. The distant mountains are purple with humidity haze. There's a little house on the pasture edge, with a cinderblock foundation and modern-looking glossy log sides. Reminds me of a hunting cabin my uncle used to have. There's an SUV parked in the muddy yard in front of it, underneath a scraggly cigar tree.

We check out the cabin for a while, hiding behind a big oak and looking for any sign of people or guard dogs. Then James puts his finger to his lips and we creep closer. He's a brave boy: he even slips carefully up the steps and onto the porch to peer in the windows. "Empty," he mouths silently, then gestures and we head over the other side of the hill and down into a high-grass meadow.

The slope's very steep. I can hear the purling of water, and sure enough, here's a brook, which we follow through low bushes and orchard grass. After ten minutes of descent, the sound gets louder: dull splash of a waterfall as the stream disappears over a ledge. We crawl down slanted rock alongside the cascade, careful on the slippery stone. James is solicitous, steadying me, his hand on my shoulder. "Careful!' he whispers, grinning.

When the land levels out, James grabs me by the hand and tugs me under the rock ledge and into cool air behind the waterfall. He points. "Check this out!" he says in triumph.

There, propped up on gravel, is a still, its copper gleaming in the gloom behind the rushing band of clear water. I recognize the basic setup from *The Foxfire Book*: still-kettle leading to worm and over into barrel, where cool water condenses vapor into 'shine. There's no fire going, which is a good sign. Despite the SUV parked up at the house, hopefully there's no one around.

"Gotta get some pics," says James, pulling a digital camera out of his backpack. "Dr. Kinder's gonna love this."

I examine the still for a few minutes, touching its copper gleam here and there, enjoying the cool created by the falling water. Then, leaving James to take his photographs, I stride out into the sloping meadow, where the heat recoalesces around me. There's a bobwhite calling somewhere. The shadows are lengthening.

Suddenly I'm nervous. "Hurry up, James," I say. "Light's running out." He's angling around the still, snapping shot after shot. I tug at a piece of broomsedge, tug off a few silky seeds, watch them drift slowly off on the warm breeze. Will it never cool down? A trickle of sweat slides down my side. I wish James would take his shirt off: I want to see that nipple ring glowing in the dying light.

Finally he's had enough. He strides over to me, camera strap over one shoulder, a happy grin on his face.

That's when we hear another voice. Not the waterfall, not the bobwhite. Someone says, "Keep real still, boys."

There's a chubby man with a red beard standing only a few feet above us, on one of the rocks alongside the waterfall. He's got a shotgun, and it's pointed at our heads.

He hops down a rock or two, surprisingly agile for such a large man. "Why'nt you boys just put your hands in the air?" he says, with the tone of an old friend offering advice. "And keep yourselves real still, 'cause there's an unfriendly serpent about two feet from you."

I grab James by the shoulder, and we look around frantically. Yep, there it is, a fucking snake right behind us. Copperhead, without a doubt. I push James behind me, start looking for a rock or stick.

"Now, y'all heard me, right? Hands up, if you please."

Great. Hands up, and a poisonous snake at my feet. The copperhead's curled up, poised to strike. I back up into James, my bare back against the wet fabric of his undershirt, and he mutters "Holy shit" into my ear.

"Now, don't you all worry about Matilda here," says the fat man, who's only a few feet from us now. With the barrel of his gun, he gently nudges the snake. A few half-hearted strikes at the metal, and the copperhead disappears into a stand of milkweeds.

"Now, all y'got to deal with is me," he says, pointing the gun at us with one hand and rummaging in his back pocket with the other.

"You, boy," he says, nodding at me.

"Me?" I croak. My throat's dry with fear. God, I don't want to look like a coward in front of James.

"Yeah, you. What's your name?" He smiles. Sixty or seventy pounds ago, he was a hot guy, I can't help but think, even as I'm trying not to piss my pants. His chest and arms are even bigger than James'.

I clear my throat. "Greg, sir," I say. *Always be polite,* I hear my mother advise.

"Greg, I'm Keith." He's holding something metallic toward me. Not a flask. Handcuffs. "What say you put a pair of these on your buddy? What's his name?"

"Uh, James, sir." Tiny, cowardly tremors are running up and down my thighs.

"James, turn around and put your hands behind your back. Greg, cuff him."

Keith steps up to me, the barrel of the gun in my face. He stretches out his arm, I stretch out my arm, and the cold metal slides into my palm.

I turn, and James is staring at me. His eyes are hard. He wants to rush this guy.

"James, turn around," says our captor, a little less friendly.

"Do it, James," I say. "Remember, you said your cousin would help us."

James nods. "Yeah, right. He'll show this asshole who's boss." Holding onto that likelihood, he turns his back to me and puts his arms behind his back. I fumble with the cuffs just a second—never handled cuffs before—then click them around one wrist. James sighs, hangs his head. I click on the other cuff. The thick muscles of his arms flex and relax, flex and relax. He looks beautiful this way, and suddenly I realize I have a hard-on. We might die here on this mountainside, and I have a fucking hard-on.

"Tighter," commands Keith. "Good and tight." I click the cuffs up a few more ratchets. James sucks in air and winces.

"All the way, boy." Keith is sounding impatient. Another couple of ratchets, till there's no room left, till James' back stiffens and he groans.

Keith chuckles. "Now that sounds about right."

The gun taps my spine. "Your turn," says Keith.

I put my hands behind my back. There's a rustling of boots through boomsedge, then metal on my wrists, then pain, as Keith tightens the cuffs till there's only a millimeter or two of hair and skin between the steel and the bone.

"I'm from over Kentucky way, actually. New around here. I never heard of your cousin."

Keith is sipping on a Miller Lite, making himself comfortable in a big armchair, the gun resting across one knee. James and I are sitting side by side on the cabin's leather couch, trying like hell to talk our way out of this. My hands are very, very cold. My fingers are tingling. James' must be too. How long after blood flow stops does gangrene set in?

"Listen," James tries again. "Cousin Steve has been helping Mr. Martin run this operation for years. You just got to call Martin and check my story. He can call Steve, and he'll vouch for me. We ain't here to turn you guys in. We just were curious. Had some of your all's good 'shine and wanted to see the still."

He's said all this once before, but Keith isn't too interested. He finishes his beer and says, "You're fulla shit, kid."

"Fuck you," says James.

Keith looks at him and smiles. He gets up, walks over to the fridge, lays the gun on the kitchen counter, pulls out another beer, and pops it. He tips it back and swigs. We watch his throat pulse as the beer runs down his gullet.

Then he takes the beer can and throws it at James. It hits him just over his left ear.

"You big, dumb, fat motherfucker! You pig-fucker!" James shouts, on his feet. In a second and a half, he's got Keith pushed up against the counter and is butting his head into the fat men's chest.

Keith grabs James by his thick hair. He slams him against the fridge and holds him there with the bulk of his belly. He commences to punch James hard, once in his stomach, once in his side, and twice in his handsome face. By the time I've pushed through the paralytic shock and am on my feet, Keith has tossed James on the floor, kicked him in the gut, and then drawn a Bowie knife from his boot.

"You just set down, Mr. Greg," Keith says, rubbing his belly and waving the long knife blade my way. He kicks James again. James doubles up and moans. Then Keith's boot crashes against James' head, and James lies still.

I'm shaking so hard it's hard to speak. I can't feel my hands at all now. There's blood all over James' face.

"Sir," I say, as calmly as I can. "You'd better check out our story. If you kill us and later it turns out that we were telling the truth, there'll be hell to pay. James' cousin Steve will track you down. He'll feed your liver to his hogs."

Keith strides over and backhands me hard. I stumble backwards, shake my head, and marigold petals drift across my vision. He slaps me again, harder. My lip splits. I fall to my knees.

"You're probably right," he says. "Now where's my goddamned cellphone?"

James starts coming to about the time I've finished tying his hands behind his back and have started into wrapping rope around his boots. I've convinced Keith that he wants us neither dead nor permanently damaged till he's discovered how true our story might be. He's let me beg for a good while before agreeing to replace the cuffs with less cruel restraints. He's released me, let me uncuff out-cold James and rub the color back into his hands a bit, before several tossed lengths of rope hit me upside the head, and Keith directs me on how to bind my friend.

James is lying on his back. His knees are bent. There's dried blood on his forehead. One eye is swollen half-shut. Blood trickles from the corner of his mouth, blood stains his undershirt. Even here and now I want to kiss him, I want to lick the blood from his face. Maybe *because* of here and now, since I don't know how much longer we have to live.

"Tighter," growls Keith over my shoulder. I cinch the rope around James' ankles as tightly as I can. James grunts, opens his eyes, and shakes his head. He looks up at me.

"What you doing, Greg?" he mumbles.

"I'm tying you," I say. It's hard to talk with a busted mouth. "We gotta stay here tonight."

"What the fuck?" James says. He struggles a little, finds his hands bound, rolls over onto his side, and says, "Let me loose. Please, man. My head hurts."

He sounds like a little boy. My eyes are suddenly wet. Goddammit. I clear my throat. "James, we gotta stay here tonight. Keith's cellphone don't work. He's gotta leave us here and go talk to his boss."

A silver gray roll of duct tape skids across the bare floor. "Okay, Greg, think it's time to add a good bit of this." The gun nudges me again, bumps down my backbone. "Don't want you boys to get loose and get bitten by snakes, now do we? Them copperheads hunt after dark, y'know. Mountainside's crawling with them."

"James, we're gonna be all right. Your cousin will probably be back here in a few hours, and he'll make sure we get home."

James licks his lips. He nods. "Yeah, okay."

"Get to the tape," Keith says, tapping the gun barrel on my head. "Wrists, then ankles."

"Roll over, James," I whisper. "Please roll over." James nods, rolls over on his belly, and gives a long sigh, the way he does when he's exhaling smoke.

When I pull off a length of tape, the sound is loud, like metal ripping, or a tree branch torn off by high wind. I wrap a three-feet piece around James' roped wrists, and James arcs his arms up to help me. I can feel him trembling.

"More," says Keith. I tug off another piece of tape, and there's that tearing sound again, so sharp in the cabin's silence. Countryside is so dark, so quiet. When you get used to that, you just can't abide cities with their lights and their noise. I wonder if Keith will do the digging, or untie me long enough to do it. Will he bury us in the woods or in the cellar?

"Nice. Now his ankles. About six feet worth. I got another couple a' rolls if that one gives out."

When James is finally secured to our captor's satisfaction, Keith opens another beer and swigs. "Want some?" he says.

I'm on my knees beside James. I look up at Keith and nod.

"Take the rest," he says, handing me the half-empty can.

"May I give him some?" I ask.

"Yeah, sure."

James is lying on his side. I pull him up into my arms. Who would have ever thought that a man could look this handsome with so much blood on his face? He smells like cigarettes, iron, and freshly plowed earth. He's really shaking now. Or is that me? I hold his head in the crook of my arm and give him small sips. "Thanks," he mumbles. I pour a little too fast, and James chokes a little. Beer foams up over his split lip, drips down his bearded chin and onto his wifebeater. "Sorry," I say, and wipe the beer off his chin, brush some crusted blood from his cheek.

"Cute. You look like brothers. Or morphodites," Keith laughs. "One other thing, Greg, then you can relax, 'cause it's about time for you to be tied."

I look up at Keith. He's smiling. It would be a great smile without the cruelty in it.

"Tear that undershirt off him," Keith says.

I look up at him, confused. I sure as shit have been wanting to see James bare-chested for weeks, but I doubt that Keith is arranging all this to cater to my fantasies.

"Go on."

I tug at the top of the undershirt, curve of white against black chest hair, wet with blood, spilt beer, and fear-sweat. It doesn't give. My eyes meet James'. *I love you*, I want to say. I'm only twenty. I've never said that to a man before. Now I'm wondering if I'll ever get the chance.

"Oh, for God's sake. Get to it!"

The wifebeater rips straight down, like the scar a lightning bolt leaves in an oak. "Here," says Keith, handing me a pocketknife. "Cut off the rest." Carefully, I slip the blade under cloth and sever the straps running over James' shoulders. I pull off the undershirt and stare at his bare chest, the wave-swell of hairy pecs I've been wanting to see, touch, and taste for weeks. The nipple ring glitters like gold dust, brightness rimming a lunar eclipse.

"Stuff half of it in his mouth."

I look up at Keith. My knees are aching. "No one will hear us all the way up here," I say.

He slaps the slide of my head. "Just in case. I don't want any confabs in the basement while I'm gone."

I stare at James. His eyes are wider than I've ever seen them. He's panting a little, starting to panic. He licks his split lip and shakes his head.

"Open up." Keith presses the gun's mouth against James' forehead.

"C'mon, buddy. Your cousin'll be here soon," I whisper.

James opens his mouth and closes his eyes. I push the fabric in, inch by inch, till his mouth is stuffed full and his cheeks are bulging.

"Looks like a greedy goddamn squirrel!" Keith guffaws. "Now finish him up with tape. I'd say about five, six feet worth."

Four layers of tape cover James' mouth by the time I'm done. He gives a muffled sob, his chin pressed against his bare chest. His shoulders start to shake violently, he's right on the edge of tears. I grab one arm, tip his head up. His beard is wet in my palm. *Not now. Not with him here,* I say with my stare.

"Sweet," says Keith. "Now, put the rest of his shirt in your mouth."

James takes a long breath, and his trembling eases up. I pick the other half of the wifebeater up off the floor, ball it up, and push it between my lips until it's packed in tight. My split lip throbs.

"Tape yourself," Keith says, handing me the silver roll.

There's that sick ripping again. What kind of sound does a knife-blade make entering or leaving a man's chest? Does a body make tiny noises when it rots in the ground? I press the end of the tape over the left corner of my mouth, then pull it across my lips, then over my ear, then across the back of my head. This is gonna hurt like hell when it comes off our beards, I think.

It's not till later, when I'm gagged as tightly as James, when I'm bent over the back of the couch and getting my hands roped behind me, that I realize that the duct tape may never be removed.

This is my world now: James' face, the cinderblock wall behind him, and a small window at the top of that wall, full of blackness broken occasionally by flickers of what must be heat lightning.

We're lying side by side, face-to-face, on a mattress in the basement.

Before he left, Keith dragged each of us down the stairs, then taped us together at the feet, knees, waists, and chests. Once we heard the car drive off, we struggled for a good while, cursing and rolling around. But the thought of rolling off the mattress and having to spend the rest of our time here on the cement floor has occurred to both of us, so our struggles have been as circumscribed as our limbs.

I can't see much, but my other senses are swamped. James' bare torso is pressed tightly against mine. Our chest hair and sweat mingle, his rank scent fills my nose, his gagged mouth bumps mine, his frustrated groans fill my ears, and, occasionally, if I keep very still, I can feel his heart beating against me. My mouth is stuffed full of the taste of his undershirt: salt of his torso sweat, rusty taste of his blood mixed with split beer. If I have to die, I'll die with the taste of James on my tongue.

It's surprising how much two men can communicate with their eyes, especially when those men are only inches apart. My right arm, the one beneath me, has gone numb. I grunt, cock my head, and we roll slowly over until we're resting on our other sides. We've been rotating like this for hours, trying to get as comfortable as our situation allows.

Thunder in the distance. The window lights up. In the brief flash, I can see James' face clearly: hair fallen over one eye, black beard bristling over the edges of gray tape. It's like looking into a mirror. But there's an added urgency in his eyes, something I don't understand.

"Uhhh!" James says, pushing against me. We roll, but this time only half-way. Now I'm lying on top of him.

He closes his eyes and shakes his head again and again. He's cursing softly, I think.

My cock has been hard for hours, needless to say, ever since Keith taped us together, but in this position, stretched out on top of James, I feel like I'm going to come any second. I know that James can't help but feel my erection jammed against him, and that mortifies me, but there's nothing I can do about it, feeling his warmth and his helplessness pressed against me in this forced intimacy.

But he's distracted by something else, and the sudden warm wetness spreading against my crotch lets me know what. He's pissed his pants.

"Uh uh uh!" *I'm sorry.*

I bump his chin with mine. He opens his eyes, shame-faced. I shrug my shoulders and roll my eyes. *Big deal, man. What else could you do? Excuse yourself and head for the outhouse?*

Under this latest humiliation, James finally breaks down. He shouts once—"UmmmMMMMmmm!"—and then starts to cry. I rub his gag with mine, but that doesn't help. I nuzzle his ear, his bloodstained, tear-wet cheeks, and then my own tears begin. The only good thing about having our mouths taped is that we won't be reduced to calling for our mothers, the way dying soldiers are said to do sometimes. I push my face against his and let the sobs break out of me like a spring flood.

We're still crying when I start grinding my hard-on against him and rubbing my chest against his. I wish I'd had the guts to tell him how I felt about him, and now I can't tell him anything with any clarity. But, by God, this side of the grave I can show him. I push my mouth against his as if we were kissing through the tape, I rub my mouth against the blood on his cheek as if I could lick it off like raspberry moonshine.

James couldn't pull away even if he wanted to, but he apparently doesn't want to, because he's nuzzling my face now, and I can feel not only his piss moistening my jeans but his own hard-on bumping against mine. He sobs harder, arches against me again and again. The window glimmers once, twice — a summer storm must be moving in — and in that intermittent illumination our eyes lock. *You're beautiful,* I want to say, try to say with wet eyes. *You're strong and wild and brave, and you're beautiful beneath me. If we have to die, it'll be side by side, and that'll be a better death than most.*

It doesn't take either one of us very long to shoot. Our crotches grind together for only a couple of minutes before James starts jerking spasmodically beneath me and moaning. Our foreheads slam together painfully, and then I feel my cum cresting, filling my briefs with hot spurts. James is right behind me, apparently, because now he roars against the tape, shakes his head back and forth, slams his hips into mine, and then goes limp.

I lie there for a full minute, tears finally run out, watching his face lit by lightning. He looks exhausted, I feel exhausted. Beneath all those layers of tape, he seems to be smiling. But then it occurs to me how heavy I must feel on top of him, so I grunt and cock my head, and we roll onto our sides.

We lie there for a few minutes just staring at one another. Then I gently bump his tear-moist chin with mine.

"Um umm um," I grunt. *I love you.* I wish he could hear me clearly. It's important that he know.

James arches one eyebrow. Then his eyes fill with understanding. He nods, nestles his face against my shoulder, sighs a few times, and soon his breathing slows with sleep.

For a second I think it was the light that woke me. It's orange-red sunrise, a shaft of it slanting through the basement window and stroking James' bruised and sleeping face.

But then I hear more car doors slam outside, and footsteps on the porch.

James' eyes are open now. He groans, and we both start to shiver.

I don't know which it will be. A circle of men around us. Knives?

No, bullets in the head. Wrapped in tarps, hauled out into the woods. Buried together. The slow rot melding, feeding weeds and trees. Bones spending the long night nestled together in one grave. Let it be one grave.

Or Cousin Steve tromping down the stairs. "Jesus Christ, James! You dumb bastard! You've got yourself in a fix, boy. But we've talked it all out. Once y'all are cut loose, I got some sausage and egg biscuits upstairs and some decent coffee."

After that, anything's possible. What I want's a house together, some old farmhouse with lots of sugar maple trees that turn orange-red in autumn, or red maples with leaves the color of raspberry moonshine. Tying James up gently and making love to him for hours. Sucking his cock in the shower. The fresh-baked bread my daddy taught me to make, and pots of brown beans. Watching fireflies and heat lightning out on the porch, James' head in my lap, his soft beard beneath my fingers.

A key rattles in the basement door. James takes a long breath and rests his face against mine, brow to brow, mouth to mouth. Our eyes lock and hold like clasped hands. The door creaks open, a light's clicked on, and heavy boots sound on the stairs, descending into the earth.

HURTS LIKE HELL
MEL SMITH

It was going to be a slow night. After six years, I could smell it. I needed money bad, though. I couldn't waste my time on window-shoppers. I needed the kind of money that came from being taken home and getting abused all night. I needed to do something that would attract that kind of attention. But what?

While I thought, I followed an old guy into the bathroom and sucked him off. The old fucker couldn't get it up and blamed me. He tossed a couple of ones in the toilet and turned to leave. I yelled at him to keep his fucking money and buy himself some Viagra.

Asshole.

I fished out the bills and dried them under the hand blower. Smoking limp cigars in the fucking toilet all night definitely wasn't cutting it.

Then it came to me, like a flash. It always happens like that. I'm brain dead 95 percent of the time, then — BOOM — for five seconds I'm a fucking genius.

I walked to the McDonald's and bought a small soda, then walked back to my bench. I finished the soda, took off my shirt, and undid the safety pin holding my fly shut. I got an ice cube out of my soda cup and held it on my right nipple.

Instantly, potential buyers began to gather. Melted ice trickled down my body, my un-scalped dickhead hung out of my fly, and that big old safety pin was between my teeth.

It took several ice cubes, but I finally lost all feeling in my nipple.

I held up the safety pin for the growing crowd to see. I popped it open then put the point against the side of my nipple.

People shouted, "Do it!"

I locked eyes with a likely pair in the back and slowly pushed the pin in.

Jesus Christ, that hurt like hell!

I did my best not to rip the thing back out and start screaming like a baby. I gritted my teeth, pushed through to the other side, and hooked the safety pin closed.

I was still staring at those two in the back. One had reached over and was rubbing the other one's crotch for him.

The crowd cheered. "Do the other one!"

A weaselly guy in front dropped to his knees and tried to nibble on my foreskin.

The guy rubbing his buddy's crotch reached through the crowd, grabbed the weasel by the back of the shirt and tossed him away. Then he took a hold of my safety pin and I got to my feet fast. They led me to their car, the crotch-rubber dragging me by my freshly speared nipple.

Both of them were huge and ugly as shit, only the guy with the prewarmed crotch looked like really, really, really ugly shit.

We got in the car; all three of us in the front seat. We negotiated the terms—basically "You pay me what I need and you can do anything you want"—then Ugly pulls out his meat.

Now, I've been doing this for six years and I've seen some pretty bizarre dicks before, but Ugly's stick took the grand prize. It was only about five inches, but that was across. Lengthwise it was about four.

"You sure you didn't put that thing on wrong?"

I could tell Ugly wasn't laughing as he pushed my head down to his plank. I got as much as I could in my mouth and the fucking thing started swelling.

Uglier was pulling my jeans down and started shoving something up my ass. From the way my hole was tearing I was pretty sure it was a plastic model of Ugly's stick.

They worked together on both of my holes like they were rehearsing a dance. Then Ugly started grunting and his dick got even fatter. Uglier shoved the plug hard up my ass, Ugly exploded into my mouth, my windpipe closed off, and I blacked out.

I woke up in a sling with my hands and ankles tied. I didn't feel so hot. Something nasty was nesting in my mouth, my tit was on fire, and my asshole was throbbing so hard I could hear it.

I was dropping back off to sleep when the Ugly Twins came in. I tried not to laugh. Those damn leather costumes are hard for me to take seriously.

They skipped the pleasantries and Uglier stabbed a safety pin through my other nipple. I got serious real fast. It was ten times worse without the ice and I couldn't keep back the tears.

Uglier closed the safety pin. A chain was attached to it. Uglier connected the safety pins with the chain. The chain was exactly the right length, pulling my nipples toward each other but not enough to tear the safety pins out. Hopefully.

Concentration was hard with my tits skewered together like that but then, I don't think they were expecting me to do much besides lie there and take it.

The sling was hooked up to this pulley system. Ugly worked some ropes and my head went down while my ass went up. Then he stuck that fucking four-by-five in my mouth again, and Uglier popped out the butt plug. I didn't realize I had such a tight grip on the thing and the pain of having it ripped free made me chomp down on Ugly.

He yelped and pulled out then he yanked hard on the chain between my nipples. I yelped back, apologizing. He stuck himself back in.

I couldn't see what the hell Uglier was doing, but he was mighty busy with my asshole. Soon there was no mistaking that he was preparing to fist me.

Now, being fisted is never my favorite thing, but there are ways of making it less painful. Uglier didn't know them. Either that, or he didn't give a shit.

With the amount of pain I was in, I thought for sure Uglier had that arm of his in up to the shoulder. Between that and Ugly's fire hydrant making it impossible to breathe, I was close to passing out again.

Then Ugly pulled out of my mouth and all I had to worry about was how much more of himself Uglier planned on cramming into my chute.

I closed my eyes and did some relaxation exercises I read in a magazine once. The article forgot to mention that they weren't effective during fisting.

Ugly joined Uglier at my hoisted-up ass. He was whacking that weird meat of his, getting off on the sight of his lover with only one arm. Then—and I could not fucking believe this—he starts to wiggle his fingers in alongside Uglier's arm. He got all four fingers into me and was adding the thumb when I started screaming.

That's when I saw the belt. It was in Uglier's other hand. No doubt, he had planned on sticking that up me, too. When I started screaming, he raised the belt over his head and brought it down hard on that nipple chain.

I passed out again.

The second time I came to, I was on a mattress on the floor, my right wrist handcuffed to a ring in the wall. I'd been pissed on. It could have been by me, I guess, but I don't usually get it in my hair. Then again, I don't usually piss while hanging upside down in a sling. Whoever's piss it was, though, I was pretty well drenched in it and being pissed on, like being fisted, ranks real high on my list of Things I Wouldn't Let People Do to Me If I Wasn't Getting Paid for It.

I tried to sit up, but my ass was too sore. My left nipple was partially torn. The chain and the safety pin on the left were gone, but the right nipple pin was still in. My flash of genius was looking pretty fucking stupid by now, so I concentrated on the money I'd be getting and not on the pain.

I looked over at the sling and Ugly was in it. Uglier was working his arm into his ass and Ugly was squirming and begging and trying to get more. Uglier looked like a proud papa delivering his own baby.

After working his arm in and out like a saw, Uglier grabs a hold of Ugly's dick with his free hand and starts yanking. Ugly shoots a load that hits the ceiling and it rains back down on both of them.

Uglier pulls out his arm, unties Ugly and Ugly drops to his knees at

Uglier's feet. He licks his way up from the boots to Uglier's cock and starts munching enthusiastically.

Uglier was getting pretty worked up by now, so he grabbed Ugly by the ears and took over. Ugly stopped munching and made like an asshole, and Uglier fucked him hard. He pulled out, made a noise like a dying elephant, and practically suffocated poor Ugly with the thickest wads of cum I have ever seen. Ugly ended up looking like the Incredible Melting Man, strings of creamy spunk stretching from his face to the floor.

Ugly left and Uglier came over to me. He stared down at my limp dick. I knew he was wondering. They all do.

Ugly, who I figured had gone to unclog his face, came back still trailing cheese and carrying—hang on now—a pig. A live one.

It squealed this horrible pig squeal, and Ugly kind of holds it down on the mattress in front of me, butt end in my face.

"Fuck it."

I looked up at Uglier. "What?"

"Fuck the pigbottom."

Now that's getting just a little too literal for me. "I can't."

"Why not?"

"Even if I was attracted to the pig, which I'm not, I can't get it hard."

"Bullshit. We're paying you to fuck the pig, so get yourself hard and fuck the pig."

"I can't. I swear."

They didn't believe me.

They tied the pig up and they went to work on me. They sucked, licked, whacked, slapped, tugged, jerked and choked my dick, but it wouldn't budge. It never did. In all these years, I'd never been able to get it up, which left me with few options as a prostitute. Except for the occasional enema job, I was pretty much the designated fuckee. For once, I was mighty grateful for that limp dick.

Ugly took the pig away. The pig seemed grateful, too.

After that, they amused themselves until morning with my body.

By the time the sun came up, I hurt like hell and smelled twice as bad. They paid me my money, plus a hundred dollar tip. We made an appointment for me to come back in two weeks. I knew it would take that long before I could handle them again.

I asked if I could shower, but they said they didn't want me in any other part of their house. They gave me a bottle of water and made sure I went out the back door.

I was going to use most of the water to clean off with, but it tasted so good washing down all their garbage that I ended up drinking it instead.

It was a long walk home, and I had to stop a few times to rest.

I was too old for this shit. At eighteen, I couldn't compete with all the little drumsticks on the street. Fuck-toy was the only thing my old man had trained me for, though, so more and more I was doing hard-core scenes, and it was wearing me down.

When I was a block from home, I went to the back of a gas station I knew. They had a hose in back and I stripped and showered, rinsing off all the piss and bloody debris. I took out the safety pin, dried myself off with my T-shirt, and got dressed.

When I got back to the apartment I opened the door slowly, in case Benny was sleeping. He wasn't.

"Hey."

"Hey."

"Rough night?"

"Not really."

He knew I was lying. Benny always knew when I was lying. It made not telling the truth so much easier.

I went to the bed and kissed him. He looked worse than when I left him last night, but I didn't say anything.

"You're bleeding."

I looked down at the stains on my shirt. "Not anymore."

I turned away and headed for the hot plate. I didn't want to see his eyes. I knew what they would look like—a hundred miles deep of Hershey's chocolate, swimming behind tears.

In my life I'd been fisted, whipped, fucked, beaten, and shocked in the balls with a cattle prod, but nobody ever hurt me as bad as Benny did when he cried. The first couple of times he did it, I beat him up because it scared me so bad. Nobody should have the power to inflict that kind of pain on someone else.

The first year we were together, I left Benny a lot. But I couldn't get away from those eyes. When we were separated, every john would look at me with them. So I would go on back to Benny since I couldn't escape from them, anyways.

It took a while, but I finally figured out that the only way I could keep them from hurting me was to not make Benny cry. Sometimes, though, that wasn't possible. Especially lately.

I started making breakfast.

"I made enough last night to get your medicine for next month."

"Did you get tested yesterday?"

"I was going to, but they were too busy."

"Tony, you promised."

"I know, but I couldn't. I'll do it tomorrow when I pick up your stuff."

"Promise."

"I promise! For Christ's sake, it's not like it matters anymore. Stop nagging me."

"It matters to me."

"And that's why I'm going to do it, so shut the fuck up."

We were silent while I made breakfast.

When I took him his plate, he smiled an apology at me.

I sat on the lawn chair next to the bed and ate.

"Do any hot guys last night?"

"Five."

"All at once?"

"Damn straight."

"What did they do to you?"

"Well, first, they got down on their knees and worshipped me like the god that I am."

Benny giggled. I tried not to smile, but I couldn't help it. Four years we'd been together, and that giggle still drove me wild.

"What did they do next?"

"They licked me from head to toe, taking turns with my monster tool. When it reached its full four-foot length, they lined up on it, and I roasted them like marshmallows."

"You fucked all five of them at once?"

I nodded. "A sixth guy came along and there was room for him, but the other five wouldn't let him on."

He was giggling uncontrollably now and it almost made me cry, he looked so normal.

He wiped away tears—the kind of tears that didn't hurt me—and his eyes were sparkling. "Were you able to get it up at all?"

I shook my head. "As usual."

Benny put down his plate. "Come here."

I took off my clothes and shook my head in amazement at the boner soaring up from my crotch. How did Benny do that?

He made a noise, and I knew the welts must still look bad.

I sat on the edge of the bed then slid in beside him. I tried to prepare myself, but the feel of his fragile bones bumping against my body was still a shock.

"What the hell happened to your nipples?"

"I cut myself shaving."

Benny didn't laugh. Those chocolate eyes started swimming and it was too late to look away.

He fought it for a little bit then blurted out, "If it wasn't for me..."

"Shut up!" I swung my legs back out of bed. "Don't start that shit again! I swear to God, I'll leave you for good."

He was silent for a long time. I wanted to lie back down—I needed to feel those bones against me—but I was too afraid of the eyes.

Then he touched me, with just the tip of one finger at the top of my asscrack. It was like pushing a fucking button. Benny knew every damned button, switch, and whistle my body contained. He was the only person who'd ever been able to find them. Or maybe he was just the only person who'd ever taken the time to look.

My body was rigid as he slid his finger down inside my crack. He burrowed in and located my hole. He wiggled his finger around and erased all my pain. He kissed that spot at the top of my crack and I rolled into his arms. We kissed and Benny's hand closed round my cock. He tugged it once.

Benny and I had signals to tell each other what we wanted. One tug meant he wanted my cock in his mouth.

Of course, these days I wouldn't let him take me into his mouth. I was too afraid I was carrying something that would make him even sicker. But whether his lips were around my cock or just on it, the result was always the same. Benny made me forget.

I got up and kneeled over his face.

He played with my precum, spreading it on my dickhead with his finger. Sometimes he would try to get it back into the piss slit. I wouldn't let him taste it anymore, but he put his finger up to his nose, closed his eyes, and inhaled. I always felt so fucking proud when he did that, like I was a god or something, and anything from me was sacred to him.

He opened his eyes and held his finger up to me. I licked myself off of him, tasting what he missed so much.

He held the head of my cock with one hand, the tip of it resting against his palm. He licked down the underside of my shaft, then kissed his way back up. He put his lips along it sideways and slid them down to my balls, his tongue tickling me.

I closed my eyes, and I forgot. There were no johns, no tears, and no sickness. There was just Benny.

He pulled one ball into his mouth with his tongue, and his free hand played with the other one. He pinched the skin and rolled the whole thing between his fingers. The one slid out of his mouth and he sucked in the other, teasing the first with his fingers.

I was ready too soon. It was going to happen too fast. I needed this to last.

I touched his hair and was suddenly relaxed. It always did that for me. It wasn't as thick as it used to be, but it was still silky soft.

I opened my eyes and he was looking up at me. I brushed back his hair and thought how beautiful he was. That would never change.

His mouth released my balls and his tongue slid up my cock. He was squeezing the head between his fingertips and his tongue ran underneath the ridge. It was a light touch at first, but soon it pushed hard, as if he wanted to pop it off like a bottle cap.

He wedged two fingers against the ridge and scissored the end of my dick between them. With his tongue stroking fast up and down my shaft and flicking wildly around my balls, he squeezed those fingers tight.

I held on to him and rocked on my knees as my glans fucked his fingers.

He worked the thumb of his free hand into my asshole and held it there. With every rock forward, I fucked his fingers and with every rock back, his thumb fucked my hole.

After an eternity I screamed, both from pleasure and from the pain of my returning memory. I climbed off of him and I ripped back the covers. I stood at the foot of the bed with my bursting dick in my hands and I came all over the bottoms of Benny's feet. His toes wiggled and his feet squirmed and there were no signs of illness as Benny's giggles brought me joy.

Then he started coughing and it took me ten minutes to calm him down.

I got him some water and washed his face off with a cool rag, then I slid in beside him again.

He laid his head on my shoulder and lightly touched my sore nipples and several of the welts. "I'm sorry."

"I know."

"I love you."

"I know."

I took a deep breath and I looked into Benny's eyes.

It hurt like hell.

TAMPING THE DIRT DOWN
PATRICK CALIFIA

"Your father is dead."

It was my grandmother's bitter voice, message number three on Wednesday's voicemail. How had she tracked me down? My family had disowned me after that terrible day at school when I took my shirt off to force my guidance counselor to admit that I had been burned with an iron and then beaten with its cord. Before I was whisked away to foster care, my father's mother told me it was my fault that the family had been broken up and disgraced, and I'd never hear from them again.

It made me cry, but they were tears of relief.

No—wait—come back from the past. She was telling me when and where the funeral would be. Another person took over my fingers, picked up the pen, and wrote down the facts she recited. The message ended with the sharp sound of her phone, banged down into its cradle. She hadn't greeted me by name, and she didn't say goodbye.

Was I in shock? She said the prostate cancer had finally gotten him. So he had been eaten alive from the asshole up, I thought with grim relish. That had to hurt. I wondered what it was like for someone who was so good at inflicting pain to be trapped with a lot of it, unrelenting, day and night. And the terror of death.

I knew what that felt like. And I'd had to hustle my own medication for the agony. No doctor was going to write me a prescription. Because children are so resilient, don't you know. They forget, and outgrow trauma as easily as they grow out of shoes and T-shirts.

The only thing I forgot was why the hell I packed my best courtroom suit and bought a plane ticket immediately, so I could arrive in time for the viewing. That maxed out my only valid credit card. No price break for purchasing your fare thirty days in advance, and I wasn't going to a major city, either. I would have to change planes three times to get there, rent a car, and drive for an hour and a half. I must have slept, called my boss, gotten someone to feed the cat and water the plants. But I was on autopilot. My memories had claimed me, and I was sleepwalking through both day and night.

But I snapped to, wide awake, at the front door of the mortuary. The world was full of bright colors; infused with heavy, damp Southern heat and the smell of hundreds of rapidly dying flowers. Someone had opened the door, tamping a cigarette out of its pack, and he looked surprised and happy to see me. The cigarettes went back into the inside pocket of his leather jacket.

It was my older brother, Joshua. I saw his lips form the first letter of my name and almost whinnied in terror. For no reason at all, I had the irrational fear that he would call me Nelly. But that was my dad's slur, his excuse for hurting me. My brother saw me only as a man, my masculinity equal to his own. He made sure of that. To all intents and purposes, he was the one who raised me, who taught me to be a man.

"Ned," he breathed excitedly, and took my hand. Instead of shaking it and letting go, he drew me across the threshold and into his arms. There was too much fabric and leather between our hearts, not to mention history. But I could smell his sweat mingled with the lime deodorant he had been using since high school. It was the smell of safety. He looked nothing like our father. I am the short, dark-haired son. Joshua was tall and blond. We had been told he took after a deceased uncle, but I always suspected he resembled the mother who ran off when I was too little to remember her. I never saw a picture of her, and we were rigorously kept away from her side of the family.

I held my brother tight, as if he was the mast of a ship and I was a sailor caught in the rigging by a sudden storm. He held me too, gently and tenderly. There was no squeeze or pat on the back to let me know it was time to disengage. Instead, he held me patiently, and I relaxed into him, trusting his love. I was the one who finally pulled away, afraid we would attract too much attention. But as I looked up, past his leather-clad shoulder, I saw that everyone was keeping their distance, and no one was looking at us. So when he drew me close again, I went willingly, because he was my only ally in this sedate but vicious mob.

"I know why you came," he whispered in my ear. His voice was as intimate as a kiss. "He really is dead. Come and see, so you can rest easy."

We went arm-in-arm to the coffin and stared at its contents for a long time. The other mourners held back or circled around us. That was my old man, all right. Even in death he looked dangerous. No amount of putty or Krazy Glue could erase the lines around his mouth and between his eyes that made him look angry with the world. He didn't look like he was asleep. He looked like he had just closed his eyes for a second because he was exasperated with me. His eyes would open and his hand would come up—

I realized I was flinching away from the ornate metal box and its gruesome contents. "Lean over and give him a good hard poke," Joshua whispered in my ear, like a miniature devil in a cartoon. "I had to. Just to make sure. Go on—it'll look like you're kissing him goodbye."

So I leaned over, put my face into a harsh bath of embalmer's chemicals and cosmetics, and stuck my forefinger into my sire's chest. A split second before I actually touched him, I sensed that I would encounter nothing but inanimate matter. But I shoved him anyway, a minute savagery, and he did not react. I was suddenly so happy and dizzy I might have tumbled face-first into the coffin if Joshua hadn't grabbed me. As if Dad would ever let me be on top.

"Steady there, Ned, steady," he said, as if he were talking to a hand-shy dog. He led me to an alcove where there was a blue velvet loveseat shielded by a braided ficus in a faux Chinese pot and two palm trees. But I didn't let him sit down. I pressed him to the wall and burst into tears.

We both cried. Loud, unmanly tears. Little boy wails. If Grandma saw us, she probably thought we were repenting of our wicked ways, the ruination of her favorite son. But we were sharing a childhood full of humiliation and fear, and giving vent to everything we had to hide so we could live among normal people and pretend to be as careless as them.

Joshua had one hand around the back of my neck, and the way he stroked my hair felt incredibly good. What a rebel he was to come to a wake in a leather jacket, jeans, and boots. He looked like a modern Viking, while I looked incongruous—like an auto mechanic who has dressed up for church. He smelled like a strong, healthy man who needs to get laid. I always notice what men smell like. I've spent enough time nosing around in the dark to get good at it. Joshua leaned forward, scorning all discretion, and licked the tears from my face. Between us, even through a layer of underwear and my wool slacks, I felt his cock twitch, then slowly thicken.

"All these people knew what was happening to us," he said, holding my head in both of his hands and turning my face this way and that so he could look at me and lick the tears on the other cheek. Oh, that indiscreet whisper, that soft puff of air that made me long for his imperious lips upon my own. My knees felt weak. "They knew then, they know now, and yet they'll put him in his grave as if he was a good man who deserved their tears and their prayers. And they'll to go their own graves denying that he's a twisted psychopath who tortured his own children, punched them and put cigarettes out on them, and put them to bed with tears on their faces and his thick, stinking spunk in their butts."

He pushed his hips forward. I gasped, but I didn't move away. I had, after all, been taught not to try to escape. Maybe it was perverse of us to get excited as we discussed the wrongs our father had inflicted on us. But if we could get any pleasure out of the past, so what? That was our business. Reparations.

"Fuck them all!" Joshua said, loud enough to be overheard. A passing cousin flinched but rapidly rearranged her face and hurried past our niche.

"I already got a room for us," Joshua told me, as if he had known, without talking to me for all of these years, that I'd be here, and I would need him to shelter me. We left the funeral parlor holding hands. Grief gives men permission to break the usual rules about not touching one another, and Southern men are more prone to emotional breakdowns and grabbing one another than Yankees, but we were pushing the boundaries of what could be justified by crazed grief.

He was driving a vintage Mustang convertible that he'd restored himself. There was a new fifth of Jack in the car, and I unscrewed the cap and tilted it to his lips and then my own. The bottle's slick glass stem reminded me of a slim cock, barely breaching my mouth. The liquor burned like a hot poker going down my throat, so I had to have some more, to dull the pain of the first slug. Joshua kept his right hand on my knee as he drove. We fell into our old pattern. I shifted, he steered. We drove to his motel through the dark streets of the hellish little town that robbed both of us of our belief in any hell hereafter.

We were laughing and drinking and breaking the speed limit so blatantly that we were lucky the police didn't pull us over. But there weren't many cops, I guess. This was a town were people still didn't lock their doors at night—unless they were locking a kid into the shed. Spiders like sheds.

But there were no spiders in Joshua's Eezy-Breezy Motel cottage, which consisted of a room barely big enough to house the bed, a bathroom with a shower and no tub, and a small kitchen. He said he was hungry so I went to the refrigerator and found our staples: eggs and frozen potatoes, butter and cheese. I made him a big plate of scrambled eggs and fried potatoes, and it was so good to see him put food that I had cooked into his mouth that I ate some myself. Then I tried to claim the bottle again, but he wanted it first, and so we had to wrestle for the next drink.

Joshua made me wait to get pinned. I wasn't quite drunk enough to have an excuse or the courage to just beg for his dick. So I struggled with him, honestly pitting my strength against his. He seemed to have a counter for any move I made. My hands couldn't get a grip on him. They just slid over his muscles, and betrayed me by wanting to linger there, hold onto his biceps or his ass. I was out of breath and hard as a teenager who just went to second base. Joshua had me down on the bed with my legs spread and my hands pinned over my head. "You want a drink?" he asked, hoisting the bottle with his free hand.

"Yes, you fucker!" I said, laughing.

He took a pull on the bottle, then held his face over mine. His raised eyebrow asked me a question. I felt a change come over my face as I melted into submission. My mouth fell open and he covered my lips with his own. We kissed around the whisky, sucking it off one another's tongues. The feel of his probing tongue and his hand tugging at my zipper made me squirm. My breath came out in short gasping whines.

He got his hand into my fly, that competent hand that had shielded me from schoolyard bullies, from every hostile force except our father. What he found there made him shake his head at me and grin. "You want more than some Jack," he said.

"Yes," I told him. "I want Joshua."

He played with me, working my cock with his hand while we kissed again. "If you let my hands go, I'll unbutton my shirt," I whispered. He rolled to one side, and I sat up and tore my shirt off, hunched awkwardly out of my pants. They would get wrinkled, and I needed to wear them to the funeral tomorrow. But let them lie on the floor. I had something more important to do.

Joshua was sitting on the edge of the bed. While I was getting naked, he had taken his dick out. I wondered how many places it had been, that proud rascal. Well, I had no grounds for jealousy. I had gotten busy as well. Sex doesn't fill the hole in my spirit, but it mercifully turns my vision away from it for a while. Maybe I had learned a trick or two that would make Joshua even happier to see me.

He poured some whisky into his hand and worked his cock. That had to burn his pisshole, I thought, but he didn't seem to care. Maybe there was so much precum that it kept the alcohol away from his meatus. "I don't have to slap you to get you to suck my dick, do I?" he asked gravely.

I stiffened, surprised by this phrase from the past. The night before I had gone to the guidance counselor and demanded that she report my father, he had gone crazy on me. When he came into my room, I had gotten some weird freakish fag courage from somewhere, and I told him, "You don't have to slap me to get me to suck your dick, old man."

"No, Joshua," I whispered, kneeling and tonguing the head of his cock. "You don't have to slap me. But I'll probably do a better job of sucking your dick if you do."

He hit me without any hesitation. That's how you know when someone really wants to hit you, when they go after you as soon as they have permission. Sadists must walk around with a perpetual mental hard-on, seeing potential victims where other people see strangers or co-workers or friends. Joshua had once been a very angry young man, and I was used to being hit. I liked it when it came from him. I could comfort him by siphoning off his rage so it didn't get him in trouble outside our house.

"You know I used to listen to him working you over," he said. As lust filled him up, his Southern accent came out. I was only listening with half an ear. I had a third of his cock in my mouth, and it tasted so good I wanted to bolt down the rest of it. But I teased both of us, sliding his shaft in and out of my throat, giving him only partial access. He kept on talking, caressing my head. I wished it was shaved so I could feel every callus on his fingertips. "I used to feel so guilty because I'd get turned on listening to him hit you with that belt. I would try to keep my hands off my cock, sit on them, bite them, until my balls were blue. But I'd always lose. I'd jack off when you'd start to cry. And I'd make myself come before he let you go, so you wouldn't see me do such a sick thing."

I let his dick slide far enough out of my mouth to allow me to say a few words. "But one night your timing was off," I reminded him.

Joshua's hand moved to my neck and he forced me forward, taking charge of the blow job. "Things have never been the same since then, have they?" he mused. His cock fucked my throat, and the further it went into me, the harder my own dick got, until I knew exactly what he meant when he said it was impossible to keep his hands off his own cock. But I didn't touch myself. I knew the rules. I was the one who had made them up in the first place.

"You want to jack off, don't you?" he teased. His voice had just the right derisive edge. He was aroused by his power over me, my willing surrender, and the humiliating evidence my body gave him of how much I enjoyed it. I gasped or grunted some affirmative response, feeling tears start to flow down my face. He would allow me to suck and lick at him for several minutes, then he would push past my ability to caress him with my tongue and deliberately make me gag. I didn't care what happened to me, if my throat got raw or I choked on him. I just wanted the taste of his dick ground into my mouth, so I would never be able to get it out, so I would always be able to taste him there.

"Show me your cock, little brother," he ordered. I put both hands at the base of my dick and tipped it up so he could see its ruddy rigidity. "Nice," he complimented me, hips swaying as he fucked my face. "Do yourself while I watch," he gasped, close to coming himself. My fist moved slowly. I had to hold myself back. It was hard to monitor my own body when his sex had taken over. I wanted all of me to be absorbed in servicing him, as if there were only one cock between us.

"Are you going to come with your big brother?" he asked. I nodded, made slobbery pig noises, begged him with my eyes. "Don't you dare shoot until I tell you," he warned. "Oh, suck me!" He grabbed my neck with both hands and screwed me roughly, sharp deep thrusts that I felt in the pit of my stomach. My cock was so ready to come that I had to stop stroking it. I could feel the moisture leaking from the head of my cock, imagined it running down the shaft to coat the crack of my ass with its slickness.

"Do it good. Do it like a big boy. I want to see my little brother shoot," he commanded, speaking in short, harsh phrases. We were both out of breath. His salty cream flooded the back of my palate, and I aimed my dick at myself, leaving white spatters all over one nipple.

Joshua slid out of me. He put his hand on the top of my head and tilted my torso back. With an index finger, he scooped cum off my chest and fed it to me. "See how much good stuff you've got in that little pecker of yours?" he asked. God, how weird is it to be turned on when somebody talks about your dick being small? But I was. I sucked cum off his fingers as if they were extra cocks and I could make them shoot. He laughed at me, pleased with himself and with me, and when my chest was clean he gave me a drink, took one himself, and then dragged me up onto the bed.

We slept. My body was more relaxed than it had ever been. I hadn't seen Joshua after that day in school. I got sent to a foster home, and he was placed in a group house. There were so many times I had wondered where he was. If I had really tried, I probably could have tracked him down. After all, my grandmother had managed to find me. But I had been afraid that this would happen even though I had never stopped playing these games. I was afraid he would call me a freak and turn away from me in disgust. I was equally afraid he would put me on my knees and dominate me again. Hell, I didn't even know if Joshua was gay, like me! But my body and my psyche didn't care about any of this bullshit. I slept cradled in the hollow of his shoulder, curled up against my brother's clean and sexy body. We were like two wolves safe in their underground den.

The next morning we started to fuck again as soon as we woke up. This time he tied me up with cords he cut from the blinds, and teased me with his hands and mouth until I was beside myself, ready to say or do anything if only he would let me come. But once more, I was not allowed to orgasm until he had his cock deep down my throat, and I was gulping down his load. He had pinched and bitten my nipples until they were painfully alert, and I felt both shame and exultation when he fondled my chest and I got hard once more. I would have been a girl for him. A dog. An alien. Anything he wanted, any place, any time. He was that good, he knew me that well.

I felt like I was being trained. But training implies an ongoing relationship. That had never happened for me, and it certainly was not a possibility with Joshua. But a boundary like that was hard to remember when he pushed me into the shower, aimed his cock at me, and pissed all over me, then made me kneel to jack off with his piss and swallow the bitter remnants from his softening meat. Impossible to hold any part of myself back from him when he shoved his boots in my face and made me lick them, my ass in the air, groveling and weeping to make him believe that I really did belong to him.

Then he slid the belt out of the loops of his jeans, doubled it over, and made me kiss it. "I thought you might like this," he said easily, hitching up his pants. The first hit almost flattened me. But I'd been told to keep my butt up for this belting. I tried every trick I had learned long ago to get me through the pain: panting, holding back my screams, letting my screams go. But it didn't stop what was happening, and I couldn't take it. I couldn't take it, but I had no choice, it wasn't going to stop.

That was when I found a door I hadn't seen for many years. I opened it up and fell through to the other side. There were the same amazing colors, the music, the sensation of dancing on air while being filled with boundless serenity. The longer I was suspended in this place, the better it felt to be there. When I cried out, it was because my human body could not contain so much ecstasy. My mind was not schooled to feel so much joy.

So Joshua came to get me. Pushed his arm through the door, grabbed me by the scruff of my neck, and hauled me back to his room. I laid face down on the bed, sighing while he fondled my welts. "I think we might have missed the funeral," he said.

"Shit," I replied.

"Do you care if we miss the rest of it?"

I thought about it. Seeing the monster's corpse laid out, frozen by time's justice, had done me a world of good. But he was still above ground, and while he was in the world, he might still have the capacity to do harm. "I think I need to see him buried," I whispered.

Joshua nodded. "Okay," he said. "Let's go." He offered me a hand. We quickly showered and dressed, then climbed into his car, ignoring the maid who had been trying to get into the room to change the towels all day. She glared at us as we drove off. I wondered what she would think about the mess we had made in the room—the piss on the bathroom floor, faint lines of blood on the sheets from where I had rolled over after he belted me, cum on the pillowcases. I became silently fierce with the need and righteous power to defend us.

"What the hell are you grinding your teeth about?" Joshua asked. I didn't reply. He sighed and put my hand on the gearshift. Sliding across the seat to get closer to him, I felt much better. I was so far under that I didn't question where we were going. He seemed to know what he was doing, and I didn't want to worry about it. All I could really think about was his cock. When would I see it again? When would I taste it again? He used me hard, and it only made me want him more. Was I one of those horrible bottoms who becomes a black hole, sucking the life out of any top in arm's reach? Or was this just one of the masochistic joys of slavery, to have your need brought to the fore, and keep it in consciousness without being able to sate it? It certainly made me attentive to him. For example, I had brought the whisky along. There wasn't much left in the bottle, but we downed it before we made it to the graveyard's parking lot.

The Mustang ground out a place for herself in the gravel. Dust hung in the air like the aftermath of a bombing. It was getting late. Soon the sun would go down and insects would begin to bite.

There was no gatekeeper or overseer to give us directions. But it wasn't a very big cemetery. We went hand-in-hand up a grassy hill, and sighted our kinfolk not far off, gathered around a red granite tablet that was half as tall as I was, thick as a loaf of bread, and as wide as my outstretched arms. Now we knew where the estate's funds had been invested. I guess no money had been put in trust for me to pay for therapy. I told Joshua what I was thinking, but he didn't laugh, just looked at me queerly, as if I had gotten too much sun. Note to self: do not babble to your stressed-out Master Brother Sir at the perpetrator's burial.

Nobody acknowledged us, but we made a place for ourselves among them. I gave grandmother a little wave, and she pointedly turned her head away from me. Why had she called me? Did she invite me to come home just so she could shun me? My father's cruelty had to come from somewhere. Or someone.

The closed casket was lowered into the ground with slings and an automated hoist. When it hit the bottom of the grave, the slings were dragged out from underneath it. Everyone took turns throwing a handful of dirt onto the coffin lid. I hurled mine like a baseball. Don't tell me I throw like a girl, you bastard. Never again. I'll never hear those taunts again. Nelly. Sissy. Fag.

But I'll always have to wonder how much he has to do with what I have become.

The mourners drifted away, leaving the coffin still exposed in its pit. Joshua and I lingered. A white-haired man in overalls and a black man in brown pants with stained cuffs were going to shovel the dirt in. There was a roll of sod to lay over the earth. "We'll take care of it," Joshua told him, and put a shovel in my hand. "We're part of his immediate family."

The two workmen shrugged and gave up their tools. "Guess we get to go home early," one of them said. They bummed a cigarette apiece off of Joshua, then trundled off to the parking lot, where I had seen a pickup truck and a van parked side by side.

"Put your back into it," he ordered me, and I dug into the first chunk of brown soil. It was heavy with clay, and I twisted my shoulder heaving it into the hole. "No," Joshua said, correcting my posture with a hand on my shoulder and another on my hip. "Put the weight here. Then pivot. I don't want you to hurt yourself."

We were high enough from having sex to giggle together at that one. Then we went to work, unable to talk much. An evening breeze had come up that threatened to blow dirt back into our mouths. I felt a quiet happiness, the way I used to feel when Joshua and I managed to sneak off together to play ball or go fishing. The more bizarre aspect of what we were doing I forced beneath the surface of my awareness. Besides, it was hard work; it takes an amazing amount of dirt to fill a grave.

Once we were done, Joshua took my hand and put another hand on my waist. "Shall we dance?" he asked, and stepped onto the grave. I followed his lead without thinking. "We have to tamp the dirt down," he explained, and kissed me on the forehead. Up and down we went, I think we were waltzing, but I don't know anything about ballroom dancing. Or disco, for that matter. I pirouetted, Joshua let me go, and bowed to me. I wasn't even tempted to drop a curtsy. I bowed as well. Then he motioned for me to help him shift the huge roll of turf and position it properly over the bare ground. We somehow managed to shove it into place and then unroll it. The dirt hadn't settled yet, so it wasn't level with the rest of the sward. It looked like a green toupee.

Looking around, I realized it was completely dark, and we had no flashlight. Would we trip over headstones as we walked back to the car? I jumped when Joshua's hands found me. He caressed my back and chest, then began to peel off my T-shirt. I resisted, and he grabbed me and bit me on the neck, hard. "If somebody shivers when you walk on their grave, what do you think they do when you fuck on it?" he hissed.

If I had fought with him before giving him that first blow job in the motel, it was child's play compared to the combat we engaged in now. I swung at him, clawed and kicked, bit and poked at his eye, pulled his hair, had no compunction about using any dirty trick I could think of to get away from him. But he was bigger and stronger than me, and he was my older brother. He had been the one I ran to when I needed ice on a burn or a bandage on a bleeding wound. He had let me sleep in his bed. He had given me my first *Playboy* magazine, seen my first ejaculation, and been the first one to show me how to take away the pain of degradation and turn it into pride and pleasure. Pride in my ability to give him pleasure. Delight in cheating my father by letting Joshua do the same things that he did, but doing them willingly, with love.

Bit by bit he got my clothes off. Hold by hold he took me down to the ground and pinned my hands at my sides, sitting on my stomach. He had kept my necktie and used it to bind my wrists together. Put it once around my neck, then around my hands, so they were held up under my chin, and I could barely breathe. Then he slapped me, once with the flat of his hand, once with the backhand. Even in the dark he knew how to find my vulnerable face, twisted with tears, aching for his approval. My face rang like the hollow bowl of a Tibetan bell. I wished that he would hit me again.

"Don't fuck with me," he warned me. Then he said in a softer tone of voice, "Because I'm going to be fucking you."

The grass tickled my bare back so much that I wanted to shriek.

Joshua's weight on me was almost welcome because it forced the blades of grass to lay flat and stop flicking my sensitive skin. "On your back where you belong," he recited. "Now you say it. Say the words, Ned."

I was weeping. "No," I choked. "Stop this. I won't. I don't want to."

"We have to," he said. "Don't you understand? We have to, or it will never be over."

Then he was quiet, and perhaps because I can never stand a long silence, I broke its ominous spell. "I am on my back," I said, pronouncing each word with difficulty. "Where I belong."

He parted my legs and lifted them, bent my knees. He was holding onto my ankles. His cock brushed the crack of my ass. I shivered, grateful for the warmth of the night and its rural depth. There were no house lights, streetlamps, or passing cars to break up our camouflage and expose us. His cock bobbed up and down, moving as he swayed his hips, maneuvering the hard shaft, keeping it near my asshole.

"I'm going to rape you, Ned," he told me. "Come on, little bro, it's not like you never had anything up your ass before."

I gasped. He had used one of the words that triggered both ambivalence and desire in me. Rape. Did I want to be raped? If I wanted it, was it rape? What if I didn't want it when it began, but did want it when it ended? Lust began to tinge my fear, like two watercolors mingled in the same brushstroke. His cock was slippery. Had he managed to spread some lubricant on himself? I wouldn't have been surprised; he was still fully clothed, in his leather jacket, fly open. Only his cock was naked, while I was bare-assed, stripped, tied, and spread wide.

He used the tips of his fingers to push the head of his dick down, where it would find an opening. He moved forward. I moaned when the cockhead grazed my hole. "See?" he whispered huskily. "You do like it. Why shouldn't I fuck you, Ned? Everybody else is, aren't they?"

"No!" I replied, even though it was a lie. I couldn't count the number of men I'd bent over for or crouched above, hoping the frantic motions of their cocks would erase my misery.

"Got you," he said when the head of his dick made it past the first sphincter. I twisted, trying to break away, but he held me fast. His hard thighs made contact with the bruises on my ass, and I opened to the pain and opened to his cock. He sailed forward, then grunted as he hit bottom. I was plugged. Breath raspy. It's a sensation you can never quite remember when you're jacking off, and even a dildo in your butt doesn't replicate it. It wasn't just his size, although that was nothing to take lightly. It's the man's presence behind the cock that moves me so much, the feeling of his need inside me, his intention to possess me.

"Oh, Joshua," I said, longing to touch his face, his arms. Strain to embrace him and strain to escape made every muscle in my body pop out. He fondled me, especially my tits, reminding me that he could elicit whimpers and pleading when he twisted and tugged my nipples. He kept his cock hard yet barely moved inside of me. I think we both enjoyed prolonging that moment of first contact, the break-in. But he finally had to threaten to take his thick rod away from me, make me cry to think it would be gone, convince me he was going to let me go, then plunge back in, laughing at my resistance and surrender.

He leaned forward and put his face close to mine. "We're tamping the dirt down, Ned," he said, his cock stirring my ass and heating it. "I'm going to fuck the shit out of you. All of it. We're going to leave it right here."

And that is what he did. I have no idea how long he tormented me. It seemed to last for hours. I raged, I screamed, I cried, and I laughed hysterically. Through it all his cock kept him connected to me, abided with me, schooled and tended me. Was this how the man possessed by evil spirits felt when Jesus chased them all away? For years I had run away from my feelings. Now there was no way that I could escape them, no matter how terrible they were. And Joshua didn't care if it hurt me. In fact, that was what kept him hard. He loved healing me because it meant he got to put his hand inside the torn and bloody places and explore them as much as he pleased. I had no idea why anybody would want to know that much about me. But he did, and I clung to him mentally, since I could not use my poor numb hands to reach him, and he did not leave me.

I felt light enough to lay my heart on the scales of the afterworld, with a feather resting in the other pan. The house of my existence was empty but clean. I told my brother so. I thanked him with eloquent incoherence. He grinned, or was he biting his lips?

I hissed, "No!" when he backed away from me, and left me empty and himself unsatisfied. But he was not finished with me or with the shadowy trench in his own psyche.

Joshua lifted his weight from my body, flipped me over, and untied my hands. I could barely feel my fingers, and I knew I would have a ligature mark around my neck that would be hard to hide from airport security. The perfect cock, a cock I had grown up with, a cock I had envied as a small boy and now coveted, edged back into my body and then swayed confidently within me. How could I have forgotten its length and circumference, the fact that his cock got so much bigger at its base, how the huge knot of his cockhead compressed my prostate, the kinks and eventual smoothing-out of my own passageway?

There was no more teasing. We fucked as hard and fast as we could without losing the bridge of flesh between us. Joshua seemed to swell inside of me, and I knew my ass was raw, and didn't care. I would trade the integrity of my skin for Joshua's release. This tall, blond man, stranger/brother and witness to my ruin, had made me as untroubled and insubstantial as the air. I would die to make him fly with me. So I reached for him with my words, binding him to me as he had merged with me. "Please take me," I said at last, exhausted but happier than mortals should be. "It's all I can give you, Joshua. But you've got it. All that I am. All that I ever was."

"And all that you ever shall be," he said through gritted teeth, and made those small quick motions that sometimes herald a fountain of jizz. "Come on his face," Joshua urged me. "Shoot all over the dirty bastard. Make him take your load."

The indecency of it was inspiring, but I had waited so long to come, it was hard to bring myself off. The urgency of Joshua's thrusts had me facedown on the unrooted grass of my father's grave. I knew a smothering moment of terror as those green shoots brushed against my face. I expected something evil and insubstantial to come out of the ground and enter me, pollute and occupy me, dethrone me from control over my own flesh and blood. But all I could sense was the quiet decency of earthworms and beetles. There was no one here but two brothers, master and slave, equals and survivors. We had nothing but each other and the precious moment that was about to pass forever, the moment of our union.

Impatient with my delayed spurt, if only because it meant he had to delay his own climax, Joshua finally spit in his own hand, wrapped it around my cock, and made me shoot with just a few expert strokes. "Take that," he whispered as the white jets left my body. "Drown in it. Lick it up. Tell me you like it!" After all the cum we had milked out of one another, I don't know how much cream he had left in his balls, but his orgasm was a long one. I took his load with my head bowed, honored to be soiled by it, wishing it could go on forever.

Some moments passed that I can't remember. Eventually I realized I was no longer in Joshua's embrace. I was panting from the huge energy drain that follows coming. I felt like I could fall down on the ground and sleep right there. But Joshua still needed me. He was beside me, on his knees, bent over, pounding the grass. "Tell me you like it!" he shouted. "Tell me!"

This was no time to crawl around in the dark, patting the ground to locate my underwear. I found my pants and a shirt and yanked them on. I went to Joshua, knelt beside him, and put my hand on his shoulder. "There's nobody here but me," I whispered. Then my voice got more confident. "Us. But I'll tell you how much I like it." I leaned over to nuzzle the blond whiskers on his cheeks. "I'll always be here to tell you I love it. And you."

Then I led him away.

The Mustang had a full tank of gas. We would need every mile we could wring out of it.

TEN APOLOGIES
WAYNE COURTOIS

Nothing is easier than getting lost in a strange city. It might begin with a view from above, through a break in the clouds: unfriendly towers nestled in a loop of highways. From there it takes you down to the ground, carries you through an unfamiliar airport along with the black carry-on bag that is your only anchor to the life you've known. Outside, the street smells of burnt rubber and exotic sweat. You haven't traveled that far, but you might as well be in a foreign country, or on another planet.

The cab will take you to the appointed corner, you don't have to worry about that. Yet the ride is disturbingly long; you sit for what seems like many miles, staring through the abused back window at block after block, each one identical to the last. How does anyone find anything here?

Long before the cab finally pulled to the curb, Drake was wishing he'd bought a street map. Confusion set in as soon as he wedged himself into the noontime crowd, all of them wearing sunglasses, all with sweat rings under their arms. He had memorized directions to the bar where he was supposed to meet Nick — *Have him drop you off at the corner of Main and Somerset, walk west on Somerset three blocks* — but which direction was west? In Manhattan you could align yourself with the compass pretty easily: walking toward downtown, you were going south. Heading toward midtown, you were going north. It was about the only logical thing about New York, but at least it helped.

Probably he could buy a street map at any newsstand or fruit market, but he resisted the impulse and let himself drift with the crowd. There was a hypnotic quality to the sea of bobbing heads, all of them facing away from him, focusing forward, never turning right or left. He couldn't recall feeling this mesmerized at home, as thick as the crowds were there, because he always had some personal agenda urging him along. Now his agenda would be partly, or mostly, or totally that of someone he had not yet met face-to-face.

Before he knew it he had walked several blocks, without seeing the sandwich board with Jack's Bar written in script. He had to turn around, but it would be so much easier to keep drifting in this direction...what if he just kept on drifting? How many possibilities lay ahead?

When he got tired of musing, tired and hot, he turned around. It took twenty minutes to retrace his steps to Main and go three blocks beyond that, where he finally found Jack's Bar. It looked like a throwback to the seventies, with potted ferns hanging in the windows, and from the outside it seemed very crowded. Drake spent several more minutes on the sidewalk, fighting with himself over whether to go in.

Why did Nick specifically tell him to get dropped off on the corner?

Because that way, no cab driver could testify that he had been dropped off at Jack's Bar.

And why meet at such a crowded place?

Because he would be less noticed in a crowded place. Less likely to be remembered.

He almost turned back. He could easily put this episode behind him, lose any risk of getting in over his head, take the next flight back home. Then someone pulled open the bar door, and the air-conditioned draft ruffled his hair, teased the collar of his shirt. Suddenly he had never been so aware of his own body, the body that had always told him what to do. He took out a handkerchief and wiped his sweaty forehead, felt the unbearably hot sidewalk through his sneakers. He pushed through the door.

It was a straight place, with men and women paired up evenly along the bar. Tables toward the back. Drake headed in that direction, aware that a few of the men, straight or not, were giving him the eye. It always happened. They would notice his physique first, then his deep blue eyes, then the faint dimple in his chin. There was a small gap between his two front teeth—nothing disfiguring, it charmed the hell out of guys when he smiled. He usually took it in stride, but right now he was damned grateful for the attention. He shouldn't have felt that he wouldn't be noticed.

Nick sat alone at a corner table. Drake placed him by his ex-Marine build and graying crewcut. Dark eyes. Drake had seen those eyes before, in the faces of certain boys and men, appearing out of nowhere, fixing him with The Look—a look that said *I know how ticklish you are.*

The two men nodded to each other, and Drake took a seat, setting his small canvas bag on the floor. It contained a change of clothes, his personal care items, and the magazine with Nick's ad, its bold headline circled: MASTER SEEKS TICKLISH SLAVE.

The ad would be a clue, if the bag was found and Drake was not. Is that why he had brought it? Clues would be scarce. He had taken an indefinite leave from work, just for this trip, and had not told anyone exactly where he was going.

The first words out of Nick's mouth were, "You're late," followed by a small, tight-lipped smile.

Before Drake knew it he was stammering.

"I...I'm sorry. I d-didn't..."

"I'm sorry, *Sir.*"

Now he was tongue-tied. The voice like a bark, the smile tight. Here was a master of discipline, the real thing, the absolutely real, fucking terrifying thing.

"Ha!" Nick smiled for real, his face opened up; he leaned back in his chair and became a friendly guy who liked to have fun. Just like that. "You should have seen your face."

Drake passed his hand over his forehead, wiping away his dark thoughts, and managed a smile himself. "I'm sorry. I think maybe the heat has gotten to me a little."

"Well, relax. Have a beer."

"Thanks, I will." Relieved, he took a deep breath. He was okay, except for his hands, which seemed to be trembling a bit. He placed them on his knees. When his beer came he gulped down half of it, then lowered the mug to find Nick leaning toward him again.

"You're not wearing what I told you to wear," Nick said, with his earlier, tight-lipped smile. "I told you to wear a tank top. Something revealing. And shorts. And sandals on your bare feet."

Drake looked down at his clothes as if he were seeing them for the first time. For some reason he had decided to wear one of his white business shirts, buttoned to the collar, and his brown corduroy jeans and white sneakers. "Sorry," he said, his face reddening. "I just—"

Nick waved a hand. "Ah, forget it. I'm just kidding." He leaned back, his hand resting easy on the back of the chair. But his eyes had that look, and his next words sent a shudder up Drake's spine: "Don't worry, you'll suffer for it later."

Drake took another long drink, if only to avoid looking into Nick's eyes. As much as he had wanted this, had formed fantasies and dreams around it, he was no longer sure he could stay.

Nick seemed to sense his uncertainty, but it didn't stop him from leaning forward and saying, in his deep rumbling voice, "Tell me more about your experiences. The ones that really drove you crazy."

Drake looked around. Already the lunchtime crowd was thinning, they were alone in their corner of the dining room. Maybe if he started talking he would calm down. So he began.

Drake had always been ticklish, always, and from the beginning there were certain boys who could always tell, who would give him The Look. They couldn't wait to get him alone, but most of the time they were satisfied with a few jabs to his ribs, enough to make him giggle. Then there was a cousin he played some tickling games with. But his first taste of real torture was filed in his memory under one name: Rodney Cole.

When Drake was in the sixth grade he was intensely aware of Rodney, a redheaded boy a year or so older. He seemed to be always staring at Drake, and Drake instinctively kept away from him. He would watch from afar, though, as Rodney tickled other boys on the playground, as many as he could grab, quickly rendering them helpless. They tried to struggle but Rodney's greedy fingers made them weak. He would sneak up behind a boy and before the victim knew what was happening Rodney would have his hands inside the boy's shirt, going for his ribs. What happened next, as Drake watched, was always the same: soon the laughing victim would be too weak to stand, sinking to his knees and then flat on the ground. That was when Rodney really had him, because then it was easy to straddle his victim and tickle-torture him from his neck to his waist. Sometimes other boys stood around and watched—it *was* amazing the way Rodney could make kids kick and scream—but no one interfered, because they were all afraid of Rodney and his strong, sure hands.

Watching these tickle attacks always gave Drake strange sensations. He wanted to get closer, to see better, to hear the voices of the victims shrink to a hoarse whisper begging Rodney to stop. Then one day Drake did get closer, hiding behind some bushes as Rodney tickle-attacked a younger boy named Charlie who was spread out on the asphalt right by the school's front door. There was no one else around, classes were over, and everyone else had gone home. It was fall, and Drake was surprised to see that the victim was shirtless. Then he realized that Rodney must have stripped off Charlie's shirt; it was lying on the ground nearby. Where did Rodney get such nerve? Maybe the ticklishness of this particular kid egged him on, for Drake had never seen a victim react like this, screaming and screaming until he completely lost his voice, his face a mask of hysteria, tears streaming from the corners of his eyes. *This is what I've been missing,* Drake thought, *because I never got this close before.* In spite of Charlie's struggles he was no match for Rodney, who was bigger and so quick with his hands and fingers. When he touched— whenever he *threatened* to touch Charlie's bare belly or ribs or armpits, Charlie would desperately struggle, but it was no use.

Drake leaned forward, closer, his fingers digging among the leaves of the bush to get a better view. *He's tickling this kid to death.* Drake's own breath was coming quickly, as if he'd been running, and he had a strange sensation between his legs. The very thought of tickling tended to make him tingle all over, and make his penis get hard. The quickening of breath, the excitement he felt now, was more intense than ever before.

Then Rodney did something Drake had never seen him do. He stopped tickling Charlie's bare torso and turned around, awkwardly, on his knees, still straddling his victim but facing his feet. The poor tickled boy was gasping for breath, so weak that he couldn't struggle, couldn't even lift his hands off the ground as Rodney unlaced his sneakers. When his socks came off too, Charlie raised his head with a great effort and croaked, "Oh, *no!* Don't tickle my feet!"

Drake's breath came even more quickly now. He knew of very brief foot-tickling scenes in movies and TV shows, but he had never witnessed the kind of fierce, prolonged foot tickling that he anticipated now. As the victim's pale, naked feet began to wriggle in Rodney's hands, Drake felt he might faint.

Charlie's feet were, if possible, even more ticklish than his belly and ribs and armpits. The boy croaked out shouts of laughter, his arms waving feebly as he tried to twist from side to side to escape Rodney's fingers. Sometimes Rodney would tickle one foot with two hands, his fingers moving so fast they were a blur, and sometimes he'd tickle both feet at once, never missing his targets no matter how they wriggled. Now he was taking one foot, bending the toes back with one hand and tickling the sole with the other, sending fresh spasms through Charlie, who had again lost his voice completely and could only gasp. *It's only a matter of time*, Drake thought. *Nobody could stand to get tickled that much. The kid's gonna die or go crazy.*

And it did seem like a *long* time before Rodney finally took a break from tickling Charlie. His legs were probably cramped from kneeling so he moved, from straddling Charlie to sitting by his side. This was Charlie's chance to escape, but he was too weak to try. He lay completely still except for his head moving a little, his chest expanding as he drew in deep agonized breaths. His skin had many marks left from the pressure and friction of Rodney's fingers. His ribs had been tickled so much that each one was outlined in red. Rodney sat and studied his victim, sometimes reaching out a finger to prod a rib or the side of his belly, raising few more exhausted giggles. And for the first time since the tickling began, Rodney spoke to Charlie.

"You know what I think?" he asked. "I think you could be a slave. I think I could make you do whatever I want, 'cause if you don't I can tickle you to death." He shook his head. "You think I just tickled you? That was *nothing*. How'd you like to get tickled for a whole *day*?"

Charlie tried to speak, but couldn't. When he opened his mouth only a few gasps came out. Rodney poked him again, and again and again, in his poor abused ribs, and the gasps came more quickly.

"Maybe I'll tickle you some more," Rodney said. "You can't do anything about it. Maybe I need to get back to these feet."

Now Charlie's eyes opened wide in terror, and he managed to croak again, "No...no...don't tickle my feet!"

"Oh shut up, I'm not even touching you yet." But Rodney was getting ready to, he was once again facing Charlie's feet. Drake leaned forward. His penis was stiff, and it hurt when he leaned forward, but he had to get as close as he could to see the kid get tickled again. Unfortunately Drake leaned a bit too far, lost his balance, and fell against the bush, making a loud rustling sound.

Rodney Cole looked up.

For a second Drake and Rodney stared at each other.

"Hey, you," Rodney growled.

That was all Drake needed to hear. He ran, taking to the overgrown field behind the school, nearly tripping several times over the dense undergrowth but never stopping, for he could hear Rodney's footsteps crashing behind him. He ran faster than he ever had before, pushing through milkweed and goldenrod, his breath coming fast and hard. Finally he had to stop, when he had no more breath. The thought of what might happen if Rodney caught him made him dizzy.

But Rodney didn't catch Drake. He gave up and went back to the ticklish victim he had left behind, who still had a long afternoon of torment to endure.

Drake could hardly sleep that night, worrying that Rodney would be out to get him now. Drake had spied on him, which was a bad thing to do. Rodney would want to punish him for it. There was only one kind of punishment Rodney gave out, and when Drake tried to picture his own ticklish body at the mercy of Rodney's fingers, it made his breath come hard and fast, and his penis stiffened again. He was terrified and excited in a way he'd never been before.

The few kids who walked to school often used the field as a shortcut. The grass and weeds were high, but over the years some footpaths had been trampled out. Walking down one of these paths the following morning, Drake felt uneasy. As the path twisted through the brush it was sometimes difficult to see more than a few feet ahead or behind. A couple of times he stopped to listen, but the sounds he heard seemed to come from birds or small animals; they weren't footsteps, after all.

He made it to school all right, but all day he worried, frightened and excited, because Rodney might try to get him after school. Because they were in different grades, Drake wouldn't see Rodney until recess, and up till then he tried to convince himself that maybe his nemesis had skipped school. But at recess Drake caught a glimpse of him. Rodney was standing across the playground, near the edge of the field. Drake stood right by the school entrance, near the steps; he didn't dare go far away. But when Rodney turned his head Drake knew, even from that distance, that his worst fears were going to come true. Rodney was giving him The Look.

There wasn't a lot of foot traffic through the field after school, because most of the kids lived farther away and took the bus or rode with their parents. Drake hoped he would catch up with somebody, though—maybe several kids he knew, offering safety in numbers. As luck would have it, though, he was alone as he entered the footpath and didn't see or hear anyone else around. He tried to breathe normally, tried not to think about Rodney's fingers. He tried to keep even the *word* "tickle" out of his thoughts. But the more he tried not to think about...getting tickled, the more nervous he got, and the word multiplied in his mind: *tickle, tickled, tickling, ticklish...Please don't tickle me. I'm too ticklish. Stop tickling me! Stop!*

Drake walked faster. He couldn't escape his thoughts, and with every step he took he was aware of his hardening penis. After a while he stopped, for he had been so preoccupied he hadn't kept track of his surroundings, hadn't been listening for treacherous footsteps. He tried to slow his breathing down so he could hear better.

Was that a noise behind him?

In a second it was gone. Probably an animal. He was in that part of the field, though, where he couldn't see very far ahead or behind. He took a step, still listening.

That sound again. A footstep?

Drake kept walking. With every step he took there was a noise behind him. Was it footsteps or not? If only he could be sure! But whenever he stopped walking, all other sounds stopped too. *Maybe it's okay,* he thought. *Maybe it's a friend behind me.* But he could not force himself to retrace his steps, to see exactly who else might be on the path. So he started walking again—slowly, then a little faster, then faster still. He could *swear* that, whatever noise that was behind him, it sped up whenever he did. Terrified, he started running.

And there were running footsteps behind him.

Hunh Hunh Hunh. Drake was panting as he ran across the field with someone right behind him but he *didn't dare* look. If he could just keep going for a couple of minutes, he'd be home free.

Then he stopped.

It wasn't the sound of footsteps that had stopped him, but a voice. A growling voice.

"Hey, you."

Drake had to turn around.

Rodney had The Look in his green eyes. It chilled Drake through and through.

"Sorry, pal," Rodney said, pushing up his sleeves as he approached, "but you're gonna get it. There's no way out of it."

Drake stumbled backwards. He tried to sound brave. "What are you talking about?"

Rodney shrugged. "Nothing much. You're just gonna get tickled, that's all. You're not scared of getting tickled, are you?"

Drake could barely speak, it was as if he had something caught in his throat. Finally he managed to say, "No...'course not. I'm not ticklish." Did he look as scared as he felt?

"I wish you hadn't said that. Now you'll have to eat it." With that, Rodney, who was suddenly very close, pushed Drake so that he stumbled once more, then sat down hard on the ground. Before Drake knew what was happening, Rodney had grabbed his long-sleeved T-shirt and was pulling it off over his head. Drake was surprised, as surprised as Charlie must have been, by the feeling of cool air on his bare skin. And he was shaking, not from the coolness but from fear. This couldn't be happening. He *knew* it couldn't be happening. It was like he was watching somebody else, some other kid being handled by Rodney like a toy, dragged over to the edge of the path, back against one of the few trees that stood in the center of the field, his arms pulled straight up, then his wrists tied together with a long piece of twine Rodney pulled from his pocket. He tied the other end of the twine to a branch, so that Drake was sitting on the ground with his bound hands above his head, completely exposed, his legs straight out in front of him. Rodney knelt at Drake's feet, and Drake sensed the strength and agility of the older boy's fingers right through the canvas of his sneakers as Rodney began to unlace them. If he was trembling with fear before he was quaking now. His cousin had briefly tickled his ribs and armpits, but *no one* had ever tickled his feet. And he knew his feet were ticklish, knew it every time he put socks on and the cloth sliding across his sensitive soles took his breath away. He couldn't walk barefoot through grass because it tickled so much, and even his mother's living room carpet made his bare soles tingle. So by the time Rodney had removed both sneakers and socks, Drake was whimpering. "It's not fair."

Rodney pulled another length of twine from his pocket. "What's 'not fair,' crybaby?" He wrapped the twine around Drake's ankles, tying them together.

Drake shivered with fear. "You didn't tie Charlie up."

Rodney snickered. "Shows how much you know," he said. "I tied him up, all right. I took him and tied him up at my house. In the garage, where nobody could hear him."

"That's kidnapping!"

Rodney snickered again, wiped his nose on his sleeve. "It was just a game. Poor kid didn't think so, though."

Drake felt faint again. "What...what happened to him?"

"Well." Rodney shook his head sadly. "You notice he wasn't at school today. He ended up in the hospital, poor kid."

For a moment a kind of sparkling darkness passed across Drake's vision, and he thought he might pass out. When he could see again Rodney was crawling toward him on all fours, then getting up on his knees, raising his hands, his fingers wiggling ferociously. He grinned like a demon.

"*Now!*"

When Drake first felt Rodney's fingers touch his sides, he screamed. It was a scream of pure fear, he couldn't feel anything else yet. But right on the heels of that fear came...*the tickling*...and oh God, Rodney's hands didn't care *what* they did, they were all over him like wild animals, squeezing his ribs, prodding his armpits, poking his belly...moving so fast that each finger's attack was a surprise, and Drake, laughing hysterically, could only watch Rodney's face through watering eyes. It was the face of evil.

Now Drake was screaming, filling the air with screams, filling the sky, until everyone in the world must hear him being tickled to death. When Rodney finally stopped Drake's body went slack, as slack as it could with his hands still tied over his head. He took in a bushel of air and let it out, feeling his lungs move against his mauled ribs.

He sensed dimly, with tears and sensations clouding his vision, that Rodney was no longer leaning over him. Oh, thank God! But he didn't have to look far to see where Rodney had gone.

He was down at Drake's feet.

Before he knew what he was doing Drake was talking, his voice so hoarse it was little more than a croak. "Hey, Rodney? Don't tickle my feet, okay? Look, I'll do anything you want." He struggled against the twine binding his wrists and ankles. "I'll even help you tickle other kids. I mean it. We could do it together, we could be a team..."

Rodney looked at Drake, looked him in the eye, but his smile was not promising. "Sounds like you think your feet are ticklish."

"No!" Drake almost screamed again. "No, no, they're not! So don't touch them, okay? Please, Rodney, don't, okay?" Drake twisted to his right and left as far as he could, but it was no use, he could barely move at all. He looked up to the sky and saw, as clearly as if it was written across the blue, that he was lost. There was no use begging, or promising, there was *nothing* he could do. His body went slack again, and to his surprise a sound came out of his mouth. It was a giggle.

"What's that?" Rodney asked. "You think this is funny?"

He still hadn't touched Drake's feet, but he was *so* close...Drake giggled again, he couldn't help it. Fear itself was tickling him. "Please, Rodney, don't..."

"You *do* think this is funny!" With that Rodney drew his fingernail right up the center of a bare helpless sole.

Drake's whole body convulsed, and he was giggling again, so fast he could hardly breathe. "Please...ha ha...don't...oh ho ho...n-n-no, Rodney...aha ha ha..."

"Well, since you think this is so damn *funny*, I guess I'd better get to work."

"No! Hahahaha *stop*...!"

And Rodney did work on Drake's sensitive feet as he screamed with laughter again, his voice high-pitched, hysterical. Rodney explored and tormented the soles of those feet, then the tops, then the toes and the spaces between the toes. Just when it seemed like Drake couldn't possibly laugh or scream any more, Rodney would find a new ticklish spot and lovingly torture it with his fingertips and nails. He finally stopped only when he had to shake out his hands and stretch his fingers. Drake still croaked out hysterical cries and laughter.

"C'mon, I'm not touching you right now," Rodney said.

Drake couldn't help it, he *couldn't* calm down, not *ever*.

Rodney got up and stretched his legs. "There's one thing I forgot to tell you," he said.

Drake gulped air, tried hard to control his breath, but it was as if his body no longer belonged to him, he couldn't tell it what to do.

"I forgot to tell you," Rodney said, "that there was soccer practice this afternoon, and it should be getting over right about now."

Drake wasn't looking at Rodney, he was looking at his poor tormented feet. He could swear they were still being tickled, that the air itself was tickling them. As for what Rodney was saying...what did soccer practice have to do with anything?

"Some of the guys will be walking home," Rodney said. "They should be cutting through here any second now."

"Guh...guh..." He could only croak now. He was trying to say, *Good! They'll help me! They'll cut me loose!*

"I told the guys that we'd be here," Rodney said. "They sounded real interested."

They'll kick your butt, Rodney! You won't be tickling kids to death anymore!

"I told them," Rodney said, "that I was pretty sure you were ticklish."

Slowly it dawned on Drake what Rodney really meant. "No..."

"Oh, yeah." Rodney got to his feet, dusted off the knees of his jeans. "I think I hear them coming now."

"No!" Drake couldn't hear much over his own breathing. But he tried to hold his breath and listen, even though his lungs still ached for air.

And there *was* someone coming. Footsteps...more than one set of footsteps kicking through the brush, stomping toward the path.

And voices. Deep voices. Older boys, older than Rodney.

Drake tried to roll from side to side. "Let me go, Rodney. Come on."

In another second they broke through onto the path. Three high-school freshmen, still wearing their red shorts and white T-shirts from soccer practice.

"Hey!" one of them said. He had hairy legs, and the beginnings of a mustache. "What have we here?"

"Looks like Rodney's been up to his old tricks." This second boy, shorter with blond hair, had an evil grin.

"Oh, yeah!" This was the darkest boy, the hairiest boy, his chest hair curling up around the collar of his T-shirt. He rubbed his hands together. "Looks like kind of a *ticklish* situation!"

The boys laughed as if that was the funniest thing they'd ever heard, and Rodney laughed too. "He's all warmed up for you," he said.

"Yeah, we can *see* that."

Drake wondered what they meant, but when he tried to move, to squirm around, he knew. His dick had gotten hard, and as his brown corduroys slid down a bit it was even more obvious. There was a little tent where his lap should be.

"How big is a sixth-grader's dick, anyway?" the hairiest boy asked.

"Gets bigger when he's tickled, I bet," the blond one said.

Drake kicked, or tried to. "Leave me alone!"

The boys came closer...and closer. They were laughing, mocking him, *Awww, leave me alone!* He watched in horror they stood right above him.

"Please," he said.

Awww, please! Pretty please!

And then they were on him.

The three soccer players tickled Drake's belly, sides, ribs and armpits, while Rodney tickled his feet. Drake laughed, screamed, and cried. He couldn't struggle with eight greedy hands on him, each of them working to drive him crazy. And though he stayed aware, agonizingly aware of the punishment inflicted on his ticklish body, the wild sensations filling his head made him wonder, after a while, if all of this was really happening or if it was some kind of dream. It had better be a dream, or else he might not survive. With so many strong hands driving at him his body just might break in half. But even if it did...even if his body broke in half, and then into more pieces, his tormentors would just keep tickling—tickling the pieces into more and more pieces, until they had tickled him to dust.

In his specially equipped torture chamber, Nick had Drake tied to a St. Andrew's cross. He was naked, except for a leather cockring and ball stretcher, and there was a ball gag in his mouth. His body glistened with sweat, for Nick had been tickling him for about two hours. Neither man had been able to keep track of the time; to Drake it was more like two hundred hours, while Nick, in a trance, felt they had just got started on a long, long journey.

After a brief pause Nick began again, digging his strong fingers into Drake's sides as he screamed helplessly. When he could organize a thought, when it was possible to put one word after another in his mind, it always came out the same: *He's tickling me to death!* His heart was pounding so, he couldn't last much longer. Would he even have the strength to beg when Nick removed the gag for "begging time," as he had done twice already? *Please, Nick, no more, I can't take it, you're killing me, oh God, stop. I'll do what you want, you can fuck me, I'll suck your dick, anything, oh God, oh please, stop. Take my wallet, my credit cards, keep my clothes, throw me out on the street naked, anything! I'll be your slave for the rest of my life I swear to God...*

And at that point Nick said, "You're right there. You *will* be my slave for the rest of your life...which might not be long."

During his next lucid moment, Drake wondered why he had to endure the ball gag. As Nick had promised, his loft was in a building that stood off by itself in an old warehouse district; no one could hear Drake laugh, scream, and beg for mercy. Then he realized that the gag was just part of his torment, making him feel more helpless.

He wondered, too, at his body's capacity to take punishment. How come it didn't shut down, why didn't he get *numb* after a while? How much could his nerve-ends take? If his body could last this long, it would no doubt outlast his mind, which was swimming, fading in and not-quite-out of consciousness. As Nick attacked his insanely ticklish armpits, Drake even thought, as he twisted his head toward a far corner of the room, that there was someone else there...someone he recognized, though he couldn't at first put a name to the figure that stepped forth from the shadows. It was a young guy...just a kid, though big for his age. He had red hair and green eyes, a striped polo shirt.

It was Rodney Cole.

Oh God, I'm going insane!

Rodney looked around, not knowing where he was. If he saw Drake, he gave no sign. Drake struggled but could not move an inch, couldn't make a sound except for the hoarse screaming stifled by the ball gag.

Rodney! he thought.

To his surprise Rodney looked at him, his eyes narrowing. Surely he recognized Drake, even after all these years; he knew what was happening, could *see* what Nick was doing to him.

Rodney, help me! He's tickling me to death!

Rodney came closer. He looked from Drake to Nick's trancelike expression and quick strong hands, then back to Drake again.

Rodney...!

Rodney could hear him, he knew it. He could hear his thoughts! *Rodney, I'm begging you, make him stop...!*

Rodney came closer, till he was nearly touching Nick's shoulder. His eyes were dreamlike as he shook his head sadly at Drake.

"I'm sorry, Drake," he said. "I'm really sorry. But I can't stop him from tickling you."

Why, why, why?

"I can't help it, Drake," Rodney said. "I love watching him do it. I love it too much. I can't make it stop."

Nick obviously did not hear the visitor's voice, or see him as he turned around to reach for one of his tools, a powerful vibrator with a rotating head of firm but feather-like bristles. Drake's eyes widened. *Oh no...not my balls...not again!*

It was true, the head was approaching his tautly stretched balls, and Rodney was doing nothing to help him!

But wait...over in the corner, where Rodney had first appeared... someone else now stepped forth. And another, and another.

The three freshmen soccer players who had helped Rodney tickle Drake on that afternoon so long ago. Like Rodney, they hadn't aged, and they still wore their red shorts and white T-shirts.

You guys, help me! He's tickling me to death!

At first, like Rodney, they didn't seem to know where they were. But they soon focused on Drake. Their mouths were open as they stood there, staring.

Help me, you guys!

One after another the three boys shook their heads.

"I'm sorry," said the one with the brown eyes.

"Yeah, I'm sorry too," said the blond, not bothering to hide his cruel smile.

"Me too," said the hairiest one. "We're sorry we can't stop him. But we love it too much. We have to watch...and watch!"

Where did you guys come from? Are you real?

Rodney shook his head sadly. "Not real enough."

By the time Drake was sixteen and a junior in high school, he was certain of one thing: he was gay. He had grown, filled out in more ways than one, with hairy balls and a dick that hung low, and he was horny a hundred percent of the time.

His teachers had him pegged as a daydreamer, but at least his daydreams were practical. Rather than worry about how he had become a fag, or fretting about what would happen when he grew older, he focused instead on one immediate concern: as much as he handled his own hard cock—he was probably the secret jackoff champ of the world—*when* and *how* was he going to get his hands on somebody else's? He had never touched another guy, not in a sexual way, but he wanted to so badly it made his fingers ache as well as his balls.

At night he lay in bed with an old gym towel clenched by his side, summoning up thoughts that made the sheets rise and his dick start leaking. (He always put out a lot of what he would later learn to call precum.) He often pictured that afternoon in the field with Rodney and the soccer players. What had filled him with shame at the time, when they had finally left him alone and he had struggled to make it home in his weakened state, was that the older boys had opened his fly to expose his little hard dick, making fun of it while they were tickling him. It was too humiliating to think about—until recently. Nowadays, as Drake teased out images and feelings from the assault, he kept seeing those older boys and how excited they had been, their shorts stretched out in front of them till they looked ready to burst. Swollen crotches had bobbed and weaved above Drake as those bastards kept changing positions, each of them making sure he got a chance to tickle every inch of Drake from his neck to his waist. Their hairy hands had darted in and out of sight, their hairy legs had brushed against him ceaselessly; and as their shorts stretched and twisted some more Drake had glimpsed the taut white pouches of their jockstraps.

The least those guys could have done was haul out their cocks and jack off all over me. It hadn't happened, but alone in his bed Drake pictured the sight, both his imagination and his right hand working overtime till the gym towel was soaked and he was exhausted.

So, okay, he was obsessed with getting his hands on what lay behind those jockstraps. The one place he was sure it would *not* happen was the high school locker room, which he had to visit three times a week, for gym class. The room itself wasn't much to look at—it was just the basement downstairs from the gym, with rough concrete walls and no illumination except for bare bulbs hanging overhead—but the view was spectacular: the naked bodies of other perpetually horny teenaged boys. Drake tried to be very, very careful not to look at them. When that became difficult, he started the habit of getting to gym class early enough to change up and be on the gym floor before the others even arrived. That left him with the problem of dealing with the locker room after class, when the boys all showered; he handled that by dashing in and out of the shower room, practicing his quick-change act, and beating feet to his next class.

Most of the time, in gym, the rest of the boys played basketball or volleyball while Drake worked out with the free weights. It was unusual to be excused from team sports so often, but Coach Doyle—a big, burly man who always had a five o'clock shadow—took a special interest in Drake. He often watched closely as Drake did his presses, and Drake was pleased to show that he had good form and was building up strength. He tried not to smile, though, or say much during gym class. He *especially* didn't want to reveal himself to Coach Doyle, who tended to wear very tight shorts. Another attractive bulge, not to mention hairy legs.

Everything was fine until Marshall Carter came along. A new boy

OUT OF CONTROL

whose family had just moved to the small town, Marshall was assigned to the same gym class. Drake got the shock of his life when he arrived at the gym one day, early as usual, and bustled down the stairs. This time he wasn't the first to arrive, for Marshall Carter was already there, standing stark naked in the middle of the locker room floor. "Hi!" he said, grinning at Drake and extending his hand. "Just call me Carter, everybody does."

Drake almost swooned. He had noticed this new boy around school, and had overheard some of the boys on the basketball team admitting — grudgingly, in mumbles and mutters — that Carter had the biggest cock any of them had ever seen. Not only that, but while some of the dark-haired boys were hairy all over, Carter was the first blond boy Drake had seen with great amounts of body hair. It covered Carter's arms, chest, belly, and legs, and it *glowed* in the light, under the naked bulbs that hung from the ceiling. He was tall, too, and broad-shouldered, his chest and abs well defined.

And that cock...Jesus God. It was long and smooth with a slight curve, and reminded Drake of nothing so much as the giant slide at the amusement park. He was ready to buy a ticket and climb on.

He was also scared to death. "I—I can't stay," he said, and ran for the stairs. As he pounded across the gym floor toward the exit, he realized he was skipping gym class for the first time ever.

After spring vacation Drake's schedule changed. Gym was now the last class of the day, three times a week. He was never in a hurry to leave school at the end of the day, not looking forward much to the walk home that took nearly an hour. So after gym class he didn't rush to get dressed the way he used to. He didn't have to worry about getting a boner in front of the other guys, for they were the ones who rushed like hell now, eager to get out of school. Now Drake was often the *last* boy out of the locker room, instead of the first.

Then came an afternoon when Drake was running even later than usual. Coach Doyle had kept him after class a little bit to show him some stretches that would help keep his muscles from aching. In these warm days of spring Drake was so horny he couldn't stand himself, and it didn't help to have the coach, in his famous tight green shorts, standing so close to him. It was a relief to head for the stairs. Maybe he *would* rush today, jumping in and out of the shower so he could get home, take out his jack-off towel and get it soaking wet.

His plan didn't quite work out. The shower felt good, the strong jets of water massaging his muscles, and he stood under it for a long time. He had his eyes closed, the water playing on the back of his neck. Then the shower next to his came on and he nearly jumped. He looked over and there was Carter, of all people! Grinning at him as he soaped up

190

his chest.

"Hi!" he said.

Drake quickly turned off his shower and grabbed his towel from the hook on the wall. Instead of drying off at the shower-room exit, where he would be seen, he went back into the empty locker room to towel down, all the time thinking: Why was it that Carter was also here late? He'd left the gym class with the other guys...

"Hey, how you doing?"

Drake spun around, dropping his towel. There was Carter, dripping wet, grinning at him.

"Oh, hi." Drake bent over and picked up his towel. He would finish drying himself and get dressed in record time.

Carter was toweling down too, but he didn't face his locker while he did it, he just stood there facing Drake. "Hey," he said, and Drake noted, for the first time, Carter's rich, deep voice. "I seen you working out with the weights."

"Yeah," Drake said, sitting on the wooden bench so he could dry his feet. "The coach lets me do that."

"Keeps you in great shape, huh?"

Drake looked up at Carter. There he stood, wincing as he dried the inside of his ear, not even covering himself with the towel. He was the single sexiest guy Drake had ever seen in person. He wanted to stick to his plan, to dress and get the hell out of there, but he couldn't help looking, just for a few seconds. As Carter used the towel on his chest, arms and legs, his body hair grew resplendent again. His beautiful cock swayed back and forth.

"Hey, you know what?" Carter took a seat on the bench, with about two feet separating him and Drake. "There's something I've always wanted to know about you muscular guys."

Drake was suddenly aware of himself, sitting there with his mouth open. He looked away, fumbled with the combination lock on his locker. "I'm not any more muscular than you are."

"Are you kidding? You've got a build some guys would die for." Carter slid down the bench, a little closer, a little more. "Anyway, I was wondering...are you *ticklish?*"

Drake turned around in sheer surprise, and Carter took the chance to reach out and tickle his armpits. "Oh, don't," Drake gasped, as Carter's fingers, thrilling and agonizing, moved down to his ribs. "Don't tickle me...!"

"Oh, yeah," Carter said, grinning. "You're ticklish, all right."

Drake squirmed, desperate to get away. He couldn't stand it, if he were tickled for *one more second* he would start laughing helplessly.

But Carter's fingers kept up with Drake's efforts to escape, they dug into his ribs even harder.

"I can't take it...!" Drake's voice rose in pitch and he broke into laughter, nearly hysterical. To be *tickled* by a sexy guy like this! Drake was struggling, not only to escape from Carter's tickling fingers, but to keep his groin hidden. He was growing a hard-on and was desperate to keep it out of Carter's sight.

"Kitch-kitchy!" Carter was incredibly quick, darting his fingers along Drake's ribs and sides, down toward his waist.

It was unbearable. He had no choice but to swing one leg over the bench in an effort to get away. When he did, his huge prick swung in the air between them.

Carter stopped, but only for a second. He licked his lips. "Someone's getting excited." His hands took up where they left off, darting all over Drake's incredibly ticklish torso. By now Drake was begging, whenever he could get a word out: "Please stop...oh, no...oh God..."

Carter dug his hands into Drake's armpits. Weakened by laughter, Drake felt himself falling...falling till his back hit the wooden bench. Now Carter was above him, straddling the bench, still tickling, tickling Drake on his belly and ribcage and underarms. Drake was helpless, he tried pushing Carter's arms away but it was no use. There was Carter's grinning face...and there, farther down, was Carter's enormous hard dick nearly touching his own.

"What are you boys doing!"

Trapped as he was, Drake couldn't look around, but he knew the voice of Coach Doyle.

Carter jumped back, his heavy dick swinging to the left and right.

Drake wanted to jump too, to cover himself, but he hadn't recovered from the tickling. For now he could only lie where he was, giggling softly as his nervous system very slowly calmed down.

"Oh, I get it," Coach Doyle said, his voice closer now. "You've got a live one, huh, Carter?"

Drake was not thinking clearly, but he *had* to get up, try to escape. He struggled to sit, and was nearly upright when he got the shock of his life. Coach Doyle had grabbed his wrists and pulled his arms upward.

So far Carter had not said a word to the coach. He had not even tried to cover himself. And instead of retreating he was straddling the bench again, reaching out for Drake...the coach held on to Drake's wrists, pulling them up, totally exposing Drake's vulnerable belly, sides, ribs, and armpits. "Oh, God!" Drake hadn't experienced anything like this since Rodney Cole had tied his hands over his head. Soon he was shouting hysterical laughter, no longer caring that his hard dick rode high on his belly as Carter tickled and tickled him.

It didn't help that the coach was now coaching. "Get his ribs, Carter!" he cried, tightening his grip.

Carter worked his way up from Drake's ribcage to his underarms, those deep pits now stretched wide. Drake heaved and bounced on the wooden bench as Carter attacked those pits. Through tears he could see Carter's evilly grinning face, and when he tipped his head back he could see the coach's face also, with the same evil smile.

"Hey, I've got an idea," Carter said. He stood up, and his dick was standing up too, harder than before, nearly touching his belly. But instead of coming closer he turned away, facing the foot of the bench.

Oh, no, not the *feet*...Drake wanted to beg for mercy, but he was too busy catching his breath.

"That's it, Carter!" The coach's low, deep voice was filled with urgency. "Let me see you tickle those feet!"

It was simple, so simple for Carter to trap Drake's ankles in an armlock and begin to explore those bare ticklish soles.

"Oh, no...don't do that...please don't...I can't stand it..."

Pleading not only didn't help, it actually encouraged his tormentors. Yet Drake couldn't stop begging, his life was at stake. How much at stake he very quickly learned as Drake raked his fingernails up and down those trapped soles. Drake threw his head back and roared. It was full-throated, panic-stricken laugher, completely hysterical. He swayed back and forth in ticklish agony.

Finally he managed to squirm completely off the bench, his butt hitting the cold cement floor. Carter lost his grip, and the awful foot tickling was over. But the coach tightened his grip on Drake's wrists, and now Carter was on him as he lay back on the floor, more vulnerable than ever. Carter tickled Drake where he knew he was most ticklish, but there were other ticklish spots to find, ones that Drake had never thought of. Carter tickled Drake's belly and abs, then reached farther down to tickle his groin, fingers working busily in the pubic hair on either side of his huge boner. Drake couldn't *believe* what was happening. And that wasn't all: Carter's fingers explored more, tickling, tickling till they were on Drake's sensitive balls.

"That's it! Get those balls, Carter! Work 'em!"

Drake's balls were large, low hangers, and Carter got them, tickling them, tickling under them and between Drake's legs, as Drake howled and bounced helplessly on the floor, each move he made only exposing him more to Carter's searching hands. Carter was even able to reach partly under Drake so his tickling fingers found Drake's asshole. The surprise of it made Drake lift his knees, unintentionally inviting a full assault.

"Tickle that asshole! Come on!"

That was how the tickling went, all in between Drake's legs from his asshole to his balls and back. Through a haze of delirium Drake was learning what it was like to surrender the secret parts of his body to the pleasure and amusement of men.

After what seemed like hours, the coach finally released Drake's wrists, and his aching arms fell to the floor. He lay there panting.

The coach looked at Carter, who was kneeling on the floor, his cock fully erect, and then at Drake. He shook his head in wonder. "Jesus, you're hung like horses, both of you." He took a few hesitating steps toward the stairs. "All right, I'll let you boys finish this by yourselves."

Drake lay on the locker room floor in a post-tickling trance, helpless as a baby, his body seeking to recover from a million jolts and violations, his mind not yet reconnected to reality. He moaned, he tossed his head from side to side as if he were still being tickled, and in fact he could still feel Carter's merciless fingers. He wasn't surprised when he opened his eyes and there Carter stood, watching him, taking in the indisputable fact of their two huge, aching erections. Even the *coach* had said they were both hung like horses.

There was something different about Carter, it took Drake a few seconds to focus on what it was: Carter was holding out his hands and they were shiny, even in the dim light of the locker room. He had put something on them, they looked wet and greasy. Drake thrust his hips upward, or rather they thrust themselves, his need was so great. He was going to *die very soon* if Carter didn't touch his cock, and before he knew it he was begging, breathlessly pleading as he had done when Carter was tickling him: "Please, Carter...touch me...take my cock, take it in your hands...jack it, jack me, jack me off..."

When Carter's fingers finally closed over that hard-on that had been throbbing for so long, Drake felt he might pass out. His body moved through no conscious will, writhing, thrusting as Carter pumped his cock with both slippery hands. Drake watched his cock being worked on and he wanted it to last, it felt so good and looked so hot, but he was too excited and knew that in a few more thrusts he would come. So he braced himself for the explosion that sent great jets of cum into the air and all over his belly and chest. He didn't know it was possible to come so hard and so long, he was gasping for breath again as he pumped out still more cum that flowed over Carter's hands.

Carter stood up, his own great hard cock rising into the air again. He touched himself, lathering Drake's cum all over his huge red dick, another sight unlike anything Drake had even imagined. His body acted again with a will of his own, propelling Drake up onto his knees. He reached out for that cock and began pumping it with both hands. It was the first time he had touched another cock, and it was even better than he'd imagined: the cock huge and rock-hard and yet still somewhat pliable; the thin, slick flesh pulsing between his fingers, first the shaft and then the head, then back again, slowly, and again and again. Drake rolled the fat dickhead between his palms like a Boy Scout trying to start a fire, while Carter moaned and cursed aloud, it felt so good. Then

Drake went back to stroking, pulling, yanking on that shaft that he didn't take his eyes off for a second. And when Carter came, great spurts of cum splattering across Drake's face like warm gravy, Drake was laughing—not from tickling this time but from sheer joy. He laughed and laughed as he pumped Carter completely dry.

After that long afternoon in the locker room, Drake had wondered if Carter would be willing to fool around again sometime—like the very next day, if possible. But fate had other plans. Carter didn't spend much time on any one boy; he wanted to tickle as many guys as possible. He methodically moved through the junior class until he had had every single sexy ticklish guy. No one really spoke about it, but there was an understanding among them that they all knew what it was like to "stay after school with Carter." Drake never heard any mention of the coach in these mutterings and mumblings.

At the end of that school year, Carter and his family left town as quickly as they had come. They moved to California, someone said. Drake was left horny and adrift, not picking up any vibes from other boys that they might be interested in tickling him to death.

Nick kept Drake tied up in different positions throughout the day and night so that his muscles wouldn't get too sore. He put skin lotion on his slave so he wouldn't be tickled raw, and gave him throat spray so his throat wouldn't get sore from laughing and screaming—though over the past several days Drake's voice had shrunk to a croak and he didn't know if he'd ever speak normally again. When it was mealtime Nick released him from the St. Andrew's cross or the rack or the stocks or the chair, hooked a leash onto the dog collar and led Drake on all fours to the kitchen area of the loft. Drake's food bowl would have something like crumbled hamburger in it, and he would eat greedily till the end of mealtime. The end of mealtime was always the same: Nick would sneak up behind Drake with a feather, an enormous white plume, and without warning plunge the feather between Drake's legs. He would tickle his tender inner thighs; his cock, kept perpetually hard by a leather cock ring; those balls, stretched for tickling; and that asshole, which was even more feather-sensitive than those balls. Before long Drake would collapse in a giggling heap. "Oh don't," he would croak finally, "don't tickle my asshole anymore, please..."

The feather didn't stop for a second. "What did you say, slave? What was that you said?"

"Oh...I said...I said, 'Please tickle my asshole, Sir. Tickle it all you want, then tickle my balls some more.'"

"I *thought* that was what you said. Well, you'll be begging me more before I'm through—begging to get back on the rack again, just to get away from this feather."

Sometimes Drake heard these remarks, sometimes he didn't. He was in the zone, where he spent most of the time these days. He was a tickle slave, taking more punishment than was humanly possible and repeatedly forced to beg for more. Nick muttered and sometimes shouted his threats and demands, and Drake either croaked a response or said nothing; but this was not the real world, not anymore. The real world was a world of pure feeling, often agonizing, always horrifying. In the real world all of Drake's ticklish nerve-ends spoke to him, it was their voices sometimes bubbling up in his throat, croaking out screams of laughter and begging and pleading. Those poor ribs, those poor arm-pits, those poor, supersensitive feet—they cried out desperately as Drake watched, both victim and observer, wondering what in the hell could happen next.

He was only mildly surprised when Marshall Carter appeared—or Marshall's ghost, or spirit, or whatever these apparitions were that could step out from the shadows of the torture chamber at any time.

Carter was still a well-endowed seventeen-year-old, naked and resplendent in the sun coming through the skylight, illuminating the golden hair on his arms and legs and chest. And his dick, that beautiful, hard dick that Drake had once taken between his trembling hands, still swung heavy through the air. "Carter!" Drake said. "I thought you were in California."

Carter laughed. "Man, I've been all over the world by now. I joined the Navy right out of high school, and I've tickled guys in more countries than you ever heard of!"

"You still look like you're seventeen."

"To you I always will be."

"Well, look what's happening now," Drake said, shaking his head, involved and yet not involved as Nick's cruel fingers tickled his bare torso, stretched to the limit on Nick's rack. "This guy is tickling me to death, you know?"

"I know, I've been watching. Look, Drake, I'm sorry, I'd stop him if I could, but I can't. I'm just a spirit, to begin with, and then...I love watching him work you over. I want him to keep going and going and never stop. Sorry, man."

Drake just shook his head. It didn't matter. His life was not in his own hands anymore: it was in the hands of a tickling maniac, and the odds of his surviving just one more day weren't too good. "It's just my fate," he said, barely able to hear his own words over the sound of Drake, the other Drake, screaming on the rack. "Listen to that. I'll be even more hoarse than usual by tonight."

Carter stared at the rack where Drake was stretched out, his ribs showing in sharp relief. Nick was playing those ribs like percussion instruments as Drake screamed and screamed again. Carter wiped his mouth with the back of his hand. His hard cock seemed to have gotten even bigger. There were tears in his eyes as he said, "Man, I wish I could tickle you. I wish I could tickle a big load of hot cum out of you."

Then another voice came out of the shadows. "Me too," it said. "Hell yeah, me too."

Drake strained to see. "Coach *Doyle*?"

It was the coach, all right—as burly as ever in his tight green shorts, naked to the waist, a silver whistle gleaming from the center of his hairy chest. "Listen, Drake, I'm sorry too. I helped Carter tickle a lot of boys in that locker room after school. It was a shameful thing to do. Afterwards, they were all too scared to tell anybody. So I kept on doing it. I couldn't help it. You were all so damn ticklish, and so young and strong...you bucked like horses. I'm retired now, and I'll never see a sight like that again."

"Well, look, Coach," Drake said, "here's your chance to do a good turn. Just get Nick to stop tickling me. Please."

The coach shook his head. "No way. I'm just like Carter, I love to watch. It's taking my breath away, seeing what he's doing to you." He leaned closer to Drake to make his final pronouncement: "You better pray, Drake. Pray that Nick lets you go." Like Carter, the coach also had glazed eyes by now, and had to wipe his mouth. "And while you're at it, son, pray, pray to the Lord God Almighty that I never get my hands on you."

In 1979 Drake was living in New York. He had a bachelor's degree in journalism, an entry-level job in corporate communications at a major bank, and a tenement apartment in the East Village. But mostly what he had was sex. Sex was everywhere—in the bathhouses, the bookstores, the porno theaters, and parks. He had sex with more men, in more places, and in more different ways than he'd ever thought possible. And whenever he began to worry that he might be a sex addict, some sizzling piece of male flesh would catch his eye and he would be off, following gladly wherever his dick led him.

It led him one night to a porno theater on Third Avenue. He skipped the film and headed directly downstairs to the back rooms, craving the kind of anonymous sex that could only happen in pitch dark, with nothing but the occasional flash of a cigarette lighter to show what—and who—he was doing.

In the first room, there were waist-high benches along two walls where guys tended to pair off. The other walls were bare except for the men leaning against them, sometimes packed pretty close together. The place smelled of smoke and dirt and cum and poppers. It was earthy, it was hot. Drake walked the length of the room letting his hand brush against one taut denim-covered basket after another. *Flash* went a lighter, a cigarette glowed, a pair of brown eyes sized him up. Drake moved on, feeling the occasional hand against his own crotch. Later on there would be more naked bodies than clothed; he knew enough to leave his wallet at home.

The second, larger room was just as dark. There were a pair of fake jail cells in the far corner, for guys who were into that kind of fantasy. Drake didn't intend to make it that far. He stopped, feeling up crotches, and as two guys moved in on him he was so hard he thought he'd burst the buttons on his Levi's 501s. An open mouth covered his, he tasted tongue and hot breath. A pair of hands worked at those buttons. Near the center of the room was a raised, carpeted platform where a guy could stretch out and get worked over. Drake moved slowly toward the platform, never losing contact with the hands that were groping him. In no time his jeans were around his ankles — he wasn't wearing underwear — and he stripped off his T-shirt, letting it fall somewhere near his feet. He lay down, letting the raised back of the platform support him, and spread his knees. His long, hard dick was ready for contact and it wasn't disappointed; one hand gently stroked the shaft while another caressed his balls, and he was sure they were two hands from two different men. Again the hungry mouth, a tongue lapping the back of his throat, and now there were hands on his hairy pecs, sliding down along his sides. When a hot mouth closed over his cock he gave a shout, it felt so good. There were still hands on his chest, roughing up his nipples, and that pair of hands caressing his sides — how many men were doing him? Three? Four? In the dark it was easy to lose count of hands and mouths and cocks. He reached out and found a hard one, began stroking it. Another nudged his left hand, and he grabbed that one too. There were at least four pairs of hands and as many mouths moving over him. The air was filled with hard breathing, moans, and soft, satisfied curses.

More hands moved in, more cocks. One gently pried at his lips and he took it in, thrilling at the feel of the dickhead against his palate. His own dick was slick with saliva and precum, and he didn't know how much more handling and sucking it could take before he'd shoot. The cock in his mouth couldn't take much teasing at all, a sudden hard thrust and hot cum coated his tongue, dribbled down his chin. If his hands were free he would have caught the last drop and licked it from his fingers. But none of him was free, his hands were full of cock and there were hot impatient hands on his arms and shoulders and chest and belly...

But what was *this*? Something different...those fingers moving across his abs. That wasn't unusual, guys were all the time feeling his abs, worshipping them...but this time the fingers were...more than touching, they were...*tickling*. Oh God, he couldn't stand it! Any second he was going to burst out laughing. He squirmed as much as all those hands would allow, praying the maddening sensation would stop. Of course it would, no one was tickling him on purpose, it was just that he was *so* ticklish...

But the tickling didn't stop. Helplessly he slid down farther on the bench, and felt a sudden rush of heat to his groin as he realized he hadn't been tickled in a long, long time. The last guy who had really tickled him to death was Marshall Carter, in high school. Now *that* was a memory to make the rush of heat to his groin even more intense, and before he knew it he let a giggle escape his lips. Could it even be heard above the groaning and moaning and sucking all around him? He squirmed some more, giggled a little louder...he couldn't help it, the fingers were digging in harder.

"What was that?"

"Hey, he's *ticklish!*"

"Where?"

"Poke him *here...*"

"Hey, yeah!"

More fingers moved in, mercilessly probing his abs and sides. He squirmed, he let go of the hard cocks he'd been pumping, but it did him no good: strong hands grabbed his wrists and pulled his arms up, just as Coach Doyle had done so long ago. "No, no," he cried, already nearly breathless with laughter, "don't tickle me, don't!" His legs were pinned down too, there were bodies pressing in on him from all sides. He'd never survive if they *all* started tickling him...But just as on that long ago day in the locker room, or long before that, when Rodney Cole and the three soccer players had tortured him, he didn't have any choice. Before long he couldn't speak, couldn't plead anymore, all he could do was laugh. As scared as he was of laughing, of letting them know just how ticklish he was, he threw his head back and roared hysterically as all those hands attacked his abs and sides, ribs and armpits.

Maybe it was the darkness—not being able to see his attackers—but he was more ticklish now than he'd ever been in his life. He screamed with laughter as fingers clawed into his armpits and knuckles mashed his ribs. The screams only brought him more punishment: a finger found its way into his navel and twisted and drilled into his guts. His groin was now the property of at least twenty fingers, and his balls were being twiddled like mad. More hands made mincemeat of his inner thighs. No part of him was safe, not even the ticklish spots behind his knees.

It was only a matter of time—insane time, tickled-to-death time— before they lifted up his feet and he felt, along with everything else, greedy fingers working at the laces of his sneakers. The sneakers were pulled free, his socks nearly torn off, and his jeans were gone altogether.

OUT OF CONTROL

Oh Jesus, don't tickle my feet! He tried to say it, but his words were broken up by laughter, hysterical laughter that became more hoarse and yet more high-pitched as fingers attacked his soles and toes and the tops of his feet. Soon each breath he managed to take escaped as a high keening wail, and they kept on tickling him.

Then he heard it again—the same deep, rasping voice that had said, "Hey, he's *ticklish!*" and then, "Poke him here." The voice and the hot breath that came with it was right in his ear, and this time it was saying, "Tell me what they're doing to you."

Was he serious? Drake couldn't believe it. All he could do was laugh, and if he was able to get a word out here and there, it was to beg for the tickling to stop. Now this guy wanted him to *talk*. Drake shook his head, his mouth stretched wide with hilarious laughter.

"If you don't talk," the raspy voice said, "then you get *this*."

Now Drake felt something he had truly never felt before, as two fingers—two thumbs, more likely—stabbed deep into his exposed armpits. They were like pile drivers, and the jolt made his entire body stiffen and tore loose a yell from deep down in his throat. All Drake could think, when he recovered enough to form a coherent thought, was that he now knew what electroshock treatment must feel like.

"Talk to me," the voice rasped again, "or you get the *thumbs*."

"Oh...Jesus...please *don't*." It took every effort of will just to get those words out, with so many hands tickling him.

"What are they doing to you?" the voice rasped.

"Oh...God...tickling...my *feet*...!"

"Yeah? What else?"

Some generous guys had been free with their pocket lube, and Drake's groin was now all slicked up. They were slicking up his abs as well, giving a new, *slippery* feel to the tickling that had Drake sputtering helplessly; he was no more capable of forming words than an infant.

"What else? What *else*? Tell me, or you're going to *get* it..."

Again the thumbs drilled into his armpits, and again the jolt was so bad that Drake thought his spine would crack.

So he was trained to narrate what they were doing to him, struggling to get out the words as he also laughed and screamed and begged and panted.

"Tickling my...*balls*! And...oh shit...aahhhh, sticking their fingers in...my bellybutton! Hah, hah, hah, can't...*stand it*...OH my ribs, tickling my ribs, Jesus Christ...oh fuck, they've got my thighs...and...*what*? What are they doing to me...?"

They were moving him, adjusting him, lifting his legs. He was their helpless toy, they could bend and flex him however they wanted and he was too weak to defend himself. Lifting and spreading his legs....

"What are they doing to you, *what*?"

"Jesus *fuck...oh no...*tickling my *asshole!*"

Slippery fingers, dozens of them, teased and prodded his asshole, stretching, exploring, poking...there was no way he could speak now, his cries were reduced to a pathetic wailing as they twiddled his anus, palped his scrotum, squeezed his thighs, violated his navel...and there was still the same steady tickling of his feet, sides, and ribs.

He knew, insofar as he was capable of knowing anything, that it would also come again, the *jolt* of thumbs screwing powerfully into his armpits...and so it *did*...

And Drake woke, as if from a dream. But the tickling wasn't a dream. He knew it was real, still happening, might be happening *forever*. He could hear the high-pitched wailing of his voice, broken by fits of panting. And yet he was distanced from it now. He looked around, and instead of his tormentors he saw only darkness.

He remembered how, as a kid, he would go swimming in the lake at night, plunging deep under the water, into absolute dark. He felt that way now, suspended, weightless, unable to see anything but his own luminous skin. And all around him, below, beside, in front, and behind him, there were little fish. Little invisible fish, all nibbling at his flesh.

He felt no sense of panic. He could breathe, even here, deep under water; and he would survive. He could let the fish do what they wanted, nibble till there was nothing left of him, as long as he remembered to breathe.

When he surfaced again, his cock was harder than it had ever been, leaking precum all over his belly, which slickened his ticklish skin even more, intensifying his torment. He was so weakened by the tickling that he didn't know if he could escape even if they did let him go; but his sexual response was stronger than ever, and when someone grabbed his cock he yelled, his hips thrusting upward all by themselves. One hand pumped his shaft, a mouth closed over his dickhead, and...yes, someone was *licking* his balls now, and more greedy mouths were licking his soles and sucking his toes...

He could no longer separate the sensations, the sucking and jacking and tickling, the licking and poking and stroking. His body had become one nerve that was being stretched to the breaking point. And just when he felt that he really *would* break, his groin began to heave, his cock shook, and he came, filling one hot sucking mouth and then continuing to shoot. Every one of his tormentors slurped from his cock as if it were a drinking fountain. "Yeah!" they were crying, over and over. "Yeah, yeah, *yeah!*"

He didn't know he could shoot that big a load. His balls had been turned inside out. As the hands and mouths gradually withdrew, he panted and moaned and offered whispered prayers and curses to the dark. Though he lay perfectly still he felt he was falling, tumbling down and backwards, headed toward inescapable fate.

It wasn't over. Far from it. Collective male lust was a force of nature swirling through the humid, dusty air, rocking the floor, shaking the walls. A hand raised his head, shoved a bottle under his nose. It wasn't his bottle of Rush, it was genuine amyl, and it took the top of his head off.

A familiar raspy voice spoke in his ear: "Wake up! Some new guys have come in, and they're dying to meet you!"

It was three o'clock in the morning, and Drake was sitting on the floor outside the back rooms, leaning against the wall by the men's room door. He had found his jeans and his sneakers, but his socks and T-shirt were lost. Well, he had had to go home shirtless before, he didn't mind as long as it was warm outside. But it would take him a while yet to fully recover. His eyes were red and swollen from tears of laughter, his throat felt raw, his ribs were sore, the soles of his feet tingled, and his cock, balls, and asshole were almost unbearably tender. Every minute or two his spine gave a shudder, and a weak, hysterical giggle escaped his lips, as if they were all tickling him still. Guys walked past him, leaving him in peace but still eyeing him hungrily and muttering to each other about what had happened in the farthest dark room.

"Never saw a guy get that kind of treatment ..."

"Did you see how ticklish his feet were? Jesus!"

"Never saw a guy come like that, either. Fuckin' *puddles* on the floor!"

Drake tilted his head back against the wall, sighed, shuddered, and gave in to a few seconds of soft helpless laughter. When he opened his eyes again he found he was being cruised. A man leaned against the wall opposite him, a ruggedly handsome older man with a beard, an open shirt and a hairy chest. Under any other circumstances Drake would be interested, but for now he could only smile and shake his head ruefully: *thanks, but no thanks.* Still the man stayed where he was, openly studying Drake as though he were an anatomical chart. Drake tried to think of something to say, something not too unfriendly that would make it clear he wanted to be left alone. Before he could think of anything the other man spoke.

"How are you feeling?"

Somehow it was no surprise to hear that deep, raspy voice again... the voice of a tormentor. "Y-you," Drake stammered, "you were the one...that made me talk to you..."

"Ha! I did more than that. I *started* the whole thing!" The man's brown eyes gleamed, teeth showed white above his black beard. "You were great."

Drake pressed back against the wall. He felt naked under that gaze.

At the same time his cock, which had so recently been wrung dry several times, began to stiffen. The two looked at each other for a very long time until Drake finally said, "Wh-what do you want?"

The man stepped forward, drawing a card from his hip pocket. It was the size of a business card, but it was a personal card, with the name Emmett D'Arcy and an address in the West Village.

"Just look me up," he said. "When you're ready."

A few weeks later Drake showed up at Emmett's apartment. It was on the eleventh floor of a high-rise off Eighth Street, more than a few notches above Drake's funky East Village tenement. As he nodded to the doorman and announced himself, and as the doorman called Emmett's number, Drake found himself wondering if Emmett had hot-and-cold-running men at his place. In which case Drake had already been marked as a trick. Normally confident, he wondered why that should bother him this time. His finger actually shook as he pressed the elevator button. His phone call to Emmett had been brief, Emmett saying only, "Be here at eight." No mention of tickling. But as Drake began his ascent, startled by his own reflection in the elevator's mirrored wall, he knew full well what he was doing: for the first time ever he was deliberately stepping into a situation where he could get tickled to death.

And it didn't take long, once they were seated on Emmett's white sofa, once they had had a drink of scotch. All of a sudden Emmett lunged, and Drake, who had been sitting half-turned toward him, was easily caught off balance. He gave a shout, and then Emmett's hands were everywhere, not only tickling but undressing him at the same time, so that before he knew it he was buck naked on the white carpet, screaming with laughter and begging for Emmett to stop.

It didn't take long, either, for Drake to discover that Emmett was also ticklish, and that he could freely take revenge on his tormentor. It was a new experience for Drake to tickle a man to feverish exhaustion. Recalling how Emmett had drilled his thumbs into his armpits, Drake learned the technique also, saw how he could make Emmett's body go limp, his eyes roll upward, his jaw slacken as he panted deliriously. He also learned how to make Emmett scream by applying the bristles of a hairbrush to his lower back.

They spent a year testing each other's limits, mostly on weekends. Sometimes they would stay in Emmett's apartment from Friday evening through Sunday night, naked the whole time, ordering in Chinese food when hunger overtook their desire to play. They grappled and stumbled and rolled through every room, from one end of the apartment to the other. Drake tickled Emmett's ribs on the dining room table while Emmett's feet kicked over half-empty cartons of Kung Pao Chicken and Beef Broccoli. In the kitchen, Emmett learned which gourmet utensils worked best on Drake's feet. When they tired of all the other places, they tumbled into Emmett's extra large bathtub and literally tickled the piss out of each other.

The joys of bondage soon followed. Drake suggested it first, remembering how Rodney Cole had tied his wrists and ankles. Emmett balked, till Drake reminded him of how, in that back room in the basement of the porno theater, he had been as good as bound, kept immobile by many strong hands. Emmett owed it to him to at least give it a try. And so their mutual torture reached another level, and another and another, as they learned the most ingenious ways of rendering each other helpless and vulnerable. The bondage naturally led to role-play — the interrogator and the spy, the leatherman and the delivery boy, the older brother (Emmett) making his younger brother suffer for telling a secret.

The sex that they had, jacking or sucking each other off, was great, but it was the tickling that they took to greater and greater extremes, till there was nothing they would not do to each other to slake their thirst for stimulation. On a Monday morning Drake would move trancelike through his day at the bank, where he was now an Assistant Vice President, his head filled with images of the night before — how, for example, he had hung by his wrists from Emmett's ceiling, naked and gagged and blindfolded, while a vibrating butt plug threatened to split his ass open and Emmett tickled his dickhead with a felt-tip pen in one hand and a camel's-hair brush in the other. This was Emmett's favorite game, and he could spend hours at it. With the felt-tip pen he wrote multivolume novels on Drake's knob; with the brush he recreated an impressionist's entire life's work, paying special attention to the piss-slit and rim of that German helmet.

Though he always craved being tickled, no matter how excruciating it was, Drake also couldn't get enough of tickling Emmett. He saw their relationship stretch on for many years to come, as they found more and more outrageous ways to violate each other's ticklish skin. Strange as it was, he also felt he was in a relationship that many men could only dream about.

Then, one night, it was over.

The two of them were having dinner in a restaurant on Second Avenue near Twelfth Street. It was something of an upscale restaurant — for that neighborhood, anyway — with modern decor, lots of pastel colors and intimate lighting, and it had become one of their favorites. It was to be a typical Friday night, Drake filled with relief that the work week was over, and looking forward to releasing his tension through screams of laughter.

But everything changed when Emmett leaned over the table, nearly upsetting his wine, to say, "I've got something to tell you."

"Okay." Drake was glad to listen.

"I'm leaving New York."

Drake looked Emmett in the eyes. After a few seconds he realized he was holding his breath. Forcing himself to relax, he asked, "You mean, you're going on a trip?"

"No. Not a round trip, anyway." Emmett seemed to be receding, part of him shutting down, leaving Drake alone already. "As you know, I've been very unhappy."

No, Drake had not known that Emmett had been unhappy. How could he have known? They never really talked about anything but bondage and tickling. And that, according to Emmett, that was part of the problem. Who were they kidding—they didn't really have a "relationship" at all, there was nothing between them beyond the physical. Well, Drake wondered, what was wrong with that, as long as they were both enjoying it so much? It wasn't just that, Emmett explained. He had grown tired of living in New York, period. So he had arranged with the head office of his corporation for a transfer to the West Coast. It would be a step up for him. A great opportunity, a chance to start over.

Drake just stared at Emmett—at this hot sexy guy who had made so many of his fantasies come true, who had helped him discover new fantasies, new intensities of feeling. He had been staring openmouthed at Emmett for so long that his throat was dry; he took a sip of white wine, but it tasted bitter now. "You mean, it's over between us?"

Looking back, he would see how stupid that must have sounded. Of course it was over, had been over for some time, Emmett had just been going through the motions. And Drake, who had been so busy being tickled into a hundred different states of consciousness, had never noticed.

He folded his napkin, placed it beside his plate, got up, and left the restaurant. He would never go there again, though he would pass by the place many times and feel a chill each time he saw its name. The place was called Tempus Fugit.

He wanted to see Emmett at least one more time before his departure, but it was no use. Emmett wouldn't even talk on the phone. Finally Drake was so desperate that he sneaked into Emmett's building, taking advantage of a shift change at the front desk, and made it to the elevator and up to Emmett's floor. But something had gone wrong. Either Emmett had had to leave earlier than expected, or had given Drake the wrong date in the first place; the apartment was empty, the door was open and the white carpeting which Drake had known so well was being cleaned. Drake backed down the hallway, turned when he heard a door opening behind him. The neighboring apartment had been owned by a gay couple, whose raised eyebrows and knowing smiles Drake had encountered many times: apparently some of the sounds issuing from Emmett's apartment weren't lost on them. But they no longer lived there either, and the man who opened the door to pick up a small package on the mat looked unfamiliar. For a split second that didn't matter to Drake, he was *so close* to just walking up to this disheveled-looking stranger in a blue bathrobe and asking, *Hey, will you tickle me?* He saw it happening in his mind, saw how easy it would be. He would take his shirt off in the hallway, clasp his hands behind his head, expose his ribs and armpits. *Go ahead. Make me feel it. Give me a rush. Go crazy.* He actually took a few steps in that direction until the man, package in hand, frowned at him, then shut the door.

I'm lost, Drake thought. *I'm lost, I'm lost.*

"So that's my story."

Drake had calmed down a bit while telling Nick about his "tickling life," even if Nick's stare from across the table had made him a little self-conscious. Now he was relieved to stop talking for a while. The waiter set a fresh beer in front of him.

"Very interesting," Nick said. "That's not the whole story, though. You've been active since then."

"Yeah, that's true. I've met a number of guys through the ads. Had some wild times." Just the thought of some of the things he had been through sent a shiver up his spine. "I think I've got nine lives, like a cat. And yet...I keep looking for something more prolonged. More intense."

"Ever since Emmett you've been strictly a bottom?"

"That's right. I can't really say why. It's just..." Drake shrugged. "I just *really want it.* Even though I can't stand it."

"Sounds good to me," Nick said. He pulled some bills from his wallet, threw them on the table. He nodded toward the small canvas bag by Drake's chair. "Is that all you brought with you?"

"That's it."

"Well, you won't need many clothes. In fact, you won't need any."

Most of Nick's walls were covered with his paintings, and they made an instant impression on Drake as he stepped into the huge studio. All of the paintings were of men—specifically, naked male torsos. No heads, no arms, just a multitude of well-developed chests and abs in all sizes and colors. There was nothing conventional about them, though. They were torsos caught in motion, twisting and stretching, muscles strained to the limit. It didn't take Drake long to realize that they represented the bodies of men under torture. As he stared, openmouthed, Nick laughed.

"I've got a freshly stretched canvas with your name on it," he said.

They moved on to where, Drake was told, he would be staying. It was a room partitioned off from the rest of the loft, but still a huge room, with a skylight that brilliantly illuminated its furnishings: various tables, platforms and racks, a half dozen St. Andrew's crosses tilting toward the floor at different angles, a chair that might have come from a dentist's office. One wall was perforated with hooks that held every kind of restraining device.

"Everything but a bed," Drake said.

"Oh, you won't need one of those. You'll be much too busy."

There was a bed, though, or at least a cot, in what Nick called the "recovery room." One of the few rooms in the loft with its own four walls and ceiling, it had originally been a large darkroom, back when Nick had gone through a phase of sketching and painting from photographs. (By now, he explained to Drake, he always worked from memory, having become a genius at memorizing a man's body, right down to the number of hairs on each nipple.) When Nick had redone the darkroom as the recovery room he had installed a cot and added a toilet, sink, and shower—complete slave quarters.

After the brief tour they returned to the torture chamber, where Nick's first order to Drake was to strip naked. "And make it fast! We got a lot of work to do!"

Drake thought, *I'll never get out of here alive.*

Drake was in the recovery room when another man from his past appeared: Emmett D'Arcy.

"Well," Drake whispered, "I thought I'd never see you again."

"Why would you think that?" Like Carter, Emmett was also naked. "I've never stopped thinking about you."

"Huh!" Drake turned his head to the side. He may have slept for a while, or maybe not. When he looked up again Emmett was still there. "So what do you want?"

"I just want to say that I'm sorry." Emmett stepped forward gingerly, as if the floor were cold on his bare feet. "I'm sorry I left when I did."

"You went to California, just like Carter. I see a pattern here." Drake tried to turn over onto his side, but his ribs were sore; he tried lying on his belly, but his belly was too ticklish now; it couldn't take contact with anything, not even a sheet. So he rolled over onto his back again.

"I've missed you, though," Emmett said. "In particular I've missed your laughing, screaming, and begging. I still fantasize about tickling you to death."

Drake chuckled again. "Well, your fantasy's coming true, only it's not your fantasy anymore, it's Nick's."

Emmett came closer. His cock was painfully erect, begging to be touched. "That guy is something else. He's a fucking genius."

"Ha! Some genius...I won't last a month in this fucking place."

"Well, you've already been here a month, but I can see where you'd lose all track of time. You've been so...*busy*." With that Emmett wiggled his fingers at Drake, and Drake laughed. His laughter, even his chuckling of a moment before, had a different kind of sound now, at least to him. It sounded just a little...depraved. More than a little crazy. Something like Nick's own laughter.

"I don't suppose," Drake asked, "that you could...get him to stop? Just for a day or so? Let me catch my breath?" He held out his hand, which passed right through Emmett's image.

"Oh, hell, no." Emmett said. "Sorry, Drake, but I'm having such a good time, watching. I like seeing everything Nick does to you, because to tell you the truth, I'd like to tickle you myself right now."

"Greedy spirit," Drake said. "I think you're actually drooling."

Emmett wiped his mouth with the back of his hand. "Believe me, Drake," he said, "if I ever get my hands on you again, I'm never letting go."

Drake was in a kind of elevated sling, on his belly, his wrists and ankles chained together. For the past couple of hours Nick had been tickling his asshole and scrotum. Among many other tools he had some long, delicate wires, extremely supple, that were excellent for this kind of detail work. For the past hour at least Nick had been wearing his hearing protectors; Drake's screaming was even louder than usual.

Finally Nick decided to rest for a minute. He took the earmuffs off. Drake had stopped screaming and was panting heavily.

"You know," Nick said, "I've got a problem."

Drake knew what he had to say. His voice, when he finally found it, was no more than a croak. "Yes, Master? What is it?"

"Well, you see, I've been wanting to tickle you till my heart's content. But even though I've just about tickled the last living drop of shit out of you, my heart's not content. I must have a very big heart, don't you agree?"

With all his strength Drake summoned his voice again. "Yes, Sir."

"What I'm going to do," Nick said, "is invite a couple of friends over. Young guys. Real fucking maniacs. The kind who don't know when to stop, if you know what I mean. Straight guys, but they'll do anything to get their rocks off."

Drake's thin, reedy voice trembled. "Yes, Sir. Whatever you say, Sir."

Raul and Pedro showed up sometime later. It might have been noon, or it might have been the middle of the night. Drake, who was stretched on the rack, wouldn't know. All that Nick had allowed him to know, for at least the past several hours, was the terrain of his own ribs. It was frightening terrain, with peaks and valleys of excruciating tenderness, vulnerable to many, many different kinds of assault. Drake thought, insofar as he was able to think, that he would never make it through this parched land, his ribs were like the rippling sand dunes of the desert, a desert without end.

Then Nick showed mercy, just for a minute. Or maybe he was just answering the door. Suddenly there were other voices in the loft, out in the studio. The visitors were so loud Drake guessed they were drunk, or high, or both. Then again it was hard to tell about voices, his own screaming had impaired his hearing.

"How's it hangin'?"

"Great to see you, man. You look fucking great."

"Where's Juan?" Nick asked. "I haven't seen him lately."

The two newcomers collapsed in a fit of giggles. "Oh yeah...Juan!"

"*Hee-hee-hee*...it's not funny, really, but—*hee hee*..."

"You see, man, Juan, he's in the hospital."

"Christ, you guys didn't break his arms, did you?"

Another laughing fit.

"No, no, man...it's not...*hee hee*..."

"It's not that kind of hospital!"

"Shit," Nick said, "you guys are something else. You mean...?"

"Okay okay okay, so we tickled him a little too much. That's the breaks."

"Yeah. Hey, he'll be okay in a few months. Maybe."

"Well, in the meantime," Nick said, "I've got somebody you guys can practice on."

"Fuck, man, we don't need no practice."

Nick led his visitors into the chamber and turned up the lights. Drake trembled with fear, and with the humiliation of being presented naked to strangers.

"This is Raul," Nick said, "and this over here is Pedro," exactly as if he were introducing buddies at a card game.

"Hey!" Raul said. "Dude looks kind of wasted." Raul looked like the older of the two. His hair was pulled back in a ponytail, his otherwise handsome face bore acne scars, and like his brother he wore a pencil-thin mustache.

"*Muy guapo*. Sexy little fucker," Pedro said. He was the handsomer one, his hair cut short, above the ears, his build a bit broader. And who was Juan? The third brother, probably, the youngest one who always got picked on because he was ticklish. Drake flashed on some of the older brother/younger brother role-plays he used to have with Emmett.

"You've got some new shit since we were here last," Raul said, standing before the rack with the vast selection of toys. "What the hell is this?"

"It's a powerful vibrator," Nick said, "with a special attachment: a rotating brush with feather-like bristles." He swaggered over to the rack, grabbed Drake's tightly stretched balls and raised them up, exposing the supersensitive skin between Drake's scrotum and asshole. "Fire that bad boy up," he said, "and stick it right here. In about five seconds he'll be blubbering like a baby."

"Sounds hot to me." Raul approached with the toy, already vibrating and spinning.

Drake licked his lips and began begging. "Don't touch me, please don't touch me, can't you see what he's been doing, he's been tickling me to death, make him stop, make him *stop*, I'll do anything for you, you can fuck me, fuck me up the ass or in my mouth, fuck me all night long if you want to, I can make you feel good, I can make you come over and over..."

"Jesus Christ, this guy's a talker, ain't he?"

"I love it when he writhes like a whore," Nick said. "That's what I've turned him into, a slave and a whore." He put his face close to Drake's, took his victim's chin in his hand. "I haven't even fucked you yet, I've had too much fun tickling you. I take care of you, though, don't I, slave? When your cock is throbbing and your balls are swollen I give you a good milking, don't I?"

"Yes!" Drake nearly screamed, though it wasn't strictly true: Nick also denied orgasms when he felt like it. "Yes, Master, you're the best milker, you milk me dry! Milk me now, please, milk me all night long if you want to, I can come over and over again..."

"Aw shit, you just don't want to be tickled. Come on, Raul, bring that monster machine over here."

Pedro ran his tongue over his lips. "Maybe we can fuck him later."

When Drake woke up, or was at least aware of his surroundings, he found that he had been moved. He was now chained to a St. Andrew's cross—not a wooden one, but one made from something hard—plastic? fiberglass?—and waterproof. The cross stood in the middle of a huge rubber mat. He took this to mean that they were going to tickle the piss out of him, as Nick had done many times already. But where were Nick and his two friends?

They hadn't gone far. They came from the direction of the kitchen, each carrying a large bowl. Each of them was also naked, which surprised Drake. Pedro and Raul were even sporting leather ball stretchers and cockrings, and by the size of their erections it was clear they were having a good time. Big erections on brown bodies, how Drake had used to love sights like that.

"Hey," Nick said, "the slave's recovered. About fuckin' time. We got work to do."

The bowls were filled with steaming water. On a corner of the mat Drake now saw that three straight razors and three cans of shaving cream had been laid out. Immediately he started babbling again.

"Don't shave me please, don't shave me please, you don't want to do that, why don't you fuck me, fuck me with your big dicks..."

"Blabbermouth is at it again," Raul said. "Let's get started."

"We may as well start with that beard he's grown, it interferes with tickling his neck," Nick said. "Everything else from the neck down comes off. We'll leave that fine mat of hair on his chest, though, for aesthetic reasons."

Raul shrugged. "Fuckin' artist."

Of course it tickled when they applied the shaving cream, and the scraping of the straight razors made him delirious. Soon the cool air on his naked armpits, abs, and groin was tickling him. His balls felt as if they had just been hatched, as tender and vulnerable as baby chicks.

"I can't believe you, Nick," one of the brothers was saying, Drake was too dazed to tell which one. "You should have shaved him long before now, man. Makes a big difference, if you really want to tickle a guy. We used to shave Juan all the time. Didn't we, little brother?"

"I keep telling you, I'm not your fucking *little* brother."

Nick grabbed the water bottle and shoved it at Drake. "Open your mouth. Hydrate."

Drake sucked cool water from the bottle. It felt so good on his parched tongue.

"Take some more," Nick said. "I've got another bottle here. And maybe one more."

"What's with all the water?" Pedro asked.

"I was just thinking," Nick said. "As long as we've got him on the rubber mat, let's oil him up and tickle the piss out of him."

The next time he came to his senses, Drake could tell by the color of the sky through the skylight that it was late afternoon. They had been tickling him for—how long? A night? A day and a night? Drake felt that his body, as smooth and slippery as a newborn's, had been violated in every way.

Gradually he flashed back on some of the things Nick and his friends had done. At one point Nick and Raul were feathering him on his neck and behind his ears. At another point Raul and Pedro were teasing his nipples with tweezers. Oddly enough he had never found his nipples to be very ticklish, but those nipple nips had him babbling again, begging Raul and Pedro to let him suck their dicks, anything to end his torment. That was a mistake, for the two decided to write down everything Drake was saying—writing it on his abs with ballpoint pens. The more they wrote, the more Drake babbled, and the more they wrote, giggling all the time.

Sometimes he managed to escape, to the cool dark waters of the midnight lake. Suspended under the surface, he surrendered to the friendly, unseen fish nibbling away at him. In turn they reminded him to breathe, they helped him remember how.

Now it was feeding time. Nick untied Drake and ordered him to the kitchen area. Drake obeyed, crawling weakly toward the bowl filled with the usual crumbled hamburger meat. The other three men were in the room with him, and as soon as he finished eating the tickling would begin again, so the key was to eat as slowly as possible. If he could make it last...nibbling smaller and smaller amounts...but he was too hungry. He couldn't stop himself from wolfing down his food in just a couple of minutes.

The tickling began as it usually did, with the huge white feather dusting his inner thighs. When he tried to roll away he saw Nick and Raul both had those long, whiplike feathers. No direction was safe, but still he tried to roll, curling himself into as tight a ball as possible. It was like a crazy sports event, with the two torturers batting Drake across the floor with their feathers. It hardly mattered where they touched him, he gave a hysterical yell every time. Finally he collapsed, facedown, belly to the floor, which gave them the opportunity to sweep the feathers all over his back, from his neck to his asscrack, and then down, to the backs of his thighs and knees, the soles of his feet.

As he lay there he heard, through his delirium, someone leaving the room—the no-nonsense sound of Nick's bare feet slapping the floor. Going to take a leak, probably, and why not, Raul was taking care of Drake, wielding both feathers, giving him more than he could handle. But Nick had only left to get a tool, for as soon as he came back he shoved a greased vibrator up Drake's ass. He recognized the feel of it very well: it was the kind with a dog-leg crook in it, designed to stimulate the prostate to the max. Nick cranked it up, and Drake's dick began to stiffen. The vibrator did it every time, but Nick knew another technique too: tickling Drake's lower ribs, just the lower ones, always made him spring a boner. So he straddled Drake and dug in. The combination of vibrator and rib tickling had his slave moaning and howling at the same time. When it got too painful to lie on his engorged dick, it was all Drake could do to get up on all fours. Nick stayed with him, not missing a stroke.

Soon Raul and Pedro both got into the act. They knelt on the floor behind Drake and started squeezing the backs of his thighs. That got Drake moving—anything to get away!

It was a mad procession, Drake crawling across the floor on all fours while Nick, still straddling him, kept up the lower rib tickling and the brothers followed on their knees, squeezing his thighs and calves.

Drake didn't know which was worse, the tickling or the horniness raging through him. They crawled along, all four of them, as Drake howled and moaned and pleaded. His balls ached, his dick was on fire. "Stop! Let me jack off, please, please!"

"You know you're not allowed to do that," Nick said. "Now *move*! I like playing horsey."

They made several circuits of the wide kitchen area. The faster Drake tried to crawl, the harder he got tickled, while the vibrator buzzed his prostate till he thought he'd die from horniness.

They didn't stop till the vibrator's new batteries wore out.

"Oh, shit," Nick said. "I should have brought some spares. Well, I could stand to stretch my legs." He stood up, and when Drake looked over his shoulder he got a glimpse of Nick's enormous rod, which, like Drake's, looked ready to burst. When the brothers got to their feet it seemed a wonder that there was enough room in the kitchen for these four throbbing hard-ons.

"Please jack me off," Drake whimpered, rolling from all fours onto his back, just like a dog. "Please, please."

Nick looked around. "What the hell?" He stomped around the kitchen, shaking his head. "Jesus fucking Christ, look at this! Pecker tracks all over my floor!"

"I'm sorry, Sir," Drake whined. "Honest to God, I'm sorry, Sir, but you know I always put out a lot of precum, Sir, especially when—"

"Shut the fuck up!" Nick drew his big toe across the yellow tiles, tracing long strands of precum. To Drake's great relief he sounded less angry when he spoke again. "Okay, this is what's going to happen. You're not getting any relief yet, jackoff boy. Instead you're going to keep crawling. And you're going to lick up every bit of that jism, till this floor is shining again."

Tears of frustration rolled down Drake's cheeks. "Please, Sir..." He looked to Raul and Pedro, to see if they might help him, but the two men were off to the side, playing with each other. They had glazed expressions on their faces as they stroked each other's long, brown, uncircumcised dicks like a couple of adolescent boys discovering sex for the first time.

"I'm bigger'n you, why don't you admit it," Pedro said.

"You got a dog dick, man. Butt-ugly. No wonder you like to stick it up butts."

"Shut the fuck up. Just stroke that fucker, stroke it!"

"Oh, and one more thing," Nick told Drake. "I'm not going to waste any more batteries on you right now, but while you're crawling around I'm going to be torturing those ribs!"

It was a losing game. The more Drake licked up precum, the more he put down, especially with Nick having no mercy in his tickling. He rubbed his slave's lower ribs like Aladdin rubbing his lamp, and the pulsing sensations shot through Drake in two directions, to his brain and his cock. He licked and leaked and laughed, laughed and leaked and licked. Nick's dick was leaking too, his precum pooling up in the small of Drake's back.

Finally he collapsed, gasping, begging for water, parched from licking up sticky jism. As a rule Nick responded to these requests—a dehydrated slave was no fun—so he reluctantly went to get the water bottle.

Thank God! A precious moment of rest! Trying not to make a sound, Drake slowly rolled over onto his back. His worry now was that the two brothers might take a fresh interest in him while Nick was gone. He tried not to draw attention to himself, not to look at them directly. But a thrill of fear shot up his spine when they appeared in his peripheral vision. Their cocks were harder than ever, and they wanted to come so bad they were panting. Drake prepared himself to grovel, beg, and promise them anything, whether it was within his power or not.

But they were distracted by Drake's dick. "*Jesucristo*, look at that thing!" Pedro cried.

"One hefty *pinga*." Raul looked just a little crazy, standing there with his mouth open, drool leaking from one corner. Both of their dicks were drooling, too: more work for Drake.

Nick returned with the water bottle, and Drake was greedy with the cool, sweet water. It helped him get his voice back to nearly normal, and he made use of it, babbling again. "Please, Sir, let me come, I'll do anything you want, anything you want for the rest of my life..."

"You're damn skippy," Nick said. He looked at Raul and Pedro, who were in a state almost as bad as Drake's. "Okay," he said, "I'm not usually a democratic guy, but what the hell, let's put it to a vote. Should we let this slave get some relief? My vote is, hell no. What do you guys say?"

Raul and Pedro were in a daze, and yet so agitated they couldn't stand still. Sex hung in the hair like an impending storm, and it was time to seed the clouds. "Hell, *yes*!" they both said. Raul added, licking his lips, "We all gotta shoot, man, or we're gonna die."

Pedro turned toward Raul. "I shoot bigger loads than you do, admit it."

Raul rolled his eyes. "*Madre de dios*, who invented brothers!"

"Okay, okay, okay," Nick said. "Let's organ grind." He found a jar of lube in a nearby drawer, screwed off the lid, and swiped a generous amount on his dick, then tossed the jar to the brothers.

Drake had his hands on himself, and he was rolling, twitching, and squirming across the kitchen floor. It felt so good he couldn't stand it, handling his own cock, controlling his own orgasm for the first time in—hell, he didn't know how long. He didn't need any lube, his dick was so slick he could hardly keep a grip on it. His hips were thrusting, back arching in convulsions of lust, and even when he banged his head against a cupboard drawer he didn't stop stroking, making love to his dick with both hands—he had never loved it so much.

"That guy's a fucking maniac," Pedro said, though he was no less wild, reeling across the room as he jackhammered his dick to death.

"Jesus fucking Christ," Raul said. "This is the hottest ever, man!" He stood still with his feet planted wide, using all his energy on his slick dick, pulling it one-handed with twists of the wrist that that were skillful, long practiced, and, judging by his moans, excruciating. He didn't spend much time looking around, he was so fascinated by his own hand-and-dick machine.

Nick, on the other hand, kept looking from one man to the other. He didn't make a sound as he pumped his enormous circumcised rod, but his tight-lipped smile seemed to assert that he was still in control somehow, the master of what each man in the room was feeling.

"Ah...ah...ah!" Drake's legs were shaking uncontrollably, his heels drumming the floor. "I'm gonna..." As he shot his whole body recoiled, he was at the mercy of his own thrusts, the power of his loins jolting him backwards across the floor. And all around him a hot rain fell.

After that it didn't take the others long. Raul and Pedro were also shaking so bad they had to drop to their knees. Only Nick remained standing, his eyes closed now, his tight-lipped smile long gone as his mouth hung open, screaming soundlessly as his cock gushed like an open fire hydrant. He bent over, jacking upward, taking several spurts on his chest, then sprayed the room. The brothers came at the same time, jerking and lurching across the floor like deranged puppets. Drake got soaked as streamers of cum flew over him from three directions.

Afterwards they lay sprawled as if dropped from a great height, left with no energy to move their twisted legs. Totally wasted, Drake finally raised his head to see Nick sitting in one of the kitchen chairs, smoking a cigarette. Nick was frowning, concentrating, creating his next move. Whatever it was, it would not be good.

"Hey, help me, man." It was Pedro, who had landed on his belly and was just now stirring. "Help, I'm stuck to the floor!"

Raul laughed wildly. "You think you got problems, man? I think I accidentally tore my dick off!"

Nick had left his chair and was surveying the room, shaking his head. "I've had my share of free-for-alls in orgy rooms, but I swear I've never seen so much cum in my life." Not surprisingly, his gaze settled on Drake. "Okay, you know the drill. You're going to clean up every square inch of this floor. With your tongue. Then you're going to clean us up, too. My chest hair is so stuck together it fucking hurts to breathe, and these guys are looking pretty raunchy too."

Thank God, thank God, none of them tickled Drake as he worked. They were probably too tired. As for licking up cum, Drake considered it part of his repertoire. His seasoned palate could distinguish among the four kinds of jism he was slurping from the floor: His own always had a strong, spunky odor but its flavor was mild, a little on the sweet side. Nick's, which he had also tasted before, was more stringy in consistency, its flavor slightly bitter, like ale. It had no strong smell at all. The other two types—he didn't know which was Pedro's and which was Raul's—were much alike in taste, neither very bitter nor sweet, and real spunky-smelling like his own; but one was much thicker and almost opaque, reminding him of the beaten egg whites they used for fake cum in porno flicks. Then there were the many spots on the floor where two or three or four kinds of jizz had blended together—reeking cum cocktails, each with its own twist.

While the slave worked, his three tormentors sat in straight-backed chairs against the wall, watching him. Smoking cigarettes and mumbling. Plotting, no doubt.

All the licking, lapping, and scouring coated Drake's face with spunk from his nose to his chin, but when he was finally finished the floor looked good. Well, it still needed washing, but at least nobody was going to slip and break his neck. Eager for praise, he looked to his Master.

"All right, you piece of shit," Nick said, "don't look so goddamned proud of yourself. You've still got work to do."

Pedro leaned across his brother to speak to Nick.. "Listen, Nick, man, just let me get a shower. I'm filthy with this shit."

Raul waved a hand in front of his nose. "You sure are, man. You reek."

Pedro turned to his brother. "I don't know if I want to do this shit, man, what he's talking about doing next."

"Well, all right," Nick said. "Tell you what. Since we took a vote earlier, let's do it again." He raised his right hand. "I vote for the plan just as I described it. No changes. How about you, Raul?"

Pedro shook his head at his brother. "No, man," he said softly. "We really don't want to do this."

But Raul, wearing the same tight-lipped smile as Nick, raised his right hand.

Nick barked at Drake: "Get the hell over here!" He took the water bottle from the counter. "I filled this up again. Hydrate, and rinse your tongue real good. Then go to the sink over there and wash the jizz off your face, you fucking whore."

When Drake had followed orders he reported back for duty. Nick explained the rules. "You're going to lick the dried cum off all three of us, starting with me."

"Yes, Sir."

"That's all there is to it, except for one additional rule that must not be broken. You are not allowed to *tickle* any of us while you're doing it. Accidentally or otherwise."

"Yes, Sir."

"If you disobey and tickle any of us, even for a second, you'll pay the consequences. Each man you tickle will get you all to himself for three hours. And it won't be pretty."

"Yes, Sir!"

"Let's move in to the next room, where we can spread out."

The next room, of course, was the torture chamber. Only Pedro hesitated to go in.

"I'm first," Nick said. He hopped up on the exam table. "I'm just going to lie here with my arms at my sides. I've only got cum on my chest, so it shouldn't take long. Now get over here!"

Soon Drake was up to his nose in coarse, matted chest hair. He moistened it till it was no longer stuck down and the jizz was a funky soup warmed by Nick's body heat. Drake had to suck on that fur to really get the cum off. The male stink of cum, hair, and sweat went to his head—it reminded him particularly of Emmett—but he was very careful not to hurt his master. As far as tickling him was concerned, he didn't worry. Nick saw ticklishness as a weakness, a failing of masculine stoicism, and if his body had ever had that quality he had willed it out of existence, or at least disciplined himself so that he would never show it, no matter what. There were a couple of dicey spots when Drake got near his armpits, but Nick only twitched slightly, making no sound.

When Drake was finished Nick sat up and rubbed his chest all over. "That's better," he said. "Now, who wants to go next?" He had to yell, for Raul and Pedro were off in a corner, arguing.

Raul looked over. "I'm next!"

"Fuck no!" Pedro shouted. "*I'm* next."

"Little brother, you're getting to be a pain in the ass."

"I'm telling you for the last time, I'm not your *little* brother, shithead. I could kick your ass in half a second!"

"I wish you ladies would stop bickering," Nick said. "Have you both got your periods at the same time, or what?"

Pedro put a hand on his brother's shoulder. "Look, man, I'm sorry, okay? It's just that...I don't want to go last. I don't want to have to wait that long." He looked as if he might burst into tears.

"Tough shit. I'm the older brother, so I get to choose." He shoved Pedro's hand off his shoulder.

Pedro wiped the about-to-cry look off his face. Now he just looked grim. "It's not always gonna be that way," he said.

Raul had cum all over his inner thighs, groin, and belly. He preferred to sit on the edge of a straight chair for his tongue bath, leaning back with his lower body thrust forward. He grinned at Drake. "Remember, man, you're not gonna tickle me one little bit, or you'll live to regret it." He spread his legs so that Drake could get between them.

It was not the best situation to be in. As human beings, Raul and his brother were pieces of shit, but viewed strictly as naked males they were damned fucking hot, in a broad-shouldered, slim-hipped, big-dicked kind of way. And Raul was in a sexy position, offering up his caramel-colored thighs, groin, and belly, including that prize cock. Drake prayed that Raul wasn't ticklish, because he didn't know if he could control his own movements, trembling as he was with both fear and lust. Very carefully he moved in between Raul's legs.

Now Nick and Pedro, who had just had a private conversation, quickly and silently approached Raul's chair from the rear. Nick had a finger to his lips to warn Drake to be quiet, but he had no time to react anyway as the two men grabbed Raul's arms, pulled them back behind the chair and bound his wrists tightly together.

"Hey, you *fucks!* What the fuck are you—" Raul grimaced, he struggled to get his wrists free, but it was no use. He couldn't even move enough to sit up straighter, meaning that his vulnerable parts were still exposed to the max and he could do nothing about it.

"Go ahead, slave!" Nick yelled. "What are you waiting for?"

Oh God. Drake ducked his head and, having no choice, touched his tongue to Raul's inner thigh.

"Ahhhhh, you bastard! You tickled me!"

Drake reared back. He hadn't even got any cum off yet, and already he was in trouble.

"That's three hours with Raul, slave," Nick said. "Well, don't sit there looking stupid, get back to work."

Nearly swooning from fear, Drake got back in between Raul's legs. Afraid of returning to the spot he had just hit, he tried a little ways further up, near but not quite touching Raul's heavy balls.

This time Raul really yelled. "AHHHH, YOU BASTARD! YOU TICKLED ME AGAIN!"

Drake started babbling, with tears in his eyes. "I'm sorry, I'm sorry, you know I don't mean to, I'm trying not to...."

"That's six hours with Raul," Nick said.

"*What?*" Drake was so startled his voice, what was left of it, spiked up an octave. "You said it was three hours per guy!"

"Three hours per guy, *per tickle,*" Nick said. "Can't you remember the rules? They're simple enough, for Christ's sake."

"No! No!" Tears rolled down Drake's cheeks. "You can't!"

"Oh, sure we can," Nick said. "Don't worry, I've got a calculator."

As it turned out, it was Raul who had miscalculated. Knowing full well how ticklish he was, he had gone along with the game on the assumption that he wouldn't get tickled much, just enough to get the slave to himself for a serious amount of time. But the stress Drake was under — terrified of tickling Raul, and *dying* to tickle him at the same time — was so great that, when he accidentally tickled Raul's balls and he yelled again, and Nick said, "Okay, that's nine hours with Raul," Drake snapped. He'd never survive nine hours with Raul, so *what the hell*! He leaned into his work, letting his tongue take off like a whirligig all over Raul's thighs, balls, dickhead, and belly. Unable to resist the stimulation, that thick brown dick was growing hard again, as Raul yelled a blue streak of cusses, insults, and escalating threats.

"AAAH, YOU BASTARD! YOU MOTHERLESS PRICK, YOU'LL PAY FOR THIS! OH JESUS, DON'T DO MY BALLS LIKE THAT! I'LL GET YOU BACK A THOUSAND TIMES OVER, YOU CUNT!"

Nick was highly amused by Drake's transformation into a ruthless tickling machine. "It's kind of hard to keep score," he said, "when the tickling never stops!"

"AHHHH, NICK, YOU SICK FUCK! CALL HIM OFF, YOU PUSSY! HE'S YOUR SLAVE! AHHHH CALL HIM OFF OR I'LL KILL HIM, I SWEAR TO CHRIST! MAKE HIM STOP OR I'LL KILL YOU TOO, MOTHERFUCKER!"

"Maybe you should gag him, Nick," Pedro said.

"Naw. It doesn't matter, nobody can hear him. Besides, it's amusing."

Raul did not take kindly to this. At the moment Drake was stretching his navel with his fingers and reaming it with his tongue.

"AHHHHHH I'LL AMUSE YOU, YOU DICKLESS TURD! I'LL AMUSE THE SHIT OUT OF YOU WHEN I GET OUT OF THIS! I SWEAR TO GOD!"

"Take it easy, big brother," Pedro said. "I'm going to help." He crossed over in front of Raul, standing just behind Drake. Surprising everyone, he reached down, grabbed Raul's ankles and pulled his legs up, spreading them wide. "How about a little asshole play? I happen to know it's a bad, bad weak spot."

"PEDRO, WHAT THE FUCK ARE YOU DOING? I'LL KILL YOU! I'LL TORTURE YOU TO DEATH! I KNOW HOW TO DO IT, TOO ...!"

Pedro looked grim. "Funny, that's exactly what you told Juan, just before you put him in the hospital."

"*VETE AL DIABLO*, THAT WASN'T ME, THAT WASN'T MY FAULT! IT WAS *BOTH* OF US!"

During this exchange Drake moved to a slightly better position. It was true, with Raul's legs pulled up like that Drake had easy access to his ass.

"PEDRO, WHAT THE FUCK ARE YOU DOING? AHHHH YOU BETTER NOT TOUCH MY ASSHOLE, YOU FUCKIN' PERVERT! I'LL HUNT YOU DOWN AND KILL YOU, YOU FREAK...AHHHHH!"

Drake's tongue had hit the mark. Raul's tight little never-been-fucked asshole was easy to tickle, he only had to stick his tongue just slightly in and Raul was writhing and yelling like never before.

"AAAAHHH NICK, YOU SHIT STAIN, YOU CALL THEM OFF OR I'LL MAKE YOU REGRET THE DAY YOUR MOTHER GOT KNOCKED UP IN A WHOREHOUSE! YOU'LL BE EATING MY SHIT THE REST OF YOUR LIFE, YOU SCUM-SUCKING FAGGOT!"

Drake stuck his tongue a little farther in. It was so easy, and the taste was tolerable. Also—*what the hell!*—he reached up and started tickling Raul's sides.

That got him. In a few seconds Raul was gasping for breath. His hard dick prodded his belly, coating it with precum. Soon he was on the verge of blacking out, his eyes about to roll up in his head.

"Hey Raul," Nick said. "I've got a proposition for you. We'll turn you loose, if you promise to behave."

Raul only gasped and moaned.

"I'll show you. Slave, stop tickling him!"

Drake obeyed.

"Okay, like I was saying, you have to promise..."

"I PROMISE I'LL CUT YOUR DICK OFF AND MAKE YOU EAT IT, AND THEN I'LL SHOVE YOU BACK INSIDE YOUR MOTHER, YOU—"

"Okay, okay, okay!" Nick said. "Slave, you'd better tickle him some more. Come to think of it, why don't all three of us tickle him. I'll get that vibrator we were using in the kitchen."

"OH, NO! *MADRE DE DIOS*, NO! YOU FUCKING BASTARDS, YOU'LL KILL ME!"

"Well, okay then...?"

"I'll behave," Raul said. He looked as if he might breathe his last any second. "I swear, I won't hurt anybody."

Much later, Nick and Raul were sitting at Nick's dining-room table, though his dining "room" was just an open area beyond the equally open kitchen, taking up a fraction of the space of the studio that lay beyond. At this end of the building a few narrow windows stretched from floor to ceiling, and it was possible to sit at the table and look directly down at the deserted streets. It hardly mattered, in that isolated area, whether the men were dressed or not, but Raul was wearing the jeans and T-shirt that he had arrived in, and Nick was as dressed as he ever was at home, wearing fatigue pants with no shirt. They were also barefoot, and they had Drake under the table, naked and gagged, his wrists tied to the table legs, and they were tickling him with their feet.

Drake couldn't remember the last time he'd been tickled by feet. The table top was glass, so the men could see more or less what they were doing; but for this kind of work feet were more inexact than hands, and in a way it was like being tickled by animals that didn't quite know what they were doing. This clumsiness was very effective, made the tickling seem more random, and Drake grew hysterical as the four feet slipped and skidded and bumped all over his torso, toes stubbing against his ribs, digging into his navel.

Drake had always liked men's feet, and excruciating as the tickling was, making him scream against the gag, he was also getting a hard-on from getting worked over by four strong specimens. Never mind that the feet were somewhat funky, smelling of sweat, cum, and piss, in that order; or that Raul desperately needed to trim his toenails, their sharpness giving an added edge to his torture of Drake's navel.

He was gagged because Nick and Raul, in addition to tickling him, were trying to have a conversation. Raul had an obsession that would not quit: when was he going to get Drake all to himself, and for how long? "I want him for at least a fucking *week*," he said.

"Hmmm," Nick said, "I bet Pedro will want him for even longer than that."

It was true, the tongue-cleaning session with Pedro had been a disaster. It had begun with his refusal to cooperate, and his demand that Drake be kept away from him. Nick, ever the cordial host, had complied by locking Drake in a big wire cage in a corner of the torture chamber. It was a cage meant for an animal, perhaps a large dog, and its space cramped Drake, who had to lie on his side with his knees drawn up. Still he had a good view of what happened next.

"I'm not doing a fucking thing, man," Pedro said, backing away from the other two. "I'm getting the fuck out of here."

"Okay," Nick said, "since we've been doing so well with the democratic process, let's take a vote."

Raul, grinning, raised his hand. "I vote we tie him spread-eagle to that exam table over there."

Nick raised his hand too. "Majority rules."

"Oh, no," Pedro said. "You fuckers will never get me on that table..."

Pedro was strong but his opponents were stronger, very soon wrestling the naked young man to the floor, where Raul straddled him while Nick pinned his arms straight back. Pedro's screams were unearthly as his brother gleefully tormented his ribs and armpits.

"NO! NO! YOU'RE NOT SUPPOSED TO TICKLE ME!"

In between screams, his torturers told him that they would relent if Pedro would agree to get up on the table; otherwise they would tickle him to death immediately.

Pedro had nothing to fall back on but the logic of a man in agony: anything that would stop them, even for a few seconds, would be a godsend. "All right, all right!" he shrieked. "I'll do it, I'll do whatever you fucking want, just *stop tickling me!*"

Set free, Pedro could barely get to his feet without help. His eyes rolled wildly, seeking escape, but even if he had somewhere to go he had already lost all energy to get there; he was limp as Raul and Nick manhandled him onto the table and fastened down his wrists and feet. He said to his brother, "Hey, man, you don't want to do this."

"Hmmm," Raul said. "I think I remember a certain mother*fuck* who didn't care if *I* got tickled out of my mind."

"Come on, man! I didn't mean anything!"

"That's not what you said when you turned my *asshole* over to the fucking *slave!*"

"All right, all right, you guys," Nick said. "Less talking, more screaming." His hands hovered over Pedro's taut brown belly. "I think I might start right here."

"NO! YOU'RE NOT SUPPOSED TO TICKLE ME! IT'S SUPPOSED TO BE A TONGUE-CLEANING, THAT'S ALL!"

"Christ, another yeller," Nick said.

"You get the belly, I'll get his feet." Raul said.

"No sooner said."

"AAAAAHHH NO NO NO NO DON'T DO THIS TO ME, YOU FUCKING BASTARDS! AAAAHHH HELP ME, GOD HELP ME!"

Nick had no mercy on Pedro as he worked from his belly to his groin and then up to his neck. Raul broke a fresh sweat as he labored over his brother's soles. Drake could only stare, fascinated, while Pedro strained and thrust against his bonds so hard that the table actually moved a fraction of an inch. In his own worst agonies, Drake hadn't budged the table at all.

When the ticklers stopped for a few seconds, the sound of Pedro's heaving breath filled the room.

"I should explain," Nick said. "You're right, it was supposed to be a tongue bath, by my slave, and if he tickled you then he would be punished. But then, damned if the slave didn't change the rules. Remember?" Nick bent over and began blowing raspberries against Pedro's stomach, with devastating results.

Pedro raised his head as far as he could, searched the room till his wild eyes found Drake. "YOU FUCKING SLAVE, I'LL KILL YOU, I'LL KILL YOU BEFORE I KILL THESE FUCKS, I'LL GRIND YOU UP AND *FEED* YOU TO THEM..."

Scared as he was, Drake had to acknowledge that Nick was a shrewd bastard. He had initiated the savage tickling of Pedro and succeeded in blaming Drake for it. As a result Raul and Pedro, when they noticed him at all, both glared at him as if they couldn't wait to tickle him to death, then back to life, and then to death again.

While Nick began to pry at Pedro's ribs, driving him to wordless, high-pitched screams, Raul retreated to a corner of the torture chamber and returned with something held behind his back.

"Hey little bro, I've got something for you."

Nick relented enough for Pedro to at least form words again. "YOU SOFT PRICK OF A BROTHER, YOU BASTARD, MAKE HIM STOP! DON'T JUST STAND THERE WHILE HE'S KILLING ME!"

"You ain't seen nothin' yet," Raul said. "Get a load of this." He held up a stiff white feather.

"AAAAHHH! NO! NO! YOU SAID YOU'D *NEVER* DO THAT!"

There followed something unlike anything Drake, or even Nick, had ever seen. As Raul approached with the feather, Pedro totally lost his mind. He screamed, mouth stretched wide, tongue protruding, eyes popping out of his head. Nick was so startled he jumped back. Here was a man who was not only in terror of being tickled, he was in paralyzing fear of losing his immortal soul.

"Wait a minute," Nick said. "There's something else going on here."

"He's always been like this with feathers," Raul said.

"So that's it! Pteronophobia, fear of being tickled with feathers. I've read about it, but never actually seen it."

"Watch what happens when I get even *closer*."

Pedro squirmed, wallowing in sweat. The sound he made now was a high, eerie keening, an inhuman sound, a ghost sound. His bladder let go, piss trickling to the floor.

"Jesus Christ!" Nick said. "So this is what you did to Juan? Does he have that phobia too?"

"No, man," Raul said, "just this little fucker right here." He began his approach again, slowly. "And when...I touch him...with this *feather*...he's going to...*die!*"

Pedro strained, every fiber of his being struggling against his bonds, and from his throat came another inhuman sound, an internal strangling, fear choking the life out of him. His body went limp.

No one moved. Raul stared at his brother, panic starting to show in his own eyes. "He ain't breathing. He ain't *breathing*, Nick!"

"Shut up." Nick checked Pedro's breath and pulse, lifted one eyelid. "He's breathing, he's just passed out. Christ, you guys are unbelievable. How have you managed to live around each other all these years and still survive?"

"Shit!" Raul let the feather drop and ground it with his heel. "I ought to slap the shit out of him when he wakes up, just for scaring me like that!"

So that's how it came to be that Nick and Raul were sitting at the table by themselves, tickling Drake with their feet. Pedro was spending time in the recovery room, then the shower. When he finally appeared, wearing the sweatpants and T-shirt he had arrived in, he was so pale his face was almost luminous. Seeing Drake on the floor, he exploded. "Why, you...!" Nick and Raul both had to restrain him as he kept yelling at Drake, "I'll *kill* you! I'll *kill* you!"

"Shut the fuck up," Nick said. "You're giving me a headache."

"I want him, Nick," Pedro said. "I want him so bad. Tied up. In *my* basement. For two weeks, or until he gives out, whichever comes first!"

"Here, sit down over here and we'll talk. You can get his feet."

Pedro positioned a chair where he could sit and raise up Drake's feet to rest in his lap. "Oh, yeah, I want these feet all right." He was able to trap Drake's ankles in the grip of one strong hand while the tortured the soles with the other.

Delirious, writhing under the table so far as he was able, Drake realized at some level that this was the story of his life: the men with dirty feet were tickling him with them, and the man who had just taken a shower was using his hands. Even so the funky feet and wild sensations were driving him into a frenzy of desperation and lust. It didn't help that Pedro was getting a boner, Drake's feet squirmed against it as Pedro held them pinned more and more tightly in his lap.

"I say he's *mine*," Raul said.

Nick mumbled something.

"If my piece of shit brother gets him for two weeks, then *I* get him for two weeks!"

"The fuck you do! And hell no, you don't get visiting rights!"

Drake drifted in and out of reality as the brothers argued about who would get to tickle him to death. Meanwhile Nick and Raul were having a shoving match with their feet against Drake's ribcage, and Pedro was practicing his dexterity in tickling between the slave's toes. Drake twisted desperately in his bonds, trying for some contact between his raging erection and the floor.

Sometime later Nick untied his wrists. "Come on, dickhead, I've got a plan."

The words filled Drake with dread. His legs were shaking and it took him a few tries to get to his feet.

"You can sit at the table with us," Nick said.

How long had it been since Drake had sat in a chair, a real chair with no restraints attached? It placed him at eye level with his tormentors, and for a moment it was almost like a normal scene, four guys sitting around a table, except that he was naked and the others were not. In front of him a silver cigarette case lay open, revealing several fat joints. Raul already had one lit and was passing it to Pedro, who took a few deep hits and offered it to Nick. Nick took a couple of shallow tokes and then, to Drake's surprise, pinched the rapidly diminishing joint in the center and held it out to him.

"For this next game," he said, "even the slave gets high."

Somewhere in the past there was a different Drake, one who earned a good living from a major corporation, confidently strode the streets of Manhattan, and would not hesitate to say, in any situation, *Hey, I never agreed to any drug use*. But that Drake was gone. He took the joint, full of who-knew-what kind of weed, and sucked on it greedily. He hadn't been stoned in years, and he was ready for it now, anything to relieve his anxiety. The effects were almost immediate, blooming in his lungs, sweeping through his brain. When he finally expelled smoke his anxieties went too—some of them, anyway.

Raul grabbed the joint. "Jesus Christ, I'm already so fucking stoned I can't see." Which didn't stop him from taking another deep hit.

"Ah, shit," Pedro said, "I'm feeling no pain, man."

"We don't want to get so fucking stoned we can't move," Nick said. He still took only shallow puffs, letting the smoke go quickly as if he were only holding a cigarette. "That would spoil the race."

Race?

Soon all four of them were standing in the middle of the kitchen. Nick was explaining the rules. They had shared another joint, with Drake getting the lion's share of it, and now Raul and Pedro were laughing as they tossed Drake back and forth between them, casually tickling him. He could barely stand up.

"We're going to let him run," Nick said.

Run?

"You're gonna let a slave *run*?" Raul asked. "Where's he gonna run to?"

"Oh, he can't really *go* anywhere. The loft is locked from the inside, I'm the only one who can open the door. The whole point is the chase. You two are going to chase him, and the first one who catches him gets to keep him for a week."

"How's he gonna run, man? He's so stoned he can't stand up, not to mention we've tickled him fucking silly."

It was true. As he was passed back and forth between the brothers Drake's giggling became shamelessly high-pitched. He sounded like a little girl about to wet her pants.

"That just makes the race a little more interesting," Nick said. "'Course, you guys are wrecked too."

Raul and Pedro were beyond noticing that Nick had managed not to smoke much dope at all. They were muttering things to Drake as they passed him back and forth.

"When I get you alone, bitch, I'm gonna tickle you like you've never been tickled before," Raul said, "but I'm gonna go real slow, so it takes all seven days to fucking kill you."

"When I get you alone," Pedro said, "The first thing I'm going to do is fuck the living shit out of you. *Then* I'll tickle you, but only till I feel like fucking you again." He still had a hard-on, clearly outlined down the right leg of his sweatpants.

Drake wondered if these guys knew how *funny* they sounded, like cartoon versions of themselves. It made him giggle even more breathlessly as one groping pair of hands passed him off to the other. He made up a little song: *fuck me tickle me fuck me tickle me*...was it just a song in his head, or was he singing out loud?

"You guys are fucking pathetic," Nick said. "Come on, let's get started before you all pass out." He had them line up at the edge of the dining area, Drake in the middle. "I've closed and locked the torture chamber and my bedroom, so he'll have to stick to the studio."

Pedro rubbed his bloodshot eyes and frowned at the huge, mostly bare room. "How many laps?"

"Only as many as it takes for one of you to catch him. But to be fair, we have to give him a head start. Five seconds."

"Okay, let's get this fucking shit started, man." Raul rubbed his brow, shook his head. "What it is we're doing, now?"

"When I say *Go*, the slave takes off. When I say *Go* again, you guys take off after him."

"This won't take long," Pedro said.

"The hell it won't," Nick said. "The shape you guys are in, a hundred-yard dash would take you an hour."

"This won't take long," Pedro said.

"You just said that."

Drake tried to keep track of the business at hand, with varying success from moment to moment. Somewhere something *serious* was going on, and he'd goddamn well better pay attention. At the same time a little filmstrip was playing in his mind: Raul and Pedro were tickling and fucking him, fucking and tickling him, and the speed was all out of sync like in a silent movie, and it was *funny*.

"When I say *Go*, slave."

Drake closed his eyes, and when he opened them again he saw the studio before him, as if he had just been transported there. The huge room was bare except for an easel in the far corner and those huge torsos hanging on the wall. A few of them could have been his—perhaps the unfinished one on the easel *was* his. Confronting those vivid images of male agony was a sobering experience; for a moment he thought clearly, realized he might stand a chance of survival with Nick, but if either of the brothers got hold of him it would be the end for sure.

He had to run. He had to make sure they didn't catch him. But how?

"Go."

Drake lurched forward onto the waxed hardwood floor. He had to run, but his feet weren't working right; as soon as he lifted them they fell at odd angles, as if he had never learned to walk, let alone run.

"Go!"

That was the signal for Raul and Pedro to take off after him. The sound of their bare feet hitting the wood was a great incentive, it got Drake moving again, not looking down but straight ahead this time as he tried to run. He seemed to be doing it, the walls were moving on either side of him. He tried not to think about how fast he was running or how close the two men behind him were.

"Hey, *slave!*"

"You're *mine*, you ticklish bastard!"

Raul was going to tickle him, Pedro was going to fuck him...wait, maybe it was the other way around...hell, it didn't matter, they were going to do whatever they wanted, there was no stopping either of them. Drake reached the end of the room and, with a shriek, veered off to his right.

"Okay, you fuck!" It was Raul's voice. "I've...got...you...*now!*"

Drake braced himself to be tackled, hurled to the floor. Instead there was a crash behind him, and a moment later Nick was cursing a blue streak.

"Fucking...shit-for-brains *greaser*...!"

"What the fuck happened?" Raul stood by the corner where the easel now lay like a pile of kindling and the canvas leaned beside it, torn through the center. "I thought it was *him*, man!"

When Pedro saw that Raul had tackled a painting instead of his prey, he started laughing and couldn't stop.

Drake saw his chance. While the others were preoccupied, he took off.

He never doubted that Nick was right—there was nowhere he could go. But he would try the outside door anyway. Before he knew it he had reached the shallow alcove that served as a foyer, and sure enough the door would not budge. It had at least three locks on it, each one needing a key.

But there was another door, at right angles to the exit. Drake tried it; it opened into darkness. He stepped inside and closed the door softly behind him. With a growing sense of panic he felt for a light switch. A bare overhead bulb came on and he was relieved to find himself in a large storage room. Along three walls metal utility shelves held sketch pads, rolls of canvas, lengths of wood, new and partially used tubes of paint. There were pots and jars and cans filled with brushes of all types; cans of gesso, the gluey, chalky stuff used to prepare canvases; palettes and palette knives; and all varieties of cleaning supplies. For a moment it was as if he had stepped into someone else's life, a life filled with purpose, the love of tools and work, powered by a spiritual need to create. Was all of that part of Nick?

Nick! Any second he would be here. There was no lock on the door. But there was a straight chair set against the wall, and without even thinking Drake grabbed it and jammed it underneath the doorknob.

Almost immediately he heard voices.

"Hey, slave master, it looks like your slave's disappeared."

"He hasn't gone far," Nick growled.

Drake stood in the center of the room, hardly daring to breathe, his eyes on the doorknob. When it turned, he jumped. The door held fast.

"Son of a bitch."

"Hey, slave master...!"

"*Shut the fuck up!*"

Nick tried to force the door, threw his weight against it, but it wouldn't budge.

Drake didn't want to laugh, but he couldn't help it. He took his hand from his mouth and let out a *haw haw* kind of horselaugh.

"You had better get the *fuck* out of there *right now*, you piece of shit, before I *double* the punishment I'm planning for you!"

Drake backed farther away from the door. He hugged himself with delight, danced in small circles to his right, then left. *They can't touch me.* The thought was delicious. He had to say it out loud, he just had to. "You can't touch me!"

"We'll do more than touch you...!"

"Hey, slave!" It was Pedro. "You're mine! My brother tore up the studio, so he lost the game. *Hee hee hee!* You know what that means! You're mine till the end of your life!"

"Fuck you!" Raul said to his brother. "This ain't been settled yet!"

"I'm thinking of a time-sharing arrangement," Nick said, slowly enough for Drake to hear every word. "We'll all three get to work on him for certain hours of the day. After a week there'll be nothing left of him."

Drake laughed again, he couldn't help it. "Ooooh, I'm so scared of you guys!"

Furious pounding on the door.

"I'm so thankful you can't touch me," Drake called. "I'm feeling soooooooo ticklish right now!"

Bang! Bang! Bang!

"I think I'd just *scream* if anybody touched me!"

"Enough of this shit," Nick said. "I'm going to get some tools."

"Hey, slave." Raul spoke with his mouth very close to the door, as if he were sharing a secret. "If there's any poison in there you better drink it *now*, 'cause anything would be better than what we're gonna do to you."

"Oh, please...don't *frighten* me like that. I might have a *heart attack* or something!" Giggling wildly, Drake dropped to the floor where he sat cross-legged, rocking back and forth in amusement.

For a while he didn't hear anything. It was hard to calm down, his excitement was so great. He had *won*, though he could not concentrate to figure out exactly what he had won or how long it would last. He sat still, listening for the voices in the alcove, but there were none. Was it a trick? He had to be very, very quiet...

He noticed his bare feet. What strange things they were, feet. These particular ones—*not* the cleanest feet in the world—now, where had they come from? Could he even be *sure* they were his? They looked more like funeral feet, corpse feet. So immobile and white.

The right foot lay on the floor, on its side, just in front of his left knee. Slowly he reached down to touch it with his left index finger. The finger had barely touched flesh when he felt the spark.

It *tickled*.

Now, he had always been told, had always believed, that it was impossible for a person to tickle himself, and his own experiments in that direction had been failures. So he was not ready to believe, even in his altered state of consciousness, that it was possible now.

He stared at the foot for what seemed like minutes on end. It was its own entity, separate from him. It was *not* him. When the left hand appeared again, the threatening index finger flexing, flexing, it was not part of him either. He was watching images on a screen, within a frame, and he was well removed from them. He only kept watching because— well, just because.

When the finger attacked, stroking up and down the sole, it skewed the picture, the projector fell from its stand. Drake closed his eyes and there was laughter in the room.

He shifted a bit, and now the left foot lay on its side in front of his right knee. He waited to see what would happen, and there it was, the right hand this time. All of its fingers were flexing, not just the one. The foot, suddenly alive, flexed also. It was like one of those time-lapse nature films where a flower blooms in a second.

This time all of the fingers attacked, and did not stop. Drake rocked back and forth on the floor. Someone was laughing.

"...fuck is going *on* in there...?"

Oh God, I'm *laughing*.

Sound of a hammer, and then: "So much paint on these frigging hinges..."

Just to see if they could, the right hand and the left hand began working simultaneously, tickling both feet. Drake rocked and laughed, twisted side to side, trying to get away from those hands.

"Shut the fuck *up* in there!"

That was Raul, who couldn't stand the thought that Drake was getting tickled and he couldn't watch. It was just the kind of thing that would make him furious.

Drake lay back on the floor, under the bare overhead bulb. It reminded him of a locker room. Where was Carter? He had just seen him recently, he was sure of it. "Carter? Are you there? Look at this." He raised his hands, held them between his face and the light. The fingers bloomed, they flexed, they threatened: they would be all over him, any second now.

The bulb seemed to swing from its cord as Drake rolled his head from side to side, over and over, breathless with laughter.

When Nick had finally removed the hinges and pulled the door away, he and the brothers charged into the storeroom, but they didn't get far. They stopped, several yards away from Drake, not knowing what to make of what they saw.

Drake was sitting up. He seemed to be hugging himself, but no, his fingers were busily digging into his ribs. Tears ran down his face as he gasped with laughter. He tried to speak, but his voice was nearly gone and they could not hear him.

"Jesus *Christ*," Nick said.

The brothers cursed softly in Spanish.

Nick moved slowly, warily toward Drake, like a hunter approaching a trapped animal. Drake was tickling his armpits now, his head thrown back, mouth stretched wide as air rushed from his lungs. He tried to speak again, mouthing the same words over and over as Nick grew closer, straining to hear him. When he finally did hear him, he couldn't believe his ears.

"Help me please help me!" Drake was saying. "I'm tickling myself, and I can't stop!"

Drake was in the recovery room. He woke with a start, not knowing how he had got there, though that was not unusual. The effects of the dope he'd smoked were gone, he felt tired but his head was clear—until he heard the voices. They were the same voices he had heard before, voices of his past tormentors. How rude of them to talk, to hold conversations when he couldn't even see them. His own voice was long gone, maybe for good this time, but fortunately he didn't have to speak, they could hear his thoughts. He asked the darkness, *Where the hell are you?*

"Easy, Drake, easy." It was Emmett again. He looked a little more real, more solid than before. But you never knew, ghosts could fade in and out. "Just take it easy, okay?"

Drake looked around. There was snickering Rodney Cole, off to the left along with his soccer player buddies. There was Marshall Carter, precum leaking from his beautiful big dick, and Coach Doyle. Emmett seemed to be the leader of the group, gathering them around.

Why do you guys keep bothering me?

"Take it easy," Emmett said again. "The thing is, Drake...we're going to tickle you. All of us. We're real enough now."

Drake had grown used to these voices, these spirits. They were just hallucinations, not to be taken too seriously. But what he saw next made him sit straight up on the cot.

Nick and Pedro and Raul were coming toward him.

"Hey you guys," Drake said, "I'm not alone in here. There are ghosts around. You'd better beat it."

Nick laughed. "We know all about ghosts," he said. "We see them too."

"*What?*" Drake wagged his head in confusion. "Does that mean... *you're* ghosts?"

"Listen, Drake." Nick sat on the edge of the cot. His voice was almost kind. "I'm really sorry, man. You've been a good slave. I'm sorry it has to end this way. But you see, I can start all over again, in another city. I've done it many times. Somewhere I'll find a loft, in an otherwise empty part of town, and lure some desperate ticklish stud there. And he'll never come out."

Drake looked to Pedro and Raul. "Sorry, man," they both said together, and they seemed to mean it. "But you know," Raul added, "Pedro and me, we still want our revenge, and this is the only way to get it."

"But what are you doing here?" Drake asked. "You guys aren't from the past. You're right here, in the next room."

"Yeah," Nick said, "we're in the next room. But we're also right here...with these other guys...colleagues, you might say."

Rodney Cole snickered. "More like partners in crime."

"Emmett," Drake called, "where did you go? You're probably the only guy who could make sense of this for me."

Emmett stepped forward again. "I wish I could," he said. "But nothing's made any sense to *me*, Drake, ever since I left you."

Drake sat up, swung his legs over the side of his cot. "Do you really mean that?"

"Oh, don't get me wrong," Emmett said. He sat beside Drake, took his right hand and held it—the first sign that the spirits really could touch him now. "I'm having a great career. I could become the youngest CEO my company's ever had. But my personal life has been a disaster. You see, leaving you was the biggest mistake of my life."

"Really?" For the first time in ...well, a long time, there were tears in Drake's eyes that had not been tickled out of him. "Then why did you do it, really, Emmett? Why?"

"Because I was afraid. Afraid of commitment—we've all heard that one before, right? Plus I was bothered by all the kinky stuff we were into. I had to get away, start over, try to find a 'normal' sex life, whatever that is. But I haven't found anything at all, or anyone at all who could take your place." Emmett raised a knuckle to his eye, a tear slid down his finger. He squeezed Drake's hand tightly. "I love you, Drake. I always have."

One tear rolled down Drake's cheek. "Thanks, bud. I love you too. It just about killed me when you left."

Over in the corner, Rodney Cole rolled his eyes. "Jeez, I didn't know I was gonna have to watch fag love scenes."

Emmett pointed a warning finger. "You watch your mouth. We're going to have to work together, remember that."

The dark, hairy soccer player stepped up to Rodney. "Yeah, watch your mouth. As a matter of fact I'm gay, too. I came out fifteen years ago, I live in San Francisco, and I'm fucking my brains out even as we speak."

Coach Doyle's response to this was automatic. He called out, "Hey, son, that's no way to talk to a younger kid."

"I'm not a kid," Rodney grumbled. "I'm thirty-two years old, and I'm in jail in Tuscaloosa for holding up a 7-Eleven. *Okay*?"

Emmett stood up. "I guess we have to get to work."

Drake kept his hold on Emmett's hand. "Before I let you go, I have to know this: if you loved me, why didn't you ever come back?"

Emmett sighed. He couldn't meet Drake's eyes now. "I was too proud, Drake. Too damn proud to come back looking for you...until recently."

"What are you talking about?"

"You might as well know everything. I did come back looking for you, very recently. But you had already left to come here, and nobody knew where you were." He had shed more tears, his face was glistening.

Drake covered his face. "Oh, my God. Oh, Jesus."

"So I had to give up. Imagine my surprise when I was summoned here," Emmett said. "I was even more surprised to find out—I don't even know how—what I'm supposed to do. What we're all supposed to do."

There was a stir in another corner of the room. Carter raised his hand and cleared his throat rather loudly. "Uh, excuse me," he said, "but can we kind of get started? I like this spirit stuff, and there's a lot more guys I want to go see."

Emmett ignored him. He could only watch Drake—for Drake was crying.

He had whimpered and shed tears in front of Nick many times, but now he broke down completely, heaving sobs that seemed to come from the pit of his stomach, tears filling his cupped hands like an offering. He cried for losing Emmett, and for losing his only chance to get him back; he cried for the years of emptiness, the nights spent in bathhouses and back rooms, the mornings of lonely solitude. And he cried for himself, for the senseless waste of his young life.

And yet, and yet....

"Look at it this way, Drake," Emmett said, kneeling down before his friend. "You've lived the only possible life you could, and this is the only possible end."

And yet...he thought not only of Emmett but also the others in the room—Rodney Cole and the soccer players, Marshall Carter and Coach Doyle, and Nick and Raul and Pedro. They had given him the most thrilling, terrifying, erotic moments of his life. Did it all add up to a life that had been worth it?

He had to believe it did.

As abruptly as he had started crying, he stopped. He shook tears from his face, took a deep breath, turned and confronted the whole group. "No," he said. "I'm not going to cry. Not anymore. And you know what? I'm not going to beg, either, no matter what you do to me."

Nick wore his famous tight-lipped smile. "You can't take *all* the fun out of it, Drake."

Drake lay back on the cot, spread his arms and legs wide. What irony, getting tickled to death in the recovery room.

The last thing he said before they fell on him was, "Nobody can say I never got what I wanted."

And so it was that Drake was finally tickled to death, in a room where he lay completely alone in the darkness. Only in his mind had they come back—the boys and men who had craved his ticklishness, who had strained to hear his hysterical laughter long after it had faded to croaks and whispers. They tickled him, these ten boys and men, with apologies but without restraint, the lust in their fingertips carving out Drake's very core.

He lasted several hours, only because he was able, for part of the time, to retreat to the dark lake, and the harmless nibbling fish who reminded him to breathe. Then that part of his mind shut down, and his soul began to seek a way out.

If you were on a plane that day, heading toward that same city, you might have seen the usual towers and highways, anonymous-looking, insignificant from so high up. If you were sitting on the right side of the plane, you might even have glimpsed the old warehouse district, and a flash of light just above it, as bright and brief as if the sun had thrown off a spark. That spark was Drake's soul, ascending toward its next life, hoping to find a gay-male body that would be just as ticklish as the one it had left behind. Just as ticklish, and—if such a thing were possible—just as brave.

CONTRIBUTORS

Cary Michael Bass has been a resident of Fort Lauderdale for sixteen years, where he lives with his long-term partner, Michael. He is a board member of Lavender Writes, a nonprofit organization devoted to aspiring gay and lesbian writers by providing writing workshops, assistance in publication, and presentation in public. Cary's own works trespass in the realms of fantasy and science fiction, seasoned with a splash of erotica. His story "Eight Hours a Year" was featured in the anthology *Law of Desire*. He is perpetually editing his first novel, *A Mirror's Shard*.

Tristram Burden lives and writes in Bath, England. He writes fiction and nonfiction about self-transformation and fringe spiritualities. While studying for a degree in the Study of Religions and Creative Studies in English, he scratches out a living as a life-model. He's working on his debut novel, from which this story is an excerpt, and a number of other projects.

Patrick Califia (www.patrickcalifia.com) is a fifty-year-old transman and sadomasochistic impresario. He has been writing X-rated stories about sex, domination, torture, and true love since the late 1970s, when one of his pieces appeared in the first volume of John Preston's groundbreaking gay-male sex anthology, *Flesh and the Word*. He has a new a vampire novel, *Mortal Companion*, and two new collections of sharp-edged gay male fiction, *Hard Men* and *Boy in the Middle*.

Rusty Canela is the son of migrant farmers who emigrated from Mexico in the early 1900s. He was born and raised in South Texas and has lived in Houston since the death of his lover. He has written two collections of short stories: *Los Hijos de Tonatzin* and *Heroes of Love Street*, as well as extensive field studies of gays in rural Mexico. He has been featured in *The Houston Press* and *The Houston Chronicle*.

M. Christian (www.mchristian.com) is the author of the critically acclaimed and best-selling collections *Dirty Words*, *Speaking Parts*, *The Bachelor Machine*, and *Filthy*. He is the editor of *The Burning Pen*, *Guilty Pleasures*, the *Best S/M Erotica* series, *The Mammoth Book of Future Cops* and *The Mammoth Book of Tales of the Road* (both with Maxim Jakubowski), and over sixteen other anthologies. His short fiction has appeared in over one hundred fifty books and websites including *The Best American Erotica, Best Gay Erotica, Best Lesbian Erotica, Best Transgendered Erotica, Best Fetish Erotica, Best Bondage Erotica* and...well, you get the idea. He lives in San Francisco and is only some of what that implies.

Wayne Courtois is the author of *My Name Is Rand*, a novel filled with tickling and madness. His fiction and nonfiction have appeared in anthologies that run the gamut from *Of the Flesh: Dangerous New Fiction* to *Walking Higher: Gay Men Write about the Deaths of Their Mothers*. Visit him at www.waynecourtois.com.

Trebor Healey is the author of the 2004 Ferro-Grumley Award– and 2004 Violet Quill Award–winning novel, *Through It Came Bright Colors* (Harrington Park Press). His poetry collection, *Sweet Son of Pan*, will be published by Suspect Thoughts Press in 2006. Trebor lives in Los Angeles. Visit him at www.treborhealey.com.

Unlike her story's protagonist, **Debra Hyde** is not quite the vagabond. Her mind, however, does wander among all kinds of queer story possibilities, sometimes landing in male space. You can find her erotica in dozens of anthologies, most recently *Stirring Up a Storm: Tales of the Sensual, the Sexual, and the Erotic; Best of Best Women's Erotica;* and *The Good Parts: Pure Lesbian Erotica*. Debra is keeper of the weblog Pursed Lips (www.pursedlips.com).

Reuben Lane lives in northeast London, England. His first novel, *Throwing Stones at Jonathan*, was published in 2000. His short stories appear in *Serendipity, Chroma,* and *The Time Out Book of London Short Stories Volume Two*. This is his first story to be published in the United States.

Jeff Mann (www.english.vt.edu/~jmann/) is the author of the erotic fiction collection *A History of Barbed Wire*. His work has appeared in many publications, including *Rebel Yell, Rebel Yell 2,* and *Best Gay Erotica 2003* and *2004*. He has published a full-length collection of poetry, *Bones Washed with Wine*; a memoir, *Edge*; and a novella, *Devoured*, in the anthology *Masters of Midnight*.

Sean Meriwether's work has been published in *Lodestar Quarterly*, *Skin & Ink*, and the second installment of *Best of the Best Gay Erotica*. He is also the editor of *Outsider Ink* (www.outsiderink.com) and *Velvet Mafia: Dangerous Queer Fiction* (www.velvetmafia.com). Sean lives in New York with his partner, photographer Jack Slomovits. Stalk him online at www.seanmeriwether.com.

Moses O'Hara was born in Massachusetts. After displaying an early propensity for all forms of naked fun, he was shipped off to an all-male prep school—which was somewhat akin to Brer Rabbit and the briar patch. He continued on to New York, received some sort of degree in something or other, and then wound up in Los Angeles. You can find his work all over the place—including *Chance Encounters* and *The Wildest Ones*.

Ian Philips (www.ianphilips.com) is the Editor-in-Chief (and Mama Bear) of Suspect Thoughts Press. He is the author of two collections of literotica: *See Dick Deconstruct* and *Satyriasis*. And since February 19, 2004, he is the illegally wed husband of heartthrob author-publisher, Greg Wharton.

Thomas Roche's short stories and articles have appeared in more than three hundred websites, anthologies, and magazines. His books include the *Noirotica* series of erotic crime anthologies and the collections *Dark Matter*, *His*, and *Hers*. He can be found lurking in cyberspace at www.skidroche.com.

Steven Schwartz has, for any future playpartner's reference, never threatened anyone with a loaded gun. He does, however, enjoy writing about peculiar sex, and his work has appeared in numerous anthologies and his own chapbook, *69*.

Simon Sheppard, called by *San Francisco* magazine "our erotica king," is the author of *In Deep: Erotic Stories*; *Sex Parties 101*; and *Kinkorama: Dispatches From the Front Lines of Perversion*. His work also appears in over one hundred twenty-five anthologies, including many editions of *The Best American Erotica* and *Best Gay Erotica*, and his columns "Sex Talk" and "Perv" appear in queer papers and on the Web. He can be found at www.simonsheppard.com.

OUT OF CONTROL

Mel Smith lives in Oregon with her daughter and various animals. Her works have appeared in numerous magazines and anthologies, including the *Best Gay Erotica*, *Friction*, and *The Best American Erotica* series. She is also the author of *Nasty*, a collection of her own short stories (Alyson Books, 2005) and a gay-male erotic Western novel tentatively titled *Sweetlips*, forthcoming from Alyson Books.

Matt Stedmann's erotic fiction appears in the anthologies *Men for All Seasons*, *Men in Jocks*, *Blood Lust*, and *Quickies 3*, which was nominated for a Lambda Literary Award. His erotic nonfiction appears in the anthologies *Best of Both Worlds* and *ReCreations*, which was also nominated for a Lambda Literary Award. He often wears a black leather jacket.

Out of Control editor **Greg Wharton** is the publisher of Suspect Thoughts Press. He is the author of *Johnny Was & Other Tall Tales* and the editor of numerous other anthologies, including four he co-edited with his beautiful and talented husband Ian Philips: *I Do/I Don't*, *Law of Desire*, *Porn!*, and *Sodom & Me*. They live in San Francisco with a cat named Chloe and a lot of books.